TWICE DEAD

About six feet beyond the rail, down the brush-covered slope, a figure was crouched down staring at a freshly dug mound of earth. Sticking straight up from the mound was a human arm—the hand at the end trying to claw its way to heaven.

"Did the dog dig the arm up?" Monk asked as he looked down at the shallow grave.

Fey caught MeCoy and Blades exchanging quick looks.

"No," Blades said after a second or two. "At least we don't think so."

"Why not?" Fey finally asked when it became apparent that they were not going to volunteer anything further.

"Because the sheriff's department found another body buried just like this one two weeks ago."

Other Avon Books by
Paul Bishop

KILL ME AGAIN

TWICE DEAD

PAUL BISHOP

AVON BOOKS  NEW YORK

TWICE DEAD is an original publication of Avon Books. This work has never before appeared in book form. This work is a novel. Any similarity to actual persons or events is purely coincidental.

AVON BOOKS
A division of
The Hearst Corporation
1350 Avenue of the Americas
New York, New York 10019

Copyright © 1996 by Paul Bishop
Published by arrangement with the author
Library of Congress Catalog Card Number: 95-94678
ISBN: 0-380-77862-9

First Avon Books Printing: January 1996

AVON TRADEMARK REG. U.S. PAT. OFF. AND IN OTHER COUNTRIES, MARCA REGISTRADA, HECHO EN U.S.A.

Printed in the U.S.A.

RA   10 9 8 7 6 5 4 3 2 1

Under the certainty of Heaven
There is always Tomorrow
And yet when yesterday is already Ours
What more can we Ask?

9 * 12 * 21

ACKNOWLEDGMENTS

Many thanks to Hal Blythe and Charlie Sweet—aka the fastest blue pencils on either side of the Mississippi.

Thanks as well to Clark Rex, Ph.D., who took Fey on as a patient and didn't blink an eye when I told him, "I have a character who has a problem."

I also want to recognize not only the fine men and women of the LAPD, but especially my fellow officers and detectives who work the West Los Angeles area. This story is fiction. The cops described in it and their actions are fiction. In real life the job takes a much higher toll, and I am constantly amazed by the integrity and dedication to duty that is the true reflection of the LAPD rank and file. I am proud to be counted among them.

—Paul Bishop
1995

Show me a hero, and I'll write you a tragedy.

—F. SCOTT FITZGERALD

PROLOGUE

DARCY WYATT SPUN THE WHEELS OF THE BLUE DELIVERY *van onto the loose asphalt behind Fratelli Pizza. A lone streetlight illuminated an almost empty parking lot.*

Darcy had been gone longer than he'd intended, and hoped the boss, Butt Wipe Norman, hadn't noticed. He also hoped no more delivery orders had come in. Darcy was feeling pleasantly buzzed after his exertions. Sucking down a fat dubie of Kenny's bitchin' grass had also helped to soften the edges. Maybe when he and Kenny got off they could do a couple of six-packs and have some more giggles. Kenny was warped, but he was always good for laughs.

The van stank of old pizza and sweat socks. Kenny never cleaned the damn thing out and the threadbare carpeting in the back was covered in stains and filth. A stack of bondage magazines, a shovel, a basketball, and a raft of empty beer cans bounced around in the back, mingling with fast-food wrappers, dirty workout clothes, and odds and ends of other junk.

Unlike the other Fratelli Pizza restaurants where Darcy worked, Butt Wipe Norman was too cheap to pop for an official Fratellimobile for deliveries. Darcy didn't have a car of his own, so it was a problem whenever he got called to fill in for the regular delivery guy who worked for Norman. However, Kenny also worked for Norman's Fratelli Pizza franchise. Since Kenny and Darcy were buds, he always let Darcy borrow the van for making the delivery rounds while Kenny stayed and cooked up more of the

1

round gut bombs that were making Butt Wipe rich.

Darcy liked hanging with Kenny. Kenny said they were sort of like brothers. They both hated Norman—they actually hated anybody who ever amounted to anything—and were always talking about what they were going to do to Norman some day. Make him eat shit and die, man.

Darcy jammed the steering wheel gearshift into park and jumped out of the van. Reaching back inside, he used one hand to drag out two insulated pizza delivery packs. With his other hand, Darcy grabbed his motorcycle helmet. It was a full-face helmet, scuffed and scarred. He never left it with his cycle in case somebody ripped it off. It had other uses as well.

Feeling loose, he pushed his way in through the back entrance to the restaurant.

"Hey, hey, buddy," he said when he spotted Kenny in the back hallway. "What's happening?"

"Shut up," Kenny said urgently. He held a finger up to his lips.

Darcy looked a little shocked. He'd never seen Kenny acting anything but cool, but the guy was real agitated now. Darcy dumped the pizza insulators on a counter.

"What's the matter?" he asked.

"Cops."

"Ah, shit." Darcy glanced around as if he was looking for an escape. "How'd they find out?"

"I don't think they did, man. But you gotta get outta here. They're asking about you."

"What the hell am I gonna do?"

"Take off, man. Just get on your bike and blow. I'll cover for you."

"Cool. Thanks, man."

"Hey, we're brothers aren't we?" Kenny held out an open palm and Darcy slapped it. "Get going, man."

Darcy pulled his helmet over his head and threw Kenny the keys to the blue van.

Kenny stood watching as Darcy went back out the rear door and headed toward where he'd parked his motorcycle. When Kenny heard the motorcycle kick over, he turned *and ran into the front of the restaurant. "Mr. Norman! Mr. Norman," he yelled excitedly.*

A short, fat man with a thick black mustache turned away from talking with two uniformed police officers.

"What-da-ya want, Kenny?" Norman asked. His voice was an abrasive whine.

"It's Darcy. He just took off on his motorcycle."

The two cops looked at each other and then turned to look through the front window of the restaurant when the noise of Darcy's cycle roared past.

The older of the two cops was suddenly in action, dragging his partner with him out the front door.

Kenny rocked back on his heels with a smug smile. He sure liked the reaction he'd started—it was almost as good as real giggles. Well, not really, but it was still pretty cool. If things went as planned, the real giggles would come later on tonight.

Darcy wasn't important anyway. Even if the cops caught Darcy—and Kenny always knew they would—Darcy didn't know anything that could mess things up. It had been cool manipulating Darcy's kinks—pervert see, pervert do.

Actually, Kenny figured throwing Darcy to the wolves was a good move. It got Darcy out of the way before he did find something out, and Kenny didn't need the complications of killing him without a good reason.

⬧◆⬧
CHAPTER ONE

NO REST FOR THE WICKED, FEY CROAKER THOUGHT TO herself as she dropped her purse on her desk with a loud thump. The shoulder strap snaked out and bounced off a Styrofoam cup filled with coffee. The hot liquid slopped out of the cup, immediately soaking into reports and paperwork scattered like abandoned confetti across the desktop.

Fey looked at the mess and rolled her eyes. She swore under her breath and tried to shake dark brown droplets off several of the disaster-struck documents. Giving the salvage work up as a lost cause, she threw the papers back on the desk and dropped down into her chair. She swore again. Louder this time.

"Get out of the wrong side of the bed this morning?" Monk Lawson asked as he entered the squad room from the back stairway. It was three in the morning and, except for Fey and Monk, the squad room was deserted.

Fey scowled darkly at the young black detective. "Where did you come up with this *morning* stuff?" she asked. "It's still the middle of the damn night."

Monk laughed. "Yeah, I know how you feel. I hate these call-outs. I'd only just turned off the lights and headed for dreamland when my beeper went off."

"At least you got to sleep," Fey said.

"Oh," Monk said. "Out doing the town, were we?"

Fey gave a weary shake of her head. "Not really." Her tone of voice suggested trouble.

"Problems on the relationship front?" Monk asked gen-

4

tly. For a while he'd sensed there was something not going right for Fey outside of the job.

Fey shook her head to dismiss the subject of her personal life. "This too shall pass," she said with a deep sigh, and then forced a smile.

At forty-something, creeping ever closer to fiftyish, Fey had been the homicide unit supervisor at the LAPD's West Los Angeles area for almost four years. She wasn't the department's only female homicide detective, but she was the only female supervising a major divisional homicide unit.

On several occasions she'd paid the price for being a woman in the position, but there was no way in hell she was ever going to give it up without a fight. She'd come too far, both professionally and personally, to roll over and play dead when the going got a little rough.

Some of her co-workers believed she'd only been given the position due to the department's affirmative action movement. Fey, however, didn't much care if that was true or not. The fact was that she was in the position and she was damn good at it. She'd made her bones several times over, and she'd match her unit's clearance rates against any other division in the city in a heartbeat.

West LA's detective squad room was located on the top floor of the two-story building. The front desk, the watch commander's office, records, administrative offices, and a small jail were located on the ground floor. The station's huge roll-call room, male and female locker rooms, and the officers' workout room were situated in the basement.

Two stairways led from the ground floor to the detective division. The front stairway was for civilians and led to a small lobby. Behind the lobby was a hallway housing interrogation rooms, a victim's interview room, the homicide unit's incident room, and an area designated for the CAD (computer statistics) team. The back stairway led from the center of the ground floor to a second hallway and the back entrance to the squad room. Along the second hallway, the area vice unit had a small office appropriately located across from the bathrooms. Another small office in the same hallway was occupied by a bureau narcotics unit.

One quarter of the squad room was walled off for a section of the department's bunco-forgery division. The remaining expanse of open floor was used as the detective division's work space. Various groups of desks were butted against each other like giant dominos. Each grouping represented a different fragment of the overall investigative case load—burglary, auto theft, juvenile, robbery, MAC (major assault crimes), sex crimes, and homicide.

Due to recent organizational imperatives, Fey, as the homicide unit supervisor, had been given additional jurisdiction over the MAC and sex crimes investigations as well as her unit's traditional homicide tasks. This meant far more paperwork and a half-dozen extra detectives to supervise. Somehow this translated into a hell of a lot more personnel problems, and far more call-outs, such as the one she and Monk were currently working.

Fey had been in mid-shriek when the noise of her beeper had exploded across the angry, emotional battlefield that her relationship with Jake Travers had become.

"Damn it!" Fey had cursed. She'd slid naked out of bed and began rooting around in her purse to retrieve the offending pager. What had started out as a lovemaking session with Jake had rapidly deteriorated into a slinging match even before the preliminaries were over. He'd pushed her buttons and she'd responded by pushing his. Passion had changed from lust to hurt, and hurt to anger, in seconds. Dripping with emotional blood, the spiked and dangerous rocks on which their relationship was floundering were as naked as their bodies.

When she had looked at the number on the pager's digital display, Fey could sense the call meant more trouble. The ongoing argument with Jake would have to wait. It wouldn't go away, not until they had finished tearing each other apart, but it would wait.

For some months Jake had been pressing Fey for more of a commitment than she was willing to give. With three marriages already behind her, Fey knew it was a position she was never going to place herself in again.

While Jake had not had the political strength to win election as the district attorney during the past year, he was still considered a fast rising star in the district attorney's office. Political clout was again amassing behind him, but there was much maneuvering ahead if he was to assure his future.

Jake and Fey had been lovers for several years, but he now needed the respectability of marriage for the sake of political correctness. Fey didn't think that was a good enough reason to place herself back into indenture. There was no doubt that Jake loved her—as she loved him—but Fey knew that love wasn't enough. Marriage had much more in common with a willingness to constantly compromise than it did with love. And there lay the rub. Fey was no longer willing to compromise. She had achieved her own autonomy and didn't need Jake, or anyone else, to make her complete. Conversely, she had no desire to be simply another part in someone else's life puzzle.

While Fey had called the station watch commander, Jake picked his clothes up from the floor of Fey's bedroom, climbed into his pants, and left without another word. Fey had kept her naked back turned while she talked on the phone and purposely kept the conversation going until Jake was gone.

When she heard the slam of her front door, Fey told the watch commander, Terry Gillette, that she was on her way in. That done, she hung up the phone and breathed a sigh of relief. To her mind, even getting called out to work when normal people were tucked up tight in their beds was preferable to living through the hell of a long-term relationship crumbling around your shoulders.

Twenty minutes later, she was on her way to the West Los Angeles area station.

CHAPTER TWO

MONK LAWSON SAT DOWN AT HIS OWN DESK, THE RIGHT side of which butted against the front of Fey's. "Did you get any info about this caper when you called?" Monk asked. "All Gillette told me was that you were on your way in and I better get my butt down here fast 'cause you were on the warpath."

Fey snorted. "I know Gillette," she said. "He's not that polite. He told you to get your black ass down here faster than the speed of light because I was on the rag."

Monk's grin displayed a perfect row of small ivories. "You be close, missy." His plantation jive act was suddenly in full swing. "You think we should be suing him for racial prejudice and sexism?"

"Nah," Fey said. "Too easy. Be like shooting cows with a sniper scope. I'd rather take our frustrations out on a suspect. Who knows, if we do it right, we may even solve a crime. After all, isn't that what we're paid to do?"

"I guess," Monk said, back to his regular, cultured voice. "If it doesn't interfere with the shuffling of paperwork."

Fey's knowing snort was cut short when two uniformed officers stepped in from the back stairway with a tall, lanky prisoner between them in handcuffs. Fey placed the suspect's age somewhere between sixteen and eighteen. He had long, dirty, blond hair that hung limply around his acne-scarred face. He wore a beat-up black leather jacket with metal studs on the epaulets over a dingy white t-shirt, greasy jeans, and motorcycle boots. One of the officers

8

held a white motorcycle helmet that Fey figured was also a part of the tearaway's ensemble.

"Where do you want him?" Officer Dick Morrison asked. He shifted hands with the suspect's motorcycle helmet. Fey had known Dick for a long time and admired his consistent record of outstanding self-initiated arrests. He was the kind of officer that seemed to have an instinct for being at the right place at the right time. He had over twenty-five years on the job, most of them spent working PM watch patrol. He was clearly working overtime on this caper. John Bassett, the officer with Morrison, was only the latest of the hundreds of rookies Morrison had trained to stay alive on the streets of LA.

"Just stick him in an interview room, Dick," Fey said, indicating the direction of the front hallway with a jerk of her thumb. "I understand you had to take him for an MT."

"Yeah. Santa Monica Hospital did the medical treatment. Same place we took the victim." Morrison reached out with his free hand and pulled some hair away from the suspect's face. A stretch of road rash ran down from the left ear to jawline. "Twenty-two stitches," Morrison said, pointing to the jagged cut over the suspect's left eyebrow. "And we didn't even touch him. Laid his bike down trying to get away."

"I wasn't trying to get away," the suspect spoke up for the first time. "I didn't even know you were behind me."

"Then you're blind and deaf as well as stupid and guilty," Morrison said. "Come on." He took hold of the suspect's arm and escorted him past Fey and Monk into the first interview room off the front hallway.

"You can take the cuffs off," Fey told the trio as they walked by. "Just lock the door when you put him inside and let him sit for a while."

After Morrison, Bassett, and the suspect had disappeared into the interview room, Monk again asked, "What's it all about?"

Fey picked up her lukewarm coffee and took a big sip. "All I got from Gillette is that Morrison and Bassett had picked up a possible rape suspect, and that Morrison asked for detectives to be called in to interrogate."

"I take it," Monk said, "that we get stuck with the call-out because Hop-Along is on vacation?"

Max Cassiday, otherwise known as Hop-Along, was assigned to Fey as the squad's sex crimes investigator.

Fey agreed. "Typical timing. Hop-Along gets nothing major for over a month, but the second he leaves on vacation everything hits the fan."

"It's like he knows when it's coming. But still, this doesn't sound like something that couldn't have waited until we got here at a decent hour."

Dick Morrison chose that moment to reenter the squad bay. "Maybe so," he said, apologetically, "but I've got a strong feeling about this one, and I figured you might want to jump on it right away before this jerk has a chance to get his head together."

Fey sat up and began to pay more attention. If Morrison had a hunch it usually paid off in big dividends. "Tell us about it," she said.

Morrison yawned, and Fey pushed her cup of coffee in his direction. He waved her off with a negative shake of his hand. "If I drink that I'll be too wired to go to sleep when I get home. Thanks anyway." He ran a hand over his face. "Did you see the teletype from Santa Monica PD last week where a suspect broke into the residence of a seventy-five-year-old lady, raped her, and then almost killed her by bashing her skull in?"

"Yeah," Fey said. "They had a caper with the same MO in Beverly Hills a month ago. The victim in that one was seventy-two. She survived the assault . . ."

"Barely," said Monk, interrupting. He was also familiar with the two cases. "Last I heard she was still in the hospital. Practically a vegetable. I doubt she's lucid enough to identify anyone."

LAPD's West Los Angeles area was sandwiched neatly between the separate police jurisdictions of Beverly Hills and Santa Monica. Fey always paid attention to the teletypes from the two other agencies, looking for suspect information or methods of operation that could easily spill over into LAPD's jurisdiction. Suspects didn't give a damn where the lines of demarcation were drawn.

"Are you saying," Monk asked, his mind racing ahead of the conversation, "that this guy is a possible suspect in those cases?"

"Well . . ."

"Come on, Dick," Fey said. "Give. Do we have another victim? Did this one survive? What?"

"Okay, okay." Dick held up both hands to stop the flow of words. "About nine o'clock, we get an 'ADW there now' call. The address is over on Castle Heights near The Hood. It's where those older homes are that still have some of the original owners living in them. They keep the street up nice even though the rest of the neighborhood is going to hell."

Fey nodded rapidly in recognition of the area. She threw a warning glance at Monk who had opened his mouth to say something. Monk caught the look and backed off. Both of them wanted Morrison to get on with the story, but Fey knew Dick wouldn't be rushed. He had to tell it in his own time.

"When we get to the location we're met by the victim's son. He's in his forties. The victim is in her seventies. She's half-blind and has some other health problems, but she's still mentally sharp." He cleared his throat and then continued. "The son had split from his own home after an argument with his wife and had come to his mother's house unexpectedly to spend the night and cool down. He opens the front door with a key and hears groaning noises from the kitchen. Thinking his mom has fallen down and maybe broken a hip or something, he goes dashing into the kitchen to help her." Morrison paused.

"And . . . ?" Fey urged. It was unlike Dick to be reluctant. What was coming had to be bad.

Morrison shrugged. "Well, it wasn't pleasant. When the son gets into the kitchen he sees some guy putting it to his mother who is bent over the kitchen table. Not only is this asshole raping his mom, he's also hitting her in the back of the head with a motorcycle helmet."

"Oh, shit." Fey closed her eyes and shook her head back and forth in anguish and disgust.

"Yeah," said Morrison. He took a deep breath. "Anyway, the suspect hears sonny yell out. He spins around with the helmet in his hand and smashes it straight into sonny's face. Sonny goes down for the count. When he comes around, the suspect has split. Mom is slumped on the kitchen floor, but she's still breathing. Sonny dials 911, yelling for an ambulance. The emergency operator sends the paramedics and puts out the shout for us as well."

"How'd you come up with the suspect?" Fey asked.

Morrison shrugged. "I had to get a little creative."

"It was brilliant," John Bassett said. He'd come back into the squad room and was standing next to Dick Morrison with a look of admiration on his face. It was a look Fey had seen before plastered across the mugs of Dick's trainees. Dick was the Messiah as far as they were concerned, only he had far more than just twelve disciples. "This guy is incredible," Bassett continued with his zealot rhetoric.

"Cool your jets, kid," Morrison said in a self-deprecating tone. "Any good cop would have come up with it."

Fey knew better. She may not have been Morrison-trained herself, but she had worked around him long enough to know he was one of the best at turning a nothing lead into something that could make a case.

"We followed the ambulance taking the victim to the hospital," Morrison said, as he continued his narrative. "She had regained consciousness by the time we got there, and we were able to interview her briefly after the doctors were finished." Morrison reached out a hand and snagged Fey's coffee cup, his initial reluctance to drink it overcome by his cop's constant need for caffeine.

He took a healthy swallow and set the cup down. "I told you that the victim was half-blind, so she couldn't give us much of a physical description of the suspect."

"What about the son?" Monk jumped in, trying to get Morrison to cut to the chase.

"Let him tell it," Fey said quietly.

Morrison gave her an acknowledging nod and then turned his attention to Monk. "The son was drunk when he turned up on mommy's doorstep, shocked out of his socks when he saw what was going on in the kitchen, and knocked on his heavily padded ass by the suspect. Sonny couldn't tell us if the suspect was an Indian chief or the queen of Sheba."

Monk shrugged his shoulders, but kept his mouth shut. He didn't need telling twice.

"The victim told us that the suspect knocked on her front door," Morrison continued. "When she opened it on the chain, he smashed his shoulder into the door and tore the chain off the door frame. He immediately hit her in the head a couple of times with the motorcycle helmet, and then dragged her into the kitchen and threw her over the table."

"Sounds as if the suspect knew she lived alone." Fey couldn't help interjecting, but fortunately it didn't seem to stop Morrison's flow.

Morrison took another sip of coffee. "Anyway, the victim is out of it by this point," Dick continued. "He's hurting her so bad she doesn't know which way is up or what's going on. From what I gathered, though, it looks like the suspect keeps hitting her in the head with the helmet while he's putting it to her—like maybe he can't get off unless he's beating her." He paused fractionally to change tacks. "I don't know if he was trying to kill her, but he might have done it if sonny hadn't interrupted."

Morrison paused again, and Fey looked at him expectantly.

"Is there a big clue in all this that I'm missing?" she asked.

John Bassett was squirming around like a kid waiting for the ice cream truck to arrive. Morrison favored him with an indulgent smile. "Okay, kid. You tell it."

"The big clue is that while the victim doesn't see too good, she did tell us that the suspect stunk of pizza."

"Pizza?" Fey asked. "What is that? Some new brand of manly cologne?"

Bassett looked confused. "No. Pizza. Like in take-out. You know? Cheese with pepperoni and anchovies."

"She knows, kid. She's just pulling your chain. A little police humor."

"Very little," Fey said. She was already getting punchy from lack of sleep.

"Yeah," said Bassett, as if he still wasn't sure. "Anyway, Dick asks her if she ever orders pizza delivered to her house. She says yes, and Dick asks her when the last time was. She says about a week ago from Fratelli Pizza around the corner. She always orders from Fratelli Pizza."

"You checked up on the delivery guys, right?" Fey asked Morrison directly, immediately seeing where Bassett was leading.

Morrison nodded as he finished off Fey's coffee. "Fratelli Pizza is a chain. They've got six outlets." Dick nodded his head in the direction of the interview room. "This guy works part time at four of them delivering orders."

"Don't tell me. Let me guess," Fey said. "He works out of the ones in Santa Monica, Beverly Hills, and West LA."

"And Culver City," Morrison confirmed. "I got a call in to them to see if they have any hits that match the pattern."

"How old is this guy?" Fey asked.

"Just turned nineteen."

"A little old for a delivery boy, isn't he?"

Morrison shrugged. "Hey, I didn't hire him. I just busted him. We get over to the Fratelli Pizza on La Cienega and Cadillac and talked to the manager, a guy named Donald Norman. I've known him a long time." Morrison had known everyone in the division a long time. "And he gives us the lowdown on this creep. His name is Darcy Wyatt. Rides a motorcycle to work. Keeps his helmet in the blue van he uses for deliveries so it doesn't get ripped off." Morrison paused for a yawn. "Most of the Fratelli Pizzas have their own delivery cars, but Norman makes his delivery guys use their own vehicles. Darcy doesn't have a car or a van so, when he works for Norman, he borrows this blue van from one of his buddies, a cook at Fratelli's named Kenny."

Bassett took over the story again. "While we were talking to the manager, this Kenny guy suddenly comes running in and tells us that Wyatt is taking off on his motorcycle."

Morrison shrugged his shoulders. "I think he'd just returned from a delivery in the blue van and was in the back room. He must have overheard us talking to the manager about him." Morrison was almost making an admission that maybe he'd screwed up somehow by not being clairvoyant. "We took off after him with lights and siren, but we didn't have to chase him far before he laid the bike down going round a corner. The idiot tried to take off on foot, but I turned the young stud here loose." Morrison pointed at Bassett. "And he had the asshole roped and hog-tied before you could count to three."

Morrison set fire to a cigarette, in direct violation of the squad room's no-smoking policy. He blew out a stream of gray smoke. Fey's nostrils quivered with desire. He pointed the cigarette at Fey. "I asked Gillette to call you in while we were getting Wyatt his MT at the hospital. I figured that if this thing all tied together, you'd want to get to him while the whole caper was fresh."

"Absolutely," said Fey. She felt her tiredness dropping away. This is what she lived for. A chance to crack a big nut. "The kid is right, Dick. It was a brilliant piece of police work."

"Ah, pshaw," Morrison said in mock embarrassment.

Fey gave Monk a brief glance. "You ready to do this?"

"Like you said, absolutely."

"Then let's start to rock n' roll."

Morrison sucked more smoke into his lungs. "I hope you crack this motherfucker wide open."

''No pun intended, right?'' Fey said, picking up the intentional double entendre.

She pointed two fingers at Bassett and dropped a cocked thumb as if it were the trigger on a gun. ''Now that's police humor,'' she said.

■✦■

CHAPTER THREE

IT WAS ANOTHER FORTY-FIVE MINUTES BEFORE FEY AND Monk were actually prepared to begin interrogating Darcy Wyatt. During that time they sped through the motions of gathering as much information as possible about their suspect and the cases he was thought to be involved in.

Two sleepy detectives, one from Santa Monica PD and the other from Beverly Hills PD, were pulled from their warm beds by Fey's telephone calls. In short order, they found themselves being interrogated about the rape cases in their jurisdictions. Once their initial grouchiness was conquered, both cooperated with alacrity. The incidents from their areas were hot priorities, especially the one from Santa Monica where the victim was the mother of a local VIP, and the detectives were more than happy to do anything they could to get their blotters cleared. Having LAPD take over the investigations would get them off the hot seat and leave them free to get on to other pressing cases.

''Can you talk to your victim first thing this morning and find out if they ever ordered pizza from the local Fratelli Pizza?'' Fey had asked both detectives, receiving an affirmative reply.

After she'd hung up, Fey called across to Monk. He was sitting down in front of the NECS terminals at the far side of the squad room. "One new piece of information that wasn't in the teletypes."

"Does it fit in with our case?"

"Absolutely. Both Cavin from Beverly Hills and Gann from Santa Monica told me their victims were blind, or as close to being blind as to make no difference."

"That's what Morrison said about our victim. This ass-hole certainly knows how to pick 'em. If they can't see him, they can't identify him."

"Ah, but he gets caught due to his cologne—Eau de Pizza."

"It's a cruel world," Monk replied.

Shortly after Fey talked with Beverly Hills and Santa Monica, Dick Morrison received a call from a Culver City sergeant named Olivo. Olivo had checked out Morrison's earlier request and come up with two cases in Culver City with similar MOs during the past month. Both victims were over seventy and had been raped and severely beaten. Neither had been able to provide any kind of useful de-scription of their assailant as both suffered from cataracts. Messages had been left for the concerned Culver City de-tective to get back to Fey or Monk as soon as he came in to start his shift.

Monk got busy waving his magic fingers over the NECS terminal keyboard. "Look at this," he said to Fey, as he pressed the print button. With an impatient grab, he tore free a sheaf of computer printouts and brought them over to Fey.

Fey's glasses rested on her chest, suspended by a thin chain around her neck. She slipped them on and peered at Darcy Wyatt's juvenile rap sheet.

"Here," Monk said pointing. "He's got a couple of kiddy things—vandalism, loitering, petty theft—but he's also got a prior rape arrest."

The disposition on the rape case showed that it had been dismissed in the interest of justice.

"Nothing since he became an adult?" Fey asked.

Monk handed her another printout. "Just a couple of traffic warrants."

"What about the dismissal on the rape case?"

Monk went over to a series of file cabinets and rummaged through one of the drawers. Grunting with approval, he pulled out a buff-colored envelope with Darcy Wyatt's name on the front. He slid out several reports and shuffled through them. "It occurred in our division two years ago," Monk told Fey, handing her the juvenile arrest folder. "The sex crimes unit was still being supervised by the juvenile unit back then, so you probably weren't even made aware of it."

"Wait a minute," Fey said. She pawed through the arrest folder. "I do remember hearing something about this. Wasn't this the caper where the kid living at Vista del Sur was caught trying to rape the grandmother of one of the other kids living at the same place?" Vista del Sur was a residential program for wayward children of the rich and famous.

Fey pulled a follow-up report from the file and read through it quickly. "The case was 'cleared other.' The DA refused to file." She read a little further. "The victim was uncooperative for some reason and the suspect walked."

"So much for the system," Monk said. "Sounds like the victim and her family were paid off."

"Sounds about right for Vista del Sur." Located in the exclusive Pacific Palisades area, the residential program had a tendency to handle many incidents under the table or in-house. "I wonder who Wyatt's parents are that they could afford to house him at Vista. It takes big-time bucks to keep a kid there."

"It would take big-time bucks to cover up a rape case."

"Any idea who his parents are?"

Monk took a closer look at the juvenile rap sheet. "Mother is listed as deceased. Father is Devon Wyatt."

"*The* Devon Wyatt?"

"Who is *the* Devon Wyatt, as compared to plain run-of-the-mill Devon Wyatt?"

"*The* Devon Wyatt is one of the top celebrity defense

lawyers in the business. His politics are to the left of Timothy Leary and he makes William Kunstler look like a pussy cat.''

"I'm with you," Monk said, nodding his head in belated recognition. "If you're in trouble, and you're a big enough name with money to match, he'll either get you off or cut the best deal money can buy. I've seen him on the news a bunch of times. Real smooth. I just didn't make the connection right away. If he's Darcy Wyatt's father, what the hell is Darcy doing working as a pizza delivery boy?''

Fey shrugged. "Sounds like a family split. Maybe the kid has been so much trouble growing up that daddy has cut him off.''

"Yeah, but if we arrest his kid for rape, do you think daddy will come running?

"Hard to say." Fey shrugged. "Maybe.''

"I'd hate to see the little shit walk again.''

"Yeah," Fey replied. "But he's an adult now, so maybe we have a better chance of getting him this time. We'll just have to play it as it lays.''

Twice since Wyatt had been put in the interrogation room Fey had gone in to check on him. The first time, she had let Bassett take Wyatt to the bathroom. The second time, she had provided Wyatt with a cup of coffee and a cigarette from a stale pack that she kept in the bottom drawer of her desk.

On neither occasion was Fey going through the motions simply to be nice. There was a method to her madness. Wyatt was obviously street smart. If Fey was going to get a confession out of him, she had to get him through the opening preliminaries of the interrogation without him screaming for a lawyer. If Wyatt thought she was weak or a goody-two-shoes, he might think he could pull the wool over her eyes and decide to go things alone.

Fey set the printouts and the juvenile arrest package down on her desk. She took her glasses off and rubbed her eyes. Monk was still standing beside her. He decided it was his turn and asked, "You ready to do this?''

"Let me get a fresh cup of coffee and we'll start dancing."

"You lead and I'll follow," Monk said, defining their roles for the interrogation process. He had seen Fey in action. When it came to interrogations, she was one of the best. She knew all the moves. If she couldn't get a suspect to cop out then nobody could. "I always like learning a couple of new steps."

Fey took a couple of deep breaths to gear herself up. "If Devon Wyatt gets involved in this, let's just hope we don't step on too many toes."

✡

CHAPTER FOUR

"I swear, Ash! You are the most depressing person I've ever met. Don't you ever smile?"

Ash watched as Holly hooked the back of her lacy, black brassiere and bounced off the bed to pull on the rest of her clothes. She was angry, and an angry Holly was a beautiful Holly. Beautiful and dangerous.

She'd been with Ash three months this time. A month longer than normal. He'd known it couldn't last. It never did with Holly, and he'd been anticipating the explosion for over two weeks. In many ways it was a relief.

"Aren't you going to say anything?" she asked, turning to flash her eyes at him.

Propped up against his pillows, legs tangled in sheets still warm from lovemaking, Ash knew there wasn't anything he could say that would make her stay. So, he remained silent. He had learned long ago that the best way to win an argument was to refuse to engage. If you don't play, you can't lose.

The down side was you couldn't win either.

The sound of crickets spilled through a slightly open window, and a warm breeze tickled across Ash's naked skin. The warm Santa Ana was not unusual for Southern California. Neither was Holly leaving Ash's bed in a snit after lovemaking. She was a concert violinist, as tightly strung as her instrument and far more temperamental.

Ash could find no rhyme or reason for Holly's tantrums beyond her own self-destructive tendencies. The most achingly beautiful woman he had ever met, she was both brilliant and pitiful. When she flowed her bow across the strings of her violin, her concentration and mastery was absolute. Her music had brought worldwide concert hall audiences close to rapture. She brought the same intensity to her lovemaking, but never to the sustaining of a relationship. It was there that the needed emotions were missing from her makeup. She was the edge of an intensely honed razor with one disastrous jagged nick in the blade. A flawed masterpiece.

Ash knew that in some ways, Holly saw in him a reflection of herself. His own obsession and skills on a par with her own, albeit in a totally different venue. His black depression a distorted reflection of her own emotional insecurities.

Ash didn't love Holly. If he had, her dramatic exits from his life would be more devastation than he could stand. As she used him to exorcise her own demons, he used her to keep the blackness of his own despair at bay. He had hunted monsters all his life, vanquishing them from the real world, but adding each of them to the dark pit of his own psyche. Holly provided a light in the darkness.

Since they had met five years earlier, she would blow into his life whenever she needed a dose of stability, and then out again when she'd had her fill. The incongruity of that situation didn't escape Ash, since he wasn't particularly noted for being stable himself. Compared to Holly, however, he was the Rock of Gibraltar.

He held her eyes until she looked away. "Damn you," she said quietly, and fifteen minutes later she was gone.

Ash didn't have the energy to move, so he stayed on the bed while trying to sort through his emotions.

Depression was a funny thing, he thought, the inherent contradiction almost making him smile.

This time, he knew Holly wouldn't be coming back. There wasn't enough time left. By the time she came around to returning, he would be gone.

He touched the tic under his right eye. His finger felt the nerve jump. It was infrequent, but becoming slightly noticeable. Ash was well aware of what the condition heralded. He only hoped he had enough time for one last monster hunt.

That was all he asked.

One last hunt.

One last chance to practice the skills that God had dispensed to him. One last chance to rid the world of an aberration. And now it looked as if there was one right here in his own backyard.

But Ash knew all about monsters. He knew they didn't just go away. They simply hid in the dark until it was time to come out and play again.

Eventually, he slid off the sheets and pulled on a pair of jeans. An upright piano stood against one of the bedroom's inside walls. Ash sat down on the bench and ran his long fingers slowly down the keys, picking out a blues riff. The movements of his hands were graceful and sure, caressing a lover who would never forsake him.

When the tune was done, he stood up and walked across the bedroom to open a pair of stained glass doors. He stepped out onto the balcony, embracing the night air, hoping it would dry his tears.

Twenty minutes later, he was still standing on the balcony, the natural elements continuing to act as a balm for his all-too-human pain. The soft page of his beeper penetrated the dark mood, but it was still a few moments before he moved. He'd been anticipating the summons. Even, in a morbid way, hoping for it.

It was that kind of night.

Death was calling.

And Ash was supposed to be the answer.

✦✦✦

CHAPTER FIVE

FEY BELIEVED AN INTERROGATION WAS AN INTRICATE verbal ballet. It was far different, far more complex, than a simple interview. An interview was designed strictly to get information. Compared to interrogation, interviewing was a game for amateurs. Some detectives, however, never get beyond that level. They know how to ask questions, but they don't know how to ask the *right* questions.

For Fey, interrogation was an art form. It was a complete and personal interaction between detective and suspect. Each had to give a little bit of their own personality in order to get a bit of the other's personality in return. The sticking point would come when the only piece the suspect could give back in return was the confession of his or her own guilt.

The days when interrogations were conducted with bright lights and rubber hoses had long since disappeared from the mainstream of American law enforcement. As a result, an interrogation of a truly innocent suspect was a simple, if arduous, process of maintaining that innocence. If a suspect is innocent then the truth will eventually win out. Circumstances will eventually be explained, and physical evidence will confirm the truth of the statements made within the oppressive walls of the interrogation room.

If a suspect is guilty, however, then he or she must hide that guilt as if it were the most prized of their possessions. And it is the process of misering away this guilt, stashing it amongst the deepest of mental shadows, that an interrogator must detect—and once detected, seize upon it like a loose thread that can unravel a complete garment.

A guilty suspect longs to scream the damning evidence of guilt from the rooftops. Guilt is almost a physical thing growing inside of them, forcing its way to the surface as if it were a bubble in a cauldron destined to explode on the surface. A detective who has the skills to recognize the guilt below the surface can coax and wheedle it out as if it were a timid animal in search of sustenance.

When Fey and Monk let themselves into the interrogation room where Darcy Wyatt awaited them, they were both filled with suppressed anticipation. They were hunters with their quarry firmly in their sights. They had but to find the right trigger, the correct provocation, that would gain them a trophy-sized confession.

"Good morning, Mr. Wyatt," Fey said.

"I want—"

Fey jumped right into the middle of Wyatt's first statement. "There are many things we all want, Mr. Wyatt, and we'll get to each of them in time." The last thing Fey needed was for Wyatt to say he wanted a lawyer. If those words crossed his lips, their best chance at gaining a confession was effectively over. Fey had to get him to talk to her. To trust her. To think that he could convince her of his innocence and walk away from this arrest.

Fey also knew the microphone in the room was hot. Everything being said was being recorded for later use in court. Fey and Monk had to play everything just right so there could be no taint to shift a jury's sympathy. If it even remotely looked like the police were badgering the suspect, one or more jury panel members could be turned to the suspect's side.

There would be time later to put all the physical evidence together, but a confession was still the most dramatic kind of evidence to use in court and amongst the hardest to refute. The plain fact was that in cases where a confession was obtained there was almost never a trial. With a confession in hand, the case would be pled out long before twelve members of a jury had a chance to hear it.

"I'm Detective Croaker and this is my partner, Detective Lawson," Fey formally introduced herself and Monk. "We want to ask you a few questions and see if we can't clear up this little misunderstanding."

"Do you know who my father is?" Wyatt asked, aggression oozing from him like a tangible object.

Fey was well aware of the specter of Devon Wyatt hanging over the interrogation. The fact that he was Darcy's father, however, was only mildly interesting. It may have kept him out of even deeper trouble when he was younger, but it appeared that there was currently a rift in the family.

Fey had anticipated this question and was ready with her comeback. "If you're nineteen years old and working as a delivery boy for a pizza parlor," Fey said quietly, "I don't think it's going to matter to me very much who your father is because it doesn't appear that it matters to him."

Wyatt had been leaning forward in his chair when he'd initially made his statement, but Fey's words seemed to take the wind out of his sails. He scooted back in the hard wooden chair that was opposite Fey but on the same side of a scarred table. He crossed his legs and folded his arms.

By placing both herself and Darcy in chairs on the same side of the table, her own closest to the door, Fey had not allowed Darcy to use the table as a physical or emotional barrier. With his back to the wall and Fey sitting in front of him, Darcy had nowhere to go. Emotionally, he couldn't run, and he couldn't hide.

Monk was standing off to one side. He held himself very still, almost blending into the wall of the room. His job was merely to observe, to get Darcy to forget he was even there. Center court was reserved strictly for Fey and Darcy.

By watching Wyatt's body language, Monk knew Fey's words had struck home. Wyatt's daddy had money with a capital M and power with a capital P, but it also looked like daddy had written off his good-for-nothing offspring.

If nothing else, Wyatt wasn't sure enough of the situation to believe daddy would immediately be riding to his rescue.

Fey was also watching Wyatt's body language. She'd successfully deflected his initial bluster and had changed him from aggressive to defensive. Now she had to untie the knots into which he had physically and mentally tied himself. She had to get him to the point where making a confession would seem like the only course left open to him.

Along with Wyatt's motorcycle helmet, Fey had also brought a large stack of files into the interrogation room with her. Most of them had nothing to do with the case. They were simply a prop to make Wyatt think there was a huge weight of evidence against him. Without saying anything further, she put her glasses on and began paging through the files.

"Can I have another cigarette?" Wyatt asked eventually, the silence getting to him.

Fey set aside the files and filched a smoke from the stale pack. She handed it across to Wyatt. Taking a pack of matches from a pocket, she tossed them across the table and watched as Wyatt lighted up. The match trembled slightly.

Fey made brief eye contact with Monk. He'd also seen the shaking of Wyatt's fingers. It was a sign. A sign of guilt.

"How are you feeling, Darcy?" Fey asked. Switching to Wyatt's first name was a deliberate move toward familiarity. She was well aware of the visible pulsation of the carotid artery on the right side of Darcy's neck.

"Okay," Darcy said.

"Good." Fey drew in a deep breath of secondhand smoke. Her lungs quivered in lust. She hated being a nonsmoker. "However, I'm sure you want to get home and take it easy. You've had a long night."

Wyatt looked at her directly for the first time since slipping into his defensive body language.

Fey continued on as if she hadn't noticed the birth of

hope in Wyatt's attitude. "Perhaps you can straighten out this whole situation if you answer a few questions for us."

Wyatt may have had a couple of prior arrests as a juvenile, and his daddy may be a top hot-shot lawyer, but Fey was banking that he was cocky enough to think he could talk himself out of trouble.

"You can ask," Wyatt said, copping an attitude of cool.

This was the tricky part. Fey had to get Wyatt through the next couple of minutes. If she could get a waiver, she knew she could nail his hide to the wall. "Well, before I ask you anything else I want to advise you of your rights."

"Damn straight," said Wyatt, still cool. "I got rights."

Screw your rights, Fey thought to herself without any outward change of expression. Everybody was always so concerned about their sacred rights, but they didn't seem to give a damn about their responsibilities.

"Okay. You have the right to remain silent," Fey opened the bidding with the accepted hard rhetoric, then she softened it by explaining further. "This means you can talk to me if you want, but you don't have to if you don't want to." This explanation sounded good on tape, as if the detective was going out of the way to make sure a suspect understood what was being said, but in reality it was a distraction. The rhetoric of Miranda told suspects to keep their mouths shut tight. Fey's explanation, on the other hand, also gave them the option of talking if they so desired.

Fey quickly continued. Timing was everything. "You have the right to an attorney. If you cannot afford one, an attorney will be appointed for you without charge before questioning. Do you know what an attorney is?" Again it would appear on tape that Fey was going out of her way to explain Wyatt's Miranda rights, but it was another distraction. Get the suspect thinking about how to explain what an attorney was and you got their mind off of asking for one.

"Yeah, I know what an attorney is," Wyatt stated.

"What is it?" Fey asked.

Wyatt looked stumped for a moment. "It's a dude that's

on your side in court,'' he said finally with a frown on his face.

Fey smiled. ''Good.'' She paused. She hadn't received a waiver yet, but she always waited a few seconds after advising a suspect of their rights before going after the waiver. It gave them time to forget the initial impact of being advised, and it gave the detective time to re-establish the rapport that had been established prior to the admonition. As long as the suspect was advised of his or her rights and the waiver questions were asked and answered, the law was complied with. Nothing was said about the time span involved.

''Can you get us all a cup of coffee?'' she asked Monk.

''Sure,'' he replied. He took no offense at being given the errand to run. Monk knew exactly what Fey was doing and quickly went about filling her request.

While Monk was out of the interrogation room, Fey asked a series of questions that were not specific to the case.

''How does your face feel?''

''It all right,'' Wyatt said.

That's too bad, Fey gave silent range to her thoughts, *I was hoping it hurt like hell*. Aloud she asked, ''How bad was your motorcycle messed up?''

Wyatt shrugged.

''Did the officers impound it or leave it at the scene?''

''They impounded it,'' Wyatt answered.

Fey played into giving Wyatt renewed hope. ''Well, when you get out of here, we'll see if there's anything that can be done about the impound fees.'' *Like hell we will*, she thought.

''Thanks,'' Wyatt said. He'd smoked his way through the cigarette Fey had given him and was now chewing on a hangnail. ''Another smoke?'' he asked.

''Sure,'' Fey said, and lighted it for him as Monk came back with the coffee.

When they were all settled Fey asked, ''Do you understand your rights, Darcy?''

''Yeah.''

"Do you want to give up your right to remain silent? Do you want to talk to me?" Fey asked both questions in quick succession, personalizing the issue from an interrogation into a conversation between Darcy and someone with a sympathetic ear.

"Yeah. I'll talk to you," Darcy said.

Fey let out a half-breath of relief. She was almost home. "Do you want to talk to me right now, just you and me, without an attorney?"

Darcy paused for a second, looking at Fey through smoke from his cigarette. "Sure," he said. "I got nothing to hide."

How many times had she heard that exact same lie, Fey wondered. *Your father is going to kill you when he finds out*, Fey thought as she watched Wyatt smirking at her from across the table. *You've got plenty to hide, and I'm going to find out exactly what it is.*

✦❂✦

CHAPTER SIX

FEY SIPPED HER COFFEE AND THEN SAT THE CUP BACK down on the table. "How long have you worked for Fratelli Pizza?"

"About three months."

"What do you do for them?"

"I deliver pizzas and clean stuff up."

Fey paused, fiddling with the coffee cup Monk had brought her when he'd returned to the room. "You asked me earlier if I knew who your father is. I'm well aware of who he is, but if he's such a big shot, how come you're delivering pizzas?"

"Screw my father," Darcy said. "He doesn't give a shit about me. Never did."

Fey pulled Darcy's juvenile rap sheet out of the pile of files on the table. She set it in front of her. "Looks like he's come to your rescue in the past."

Darcy shrugged. "Only when it suited him. Didn't want to soil the family name. He was the one that stuck me in that place."

"Vista del Sur?"

"Yeah. A concentration camp for juvenile embarrassments. I never raped that old lady anyway. She came on to me. I was just giving her what she wanted."

"You get a lot of that?" Fey asked.

Darcy smirked. "Sometimes. Some broads like to go slumming. How about you?"

Fey ignored the question and asked another of her own. "How many of the Fratelli Pizza restaurants do you work for?"

"I'm the relief driver, so I work at four outlets."

"When you make deliveries, do women ever come on to you?"

"Yeah. Sometimes." Darcy was now sitting in his chair facing Fey. He still had his arms and legs crossed, but he was beginning to loosen up. Fey was building his ego, and he obviously liked it.

Fey's brain was racing ahead. She was instinctively trying to read Darcy, looking for the chink in his armor. While verbally dancing around the issue of the violent rapes, she was rapidly thinking through all of the information she had received about Darcy and the crimes.

The key appeared to be the strong animosity between Darcy and his father. When Fey had first confronted Darcy, he had thrown his father up in her face. When Fey had called his bluff, Darcy had sullenly backed off behind a smug and indifferent attitude. Fey had seen all of this a hundred times before and knew that Darcy's cool exterior was as brittle as a dried twig.

If Fey's instincts were right, Darcy didn't necessarily want to be captured, but now that he was caught he wanted the whole shooting match to come out into the open. It was apparent that Darcy's father had cut the boy off and Darcy resented it mightily. But this time Darcy's situation was so bad that his father would have to pay attention again.

Darcy was clearly no whiz kid in the brains department. He wasn't some kind of sophisticated criminal. His crimes had not been plotted and planned any further than choosing victims who would have trouble identifying him visually. The rapes had been disorganized, angry, violent outbursts. And Fey was banking that the anger had less to do with sex or women than it did to a transference of the frustrations he centered around his father.

Fey had seen this transference in action before. A year earlier she'd handled a case where a sixteen-year-old boy had been badly beaten by his father. When the beating finished, the boy loaded up a rifle and went out into the residential neighborhood and shot the first male adult he came across. He couldn't face actually shooting his father, and instead had settled for an unknown father substitute. The transference in this case had a different outlet, but the process of the transference was the same.

There were other key points that clarified the situation for Fey. Despite the rift between father and son, Darcy was still a lawyer's kid. He may have been naive, but he still should have known better than to give up his rights. The little voice of experience in Fey's head was telling her that Darcy wanted to confess, needed to have his crimes made public, to strike back at his father in an indirect, yet damning, manner.

Fey had hated her own father and understood the impossible need to break through that hatred and try to find something related to love lying behind it. She also knew that there was never, ever any way to fulfill that need. It was as impossible as touching the end of the universe.

But just because she understood Darcy didn't mean she felt any compassion or sympathy for him. He had made his own choice to rape and bludgeon. The fact that he hated his father was no excuse, but Fey would let him think that it was. She would let him rationalize all he wanted as long as he gave her the confession she wanted.

"Darcy, do you know why you're here?" she asked.

Darcy shrugged.

Fey smiled inwardly. She was already halfway home. He wasn't denying anything. He was going to make her work a little harder, make her put the pressure on him so he could justify the confession, but he was going to cough in the end. Of that Fey was sure.

In the corner, Monk was holding himself very still, barely even breathing. He knew Darcy's whole attention was focused on Fey, and there was no way he wanted to do anything to break that connection. If he had been a betting man, Monk would back Fey every time when it came to getting a confession. She was a wizard at manipulation and judging a suspect's response. She couldn't win them all. Nobody could. But she won more than she lost, and in the final accounting that was all that mattered.

Fey casually picked up Darcy's motorcycle helmet and examined it. She wrapped one hand around the mouthguard and very slowly and deliberately raised the helmet up in the air over her head. And just as slowly and deliberately, she brought it down to touch with feather softness against the open palm of her other hand. The movement was silent and graceful and would never be picked up by the room's hidden microphone.

Darcy turned his head away from Fey as she repeated the movement.

"We both know why you're here, Darcy."

Fey raised and lowered the helmet again. This time it slapped a little harder into her open palm.

"You just can't stay away from those ladies you make deliveries to. Can you, Darcy?"

The helmet went up and down. Up and down.

"There's something about them. Isn't there, Darcy? Something telling you to go back and do the things you did. Isn't there?"

Raise and lower. Slap a little harder in the palm. Not too hard. Didn't want the mike to pick up something it shouldn't. The movement was a subtle intimidation. It wasn't a physical threat, but a mental one—Fey letting Darcy know she knew what he had done. She was telling him that she knew exactly, in every detail, and was only waiting for him to admit.

Fey was hitting her interrogatory stride. Under other conditions she would spend more time building her theme—giving her suspect a way to justify his crimes. Interrogatory themes allowed a suspect to buy into a rationale behind their actions that would appear to make them more socially acceptable; *she made you do it . . . if she didn't want it, she wouldn't have dressed like that . . . after what she said, you had to hit her . . . you didn't mean for anyone to get hurt, it just happened*; anything that would bring a suspect to the point of confession.

Fey didn't believe in the excuses she dangled before a suspect, but she laid them out just the same in order to get the confession. It didn't matter how a suspect justified the crime. What mattered was the confession. The crime was just as bad, the punishment just as severe.

With Darcy, however, Fey could already feel him coming to boiling point. He was jumping out of his skin, and Fey just needed to push him a little further and he would be over the brink. Like taking candy from a baby.

"Nobody has really understood the real you. Have they, Darcy?" Fey's voice had a soft, almost grandmotherly comfort in it. She knew Monk would call her a whore for getting a confession this way, but what the hell.

She put the motorcycle helmet gently down on the table and then reached out and placed a hand on Darcy's shoulder. "I can tell that about you already. Nobody really listens to you. Do they, Darcy?" The constant use of the first name established an intimate bond. Ever so gently she began to rock Darcy's shoulder back and forth. The young man's whole upper torso began to sway with the motion.

"Darcy, what you did to those ladies wasn't right. Was it?" Soft questions now. Closed ended. Not asking for elaborate answers, just a simple yes or no.

"I didn't do—"

"Yes, you did, Darcy," Fey immediately interrupted the denial before it was completed. She was in total control of the interview. "I know you did these things." Fey deliberately avoided harsh, accusatory words like rape and beat. She kept everything on track, but soft. Lull the suspect into thinking things weren't as bad as they were. "You know you did them. We have to get to the truth. And that's all I want, Darcy, is the truth. You can tell me the truth. Can't you, Darcy?"

There was a few seconds of silence as Fey continued to rock Darcy's shoulder, and then there came a quiet, "Yes."

Fey watched as Darcy's eyes scrunched closed. A huge tear broke loose. Fey knew she had him now, just needed to press a bit further.

"Darcy, you can tell me about what happened tonight." Get the most recent crime cleared and the others would follow like falling dominos. "You're sorry about what you did. Aren't you, Darcy?" Again the close-ended question with the assumption of guilt built in. Not, *Have you ever hit your wife?* but, *The last time you hit your wife, you really didn't mean to hurt her, did you?* Close-ended questions. Assumption of guilt. Looking for simple yes or no answers.

Fey waited in silence for the answer to her last question. She knew Darcy had heard her, and she was giving him time to feel the pressure of the silence and fill the void. It was a trick lawyers and reporters all learned when they went to asshole school—ask, *How do you feel now that your entire family has been killed?* and then sit back in silence and wait for an answer. We've all been trained to respond to questions to the point where it becomes a natural habit. We answer even when we don't want to because we know we're supposed to answer.

Finally, Darcy surrendered a quiet, "Yes."

Fey felt jubilant inside, this was the first admission of guilt, but her exterior remained cool and nonjudgmental. There was a hole in the dike, but now she had to break the dam.

"You are sorry. Aren't you, Darcy?" Hit the same point again.

"Yes." The answer coming quicker, easier this time.

"Actually, you really like Mrs. Mattheson. Don't you?" Fey named the most recent victim.

"Yes," Darcy replied, his eyes still scrunched closed, tears flowing silently.

"Look at me, Darcy," Fey said.

Darcy shook his head negatively, but Fey rocked his shoulders back and forth in an affirmative manner. "Come on, Darcy. Look at me."

Darcy opened his eyes.

"You went back there tonight. Didn't you? You went back to Mrs. Mattheson's house and you pushed your way in. Didn't you? And you pushed Mrs. Mattheson over that table and put your dick inside of her!" Fey raised her voice. She dropped her hand from Darcy's shoulder and picked up the motorcycle helmet again. "And you hit her in the head with your motorcycle helmet because you were angry. Because nobody understands you. Because your father doesn't give a damn about you!" She thrust the helmet into Darcy's lap. "You did that didn't you, Darcy? Didn't you?"

Tears flooded down Darcy's face.

"Didn't you, Darcy? You did that to Mrs. Mattheson!"

"Yes!" It came out on a wail of inner pain.

"And you did it to the others, didn't you? Mrs. Basil, Mrs. Cranston, Mrs. Greaves, and Mrs. Plimpton!" Fey named off the other victims. "Didn't you? Didn't you?"

"Yes! Yes! Yes!" Darcy stood up screaming, tears streaming.

"What did you do to them, Darcy?" The question was perfectly timed and executed.

"I screwed them! And I hit them! I hit them over and over! They didn't like me! Nobody likes me! Everybody hates me!" Darcy collapsed back onto the hard chair, burying his head in his arms.

Silence except for Darcy's sobbing.

The electricity in the room ebbed.

There was a knock on the interrogation room door. Fey flashed a look at Monk. If the knock had come a few seconds earlier it could have destroyed the whole dynamics of the interrogation. The interruption could have clammed Darcy up tighter than a duck's ass, blown the whole confession.

Fey jerked her head at Monk, indicating that he answer the knock. Monk was glad of the chance to move. His muscles had been cramping. He opened the door and stepped outside.

Fey sat back, watching Darcy who still had his head buried in his arms on his lap. Muffled whimpering reached her ears. She felt drained and looked over at the pack of stale cigarettes on the table. Heaven knows she could have done with a smoke right then. She picked up the pack and then set it down again almost immediately.

Monk stuck his head back in the door. "Grab your boots and saddle, partner. We've got us a cold one."

✦

CHAPTER SEVEN

FEY TURNED THE GOLD CHEVY INTO THE WILL ROGERS State Park entrance. In the passenger seat Monk was busy gathering up his notebook and pen.

"You see anybody?" Fey asked as she pointed the vehicle past the empty ranger shack.

"There's a couple of black-and-whites up there," Monk said, pointing toward the far corner of the parking lot. One of the cars was in plain sight. The other was mostly hidden by the drooping boughs of a pepper tree.

Fey cruised toward the location. She liked working with

Monk. He was still young for a homicide detective, but he was very anal retentive and took pride in what he did. He was intuitive, methodical, and rarely made mistakes. He was also happily married, which made him a rarity in a profession that tore wedded bliss apart like wet tissues in a cyclone. Monk's devotion to his wife and three young kids also relieved Fey of having to deal with a partner who was more interested in where his next lay was coming from than in solving crime. Working with partners who were constantly trying to get into her shorts—not because they felt anything for her, but simply because she was female—was a state of affairs for which she was developing less and less tolerance.

Parking the Chevy behind the second black-and-white, Fey clambered out of the vehicle. She pulled on a dark blazer to cover the Smith & Wesson .38 that hung in a shoulder holster under her left arm. A number of years earlier, the department had authorized officers and detectives to use the Smith and Wesson and Beretta 9-millimeter semiautomatics. At the same time, the department also began phasing out the S&W .38 by issuing 9-millimeter weapons to police academy recruits. But even though Fey had completed the training and owned a 9-millimeter Beretta, she still carried her favored .38 wheel gun most of the time. It had become an old friend over the years and she was loath to carry anything else. She knew it made her an anachronism, but she didn't really care.

She was certain she could hit and kill with the .38, but she wasn't that comfortable yet with the 9-millimeter. Given time she would get used to it, but she wasn't sure she had all that much time left on the job to make the effort worthwhile.

As she approached the second black-and-white, Fey was surprised to see that is was not an LAPD vehicle, but instead bore the logo of the Los Angeles sheriff's department. There was also another plain detective sedan, parked further forward, that had been completely hidden by the drooping pepper tree and other surrounding foliage.

She glanced between the roof antennas of the gold

Chevy as she slammed the door and caught Monk's eye. He raised his eyebrows in reply and shrugged his shoulders. It looked like there may be a jurisdiction dispute awaiting them. The border between LA city's bailiwick and the province covered by LA county ran along the north edge of the park.

Since there was nobody around to direct them otherwise, Fey and Monk started hiking the dirt trail that led away from the front of the foremost vehicle.

The announcement of a possible homicide had brought an abrupt end to Fey's interrogation of Darcy Wyatt. She had left him, however, in the hands of Dick Morrison who Fey knew was very capable of finishing the booking process.

Morrison had been listening to the interrogation through earphones in the cramped quarters of the tape room. He knew exactly where Fey had left off, and she was sure he would be able to effectively pick up the pieces. Morrison would run with the confession by getting Darcy to make a fuller statement, typing it out, and having Darcy read it and sign it after initialing any changes.

Several mistakes would be made on purpose in the typed confession. This would be done strictly to get Darcy to point them out, make the changes, and then initial them. The reasoning behind this procedure was that later on in court, Darcy couldn't claim he'd signed a blank piece of paper which was then filled in without his knowledge. Having him change and initial the mistakes proved that he'd read and confirmed the statement.

Fey didn't like leaving the interrogation at the halfway point, but she really didn't have much choice. Murder took precedence. In the back of her mind, however, there was something tickling her intuition. She didn't know what it was yet, but there was something there.

The confession had been clean. It had been a little easier than most, but it was still a good piece of work. Morrison had done a good job of catching Wyatt to begin with, and she had done a good job of breaking Wyatt down and getting the admissions from him. Something, though, still didn't feel quite right. It was as if a portent of doom was surrounding her mind as she reviewed the situation. Somehow, some way, she knew that she was far from done with Darcy Wyatt.

As she walked up the trail, however, she began a concerted effort to wipe Wyatt out of her mind. She would need all of her attention centered for the immediate task ahead and could not afford to be distracted. Mistakes could let a killer slip away like water through a cup of interlaced fingers.

Both she and Monk kept their heads on the swivel as they hiked, checking the ground around and ahead of them before they stepped. They were looking for anything that might be a clue. They didn't even know for sure what they had yet, but they were operating on automatic pilot, keeping their senses attuned for anything, no matter how small, that might later be able to help them crack the case.

Monk had already started his notes on the case. He'd written down the date and time they'd been notified about the body's discovery, who had told them, and the location where the body was to be found.

It was approaching six-thirty and the sun was making itself known. It was already warm, and the day promised to be another scorcher in the ongoing heat wave. The Santa Anas were slated to kick in again later in the day. On the way to the scene, the Chevy's static-ridden AM radio had spat out the information that the high for the day was expected to break a hundred and three degrees in downtown LA and the surrounding valleys for the sixth day in a row. Tempers in the city were already flaring and there was no hope of relief in sight.

One side of the trail was bordered by rough, four-foot-high split-rail fencing. Beyond the fencing was a thick tangle of shrubs and trees. The other side of the trail ran along the gradient of a hillside that reached up above the detectives' heads and then flattened out to be covered by more shrubbery—the city giving way to the rural.

The trail itself was worn from constant use. The prints of horseshoes could be seen molded into the dry dirt, and here and there droppings from the same animals testified to the trail's main use.

As Fey and Monk sauntered around a bend in the track, they were brought up short by a stream of yellow crime scene tape stretching from the fence to the hillside, where it was tied around a sturdy manzanita branch. Beyond the tape stood two uniformed LAPD officers, a uniformed sheriff's officer, a citizen in jogging shorts who was attached by a leash to a large German short-haired pointer, and MeCoy and Blades—two suits from the sheriff's homicide detail.

"Ah shit," Fey said *sotto voce* when she saw the two rival detectives.

"Lookit here," MeCoy said when he spotted Fey. "If it ain't the fabled Frog Lady herself. How's it shaking, darlin'?" His tone was lounge-lizard sincere.

"You're not even registering on my Richter scale, MeCoy," Fey replied, ducking under the crime scene tape and moving forward. "Nice suit," she said to the sheriff's detective as she got closer. "How often do you have to take it in to get the seat shined that way?"

Blades, the other sheriff's detective, laughed and got a dirty look from MeCoy in return. There wasn't much love lost between the two sets of detectives. It had less to do, however, with the rivalry of the two big LA law enforcement agencies than with straight personality conflicts. There were a number of sheriff's deputies who Fey liked and respected. MeCoy, however, always managed to get under her skin, and Blades wasn't much better.

Things had escalated between Fey and MeCoy two years earlier. While working a gang shooting in West Los Angeles, Fey had come across information that led to the suspect in a sheriff's murder case. Fey had not only come up with hard evidence, but she had also obtained a confession from the suspect. The fly in the ointment was that MeCoy had already cleared the sheriff's case as murder/suicide.

When Fey marched in with her suspect's confession and the evidence to back it up, the situation belched egg all over MeCoy's face. If the same thing were to happen again, Fey might play things differently—she already had all the on-the-job enemies she needed—but the damage had already been done and MeCoy would never forgive her for it.

"What do we have?" Fey asked.

"Well, excuse me for not getting right down to it," MeCoy said. "I didn't realize you were so serious these days, Frog Lady."

"Murder is a serious business," Fey replied mildly, not rising to the bait of her despised nickname. "Or is the sheriff's department still handling it like dark comedy?"

"You would have thought LAPD could have sent us a real homicide detective instead of a cut-rate Henrietta Youngman," MeCoy snapped back.

"Damn you're quick," Fey said. "I bet you're just a howl on the stand-up circuit. However, this is the lay-down-dead circuit we're working this morning."

MeCoy's face twisted into a smug grin. He couldn't miss this opportunity. "I've heard that about you. When somebody gets you to lay down, it's just like you're dead."

Fey didn't even let the verbal shot make a dent in her armor. "Typical sheriff's sources," she replied. "All hearsay, and never reliable."

"Children, children, please," Monk cut in to act as mediator. "Do you think we could cut the comedy act and get on with things? I've got to be in court in a couple of hours."

Fey and MeCoy glared at each other, but a silent, uneasy truce appeared to be declared.

Blades cleared his throat. "The body is over here." He gestured with his arm and the four detectives began to move down the trail. Blades pointed at the citizen in the jogging shorts, who along with his dog had been watching the repartee between the rival detectives. "That's Cory Parsons and his dog Spot. Spot found the body while he was looking for a place to crap along the edge of the trail." Blades's voice was low enough that it did not reach Parsons's ears.

Both man and dog, however, appeared to know they were being talked about. Parsons looked upset, and Fey realized that, as usual, Blades and MeCoy hadn't handled their witnesses with kid gloves. She figured she'd try and salvage some kind of rapport and shot a smile in Parsons's direction. "We'll be with you as soon as we can," she said.

"I certainly hope so. I have an important early business meeting to attend, and I'm beginning to stiffen up," Parsons said. He started a series of stretching exercises as if to emphasize his point.

Fey knew Parsons's type. She dealt with them all too often in West Los Angeles. More money than sense, and a highly inflated perception of their own importance. She was also aware of West Los Angeles area's unofficial motto, *The rich are different, and will be treated that way.* It stuck in her craw, but that didn't make it any less true.

Fey and Monk both gave their names and serial numbers to the uniformed LAPD officer who was keeping the crime scene log. The officer noted the information and added their arrival time.

"Is the dog's name really Spot?" Monk asked Blades.

"Who the hell cares," Blades replied, loud enough this time for Parsons to hear. "It's just a dog."

"Oh, good," Fey said. "He can identify mammals all by himself now. What an improvement since the last time we worked together."

Blades had his back to Fey and didn't respond verbally. However, Fey saw a dark red blush run up the back of his neck.

"Why do you always have to be so antagonistic?" Monk asked Fey in a soft voice. They were walking a few paces behind Blades and MeCoy.

"It's in my nature," Fey replied, not taking offense to the question.

"This isn't going to be any easier if we piss them off."

"I know that, but what do you want me to do? Both these guys are jerks."

Monk felt slightly odd counseling his partner, who heavily outranked him, but he persevered. "Don't let them wind you up. If they know they're getting your goat, they win. Find some way to use them. You won't get anywhere abusing them."

Fey shrugged her shoulders. "I'll try to be good, Daddy."

"Hey, I'm on your side. Don't start with me."

Fey held up both her hands. "You're right. I'm sorry."

Blades and MeCoy both stopped by the split-rail fencing that bordered the edge of the horse trail. About six feet beyond the rail, down the brush-covered slope, a figure was crouched down staring at a freshly dug mound of earth.

Sticking straight up from the mound was a human arm—the hand at the end trying to claw its way to heaven.

✡

CHAPTER EIGHT

"WHO THE HELL IS THAT?" FEY ASKED, ANGRY TO SEE someone encroaching on the crime scene. Even though Fey had spoken loud enough, the figure crouched by the gruesome shallow grave did not turn around.

"He's FBI," MeCoy said with distaste. If there was anything that could unite the LAPD and the LA sheriffs it was a common dislike and distrust of the FBI.

"Get outta here," Fey said. "He doesn't look like any FBI guy I've ever seen. Where's his black suit, white socks, and brown wingtips? Hell, he ain't even wearing a skinny tie." The figure, still crouched by the shallow grave, wore black stovepipe jeans cinched with wide buckle belt, scuffed black cowboy boots, and a black t-shirt with the sleeves rolled up. "He looks like a reject from a bad James Dean movie."

The figure finally stood up and turned around. "There were no bad James Dean movies," he said, as he carefully walked away from the grave and toward the quartet of detectives.

Blades did the introductions. "Detectives Croaker and Monk, LAPD," he said, making the appropriate pointing motions. "Special Agent Ash, FBI."

Fey felt her stomach flip-flop.

Ash stood slightly over six-two. His short blond hair had been bleached almost white by the sun and appeared to have been cut by a berserk lawnmower. His lean build was capped by deceptively broad shoulders that tapered to narrow hips and long legs. The arms that extended from the rolled up sleeves of his t-shirt were corded with tanned and sinewy muscles. His face was long and gaunt, his eyes sunk in shadows. Character lines set him squarely in his forties. Fey could almost hear the Marlboro Country theme playing in the background, almost smell the open range.

Get a grip, woman! She mentally yanked on herself. *What in the world is the matter with you?*

Ash held out his hand. It was cool and dry in Fey's as she shook it. She'd half-expected electricity to jump from it.

"I hope you don't mind," he said, knowing he was trespassing on a homicide detective's sacred territory. "I'm just here as an observer." His voice had the weary rasp of too many late nights and too many dead bodies.

Just for a second, before he removed his hand from hers, Fey caught a flash of insight—felt something of Ash's inner turmoil. She didn't know what it meant, but she instinctively knew that Ash was carrying around some heavy baggage. And there was something else . . . something else . . . and then the window closed and the image lost.

"Our watch commander notified Agent Ash when the call came in," Blades said, as if that explained everything. He looked from Fey to Ash and back again as if he too was sensing something he couldn't quite put his finger on.

Fey's first thought was to ask why the sheriff's watch commander would call out the FBI to a local murder scene? Ash claimed he was just here as an observer, but Fey knew that was a pile of malarkey. There was more to this situation than was readily apparent. Rather than make waves at this juncture, however, she decided to play along until she could establish the ground rules for this little fiasco. She winked at Monk, letting him know to keep cool.

"What's with this guy Parsons and his dog?" Monk asked, trying to get the proceedings back on a normal level. "It must have been pitch black out here when they discovered the body."

Blades shrugged. "Typical granola nut. Can't miss a morning of jogging. Apparently, he has this early business meeting he was bitching about, so he had to take his morning jog earlier than normal. He said he runs along the horse trails here every day. He didn't want to mess up his biorhythms, or some such crap, by changing his course just because it was dark. So he brings along a giant flashlight and takes his chances stumbling across the landscape."

"The dog found the body?" Fey asked.

"That's what Parsons told us. Said the early morning start threw Spot's bowel movements off. Usually, the dog runs right along with him, but today he took off into the undergrowth. Parsons figured the dog was just looking for a substitute fire hydrant and would catch up down the trail."

"I take it the dog didn't catch up," Fey said.

"Yeah," Blades continued. "Really pissed Parsons off. He had to turn around and come back looking for Fido. When he gets back to where Fido took off, Parsons shines his flashlight into the brush on the side of the trail and lights up Fido doing the doggie two-step around the grave. The stupid animal must have been having an orgasm thinking about all those juicy, freshly buried bones. Must have thought he'd won the doggy lottery."

"Good old Rover probably cost Parsons a world's record, screwing up his training like that," MeCoy said without feeling.

Fey shut her eyes and took a deep breath. These two really knew how to push things to the limit. The dog had probably been distressed and confused by his discovery—the animal's senses picking up the violent vibrations from the scene. However, Fey kept her mouth shut. If she voiced her opinion, Blades and MeCoy would never let it rest. She didn't need to give them any extra ammunition. "What did Parsons do after he found his dog with the body?"

Blades shrugged. "Chained Fido to his leash and dragged him off to the nearest pay phone and dialed 911. He made the location sound like it was in the sheriff's area, so one of our units rolled out. The deputy who caught the call wasn't sure of his boundaries either, so instead of kissing this one straight off to you guys, the dumb shit gets the watch commander to roust us out of bed and drag ass down here."

MeCoy took over the narrative in his own inimitable way. "First thing we did was check the borderline on this section of the trail. And what do you know? This baby has LAPD's jurisdiction written all over it."

Fey grunted. She knew the area, and knew the body was squarely on LAPD's side of the border. "I wouldn't put it past either of you to have moved the body when nobody was looking."

MeCoy grinned. "Yeah. You can still see the heel marks where we dragged him from our jurisdiction to yours. It was pretty tough reburying the body and getting that arm at just the right artistic angle."

Fey grunted. MeCoy and Blades would do whatever they could to hamper her, of that she was sure, but moving a body and reburying it with witnesses around was a bit beyond the pale even for them.

"Did the dog dig the arm up?" Monk asked, as he looked down to the shallow grave.

Fey caught MeCoy and Blades exchange quick looks.

"No," Blades said, after a second or two. "At least we don't think so."

It was Fey's and Monk's turn to share glances.

"Why not?" Monk finally asked when it became apparent that MeCoy and Blades were not going to volunteer anything further.

The answer, however, came from Ash. "Because the sheriff's had another body buried just like this one two weeks ago."

✦✦✦

CHAPTER NINE

"WHEN WERE YOU GOING TO GET AROUND TO SHARING this trivial bit of information with us?" Fey asked Blades and MeCoy, anger tinged with frustration evident in her voice. "Or were you perhaps just going to let us take this one over and not bother to mention it was the second in a series?"

"Hey, give us a break here," MeCoy said, spreading his hands in a gesture of innocence. "We just didn't have the chance to bring the subject up yet."

"Yeah, right," Fey said. She had her hackles up again. "There was never anything in the teletypes from your department about a body buried with the arm sticking out."

"A teletype was sent out last week," Blades said. "We kept the information to a minimum, however, because we didn't want the press getting hold of anything they could run with. We didn't need the investigation turning into a three-ring circus."

"So, did you come up with anything?" Fey asked.

Blades shook his head. "Nada. Zippo. Zilch. We're at the same place we were when the body was discovered."

"Who was the victim in your case?"

Blades looked chagrined. "We haven't identified the victim. It's a John Doe. Black. Twelve to fifteen years old."

"A kid?"

"Yeah. Sexually assaulted. Bondage shit. Buried with the arm sticking out of the ground. Just like this one."

"I'm going to want the file."

"You'll get it," Blades said.

"The complete file." Fey's voice was low and menacing. She'd had trouble in this area before.

McCoy took a step forward, but Blades put a hand on McCoy's shoulder and stopped him. "You'll get the complete file. You'll also get our complete cooperation. We want these solved as badly as you will, once you get into them."

"You're already assuming they're connected." Fey made the statement to Blades, but shifted her eyes to Ash as if he were a magnet. If the bodies were connected, the FBI agent's presence became a little clearer.

"Have to be," Blades said. "The grave scenes are too similar for the bodies not to be connected."

Fey nodded. Blades was probably right, but the last thing she needed was a serial killer on her turf. If it was a serial killer, she could lose the whole investigation to the robbery-homicide division. And if there was anything she needed less than a serial killer on her turf, it was the big boys from downtown throwing their weight around all over the place. She could feel a headache coming on behind her eyes.

The tension of the scene was broken by the sound of new arrivals. The five detectives looked over to see Lily Sheridan, the coroner's investigator, leading a parade consisting of the crime scene photographer, and two blank-looking lumps of muscle who were Lily's assistants.

"Fine time of the morning to drag my ass out here," Lily said when she was close enough. She was a big woman who didn't seem to care much about her image or the coarseness of her personality. Her blouse and slacks were creased and grubby, the tail of her blouse hanging out at the back. When she wasn't working a crime scene, she chain-smoked with a vengeance.

"Where's the body?" she asked, and Blades and McCoy moved aside and gestured toward the shallow grave.

Lily took one look and winced in disgust. "Shit," she said. "Sammy, go back to the truck and get the tools." There was no sympathy in her voice. She was not upset by the scene, but by the inconvenience of having to wait for the correct equipment before she could deal with the body. "Why didn't you tell me this was a burial job?" Lily bustled away, clearly not expecting an answer.

Fey turned to Monk. "Why don't you start by getting a full statement from Parsons? I'll get Eddie Mack organized on the photos, call in the troops, and then stay with Lily."

"Right," Monk said, taking a thin silver pen from his inner jacket pocket.

"And, Monk," Fey said, verbally stopping the detective before he could walk away. He looked back toward her. "Let's do this one slow and easy. Let's not miss anything. I don't know why, but I've got a feeling we're going to be in for a real roller-coaster ride before we're done."

Monk nodded without saying anything and moved away. He hated it when Fey got bad feelings. He'd never known her to be wrong.

Eddie Mack, the SID photographer, had a smile that reminded Fey of a kindly Santa Claus. Beyond his smile, however, he was about as ugly as ugly gets. He was short and stocky, with thick black hairs exploding unchecked out of his nostrils and connecting his eyebrows across the top of his nose. A bad case of teenage acne had left his cheeks looking like used pin cushions, and there was a large round growth on his neck. His clothes would have been rejected by most transients, and there was the constant faint smell of rank body odor whenever Eddie was within arm's length.

Fey didn't care for the man's physical appearance, but she was always glad to see him at a crime scene. His camera equipment was state of the art—all personally owned because the department claimed not to have the funds to provide what was needed—and cared for in a manner that bespoke obsessive love for the inanimate objects. The best thing was that Eddie also knew how to use all the trick stuff he carried around with him, and could produce the most extensive crime scene photos without even breaking a sweat.

"How ya doin', Fey?" Eddie asked around the wad of gum taking up a good portion of his mouth.

"Could be better, Eddie."

"Well, look at the bright side. At least you're better off than the stiff."

Fey shrugged. "Some days, I wonder." She turned her full attention toward Eddie, but not before noticing that Ash, the FBI agent, was watching her from where he stood with Blades and McCoy. It made her feel nervous, as if he was waiting to see if she made a mistake.

"What kind of shots do you want on this one?" Eddie asked. He fiddled with the light setting on one of the Nikons slung around his neck.

"Give me a full panorama set of the area around the body. Some closeups of the arm sticking out of the grave. And then a complete series as Lily uncovers the body."

"You got it."

Fey thought for a moment. "Can you also get me a couple of snaps of Parsons and his dog?"

"He the one that discovered the body?"

"Yeah."

"All right. No sweat."

Fey appreciated Eddie because he never quibbled with what you asked him to do. He'd also worked so many crime scenes that if a detective didn't ask for certain shots, chances were Eddie would have taken them anyway simply as a matter of routine.

As Eddie bustled about his tasks, Fey took a portable phone out of her jacket pocket. Flipping it open, she dialed the squad room's homicide line.

The call was picked up on the second ring. "West LA homicide, Detective Jones." The smokey voice was aggressively female.

"Brindle, it's Fey. We got a cold one out here and I need you and Alphabet to give us a hand." Brindle Jones and A.B. Cohen, better known as Alphabet, were partners on the MAC table. They doubled as the second homicide team behind Monk and his regular partner, Chip Hernandez. Like Hop-Along Cassiday, the sex crimes investigator assigned to Fey's unit, Hernandez was on vacation and unavailable.

Alphabet, Monk, and Fey had all been around West LA for a number of years. Jones and Hernandez, though, had only transferred into the division in recent months—their presence being part of a not-so-subtle move to bring more gender and ethnic diversity to the West Los Angeles detective division.

"I heard you had a stiff when I got in this morning," Brindle said. "Dick Morrison was finishing up with your rapist from last night. He said you didn't even have a chance to catch your breath between getting a confession out of the rape suspect and getting the homicide notification."

"I didn't even have the chance to take a pee," Fey said. "And some of the bushes and trees around here are starting to look pretty good."

"Bushes? Trees? I thought we worked in the city. Where the hell are you?" Brindle asked. "Wait a minute," she interrupted before Fey could tell her. "Let me grab a pad."

Several white male detectives had been forced to transfer from the division recently for a variety of nit-picky reasons. Their absented positions had all been filled by female detectives or detectives from ethnic minorities. Fey didn't necessarily view these moves as a bad thing, but she hated the manipulations that were "politically necessary" in order to accomplish the supposed ethnic and gender "balancing" of the division. On the surface, all of the detectives appeared to be getting along, but subtle tensions were also present because of the artificial way the personnel changes had been implemented.

"Okay. Where do you want us to come?" Brindle asked, when she came back on the phone line a few seconds later.

"We're on the horse trails along the west side of Will Rogers State Park."

"Isn't that the sheriff's area?"

"Murphy's law in action," Fey said. "The body is just on our side of the border."

"Shit. And to top it off I'm dressed up for court today."

Fey laughed. Brindle was a notorious clotheshorse. "I told you—Murphy's law. You'll see the parked cars from the main entrance to the park. Just follow the trail from there."

"Okay. Alphabet should be getting in any minute now. As soon as he does we'll start rolling. Anything I can do until then?"

"Yeah. Whistle up a couple of day watch patrol units from roll call. Send them this way to help with the crime scene search, but tell them not to use open frequencies." She knew Brindle was smart enough to pick up that Fey's reasoning behind this request was so that the press did not come out and start saturating the park with reporters and camera equipment.

"Right," Brindle said. "Anything else? Do you need the video camera or anything?"

"The video is in the back of my car. I'll have to go back and get it. I could do with a hot cup of coffee, though, since we're going to be here for a while. Would you mind doing a Starbucks run for all of us? You fly and I'll buy."

"You got it. Hey, Alphabet just walked in. I'll bring him up to speed, and we'll see you in about forty-five minutes."

Fey hung up without saying goodbye. Brindle Jones had come to West LA with a reputation for sleeping her way into good assignments and promotions, and she had done little to change that perspective since she had arrived. Fey thought that was a shame because Brindle had the potential to be a good detective without needing to use sex to get ahead. However, the situation didn't seem to bother Brindle as much as it did Fey.

Lily Sheridan's loud voice broke into Fey's reverie.

"Hell, Sammy. What took you so long?" The big woman grabbed one of the shovels out of Sammy's hands as he returned from the coroner's van. "I got people to see, places to go. I can't be standing around here all day waiting for you before we can play Captain Kidd and dig up the buried treasure."

Sammy's expression was long suffering and chagrined. Marty, Lily's other blank-faced assistant, looked glad that he wasn't on the rough end of Lily's tongue for a change.

"You coming to help dig up the body, Croaker?" Lily directed her comments toward Fey. "Or are you going to wait for the *Reader's Digest* version?"

"Hold your water for five minutes," Fey replied. "I want to get the video recorder out of the car and then I'll join you down in the muck."

"Great," Lily said. "Home movies. Maybe we can make some money off of this on 'America's Most Gruesome Home Videos.' I love that show, don't you?"

✦ CHAPTER TEN

THE FOLLOWING SIX HOURS TOOK THEIR TOLL ON FEY AND the other detectives at the scene. The toll was not simply a physical compilation of lack of sleep coupled with the tedium of any homicide crime scene search. The major toll was emotional. The price Fey and her co-workers paid was a sucking away of any feelings of compassion or humanity, a hardening of the soul necessary to deal with the cold, calculated humiliation and destruction of another human being.

Level by level, the horror of the scene appeared from the shallow grave. As it became clearer, Fey had to shut down her own humanity in order to deal with the atrocity being unearthed.

Every cop learns how this is done. As a rookie, you're entitled to lose your cookies at your first dead body call. It doesn't matter if the call is a gruesome murder scene or a simple natural death. If it is the first time you've come across a dead body as a cop, you have a freebie to share your lunch with the closest flower bed. But that's it. One time only. After that you better learn how to shut down, remove yourself from the scene, find something funny to laugh about, turn off every compassionate emotion.

You can't think about how you would feel if that was your husband, wife, mother, father, son, or daughter, lying there in that pool of blood with his entrails ripped out. You can't think of the body with its eyes plucked out, its breasts cut off, and a hair brush jammed up its anal orifice as human.

Once, it might have been human, but it isn't any longer. Once, it may have been someone's relative, friend, or lover, but it isn't any longer. Now, it's just so much bloody carnage. A pile of chemicals and elements. Cold clay. Ashes returned to ashes. Not human. Not a vital living, breathing, walking, talking creature blessed with the spark of life.

Now, it is nothing but a shell.

Dust to dust.

If cops don't learn how to shut down emotionally, they quickly find themselves on the overload rocket straight to the moons of madness.

A cop has two choices, shut down or go insane.

But shutting down also carries a high price tag. With each crime scene, with each victim of excessive violence, with each investigation of a death at the hands of another, with each shutting down of emotion and humanity, it makes it that much harder to turn it on again—to come back and act "normal" around noncop friends and family.

And each time you shut down, you're never able come all the way back. Shut down enough times and the switch breaks. And if the switch breaks, your emotion remains as dead as the lump of lifeless clay at your feet.

When Fey returned from her vehicle with the video camera, Lily was already standing next to the grave. She hadn't started disinterring the body yet, but had busied herself scooping up the top layer of earth in a wide circle around the grave. Fey knew that Lily would preserve the earth for later analysis to see if any traces of blood, urine, or semen had been left by the suspect before or after burying the victim.

Lily had marked out two areas near the grave that showed clear footprints in the loose earth. They would be photographed and plaster casted before Lily lifted the earth they were on for analysis.

Lily pointed the prints out to Fey. "You think they belong to your suspect, or to the guy who discovered the body?"

"They probably belong to Blades or MeCoy," Fey said

cynically. "We'll have to get paper foot impressions from all of them for elimination purposes."

"What about the FBI guy?" Lily asked.

Ash was standing at the edge of the trail watching the activity.

Fey shrugged. "Let's get his shoe prints also, but somehow I think he's a hell of a lot more careful than those other two."

"Good-looking sucker, isn't he?" Lily said.

"If you like that type."

"Right," Lily snorted. "You just play it cool. Keep on making out like he doesn't make your panties damp."

"Shut up, Lily." Fey quickly glanced around to make sure nobody was in earshot. "Is it that obvious?"

"Just to me, doll," Lily said. "And that's only because I'm also a woman. I'd let him screw me rigid in a heartbeat."

Fey had to readjust her image of Lily in a hurry. She'd never thought of the sloppy coroner's investigator as having any kind of a sex life.

"How about we keep my feelings our little secret and get on with the job at hand," Fey said in a conspiratorial, all-girls-together tone.

"Whatever you want, doll," Lily said, scooping more earth into a plastic bucket. "Just let me know how it comes out."

While Fey had walked back to her detective sedan to get the video camera, she'd also used her portable phone to call Lieutenant Mike Cahill, the detective division's commanding officer. She caught him at breakfast and filled him in on the homicide scene.

Cahill would take care of contacting Captain Strachman, who was the commanding officer of the entire West Los Angeles area. Cahill would also notify West Bureau, which had command over the four West Bureau areas—West Los Angeles, Wilshire, Pacific, and Hollywood.

At some point these notifications would result in the brass showing up at the crime scene so they could strut importantly around telling the working detectives to do exactly what they were already doing. There had been too many departmental blood baths, head choppings, and general demotions flying around recently for anyone from the ranks of captain and above to feel comfortable. They all had to see and be seen at important crime scenes. Had to make a presence in order to deflect those knives waiting to slam home in their backs. The politics at the high end of the brass heavy department were becoming even a more deadly game than normal. If you blinked, your career could be killed quicker than a ten-dollar whore in an alley with a psychopath.

Fey had to play her share of politics, but she wasn't at a level yet where it really counted. She was still an Indian, still connected to the streets. Fey considered watching the chiefs dither around until they self-destructed one of life's little pleasures.

Watching Lily disinter a body, however, didn't rate in the same category.

Eddie Mack came in for some closeups of the hand and arm that were sticking up from the grave. Lily also looked at the exposed appendage as Fey set up the video on a tripod. Once the Palmcorder was running, Fey stepped over to examine the area of the wrist that Lily was pointing out.

"Looks like the hair on the back of the arm has been ripped off," she said, squinting to get a better view of the raw patch of skin. "Adhesive tape?"

Lily nodded. "Be my guess. A little bondage to keep things interesting."

"Before or after death?"

Lily shrugged. "Have to wait on the autopsy for the answer to that one."

Very carefully, Lily began sifting dirt away from the body. As she pulled the dirt away, Sammy scooped it up into a plastic bucket.

"I appreciate your taking all the pains with the dirt," Fey said. She was aware that some coroner's investigators wouldn't bother.

"Whoever did this is a real sicko. I'd love to see you

nail his balls to the wall. The dirt is a very, very long shot, but I don't wanna be the one to overlook it.''

Fey again found herself reassessing her impressions of Lily. It wasn't very often that you came across a sloppy anal-retentive with a sex drive. ''How can you be sure the killer is a man?'' Fey asked simply to play devil's advocate.

''Give me a break.'' Lily looked up from sifting earth. ''How many female ritual killers have you ever heard about? You could count them on one hand and still have fingers left over to pick your nose and wipe your butt.''

Fey had to laugh. ''Okay, I'll concede the point. The arm didn't pop out of the grave all by itself. It was placed that way as part of the killer's ritual. Did you know the sheriffs had another one like this?''

''News to me,'' Lily said. ''With a setup like this, they should have known there would be another one.''

''I'm sure they did, and that's why they kept quiet about it. If a couple more popped up in another jurisdiction they could kiss theirs off by tagging it on to another investigation.''

''You gonna let them get away with it?''

''That remains to be seen. The fat lady hasn't sung yet.''

Lily grimaced. ''And don't expect me to either. I got a lousy voice.''

As more dirt was pulled away the body clearly became that of a white male. The corpse was naked and lay on its back in the grave. The other arm was twisted underneath the body at an unnatural angle. The grave was deeper than it first appeared, because the victim's legs were bent back at the knees, feet behind the body's buttocks.

''Didn't you say your body was a male black?'' Thinking Blades or MeCoy were standing behind her, Fey asked the question without turning around.

''Male, black, fifteen to sixteen,'' Ash answered. ''The body was laid out exactly the same with one arm sticking out of the grave, second arm under the body, knees bent, legs underneath the body. I feel quite sure that there are going to be a number of other similarities when we turn the body over.''

Fey looked over her shoulder. Blades and MeCoy were nowhere to be seen. ''Where did Batbrain and Boy Blunder go?''

Ash smiled slightly. ''They also think highly of you.''

''I'm sorry. Personality clash.''

''It happens.''

''I'm afraid it happens with me more often than not.''

''At least you recognize the fact.''

''Yeah, but I'm getting too old to do anything about it.''

''Happens to the best of us.'' Ash also turned to look behind him. ''I think your counterparts slipped away to get a bite of breakfast,'' he said, turning back.

''Nice of them to let me know. I wanted the file on their first body before I let them out of my sight.''

''Don't worry. I've got everything you need.''

One look at Ash's face told Fey the double entendre had not been deliberate. He wasn't even aware of the twofold meaning inherent in his statement. The problem was that Fey had kind of hoped the statement had been deliberate.

''When we get done here,'' Fey began asking, ''can I buy you a cup of coffee somewhere and have you explain to me how you're involved in all of this?''

''No problem.''

Fey returned her attention to Lily's efforts and saw that Eddie Mack had his camera clicking away again over some aspect of the corpse.

Getting closer Fey saw what was holding Eddie's attention. A piece of silver duct tape was slapped across the mouth of the corpse, and around the neck a length of quarter-inch white rope dug deeply into the flesh.

''Ouch,'' Fey said mildly, but looking down with disgust.

Ash's voice intruded on her thoughts. ''I think you'll find the rope runs down the back to attach to the victim's wrist and ankles.''

''I've seen it before,'' Fey said. ''The more the victim struggles to get loose, the tighter the rope around their neck becomes.''

"Basically, they strangle themselves," Ash agreed.

"With a little help from whoever trussed them up like a turkey in the first place," Lily added, throwing in her own two cents.

Lily bent over and looked up the victim's nostrils. She took a small flashlight from her belt and took another look. "It looks as if the victim has recently taken up snorting dirt," she said, as she straightened up and returned the flashlight to her belt.

"Which means," Fey said, understanding the implication immediately, "the victim was alive when the killer buried him."

❈❂❈

CHAPTER ELEVEN

"MIKE, YOU CAN'T DO THIS TO ME."

"I'm not doing anything to *you*, Fey. I'm telling you to turn this case over to robbery-homicide division because that's where it belongs."

"Pardon my French, Lieutenant, but that's bullshit. This murder occurred on my watch and my people deserve a chance at cracking the case. Robbery-homicide isn't going to be able to do anything that we can't."

"Yes they are, Fey, and you damn well know it. They can throw thirty detectives on this case right now. We can't do that. In case you haven't taken count lately, we've got three detectives, including yourself, assigned to homicide in this division, and one of them is on vacation. You and Monk are already covering sex crimes for Hop-Along, who is on vacation as well. You're also still in charge of the MAC unit until bureau agrees to give us another D-III supervisor to take that unit over. This case has the potential to get completely out of hand, especially since the sheriffs have a matching body. We don't have the personnel resources to handle serial killers or high-profile cases inhouse. They're robbery-homicide's responsibility. That's what robbery-homicide is designed to handle. If we don't give them this case, they're going to take it anyway.''

''Not if they don't find out right away about the sheriff's body.''

Lieutenant Mike Cahill threw up his hands in exasperation. ''What do you want from me, Fey? Do you want me to lie to robbery-homicide? Do you want me to lie to bureau? Lie to the chief? Is that what you want?''

''Sounds reasonable to me. Since when have they ever told us the truth about anything?''

''Fey—''

''Come on, Mike. This is the biggest case this division has seen since I took over the homicide unit. If robbery-homicide takes it away, you know what it's going to look like?''

''It's going to look like exactly what it is—following procedure for a possible high-profile murder case that requires more resources than are available at a divisional level.''

''Crap! That may be the real reason. I'll not argue with you. But it's going to look like it was taken away because I'm a woman.''

''Damn it!'' Cahill stood up from behind his desk in agitation. ''That's a load of shit, and you know it. You can't turn everything into a gender issue. You're being ridiculous.''

''Am I?'' Fey, who had been standing in front of Cahill's desk, took a step back and sat down. She took the action as much to diffuse Cahill's growing agitation as she did to not give away the fact that her legs were shaking. She pointed toward the squad room, where a myriad of detectives were intently showing no interest in watching what was going on through the open blinds of Cahill's office windows. ''Then how come everyone out there thinks that's exactly what's happening?'' Aside from sitting down, Fey had also modulated her voice. She didn't quite have the *juevos* to go nose to nose with her commanding officer.

In actuality, she was glad to find that there were still limits to her own bravura. Monk had been right—lately everything and everyone was aggravating her, and she was starting to act like a witch on steroids. Fortunately, she was still able to recognize that challenging Cahill verbally was one thing, but getting into a physical altercation with him was quite another.

Cahill had started the argument over sending the case to robbery-homicide division when Fey first briefed him at the crime scene. He had arrived at the scene along with Brindle Jones and Alphabet.

Brindle had been dressed to kill, as usual. Fey considered the outfit. As far as she was concerned, Brindle's skirt was shorter than professional, and the heels high enough to be outlawed. It never ceased to amaze Fey what this woman could get away with. To Fey's mind, Brindle's arms and legs were so skinny they could be used to pick locks, but the woman had breasts that just wouldn't quit. Store bought, was the opinion of most of her female coworkers, but that didn't stop most males from tripping over their tongues.

Brindle's ebony skin glowed in the early morning sun, her face framed by an explosion of honey-colored hair. She wore her body as if it were a coiled spring, snapping almost every male head in the vicinity to attention. The one exception was Ash. Fey had grabbed a glance at him to catch his reaction to Brindle's arrival. She was surprised to see him take one look at who was causing all the commotion, and then turn his head back toward the body of the victim.

Fey sent up a silent prayer. *Please don't let him be gay.*

In comparison to Brindle, Alphabet was a troll in training. Short, round, bald, and myopic, but with a waxed mustache to die for. His dung-brown, off-the-rack suit hung on him like a blanket covering a huge rubber ball.

He was carrying a tray stacked with large containers of café latte. He handed one to Fey, who took the top off and drank gratefully.

With hidden delight, Fey had sent Brindle and Alphabet off to search the area of the trails around the crime scene for any clue that may give them a lead. "I want any kind of trash you come across recovered and brought back to the station. If you find anything out of the ordinary, send up a shout and Eddie Mack will come over and take photos. Anything that looks like tire tracks or fresh footprints are going to have to be casted. Mark 'em and let the SID criminalist know whenever they get here."

Brindle looked daggers at Fey, but didn't argue. She was well aware of what Fey was doing. In her mind, though, if the old bitch couldn't keep up she shouldn't come out to the race. Alphabet, on the other hand, immediately went off about the job as happy as a puppy playing with an old slipper.

Fey had then turned to Cahill and brought him up to speed. The lieutenant had been silent while Fey talked, trying to take in everything she was telling him and come to a correct decision. When she finished, his first words had been, "We better call in robbery-homicide," and the two of them had been arguing ever since.

Cahill wanted robbery-homicide notified and rolling to the crime scene, but Fey distracted him as Lily and her goons zipped the victim into a body bag and began to remove the corpse.

Lily had already bagged the victim's hands and feet in plastic to retain any evidence that may be under the fingernails or toenails. She had also removed and retained the rope that had been used to bind the victim, cutting it so the knots would be preserved. Later the knots would be examined for style and comparison.

The silver duct tape from across the victim's mouth had been removed and placed in an evidence envelope. The killer had also used duct tape to bind the victim's ankles together. The wrist belonging to the arm that stuck out of the grave had marks where tape had been torn off. Fey and Lily had thought at first that adhesive tape had been used. It was clear now that duct tape was the culprit as there was still a piece wrapped around the wrist secured under the body.

All the tape had been removed and secured for analysis. If the detectives ever recovered a roll of tape from a suspect, the torn ends of the tape could possibly be matched. There would also be residue attached to the adhesive side of the tape. Most of the residue would belong to the victim—hair and skin particles—but there might also be something from the suspect, or something from the location where the victim had been held before being brought to the park.

Fey had kept Cahill's order to call in robbery-homicide successfully at bay until they returned to the station. Once there, however, the battle raged—first in the squad room and then behind the closed door of Cahill's office.

After Fey pointed out through the open blinds into the squad room, Cahill marched around his desk and briskly pulled the cords on the six Venetian blinds closed. "There. Are you happy now?" he asked.

"Closing the blinds isn't going to make anyone think any differently about what's going on in here. They all know that you're giving me a good woodshedding."

"And you deserve it." Cahill sat down in the other visitor chair, but kept the width of the office's oval meeting table between them. "I'm ordering you to sell this case to robbery-homicide, and you're fighting me every step of the way."

"Mike," Fey put a little pleading in her voice, "I want this one. If Lee Phillips was still running our homicide unit, you'd never take this case away from him if he wanted it. In fact, you'd fight tooth and nail to help him keep it."

Cahill didn't immediately reply to this foray. It hit a little too close to home.

Fey pressed her advantage. "You know I'm right, Mike. You and Lee were the president and butt-buddy of the good-ol'-boys' club in this division. Drinking buddies, fighting buddies, whoring buddies—''

"That's not fair, Fey."

"Yes it is." Fey leaned her elbows onto the table. "It's the whole point. I'm never going to be one of the good-ol' boys. Hell, I don't want to be. But I've covered your ass since I became the homicide D-III. Our clearance rate has come up to the same level as when Lee was here, even though the number of murders has almost doubled in the last two years."

"It hasn't quite doubled."

"Hey, you must be losing this argument if you're starting to pick nits. I know I was given the spot up here as a token gesture to affirmative action—''

"That's not totally true. You were also qualified."

"I know that, but I also know that pressure came down from the chief's office to put a woman in the position of a homicide supervisor. West LA drew the short straw because Lee retired and we have the lowest murder rate in the city. If I screwed it up, it wouldn't be that bad."

Cahill shrugged—not arguing. "I still want this case turned over to robbery-homicide."

"Let me finish, because I haven't screwed up. Have I?"

Again Cahill simply shrugged.

"Come on, Mike."

"Okay. Okay. You've done the job."

"Mike . . ."

"All right. You've done a good job."

"I've done a great job, damn it! Why is it so hard for you to say it? It's not like we've been married for the last two years and I'm begging you to tell me that you love me. Just give credit where credit is due."

"I'll give you credit, but—''

"No buts, Mike. Give me a week to do something with this case. Don't snatch the rug out from under my feet again. You did that to me two years ago over that case with Colby and look what that got you!"

"That's not fighting fair."

"Oh, that's fighting fair, all right, but this isn't—if you don't give me a week on this thing, I'm going straight to the department's women's coordinator and lodge a complaint. And then I'm going to start shooting off my mouth to the press. Everyone is going to believe this case was taken away from me because I'm a woman"—Fey held up her hand to stop Cahill's interruption—"even though that may not be true. But if that's what people are going to think, then I'm going to go with the flow. I'll make your life miserable. You've got, what? A year left till retirement? Do you want to put up with that kind of grief?"

Cahill gave Fey a hard stare. "You really are one tough bitch."

"And you're one tough bastard. Now are we done with the schoolyard posturing? All I'm asking for is a week. If we don't cut a break with this thing by then, I'll roll over and play dead and robbery-homicide can run with it."

"This is going to cost you big time, Croaker."

Fey knew that Cahill's use of her surname indicated she was in the deep end, way over her head.

"Okay, you got one week. If you mess this up, I'll have your head on a platter so fast the butcher won't have time to stuff an apple in your mouth."

"Jeez, I love a man who has a way with sweet talk."

"Get the hell out of here before I shoot you and put you out of my misery!"

Fey stood up, smiling. "I love you too, Mike."

"Your time is ticking, Croaker."

✦ CHAPTER TWELVE

"A WEEK? YOU HAVE TO BE KIDDING. HOW ARE WE SUP-posed to solve this thing in a week?" Brindle Jones punctuated the question with a cynical snort. "I don't see why we don't just let robbery-homicide take it over right now."

"Don't you start," Fey said. "I had to damn near sell my soul to buy us a week. This atrocity occurred on our turf. I take that as a personal challenge. If you don't like working homicide, I can get you spun over to auto theft or burglary without a second's notice."

Brindle shook her head. "No deal." Brindle had her eyes on a couple of plum positions within the department. Having homicide experience in her package was going to get her a lot closer to those goals than any assignment that was strictly investigating crimes against property. "If you say we can solve this murder in a week, I say we can solve it in seven days." She may not like Fey, but she did respect her, and she wasn't about to get left at the gate on this thing.

The way Brindle figured it, Fey was good enough and lucky enough that she stood a good chance of pulling a rabbit out of the hat somewhere down the line. Brindle had seen her boss do it before, and she wasn't about to bet against her this time. If Brindle stayed in on this she knew she couldn't lose. If the case busted open, she would make sure she hogged more than her share of the glory. If the case blew up, she could cut and run, and the responsibility would lay squarely on Fey's shoulders.

Fey swiveled her eyes around the interview room to take

in Alphabet and Monk. "Do either of you have any problems with this? If so, now's the time to put up or shut up."

Monk flashed his ready smile. As far as he was concerned, Fey's concentration and excitement were catching. He loved this stuff.

Alphabet gave Fey a conspiratorial wink and ran a handful of pudgy fingers across his bald head. He, too, could sense his blood rising to the battle. "Okay with me, boss," he said.

Ash was also in the tiny room where Fey and Monk had earlier interrogated Darcy Wyatt. His lanky frame was leaned back into a corner, cowboy boots crossed below, arms crossed above, as if trying to disappear. He caught Fey's eye, but only gave a slight shrug of his shoulders without saying anything. Now wasn't the time.

Fey seemed to relax a little. She took her glasses off and rubbed the bridge of her nose. After leaving the lieutenant's office, she had called her Indians in for a council of war. First, though, she'd had to make sure they were all on the same page of music. She couldn't afford anyone dragging their feet. Brindle was still a question mark, but Fey was relying on the young detective's ambition to keep her plunging forward.

She looked at her watch. It was only one o'clock in the afternoon. It seemed like she had been at work forever—first dealing with Darcy Wyatt, and then at the crime scene. Wasn't time supposed to fly when you were having *fun*? Still, they needed every second they could steal on this one.

"All right," she said finally, after quickly organizing things in her mind. "Alphabet, you get on the horn to the coroner's office. I want the body on a slab and fileted today. If they give you a bad time talk directly to Harry Carter. Tell him it's me asking, and see if he'll do the case personally. Stroke his ego a little. He's the best there is, but he still likes people to tell him so. And, I want you down there taking notes when the scalpels and saws come out."

"You got it, boss," Alphabet said, as he finished scribbling in a small notebook.

"Monk, I want you and Brindle to jump on identifying the victim. Lily gave me a set of prints she rolled at the scene, along with a half-dozen Polaroid closeups of the victim's face. Fax the prints, a full description, and a copy of the Polaroids to DOJ." The Department of Justice in Sacramento was a clearinghouse for information on missing persons. "The body looked young enough to be a runaway, so let's see if he's in the system. Check with our own missing persons down at detective headquarters division, and then show the pictures to our vice unit and someone from ad-vice downtown."

"I've got to go to court this afternoon on the Sanders case," Brindle reported.

"That's the spousal abuse that was filed as a felony?" Fey asked, checking her memory.

"Yeah. He thumped her good. Broken jaw and cheekbone. Third reported complaint."

"Who were the arresting officers on the case?"

"Hamilton and Hamilburg."

Fey shook her head. "Uniform patrol's answer to Cheech and Chong." The two officers were known for their standup comedy routines at divisional Christmas parties. "You just filed the case, right?"

"Yeah. I won't be needed to testify, just to coordinate the victim and wits."

"Okay. See if you can get the DA to buy off on kicking you free and keeping Hamilton as the investigating officer on the case."

Brindle nodded.

"What are we going to do about today's MAC cases?" Monk asked. The homicide would take priority, but other crimes would also be demanding attention.

"Did you look to see if there was anything pressing?"

"Just the normal paper flow. Nothing screaming for immediate response."

"Give it all to Hammer and Nails. It won't faze them

to carry the brunt of the other MAC cases while we run with the homicide.''

Police culture loved nicknames. Arch Hammersmith and Rhonda Lawless, otherwise known as Hammer and Nails, were a couple of hardcases that had recently transferred into the division from internal affairs. Their eighteen-month tour of duty with IA had twice been extended, and they were considered legendary when it came to burning bad cops—a reputation that bought them respect but few friends.

Nobody knew quite what to make of the situation when they were transferred to West LA, but it was clear that the pair had a rabbi high enough in the department echelon that they could write their own ticket. The point had been driven home when they had first been assigned to different investigative units in the squad room. The department frowned on long-term partnerships, and Mike Cahill thought it best to split the pair up. In less than twenty-four hours, however, Cahill had doubled back on himself and Hammer and Nails were a partnership again assigned to Fey's MAC Unit. No explanation was given.

Fey didn't know if they had asked to be assigned to the MAC unit, or if Cahill didn't know what else to do with them. Whatever the reason, Fey was actually glad to have them. They may be inseparable, but they came to work early, stayed late, turned in quality investigations, seemed to anticipate the unit's needs, kept out of trouble, and never complained if they were given the donkey's load of the work. As far as Fey was concerned they were just what the doctor ordered. If they wanted to stay together and work MAC, she'd give them a long leash.

Rumor control in the division, however, said the pair were still assigned to internal affairs, working undercover to investigate allegations of sexual harassment and racism within the division. As a result, most of the other detectives and officers gave the pair a wide berth. This attitude, though, didn't seem to disturb Hammer and Nails to any degree. They kept to themselves and did their job. If they were still working for IA, they had a tough row to hoe.

Fey wouldn't have minded getting Hammer and Nails involved in the homicide investigation. They had more investigative experience than almost anyone else in the unit, but that was also the reason she needed them clear to run everything else while the rest of the team worked with her.

"What if the victim was hooking?" Brindle asked suddenly. Her brain had obviously been churning. "Can we talk with the West Hollywood sheriff's station's vice unit?" West Hollywood had the highest population of homosexual prostitutes in the area.

"That's a good thought," Fey told her. "They're probably the best source, but let's not do it until we've run everything else to earth. We don't want to owe them anything. Got it?"

"You bet."

Fey finally pointed at Ash. "While everyone else gets cracking, you and I are going to have a long talk about the body that McCoy and Blades are trying to dump on us, as well as what the Feeble-Brained Investigators' interest is in this whole stinking setup."

Ash smiled slightly and nodded, but didn't rise to the bait.

There was suddenly a silent pause in the room when everyone seemed to take a deep breath at the same time.

"This one is going to get ugly, people," Fey said. "I can feel it in my water. We're all going to have to give a hundred-and-ten percent to clear this before the killer racks up a whole string of bodies." Fey took a second to let what she was about to say sink in. "As far as the press is concerned, we give them nothing. You are all deaf and dumb. If I catch any of you leaking information, your ass is going to be grass and I'm going to be the lawnmower. Are we straight about this?"

Everyone in the room nodded.

"Right now we've got two bodies that may be connected," Fey continued. "If we don't move fast, there will be more." Again she took a dramatic pause. "Somewhere out there, walking around, is a victim whose life is resting in our hands. If we don't do our job fast enough, that victim will die and the clock will start ticking on the next victim. Think about that when you start getting tired and your butts begin to drag. Don't just think about solving this case. Think about saving a life.''

The faces in the room were solemn as Fey's words hit home. Finally, there was a shuffling of feet and scraping of chairs as everyone started to stand up and move out.

"I just hope I'll have time to eat lunch before going to the autopsy,'' Alphabet said with a straight face.

"Oh, gross,'' Brindle said, wrinkling her nose. Everyone else laughed, breaking tension.

"Gross is as gross does,'' Alphabet retorted, in his best Forrest Gump impression.

"Yeah,'' Fey said, glad that Alphabet's natural humor was putting everyone back on an even keel. "Just remember, life is like a box of chocolates. It's overpriced and most things in it suck.''

⊡⊗⊡

CHAPTER THIRTEEN

As Fey reentered the squad room with Ash trailing behind her, she heard herself being paged over the station's intercom system.

"Detective Croaker, you have a visitor at the desk, Detective Croaker.'' The voice was a tinny whine, as if the human responsible for it was on life support.

"Give me a break,'' said Fey. "I've got too much going on to be messing with somebody's pretty-ass problem at the desk.'' She sat down and picked up her phone. Quickly she punched in the extension that would connect her to the volunteer who worked the squad room front desk.

"West Los Angeles Community Police Station." The same voice that had paged Fey over the intercom answered the phone.

"Ruth, this is Fey Croaker. Do you know who's at the front desk for me?"

"Just a moment, I'll ask."

"No! Wait! Ruth—" Fey was too late. The volunteer had put her on hold. *Bless their souls*, Fey thought, but sometimes the crew of older women who volunteered to answer the squad room phones drove her crazy. Didn't the woman realize Fey wanted her to be a bit more discreet?

"Detective Croaker?" Ruth asked, coming back on the line as if she had expected Fey to have hung up.

"Yes."

"The man said his name is Devon Wyatt. He seems very nice."

Fey felt the walls closing in around her. *Very nice.* The volunteer was obviously not a good judge of character. "Okay. Thanks, Ruth," Fey said. "Tell him I'll be out in a minute."

Fey hung up and slumped in her chair.

"Not a petty-ass problem?" Ash asked with a smile.

"Hardly petty, but still an ass. Do you know Devon Wyatt?"

"It's hard not to know Mr. Civil Rights in our business."

"His kid was arrested for rape last night. I did the interrogation, got the cop-out, and authorized the booking before getting called to the homicide scene this morning."

Ash laughed gently. "Sounds as if you're moving up to play with the big boys."

"I certainly know how to pick 'em, don't I?" Fey sighed and stood up. "Look, I'm sorry about this, but if I don't deal with this asshole right now, it will only make things worse."

"No problem," Ash said. "I'll be here when you get done. Can I use your phone?"

"Make yourself at home," Fey said expansively, waving her arm across her cluttered desk. "Coffee room is over there," she said, pointing.

She gave Ash a direct stare when she thought he winked at her. She looked away quickly, realizing he had a slight tic under his right eye that occasionally spasmed.

There was still something about the man that was touching her on a personal level. His eyes were an unremarkable slate-gray color, but there was a depth to them that was disconcerting. It was as if he was constantly fighting to stop himself from exploding, an outward calm belying a deep inner turmoil. She didn't know exactly what vibes she was picking up, but she knew that she had better be careful with her emotions.

The damn man made her feel very conscious of her body. During the last six months she'd lost twenty pounds through cleaning up her eating habits and three vigorous workouts a week with a friend who was a personal trainer. She'd been feeling pretty good about herself—not afraid to look at herself naked in the mirror—but Ash made her suddenly aware that there were areas that still needed improvement.

"I'll be back," she said in a bad Austrian accent, as she tried to shake off the feeling.

"You and Schwarzenegger. What a team."

"Yeah, but he's kind of like the cops. You can never find a good terminator when you need one."

Devon Wyatt sat in the same small interrogation room Fey and her team had recently used for a council of war. The same room where Fey had earlier taken Darcy Wyatt's confession. *The damn place is getting a lot of use today*, Fey thought, reflecting briefly on the hundreds of interrogations and interviews she'd done between the urine yellow walls. *If I had a penny for every lie told in this room, I'd make Howard Hughes look poor.*

"It's nice to meet you, Detective Croaker," Devon Wyatt said. He didn't take the chair on the far side of the scarred table that Fey was gesturing toward. Instead, he slid expertly into the chair closest to the door, which gave him the position of command that Fey would normally take for herself.

Fey had to smile. The man was smooth. Fey estimated him at under five-seven, but the man was clearly athletic and carried himself tall.

Dressed in a double-breasted wool suit no cop would ever be able to afford unless he was on the take, Wyatt was both dapper and confident. The cufflinks holding the French cuffs of his creamy white silk shirt were gold nuggets the size of a swollen knuckle. The subdued Countess Mara tie was secured by a two-carat diamond that flashed in the room's harsh lighting. Thick, jet black hair grayed slightly at the temples, but Fey had a sneaking suspicion the gray was touched on for effect.

"I've heard a lot of good things about you," Wyatt continued. "Jake Travers speaks very highly."

What a crock, Fey thought. Did this guy truly think she was going to buy off on this? Jake's name, however, had hit home, and Fey wondered just how much Devon Wyatt knew about her relationship with the high-ranking district attorney. It wasn't common knowledge that Jake and Fey were an item, but Wyatt might have access to that information. He probably didn't know they were on the outs, however, or he wouldn't have dropped the name in an effort to curry favor.

"I also hear you're very tough," Wyatt continued. "They say you put your own brother in jail."

Fey felt her blood getting hot. Tommy Croaker was Fey's younger brother. He was a low-life drug addict who had caused her problems for years. She'd protected him from their abusive father when they were kids, and she'd done everything she could to help him when they were older. Tommy, however, didn't want to be helped. When he broke into Fey's house, to get money for drugs, it was the last straw. Fey arrested him, pressed charges against him, and made sure he served the maximum jail time possible. Tommy was now back on the street, and supposedly straight, but he'd had no contact with Fey.

"It's good to know people are saying nice things about

you behind your back for a change," Fey said as calmly as she could. "Although you probably wouldn't know the feeling."

Wyatt's smile reminded Fey of a carnival ride attendant watching some poor kid puke his guts up on the Scramble Wheel. "And here I thought we were going to be friends," Wyatt said.

"Let's be clear and up front," Fey said in a reasonable voice. "The only thing I'm likely to get from you is grief. The only reason you're here is because your kid got booked this morning, and you want something from me that you're not going to get. We may be able to remain civil to each other, but we aren't ever going to be friends."

Devon made to interrupt, but Fey overrode him. She had taken the offensive in the interview and was not about to let Wyatt take it away from her. He was too slick. If she backed down in any way, he'd lawyer her into a corner.

"The case against your son is part of an ongoing investigation, and I'm not going to discuss it with you. After Darcy is arraigned, his lawyer can apply for discovery through proper channels. Until that time, I don't think there is anything I can do for you."

Wyatt sat back in his chair. His eyes were locked with Fey's as he crossed his legs and adjusted the sharp crease in his trouser leg. "Very impressive, Detective Croaker." His voice was filled with the mellifluous resonance that made him a killer with juries during final arguments. "I see I am going to have to reassess my estimate of you."

Fey didn't reply.

"Did you know who my son was before you interviewed him this morning?"

"Yes."

"And you didn't think it might have been prudent to call me before you questioned him?"

"Never entered my head. He's a big boy now, and he can't expect Daddy to hold his hand forever."

"With an attitude like that, Detective, I don't see you going much further in this department."

Fey laughed. "I have to tell you," she said. "The chief and I have one thing in common. We're both as high as we're going to get on this job."

"Darcy is my only son, Detective Croaker." Wyatt gave a short pause. "We have had our problems in the past, but he is still my son. I will be using every asset within my power to see that he is cleared of this ridiculous charge."

"Even if he's guilt?"

"What does guilty have to do with anything?"

"What about the women he raped?" Fey felt her anger rising and tried to put a cap on it.

"What about them? Even if he did rape them, so what?"

"Let me get this straight," Fey said through clenched teeth. "You figure Darcy should walk away from this simply because he's your son. You figure that gives him some kind of carte blanche or diplomatic immunity?"

Devon Wyatt gave a self-deprecating shrug. "I've spent the better part of my life defending justice from narrow-minded, political Golems and the trolls, like yourself, who are their tools. I've seen enough police corruption in my time to know that charges like the ones brought against my son are more often than not simply a frame to hang on an innocent party so the police can clear their blotter. The real rapist is still out there, but you don't have to worry about him now because you think you have my son to take his place and cover yourself in roses. Well, think again."

"What a crock," Fey said, voicing aloud her original thought.

"Don't even begin to think you can bandy words with me," Devon Wyatt said. "You have no chance of standing up to the weight of true justice that I represent. You have no idea the depth of the precipice on which you are standing."

Fey shook her head. "I don't believe I've ever met a megalomaniac before now, Mr. Wyatt. Thanks for the experience, but it's not one I'll want to repeat in a hurry." She was calmer now, almost awed by the gall of the man.

"Detective Croaker, police departments—especially the LAPD—have a well known reputation for taking care of their own. Well, so do I, and you will rue the day you ever decided to meddle in my affairs."

"I'm just doing my job, you schmuck. And I'm telling you right now, Darcy is going down. And he's going down hard."

Devon Wyatt smiled. "Name calling? Somehow, I expected better from you. But I'll tell you something for free. Whatever the outcome regarding the charges against my son, I will make it my personal quest to destroy everything you hold dear."

Fey came up with a shark-tooth smile of her own. "Threats? Somehow, I expected better from you."

Devon Wyatt glared at her.

"I think this interview is over," Fey said. "I'm quaking in my boots too much to carry on." She stood up and opened the door. "I'm sure you can find the exit," she said. "Straight down the hallway and through the door. Don't let it hit you in the ass on the way out."

Wyatt stood up and started to move past Fey. He hesitated in the doorway, their bodies in close proximity, but not touching. He looked up into her face. "I'm going to enjoy this," he said. The stare-down continued for several silent beats, and then Wyatt turned and strutted away.

Fey watched him until he reached the doorway that led through to the squad room's front lobby. "Wyatt," she called. He stopped and turned to face her. "You look better on TV," she said. "Somehow, I thought you'd be taller."

CHAPTER FOURTEEN

FEY'S HEAD WAS BUZZING. THERE WAS ALMOST MORE GO-
ing on than she could deal with. She had to organize and
delegate. The latter was something she still had a hard time
doing as a supervisor.

She looked at her watch. Two o'clock. *Damn!* She had
a four o'clock appointment that she didn't want to miss.
First, though, she had to get somebody to handle the Darcy
Wyatt case. If each *i* and *t* wasn't dotted or crossed, Devon
Wyatt would find a way to kick their collective butts all
over the courthouse. She also had to find time to deal with
Ash and dig into McCoy and Blades's case.

What she should do was tell Mike Cahill she needed to
borrow a detective from one of the other tables. Rape and
homicide were both high profile enough to justify reas-
signing detectives from units such as auto theft or burglary
if the need arose.

Personnel lent to other units, however, were usually
about as sharp as Nerf balls. No unit was willingly going
to give up their best and brightest. They had their own
cases to clear and couldn't afford to let their top workers
disappear for an extended length of time. Also, there was
always the fear that if a unit was able to get along without
the reassigned detective, then that unit would never get the
position back. Borrowing detectives from other tables was
sometimes done, but it always led to harsh feelings and
other problems.

There was also another dilemma. If Fey went to Cahill
and said she needed extra personnel to run her unit's cases,

it would immediately prove Cahill's point that the current murder case should be sold to robbery-homicide.

Fey quickly realized borrowing personnel wasn't an option. Her people were just going to have to suck it up and go for it. She did a quick inventory. She, personally, had to take care of Ash and deal with McCoy and Blades's case. Alphabet was at the autopsy. He'd be gone for at least three or four hours, and then he'd have to write up everything and follow any leads that were produced. Monk and Brindle were chasing down the identity of the murder victim. Depending on where that information led them, they could also be tied up for an extensive period.

At one end of the MAC table, Fey could see Arch Hammersmith was elbow-deep in paperwork. It was clear Hammer and Nails were going to be swamped handling the regular MAC caseload. Fey knew there were three separate bodies in custody for spousal abuse, and there must have been fifteen or sixteen new misdemeanor battery cases in the unit's in box that morning. All that plus the ongoing cases was going to be enough to keep the pair off the streets and out of trouble no matter how good they were. Fey couldn't ask or expect them to do any more.

She sighed. Her only option appeared to be splitting up Monk and Brindle. It wasn't something she wanted to do. Identifying the murder victim was of prime importance to breaking the case, and there were too many tangents for one detective to chase down.

Feeling slightly stressed, Fey turned to look for Brindle and found herself instead confronted by Rhonda Lawless.

"Hell, Nails. Don't you know better than to sneak up on a trained detective?" Fey blew out a heavy gust of breath.

"Sorry, boss, but I wanted to ask you about this rape arrest." Nails held out the paperwork on Darcy Wyatt. "You want Hammer and I to run with this thing?"

Fey took stock of Nails. She was forty-seven but looked thirty-five. Tall and lean with short, thick hair so black that it caught purple highlights in the station's florescent lighting. Fey had seen Nails naked in the locker room and knew that she had the musculature of a female body builder. There was nothing soft about the woman at all. She had a reputation as an ice queen, but she seemed to fit together with Hammersmith as if the two of them shared the same brain—psychic twins.

"I was going to give it to Brindle. You two have enough on your plate."

"Give me a break," Nails said. "No offense, but if you give this thing to Jones it will get screwed up nine ways to Sunday." Nails nodded her head toward where Brindle was bending over a table giving Cahill a free view down her cleavage. "If she doesn't give the lieutenant a heart attack, I'll be surprised. Why don't you just tell her to put her tits away, go home, and leave the detective work to the professionals."

Fey had to laugh and saw a rare smile cross Nails's face. "I'm sorry," Nails said. "Some days she just pisses me off."

"I know what you mean."

Brindle had heard Fey laugh. She stood up, as if knowing Nails had said something about her, and walked off. She gave Cahill a sly smile and the lieutenant almost jumped back out of her way. His face flushed as if he were a schoolboy caught looking at dirty magazines.

"Look," Nails continued. "Leave this case with Hammer and me. We've got the other MAC stuff under control, and if this case isn't followed up properly we could end up losing it. You know who this jerk's father is, don't you?"

"In spades. I just spent an uncomfortable ten minutes in an interview room with him."

"Like swimming with a shark, isn't it?"

"You know him?"

"Hammer and I have been up against him before. He's far from a cream puff, but he is beatable."

"Okay. If you want the case, you've got it, but there's a hell of a lot to do on it—"

"—Hammer has already been on to the other jurisdictions and has everything organized. Since we have the arrestee here, we're going to file all the cases with MacNamara, our DA. She's agreed to go out with us to reinterview all the victims. It will be quicker than trying to get them all to come to us. We already have SID online to analyze semen evidence recovered from the victims, and we think we can get some trace evidence off Wyatt's motorcycle helmet.''

''Whew! You two are a constant source of amazement.''

''Rabbits out of hats are our specialty.''

''I really appreciate it,'' Fey said. ''But I'm also depending on you both not to let the other stuff slide.''

''Piece of cake,'' Nails said with a shrug. ''We can handle that stuff standing on our heads.''

Fey saw Hammersmith glance up at his partner and wink. He looked like a California beach boy. Blond with piercing blue eyes, wide shoulders, and narrow hips. Except for a crooked nose, he would appear right at home on ESPN's beach volleyball coverage. The nose, however, was a legacy from his days as a gold medalist boxer in the International Police Olympics.

The team was an odd pairing, and nobody knew what they did off-duty. They were both single, so it was anybody's guess. Rumor control had them running the gamut from celibacy to heavy bondage and discipline. Fey didn't much care one way or the other. She was simply grateful for their attitude. In her mind, she could put Darcy Wyatt on the back burner knowing the case was in good hands. Either Hammer or Nails would get back to her if there was a problem. Until then it was their baby.

''Croaker, line five. Croaker, line five.'' The squad room pager intruded loudly into the air.

Nails gave Fey a nod and headed back to her partner.

Fey scooped up the closest phone and barked into it, ''Croaker.''

''Fey, it's me.'' Jake Travers's voice came down the line. ''I know you must be busy, but I just called to say I'm sorry about last night.''

''Me, too, Jake,'' Fey said, although she wasn't really, and it irritated her to have to deal with Jake's hurt feelings when she had so much on her plate already. "But I don't think being sorry is going to help fix things between us."

"Are things really that bad?"

"I think so."

"Can we talk about it?"

"Not right now. I'm up to my ears in a double homicide and a separate triple rape."

"I meant we can talk about it tonight. I'll pick you up about seven."

"Tonight . . ." The hesitation in Fey's voice was clear.

"Come on, Fey." Jake matched Fey's hesitation with his own irritation. "Surely, you haven't forgotten tonight's fund-raiser. I need you there."

"Jake, I'm sorry. I can't. There's just too much to do on this case. It's a big one—"

"They're all big ones, Fey. But there are other things that are bigger." Jake's anger was rising.

"Preening for dollars may be more important to you," Fey counterattacked immediately. "But it sure as hell isn't to me. I'm not good at simpering around and sucking up to a bunch of old men who think the height of humor is to goose the cocktail waitress."

"Fey, those old men control a lot of money. They're also married to a lot of old women who think nothing of grabbing the closest hard young prick for a quick tumble and tip. It cuts both ways. If I'm going to get the funds for a successful campaign, I need their support."

"If that's what it takes, Jake, then I don't think it's worth it."

There was silence from the other end of the line. Across the room Fey could see Ash talking into the phone on her desk. "I'm sorry," she said eventually, bringing her attention back to her own conversation. "I know how hard you've worked for this campaign, and I know I've been a bitch about it at times, but my work is just as important to me and I've got to see this thing through tonight."

"If that's the way you want it."

"It's not the way I want it, Jake. It's just the way it is."

"Okay. Okay. I give in," Jake said. "Call me later."

"You got it." Fey waited a second and then hung up. She realized neither of them had said, "I love you." They hadn't said it for a while now, and Fey knew it was no longer true. In many ways, she was relieved by the realization. She'd already made three trips to the altar that had ended badly, and she was damn glad she hadn't let Jake push her into making it four trips.

She walked back to her desk, arriving there just as Ash was terminating his own phone conversation.

"Business or pleasure?" she asked.

"It's always business when there's a monster hunt on."

"A monster hunt?"

"You don't think this killer is a monster?"

"Wait a minute," Fey said. "I know who you are now."

Ash raised his eyebrows.

"There was an article on you a year or so ago in *Police Chief* magazine—right after that book came out . . . What was the name of it? *Here There be Monsters?*

Ash cringed visibly. "Please—"

"—You're the guy that tracked down Michael LeBeck, the Vermont Vampire, and Charlie Haddock, the guy who cut all those children up in Wyoming. Something about how your mind can tap into the vibes of serial killers and figure out what they're going to do next."

Ash was shaking his head violently. "That book was total crap from the first word. The hack that wrote it was a guy by the name of Zelman Tucker. He's a reporter for the *American Inquirer*. Tabloid bird-cage lining. I refused to be interviewed by him, and the FBI refused to cooperate. Tucker made most of the book up out of thin air. The rest came from newspaper and magazine articles of less repute than *AI*."

Fey was laughing quietly.

"I'm telling you the truth here," Ash said imploringly. "I don't get into the minds of these killers. I don't operate in some kind of trance state straight out of a Shirley MacLaine biography. I might have good instincts and some luck, but what I do is simple by the numbers police work.''

"Well, Tucker, or whatever his name is, sure made you sound like Superman. You should hire him as your press agent.''

"That's the last thing I need. I just want to be left alone to do my job. I don't need someone like Tucker the Sucker making things more difficult than they are. Lives are at stake here, but every time I turn around he's there, like a leech, looking for another story.''

"He knows a gravy train when he sees one.''

"Let it drop," Ash said. There was steel in his voice.

"Whoa," Fey said, immediately serious. "I didn't mean to push buttons.''

Ash closed his eyes and leaned back in Fey's chair. "I'm sorry. There's stuff you don't know. I don't have a lot of time, and I want to catch this guy.''

Fey let that pass by without comment. She didn't want to rile the man any more than he was. She needed allies right now, not enemies.

Monk's voice cut across the squad room. "Press on line two, boss," he called out to Fey.

"Tucker?" she asked Ash.

"Or someone just as bad.''

"Let whoever it is hold for a couple of minutes and then accidentally disconnect them," she said to Monk. "When they call back, give 'em to Cahill.''

Monk grinned at her.

"Let's get out of here," she said, turning back to Ash. "I need a decent cup of coffee, and we're never going to get a chance to hash this stuff out with all these distractions.''

"You have somewhere in mind?''

"Yeah. How about Tahiti?''

CHAPTER FIFTEEN

"I CAN'T BELIEVE YOU OPENED YOUR STUPID MOUTH AND talked to that bitch!" Devon Wyatt was so mad he couldn't sit in the hardback chair that was the only piece of furniture in the attorney/client visiting room. Separated from Darcy by a Plexiglas window sitting on top of a four-foot-high wall, Devon Wyatt wanted to smash through the distorting clear plastic and throttle his son.

For his part, Darcy leaned far enough back in the chair on his side of the room for the front legs to come off the ground. He supported the position by placing his feet on the wall just below the Plexiglas. A sneer cut through all other expressions on his face as he watched his father rant and rave.

"What have I ever done to you that's been so bad? Huh? Huh?" Devon Wyatt's voice was approaching hysterics. For a man whose tactics and demeanor in the courtroom exemplified cool under fire, he was losing it big time.

"You want to screw women? I'll buy you women. You want to beat them up? No problem. I'll pay the extra. But no! You gotta go out and rape grandmas. And then, as if that isn't bad enough, you get caught and spill your guts to some dyke bitch of a cop." Devon turned to face his son, placing both hands on the Plexiglas window separating them. "Just what is your problem?" He turned away without waiting for, or even seeming to expect, an answer.

The attorney/client visiting room at West Los Angeles station did not provide much room for Devon Wyatt to pace. Each half was an eight-foot by eight-foot square, barely big enough to contain the anger that washed out of Devon Wyatt in tsunami-size waves.

"You are a stupid little shit," Devon Wyatt said to his son. "You have been nothing but grief since the day you were ripped out of your mother's stomach butt first. If I didn't know better, I'd swear your mother had been screwing somebody other than me when you were conceived."

Darcy Wyatt snorted a laugh. "The only way you know she wasn't fooling around was because when you weren't doing her, you were proving your manhood by beating her. Personally, I think the Menendez brothers had the right idea."

"You shut your mouth!" Devon was back with his hands spread on the Plexiglas.

"Where do you think I learned all my dirty little quirks, Daddy dearest? Monkey see, monkey do."

"You little asshole. Do you have any idea how much this is going to cost to keep quiet? Let alone what it's going to take to get you acquitted."

"Get me acquitted. What are you going to do? Plead me not guilty? For shit's sake, I confessed—"

"You were manipulated and taken advantage of because of your youth. You were tricked by an experienced detective into confessing because the stress of the interview was too intense. You were refused the counsel of your parent—"

"I'm nineteen—"

"With the provable intelligence of a twelve-year-old."

"The old lady can identify me."

"A blind grandma with a sense of smell? Give me a break. She'll get torn apart on the stand."

"I knew what I was doing."

"No you didn't. If you did you wouldn't have done it. Psychiatric examination will prove that your actions were beyond your control. Extensive therapy is called for, not incarceration. A few large contributions spread throughout the current district attorney campaign and a plea bargain will suddenly look like a good deal."

Darcy Wyatt shook his head. "I gotta see this. If you

think you can get me out from under this—''

Devon Wyatt slapped the flats of his palms on the Plexiglas. ''When I get you out of this it will be the last time you will be an embarrassment to me. Of that I'll make sure. And you better play ball all the way. Think about it. A young boy like you? A convicted grandma rapist? The boys inside will take less than a week to give you an asshole big enough to park a motorcycle.''

For the first time the sneer on Darcy Wyatt's face faltered. Devon Wyatt saw the expression change and grinned like a jackal. ''That's right, boy. You didn't think of that when you were spilling your guts. If I leave you to rot in this place, you'll soon be getting a taste of your own medicine. Every cop knows a con inside who'll be more than happy to take care of someone like you for the price of a few privileges, or maybe the turning of a blind eye during a prison visit dope exchange. That Croaker bitch will set you up big time.''

Darcy stood up, knocking his chair over. ''What about bail?''

It was Devon's turn to snort a laugh. It was a curious noise, almost a family trait. ''It's sitting at a million dollars right now, and they may petition the judge for a no-bail stipulation. Your balls are in the ringer on this one.''

''Get me out, man! Come on. Tell me you can get me out!''

Devon Wyatt gave his son a pitying look. ''I almost can't believe you sprang from my sperm.'' He turned and opened the door to leave the small visiting room.

Darcy started banging on the Plexiglas. ''Come on, Dad. Get me out! Get me—''

Devon let the door swing closed behind him, cutting off his son's pleas. He took a phone out of his inside jacket pocket and pressed a memory button. One of his many assistants answered the call.

''Get me everything you can on a detective named Fey Croaker,'' he said without preamble. ''I want it on my desk when I get to the office. I'm leaving West LA now.'' He disconnected without saying goodbye.

CHAPTER SIXTEEN

FEY FELT LIKE A DRINK, BUT SHE DIDN'T ORDER ONE. IT would have been inappropriate on several levels: she was on duty, there was still a hell of a lot of work to do before she could call it a day, and she didn't know how Ash would react. Eliminate any one of those reasons and a cold beer would have gone down well. As it was, she ordered tea. Coffee in this particular setting would have been a blasphemy.

The King George V was a British-style pub/restaurant with a patio eating area that sprawled out into the pedestrian walkway of the Third Street Mall in Santa Monica. It was slightly outside of Fey's jurisdictional area, which was a plus as far as she was concerned. She had originally been turned on to the spot by a detective partner who had been born and raised in England and frequented the predominantly British haunts of Santa Monica as a stopgap against homesickness.

Fey's mother had been Irish, and while Fey had never set foot on the old sod, she'd come to find an affinity for things British. Despite her genuine cowgirl ways, the pub suited another side of Fey's personality. She now used it as a private getaway when she didn't want to patronize the local cop spots in West LA. The food at the King George V was plentiful and passable, the tea strong and hot, and the management knew Fey well enough that they were happy to leave her alone if she occupied a table for an extended period of time.

It was hot in the sun, but Fey had chosen a table shaded

by an umbrella that made the heat bearable. Ash had settled down across from her and was browsing the menu. He ordered quickly, and then leaned back in his chair as if waiting for Fey to set the pace of the conversation.

They had driven to the restaurant in two separate cars, parking in a nearby lot. By mutual consent their conversation while walking to the restaurant had been small talk of the do-you-know-so-and-so variety. It was an exploratory period, one used by cops everywhere to ascertain preliminary boundaries with a new associate. The process was akin to two dogs sniffing each other's rear-ends, albeit not as blatant. The aim was the same—a determination of trust.

Blood may prove thicker than water when choosing between family or friends, but The Badge was a far tighter bind than any church vow or blood relation. Despite the public push toward the concept of community policing, what goes on within the police culture is kept as secret and separate as possible from outsiders. Spouses and friends may catch a glimpse or an insight now and then, but they are still outlanders to be kept at bay.

When a new contact is made between two insiders there is an instant recognition of mutually shared experience. This translates into an initial trust associated with being part of the most exclusive club in the world. Anything beyond those original reactions, however, has to be earned. Personalities have to blend, and a common ground of philosophy and work habits has to be established before a full relationship can be created. A cop may cover for another cop he doesn't like, but he won't trust him or work with him to advantage.

"Okay, Mr. Special Agent," Fey said. "Let me bring up my previous point. You don't look like any anal-retentive, buttoned-down, brown suit and black wingtips FBI man I've ever come across. So, who exactly are you? And while you're at it, could you take a minute to explain what the Female Bra Inspectors are doing in the middle of this investigation?" Fey's questions were pointed, but her tone of voice was not particularly aggressive. It was an opening gambit to see how much Ash would give her up front.

He laughed softly. "You don't think much of the FBI do you?"

Fey took off her sunglasses and placed them on the table. "I've known a lot of good individual agents. They've been hard workers and good detectives. As an organization, however, I can't say that I'm impressed with the FBI's bureaucracy or their attitude. If there's a more pompous law enforcement organization on the face of the earth, I've yet to find it."

"How about the LAPD?" Ash drawled.

Fey gave a shrug and a smile. "Maybe. I'll give you that there are a number of similarities. We always like to think that LAPD is number one, but I'd hate to be the one responsible for running the comparisons."

"Okay. So, are we done with the name calling?"

"Sure, but how about some answers to my questions?"

"No more bobbing and weaving?"

"No more."

"All right. I don't look like an FBI agent because I'm not anymore."

Fey remained silent, figuring she'd let Ash tell it his way. She noticed again the slight periodic tic beneath his right eye.

"I've been officially retired for over a year," Ash continued, "but since that time I've been retained as a special consultant. Full rank and pay, but a very long leash to play on."

"Sounds like nice work if you can get it," Fey said, as their food was delivered. "But you don't look old enough to be retired."

"I appear young for my age?" Ash's voice was light.

"I'm not buying it," Fey said. "You may have seen the front end of forty, but you don't look like the type to do a runner after a quick twenty years. You look more like a bury-me-with-my-boots-on lifer."

"You may be closer to the truth than you think," Ash said. He immediately regretted the statement, but there was something about the woman he was sitting with that was drawing things out of him—things he had vowed not to talk about. He tried to verbally cover himself. "Can we just accept the fact that I'm telling you the truth and skip the gory details?"

"For now," Fey said. "But you intrigue me. I'll be ringing these same bells again later."

Ash looked down at the sandwich his fingers were toying with. "I'm tentatively attached as a consultant to the FBI's behavioral science unit based out of Quantico."

"I'm impressed. Why is the attachment tentative?"

Ash took a bite of sandwich, chewed, and swallowed. "Because, in actuality, I've been given the freedom to pick and choose what cases I work on."

"It sounds as if Tucker didn't have it all wrong in his book—the rogue FBI manhunter on the trail of a serial killer, a personal, mano-a-mano vendetta." Fey's voice held a hint of impishness.

Ash set his sandwich down with a sigh and wiped his mouth with a napkin. "Tucker is a rude pain in the butt, but he's not an idiot. He knows what sells, I'll give him that. He also knows how to embellish what won't sell so that it will."

Fey watched Ash's hands as he reached up and ran them both through the short tufts of hair on his scalp. His fingers were long with distinct knuckles, what Fey had heard referred to as gamblers' hands.

"If truth be told," Ash continued, "for my first ten years on the job I was a run-of-the-mill agent at best."

"Let me guess," Fey said. "Not good at following orders? Had problems with the dress code? Didn't know when to let things go? A blind man in the minefield of politics? Did not work or play well with others?"

A wry grin escaped from between Ash's thin lips. "I didn't realize my personnel file had become public knowledge."

"Just call it feminine intuition."

"How about an experienced guess?"

"Okay. So what happened to make you a hot shot?"

Ash shrugged. "I had my law degree and passed the bar exam before signing on with the bureau. I'd continued going to school and eventually picked up my doctorate in psychology. Thus armed, I was sent over to work the hostage negotiation team and later to the antiterrorism task force."

"I know a couple of LAPD guys from our ATD unit that were assigned to that same task force. You worked out of the federal building over on Wilshire?"

Ash gave an affirmative nod of his head. "I was working the domestic terrorism side of the task force. Most people, even coppers, don't have any idea how many homegrown terrorist groups are festering among us."

"Does this lead somehow to you becoming Zelman Tucker's favorite supercop?"

"After a fashion. Have you ever heard of Robert Ressler?"

"Yeah. He's the guy that was most responsible for kick-starting the FBI's behavioral science unit."

"Right. He was the first person to take psychological criminal profiling seriously. He actually coined the term *serial killer*. Before Ressler, serial killers were referred to as *stranger killers* even if they knew their victims."

"What's Ressler to you?"

"A mentor of types. As an analyst with the terrorism task force, I initiated a project to apply Ressler's criminal profiling techniques to terrorists and their organizations."

"Sounds a bit highbrow to me."

"Maybe so, but we had some success. Enough anyway to continue the project. The biggest fish we ever caught, however, was not a terrorist."

"I remember now from Tucker's book. He had it down as your first major case. Not a terrorist, but some garden variety, whacked-out serial killer? What was the guy's name? Wilson?"

"Winslow. He was a low-level scientist working at a missile site near Point Mugu Naval Air Station just up the coast from here. We were looking at him because he had some connection with the RCP."

"Revolutionary Communist Party?"

"Yeah. One or two very dangerous men surrounded by a petty bunch of raving loonies and deadbeats. When we first took a look at Winslow, he didn't fit the profile we had developed in targeting terrorists. He appeared to be simply one of the group's numerous hangers-on. But there was something odd about him, so I kept digging away. Eventually, it dawned on me that he didn't fit the terrorist profile, but he sure as hell fit the profile Ressler had created for a serial killer."

"What did you do with that information?"

"There had been a string of disappearances of young girls up and down the West Coast over a seven- or eight-year period. I had a gut reaction Winslow might be involved, so I arranged for him to be kept under surveillance as if he were a threat to public security."

"And?"

"And I got lucky. Halfway through the second day of surveillance, we observed him stalking a six-year-old girl. The next day we caught him in the act of attempting to kidnap her. We used the terrorism hook to keep jurisdiction over Winslow. He was our fish and we didn't want to lose him to the locals, especially once he started singing."

"How many murders did you clear?"

"He copped to five, but he was good for at least double that amount."

"Impressive."

"Lucky."

"I don't think so. It sounds like it was good police work."

"You're putting too much stock in Tucker's book."

"What happened afterwards?"

"I shifted over from the antiterrorist task force to the BSU—behavioral science unit. Ressler was retired by now, but his work was still going on strong and I found it fascinating. I also continued to be lucky."

"Michael LeBeck and Charlie Haddock?"

"Or as Tucker called them, the Vermont Vampire and the Wyoming Whacker."

"The man has a way with words."

"There were also two others before LeBeck and Haddock, and one since. They didn't garner the same type of national press, but were still equally gratifying. I'd finally found my niche—something at which I was very good. It gave me meaning."

Fey finished her tea and poured herself another cup from the battered metal pot on the table. "I guess I don't understand. You were on a hot streak, but you still pulled the pin and retired?"

There was a pregnant pause as Ash fiddled with his silverware. "I had to leave to take care of some personal matters."

"And now we have what appears to be a serial killer right here in River City, and you're hooked into it as a consultant?"

Ash's expression became irritated. "Look, do you want help with this case or not? Does it matter exactly what my connections to the bureau are? You can check me out. Call Freddie Mackerbee—he's the special agent in charge of the LA office."

"I know Mackerbee. Perhaps I'll call him later, but tell me something up front. Do you have a personal interest in this case?"

"Not in the way you intend the question. I don't know the victims, I have no idea of the suspect's identity, and there are no connections I'm aware of between this case and anything else I've ever worked on."

"But there's still something personal. I can sense it."

Ash stared hard across the table. "I'm good at what I do," he said in a hard, quiet voice. "I want to do it one more time. One more time . . . before I can't do it anymore."

Fey stared back, but left that statement alone. Sooner or later, she'd get to the bottom of Ash, but right now she needed all the help she could get. "Tell me about the case the sheriffs have dumped on me," she said, levelly, as if declaring a truce.

Ash took a thick file out of the Battenkill briefcase he

had carried into the restaurant. He placed it on the table and turned it around to face Fey. "This is a copy of MeCoy's and Blades's murder book."

"Well, that should make interesting if incomplete reading." Fey took the file and began to flip through it. "Can you bumper sticker it for me?"

Sitting back in his chair, Ash seemed to be gathering his energy before talking. Most of his meal remained on his plate. Fey had watched him push the food around and break it up so it appeared that he was eating when he really wasn't.

"The body was found fifteen days ago in the hills above Pepperdine University. Shallow grave, like today's. As far as I can tell, the body was trussed and laid out exactly the same with the one arm thrust out of the grave. Blades and MeCoy figure the victim to be between twelve and fifteen. Personally, I'd say closer to fifteen or sixteen. He looked young, but I'd say he was simply immature."

"Male black?"

"Yeah."

"Doesn't jibe with the current one being a male white."

"Who knows at this point. It's the only real inconsistency."

Fey looked thoughtful. "If you're working with BSU then you're up to date with all that organized/disorganized killer stuff."

"That's right. The distinctions between the two types of serial killers are one of the main tenets of Ressler's research."

"Let me see what I remember about this stuff. Murders by disorganized killers have a random quality. Disorganized killers are less specific about their victims. They usually commit the killing with whatever weapon is at hand and usually leave the body where it can be found easily.

"Organized killers, on the other hand, choose their victims with care—looking for somebody who approximates in size, shape, age, and coloring what they have been fantasizing about killing. An organized killer will take time savoring the murders and will go to great lengths to make sure they are not caught. They understand about physical evidence and so rarely leave fingerprints or other easily identifiable goodies. They are also likely to conceal the bodies of their victims or move them from the original crime scene.'' Fey stopped and picked up her tea cup. ''Sounds like a lecture from Murder 101, doesn't it?''

Ash laughed softly. ''You've got the basics down for sure.''

''Where does that leave us with this series?''

''I think it's pretty clear our suspect is an organized killer. The way the victims were tied up and the sadistic bent of burying them alive speaks of at least some advanced planning.''

''That figures. And organized killers are the more difficult of the two types to catch.''

''Without question.''

Fey frowned. ''The ritual with the arm sticking out of the grave. Do you think the killer may be taunting the police with that quirk? Thinking maybe the graves won't be found unless the arms are left as a sign post?''

''I'd have to think about that in the overall context, but my first reaction is that the arm left sticking out is part of the killer's fantasy.''

''Was there any physical evidence in the first case?''

''Semen was recovered from the rectal cavity. Blades and MeCoy had it blood-typed and sent for DNA analysis. Beyond that there was nothing of significance.''

''Was the sexual activity conducted before or after death?''

''Before. The victim was buried alive, the same as in the new case. The sex also appeares to be consensual—no tearing of the rectum or other scarring.''

''The victim wasn't an anal virgin then?''

''It's doubtful.''

''And there's no ID.''

''Nothing from DOJ, and nobody inquiring about local missings.''

''Sounds as if the victim was probably a rent-a-boy. Those kids go missing and nobody cares.'' The alarm on

Fey's watch went off, and she reached down to silence it. She checked the time. "I'm sorry, but I have to get to an appointment. I'll be heading back to the station afterwards in about an hour. Can you start a preliminary profile on the suspect? I think we have to establish victim identity first, but until we do, we may need somewhere else as a starting point to begin looking for the needle in the haystack."

"I'll do what I can. How about we touch base tomorrow morning at the station?"

"Sounds good." Fey paused for a second, looking gravely across the table. "Listen," she seemed to fumble for the right words. "Thanks."

"No sweat." Ash winked at her. "Nobody can do it all themselves. We all can use a bit of help from time to time."

"Amen," Fey said. "Amen."

CHAPTER SEVENTEEN

"TELL ME, FEY. WHAT MADE YOU FIRST DECIDE TO COME and see me?"

Fey took a deep breath. "I've told you all this before."

"You may have told me your reasons, but you haven't accepted the reasoning yourself."

Dr. Emma Winters was physically a small woman, but her presence in the tastefully decorated consulting room was strong. At sixty years old, dark hair still fell thickly across her shoulders with a natural shape and bounce that other women would kill for. Her eyes were a riveting, al-

most unnatural violet, emphasized by large-framed glasses
that perched on a patrician nose.

"I came to you because my life is going to shit in a
hand basket."

"No. That's not why you came to me."

"Okay. Then you tell me." Fey sounded petulant—a
teenager put out by a strict parent.

"You came to me because you realized that certain areas of your life were getting beyond your control. You
may not have realized what was happening to you on a
conscious level, but you were sharp enough to recognize
the symptoms." Dr. Winters sat in a comfortable wing-
back chair with her hands folded in her lap. Fey sat across
from her in a matching chair. A low coffee table between
them supported a spray of miniature roses.

"If you say so." Fey's tone was shut down hard.

Dr. Winters rubbed her fingertips gently along the fabric
of the chair arm. "Listen to yourself, Fey. This is why you
came to me for help. Your constant verbal ripostes are the
most obvious manifestation of the forces responsible for
undermining your relationships."

"Psychobabble, gobbledy-goop. I could have told you
that without having to pay you a hundred dollars for a
shortened hour. So, big deal." She shrugged. "So, my
tolerance level for bullshit no longer registers on the
scale."

"Your antagonistic attitude, and your lack of patience,
are simply other symptoms of the dysfunction that is at
the root of your problem."

"I knew a doctor once who didn't have any patients."

"Very funny." Dr. Winters wasn't laughing. "Do you
want me to give you a rim-shot?" she asked quietly. This
was Fey's third visit to her office, and Dr. Winters had
been battling Fey's verbal defenses from the beginning.

"Oh, for hell's sake, wipe that smug smile off your face,
Doc," Fey said. "You make me sound as if I'm a talk
show candidate—'Next on "Oprah," dysfunctional cops
and their screwed-up lives!' " She stood up in agitation,
and walked around the room. A large painting full of pale

yellow ribbons billowing softly against the faintest tinge of blue breeze stopped her at its center, and she stared at it as if trying to lose herself in its whimsy.

Dr. Winters remained silent, and after a few long moments Fey returned to sit down again.

"I'm sorry, Doc. I'm just having a real hard time with this. You don't know how long it took me to work up the courage to come and see you in the first place."

"I have an idea, since you cancelled your first three appointments." The doctor's voice was soft, almost lulling. "I sensed you would come eventually, given time."

"I couldn't go to the department for help," Fey said. "They tell you that anything you say to a department shrink is confidential, but that's crap. The simple act of asking to see a department shrink puts a straightjacket on your career. I've seen it happen time and again. An officer or a detective goes to a department psychologist, and before you can turn around all of your senior officers are aware of your problems."

"Is that why you pay my bills in cash and won't allow my office assistant to bill your medical insurance?"

"Absolutely. I can't afford any trace of my association with you to get back to the department."

"And you truly believe that somebody within the department hierarchy keeps track of medical billing for mental health visits?"

"I know it sounds paranoid, but I've been on the receiving end of just that kind of information, and I don't want to be the subject of it."

Dr. Winters reached one hand across to where Fey was sitting on the edge of her chair. "Fey, you are safe here. Sometime, somewhere, you're going to have to let your defenses down. If you refuse to make yourself open to change then change will be impossible."

"You're telling me it's like the old joke about how many psychiatrists it takes to change a light bulb." Fey waggled her eyebrows, simulated a Groucho Marx cigar, and put a funny accent in her voice. "Only one, but the light bulb really has to want to change."

Dr. Winters laughed this time. A full-bodied laugh of enjoyment. "Damn it, Fey. We're supposed to be serious here. You can't keep trying to make me laugh."

"I'm not just trying. I'm succeeding."

"The only thing you're succeeding in is running away from the reasons you came to see me. If you are afraid of the dark, you can turn a light on. It makes the dark go away, but it does nothing to confront the fear."

"So, bottom line. What are you telling me, Doc?" Fey pushed herself back in the chair and tried to assume a serious expression. Her agitation level, however, was visibly rising again.

Dr. Winters's eyes twinkled gently. "We're still a long way from the bottom line. But there are some surface issues we can address."

"Such as?"

"To start with, many women involved in traditionally male-dominated professions display similar characteristics, so you are not alone."

Fey shrugged her shoulders again. "A sinking ship is still a flooding vessel. It doesn't matter how many sailors are going down with you."

"Stop it, Fey," Dr. Winters said sternly. "At least allow me the courtesy of finishing my discourse before you steamroller over it. Self-pity isn't very flattering."

That stung. Fey checked her watch. Fifteen minutes of bobbing and weaving left in the session. It seemed like forever. Why had she chosen to put herself through this? She was fighting it every step of the way, yet she felt compelled to return.

"All males have a female component of their psychological makeup called the anima," Dr. Winters continued. "Conversely, females have a male personality component called the animus. For women attempting to succeed in professions where male behavior and thinking is demanded or rewarded, the danger lies in the animus becoming the controlling factor in their personalities.

"By repressing their feminine behavior and allowing

their male side to dominate, women react to their male counterparts from the standpoint of aggressive competition—the way men generally deal with each other. In some cases this can help women to get ahead in traditional male professions, such as police work, but generally difficulties arise in two areas.

"First, if you totally repress your femininity on the job your behavior becomes out of balance—it becomes all male and you lose the advantages that your female side provides. This causes problems with male co-workers whose feminine component, their anima, is keeping their male personality traits in check. In essence you, as a woman, become more male than the men with whom you work, sometimes to the point of becoming obnoxious and disliked. You are now hindering your chances of success instead of enhancing them.

"Secondly, this repression of your femininity is not something that can be turned off the moment you're done with your work day. It carries over into your private male/female relationships. As a result, instead of your feminine side reacting to a male companion as a lover, your male side gets in the way again. Instead of a romantic relationship—female reacting to male—you have male reacting to male in an aggressive or competitive manner, which can quickly destroy what each of you is seeking." Dr. Winters paused, observing the effect her words were having on Fey. "I see you recognize the phenomenon."

"Perhaps," Fey said, reluctantly. "But what can be done about it?"

"This is not something that happened to you overnight, so it is not something that you will be able to change immediately. Being aware of the problem and understanding it is a start, but bringing your personality back into balance will be a gradual process. All behavior is carried out through roles. You must simply start to be more aware of the role that you are supposed to be playing at any given time. You cannot convincingly act the part of Hamlet in the personality of Falstaff, but an actor—aware of the demands of each character's personality—could effectively portray Hamlet in the morning and Falstaff at night. In other words, you must become cognizant of the personality demands of the many roles you play and act them accordingly.''

"It's kind of like working undercover," Fey stated. "Assuming a new identity, a new role, to convince the bad guys that you can be trusted."

"In some ways," Dr. Winter agreed. "But when you are undercover you may be playing a role totally opposite from your personal nature. You are acting something that you are not. In real life, all the roles are projected through your own personality—they become simply separate facets of your total personality. You are still true to your own values only you support them in different manners."

Fey shook her head, a bit bewildered by it all. "Is that all there is to it?"

"Of course not." Dr. Winters again leaned forward and put a hand on Fey's shoulders. "You're not going to get off that easy. What we are talking about here barely scratches the surface. Both of us know that the emotional storms causing you so much pain go far deeper." Dr. Winters tried her best to gentle Fey into the next step.

"When you first came to see me, Fey, you told me a little about the abuses you had suffered at the hands of your father. You were rather blunt about the whole situation, as if wanting to address it and move immediately on. You wanted me to believe that you have dealt with your angers toward your father, and that he doesn't affect you anymore."

Fey was silent—more than a bit afraid.

"We both know you still have many unresolved issues lying in the great morass of childhood abuses. We need to talk more about them, to bring them into the light."

"What's to talk about? My father was a sexually and physically abusive alcoholic asshole who liked to get drunk and then hit me and screw me. How much more into the light do we need to bring things?"

"Listen to your anger, Fey. Hear not your words, but what lies beneath them."

"Oh, very Zen. Snatch these pebbles from my hand, grasshopper. When you can do that it will be time for you to leave."

Dr. Winters responded in kind. "Snatch these emotions from your mind, grasshopper. When you can do that it will be time for you to leave."

As if on cue two alarms sounded. One was on the small coffee table—a soft bonging indicating the end of the session. The second was Fey's beeper. She turned it off and checked the number. It was Lieutenant Cahill's private line.

"Can I use your phone, Doc? It's time for me to slip back into character."

Dr. Winters waved a hand toward a small library table with a phone on it that stood against one wall. Fey strode over, picked up the receiver, and punched in the familiar numbers.

"This is Croaker," she said when the lieutenant's secretary answered the line.

"Hold on a second."

Fey waited.

"Fey?" Mike Cahill said, picking up the line.

"Yeah."

"I'm sorry to have to tell you this, but it's about your brother."

"Damn! What now?"

"I'm afraid he's had an overdose."

CHAPTER EIGHTEEN

IT TOOK FEY LESS THAN TEN MINUTES TO REACH SANTA Monica Hospital on the corner of Sixteenth and Wilshire. She slid the detective car neatly into an "ambulance only" parking space in front of the emergency entrance. Brisk strides took her through the automatic door. She flashed her badge at the nurse on the desk and was buzzed through into the working side of the ER.

Even though it was located just outside of her jurisdiction, Fey was familiar with the operations of Santa Monica Hospital. SMH had one of the best rape counseling programs in the city. As a contract hospital, it was also top of the list when it came to providing emergency medical treatment for rape victims and for the preparation of evidentiary rape kits.

A voice called out, "Detective Croaker," and Fey looked up to see Anson Brewbeck, a black ER doctor she knew slightly. Hospital greens stretched tightly across an impressive expanse of muscle that had almost earned Brewbeck a Heisman trophy and an NFL career. A blown knee in a Rose Bowl game, however, had brought about a change of focus from pigskin to sheepskin. There were far more grateful patients than disappointed fans.

"Is he dead?" Fey asked bluntly. Her tone was flat, icy cold.

"Whoa, slow down," Brewbeck said.

"Just give it to me straight," Fey said, catching and interpreting Brewbeck's puzzled expression. "There's a lot of history here that you don't know about. I don't need hearts and flowers.''

Brewbeck checked the chart he was carrying in one meaty hand. "Tommy Croaker is your brother?''

"Much as I hate to admit it.''

"Well, he's going to be okay—''

"More's the pity,'' Fey said. "What did he stick in his arm this time?''

Brewbeck reached out and placed his hand on Fey's shoulder. It was a professional investigation, not a personal gesture. Beneath his fingers, he could feel the iron tension running through her trapezoid muscles. "Good grief,'' he said. "Get into the doctor's lounge and sit down.''

Fey opened her mouth to argue, but Brewbeck cut her off. "Do as I tell you. Now.'' With the fingers that were on her shoulder, Brewbeck turned Fey and gave her a push in the direction he wanted her to proceed. He turned to an ER nurse who had been watching the exchange. "Stay with her,'' he said, in a half-whisper.

A few minutes later, Brewbeck entered the doctor's lounge carrying a small paper cup with two small, light blue, single-scored tablets residing in the bottom. Fey was sitting on a hard chair next to a small Formica table. The hands clasped in her lap showed white at the knuckles.

The nurse, a butterball blond in white polyester and thick-soled shoes, leaned with one shoulder against a fat refrigerator. When she saw the pill cup in Brewbeck's hand, she immediately turned to a water cooler and filled a Dixie cup from the contents.

"Take these,'' Brewbeck said. He placed the pill cup on the table by Fey. The nurse placed the water next to it.

"What are they?'' Fey asked.

"Valium.''

"I don't need—''

Brewbeck sighed. "You're wired up so tight, I'd be surprised if you could pass gas. You either take the pills, or I call your boss and tell him that in my professional opinion you're not fit for duty.''

"You're not a city doctor. You can't do that.''

"Watch me," Brewbeck said.

Fey scowled, but picked up the pill cup and tossed its contents into her mouth. She swallowed and then downed the water chaser. "Ick," she said, wrinkling her nose. "I hate taking pills." She set the empty Dixie cup down and glared at Brewbeck. "I used to think you were okay."

Brewbeck's gentle laugh sounded a deep resonance. "Given time, you will again."

"What about Tommy?" Fey asked.

Brewbeck twitched his head at the nurse. She picked up the signal and left the mismatched pair alone.

"I told you he's going to be okay, but how about you give me a little information first?" Brewbeck translated Fey's silence as acceptance. "I saw the tracks on his arms. He used to be a junkie."

"Once a junkie, always a junkie. Isn't that what they say?"

Brewbeck's massive shoulders rose and fell. "Perhaps, but he didn't fall off the wagon this time. From what I can tell he hasn't been voluntarily pinging himself for maybe a year or more."

"He just finished a county lid a couple of months back, so that's not saying much."

Brewbeck raised his eyebrows. It was unusual for somebody to do an entire year in county jail.

"I made sure he did the time," Fey responded to Brewbeck's surprise. "To cut a long story short," she said, "I spent the better part of my life protecting Tommy from both the big bad world and from himself. I know now that it may not have been the best course of action. He never learned to stand on his own two feet. I finally had to draw the line somewhere. When I did, he responded by breaking into my house and ripping me blind. I pressed charges. He went to jail. I made sure he stayed there. Life is hard."

An image of her father flashed into Fey's mind. She remembered his threats vividly. If she didn't do what daddy wanted, daddy would cut off little Tommy's wanker. That's when the protecting had started—and like the abuse, it had never stopped.

"You had any contact with him since he got out?"

"None that he knows about."

Brewbeck's lips twitched at that statement. "You've been keeping tabs?"

"He's still my brother."

"What about your parents?"

"Dead."

"No other siblings?"

Fey shook her head.

"You know about the underground raves?"

"Yeah. I also know Tommy was fronting them."

Raves were huge floating parties attended by the detritus of the Generation X set. An abandoned warehouse, or some similar deserted location was chosen as a party point. Word was put out on the street and a buzz began to cultivate. A bar was established—usually nothing more than a plank across two oil drums. A portable sound system was brought in and set up. Sometimes a band or two was procured for the gig. Around one or two in the morning the first revelers would begin to show up at the location, and the music, the dancing, the booze, the drugs, and the blood would flow through till dawn. The location was then broken down to be moved and set up somewhere else. The profits from the booze and the entrance fees fell tax free into the promoter's pocket. Fey was aware that Tommy had been part of a group managing and producing the raves.

"You knew your brother was involved?" Brewbeck asked.

"I told you, I had to stop being his keeper. I knew, but I wasn't—couldn't—do anything about it. As far as I knew Tommy was making the scene, but staying clean. It wasn't much, but it was something. An improvement . . . a promise of better things to come, maybe . . . I don't know."

"Sounds as if you've been going through the ringer with this guy for a while now."

"It's a long and typically sordid story."

"I can sympathize," Brewbeck said. "There was a black sheep in my family as well."

"No pun intended?"

Brewbeck shrugged and gave a smile. "Maybe just a little." His face took on a grimmer expression. "The problem is, the black sheep in my family is dead now and I never had the chance to make my peace with him. It bothers me."

"I don't think peace is an arrangement that Tommy and I will ever reach. The wounds run too deep."

"You have to keep trying."

Fey returned Brewbeck's shrug. "If you say so," she said. "What happened this time?"

"The good news is that Tommy's overdose wasn't self-administered. The bad news is that there were about ten others in the same condition that were brought in along with him."

"You're kidding?"

"No. Best we can tell is that Tommy and the others were at a rave in an abandoned building behind the deserted Henshy's store. Witnesses say everybody was shooting squirt guns—apparently that's the in thing right now—only somebody thought it would be funny to shoot people with PCP."

"Oh, shit," Fey said.

"Exactly," Brewbeck replied. "People were getting shot in the mouth, in the face, the eyes. The PCP went straight into their system, and the next thing you know the rave turned into a freak-out."

"How's Tommy?"

"He was one of the first to come through the ordeal. He's resting right now, and can probably be discharged in the next couple of hours."

"Did he ask for me?" Fey couldn't keep the hope out of her voice.

"No," Brewbeck said quietly. "One of the cops who brought them in recognized him, and knew he was related to you."

"Who was that?"

"Butler."

Fey knew who Brewbeck was talking about. He was a

veteran Santa Monica street cop who she'd had some interaction with in the past. "He tell you to call me?"

"Did it himself. I think he got hold of your boss."

Fey nodded. "Can I see Tommy?"

"Sure. You feeling up to it?"

"After those two Valium, I think I could handle meeting the devil himself. You could make a fortune dealing those on the side."

"Nah," said Brewbeck. "I'd hate to go into competition with the national health plan." He opened the door and ushered Fey through.

Together they walked through the ER room, down a long corridor, and into recovery. Fey saw Tommy lying propped up in a portable hospital bed. He had his eyes closed and appeared to be asleep.

She'd only seen her brother once since he'd finished his county time. She'd been there to meet him at the release gate, but Tommy had walked right past her as if she didn't exist. She'd wanted to chase after him, to tell him she was sorry for what he'd been through—what she'd forced him to go through. She knew, however, that if she tried to start protecting and helping him again it would defeat the purpose of the most difficult decision she'd ever had to make.

She'd let him walk away. It tore her up inside, but if she had to lose their relationship in order for him to change, then it might be worth it.

Watching him lying in the bed, his gaunt, pock-marked face a slack visage of neglect, she felt her stomach roll. Brewbeck was behind her. When he sensed her faltering, he placed both hands on her shoulders and squeezed.

"Don't ever stop trying," he said. His voice was soft and gentle.

Fey walked forward and took one of Tommy's hands from the top of the bed sheets. The arm it was attached to was stick-thin and corded with veins.

"Tommy . . ." she started quietly.

Her brother opened his eyes, and for the briefest of moments when their eyes collided it was as if they were young kids again and had all the love in the world for each other. But the moment passed in a flicker and the hate of the intervening years stepped through.

"What are you doing here?" he asked. His voice was high-pitched, but thick with drowsiness.

"I heard what happened. I came to see if you were okay."

"All of a sudden you're the concerned sister? Why don't you just back off? The role doesn't suit you."

Fey tried to ignore the bluster. "Who did this, Tommy? Do you know?"

"If I did, I wouldn't tell you. I don't need you to fight my battles anymore."

Fey fought to keep her calm. "I don't want to fight them for you anymore, Tommy. I want to fight them with you."

For a moment Tommy looked as if he was going to cry. "I'll fight for myself," he said, his voice now slightly choked. "Isn't that what you wanted? I don't need you anymore. You don't have to worry about me. I learned real good how to take care of myself."

"Then what are you doing laying in this hospital bed?" Fey snapped, and immediately regretted the statement.

Tommy opened his mouth and then clamped it shut. He pulled his hand out of Fey's grasp and rolled away from her onto his side.

"Tommy, I'm sorry."

"Go away, Fey. I don't want to talk to you."

Fey knew it was no good pressing it further. Tommy had always been good at finding ways to punish her when he was angry. That much appeared not to have changed. Not knowing what else to do, she turned and walked away. She felt Brewbeck watching her, and turned to face him.

"Take good care of him, will you?"

"Sure," he said. "Do you need anything?"

"Nah." She gave the doctor a world-weary grin. "I'm a tough old broad. I'll live through this." She shook Brewbeck's hand and walked away.

In the lobby of the ER room, Fey picked up the receiver

of a pay phone and dialed the squad room. When it was answered, she asked for Monk.

''This is Fey,'' she said when he came on the line. ''Anything cooking?''

''Jackpot time, boss. We just got a make on the victim.''

⌖

CHAPTER NINETEEN

IT WAS GETTING ON TO FOUR IN THE AFTERNOON, BUT THE squad room was still humming with activity. Detectives from the robbery unit had just returned from serving a pair of arrest and search warrants. They were busily taking off bulletproof vests and examining an array of confiscated weapons. Two Jamaican *posse* members with flowing dreadlocks sat handcuffed to a bench in front of the squad room lockers.

Fey looked around for her own people and spotted Alphabet sitting at the squad room's only computer. He appeared to be tediously punching out a preliminary report from his notes on the autopsy. The affable detective's typing skills still hadn't progressed past the hunt-and-peck stage. Alphabet, however, preferred to refer to himself as a biblical typist—as in ''seek and ye shall find.'' In actuality, he was proof that you may be able to propel police equipment into the twentieth century, but getting the detectives there was another story.

As usual, Hammersmith and Rhonda Lawless had their heads together at their end of the MAC table. They were surrounded by stacks of paperwork, buff-colored suspect folders, and the blue notebooks that were used to log cases.

Fey had no idea what the duo was doing, but trusted them enough to leave them to it.

Monk was sitting at Fey's desk peering at a teletype. Brindle was standing behind him with her hand on his shoulder. She was bending over, looking at the teletype in Monk's hand and managing to stick one of her breasts in his ear at the same time. To his credit, Monk appeared not to notice.

"Leave the poor man alone," Fey said *sotto voce* as she came up behind Brindle. "He's married."

Brindle stood straight up as if she'd been electrified. "Excuse me?" she said, turning to Fey.

"Oh, nothing," Fey said. She dumped her purse down on her desktop. "What do we have?"

Monk held the teletype out to Fey. "DOJ return," he told her. "They sent us twenty possibles from the description, but we were able to eliminate over half of those by using the photos DOJ faxed down. Some of the faxed photos weren't too clear, so we made some calls on the others and eliminated a couple more. By that time, Alphabet was back from the autopsy. The doctor had noted a small, port-wine birthmark on the victim's back."

"That should have narrowed things down considerably," Fey said.

"It did. However, the strange thing was that two of the missing persons descriptions that came down from DOJ mentioned port-wine birthmarks on the back. The photos were also similar."

"You're kidding?"

Monk raised his eyebrows. "You know how these things go," he said. "It's never too easy."

"Dental records?" Fey asked.

"Yeah," Monk said. "That was the clincher. Alphabet brought back a preliminary dental chart on the victim. I called DOJ and they faxed down the dental charts of our two possibles from their files. Our victim had three fillings and a missing bicuspid. One of the charts from DOJ matched."

"Outstanding. So, we have an ID. Who's the victim?"

Monk pointed at the teletype now in Fey's hand. Fey held it up to read and had to push it out to arm's length. "Help me out here," she said. "It's obvious I don't have my glasses."

"Ricky Long," Brindle said. "A fourteen-year-old runaway from San Francisco."

"Fourteen." Fey sighed heavily. "He looked a little older. What a crying shame." She felt deflated, depressed.

"That's not the end of the bad news," Monk said.

Fey waited in silence. Brindle filled in the blank. "The victim's mother is a San Francisco cop."

Fey rolled her eyes. "That's all we need. Has anybody talked to her yet?"

"She's on duty," Monk told his boss. "I talked with her watch commander. He's put a call out for her to return to the station. He'll have her contact us."

"That's going to be a fun notification." Resignation outweighed the sarcasm in Fey's voice.

"I'll do it," Brindle said.

Fey was surprised. It was unlike Brindle to volunteer for anything. "Are you sure?" Fey asked. "It's not a pleasant job. I won't stick you with it if you don't want to handle it."

"No, I can handle it," Brindle said. There was something in her voice that made both Fey and Monk give her their attention.

Brindle looked a bit uncertain under their gaze, but then seemed to gather her courage. "My father was killed in an on-the-job accident at a construction site. The way the news was broken to my mother almost killed her." The cocoa-colored skin across her model-sharp features sallowed with the memory. "I won't let that happen to somebody else if I can help it." This was a side of Brindle that hadn't been seen before.

"I don't like delivering the bad news," Fey said. "But I'm not completely insensitive."

"I didn't mean to infer you were," Brindle said. "It's

just something I feel I can do well because I've been there. Do you mind?''

Fey put up her hands. ''Not in the least. I'll even appoint you the unit's official bomb dropper, if you like.''

Brindle nodded, suddenly looking close to tears. She walked away in the direction of the bathroom without saying anything further.

Fey tried reading the teletype again. She had about as much success as the first time. ''Give me the rundown on what else we know about this kid. What's his name again?''

''Ricky Long,'' Monk told her. ''He's been a chronic runaway since he was twelve.''

''Any idea why?''

''Not at this point. Last time he was home was three weeks ago. He'd been picked up for prostitution by West Hollywood sheriffs and returned home. I called the West Hollywood juvenile unit. They remembered the case. Evidently, the kid's mother came down and picked him up. Full of concern, but frustrated as hell. She's divorced and has three other kids.'' Monk took the teletype back from Fey and checked it. ''Two boys and a girl. All older than Ricky and apparently not a problem between them.''

''All of them have the same father?''

''No idea,'' said Monk.

''Where is the father?''

Monk shrugged. ''Haven't gotten to that information yet. Are you thinking possible suspect?''

''I doubt it,'' Fey said. ''Unless we can prove some kind of a tie-in to the sheriff's victim. But who knows?''

Monk pulled out the murder book he'd started on the case and made a note. ''I'll check it out.''

''Talking about the sheriff's victim, did DOJ come up with anything there?''

''MeCoy and Blades had already done a run-through, but I did it again. Nothing so far.''

''Any possibles?''

"The sheriff's victim was a male black. DOJ sent us down six files to look at, but Blades and MeCoy had already eliminated them. There was nothing new."

"Okay," Fey said. "I want them eliminated again. Have you seen a copy of the sheriff's file yet?"

"Yeah. That FBI guy—Ash. He left us a copy."

"Good. Go through it with a fine-tooth comb. Whatever Blades and MeCoy did, I want redone."

"Wow. That's going to be a lot of work, boss."

"Do you trust them to have done it right?"

Monk blew air heavily out through his lips. "Point taken. I'll get on it."

"Don't do it all yourself," Fey told him. "Delegate some of it to Brindle and Alphabet. It's a hard lesson to learn, but you'll kill yourself otherwise."

"I think that sometimes you forget to take your own advice."

"That's twice today you've pulled me up about my professional conduct. Don't push your luck too far."

Monk looked stricken. "I . . . I didn't—"

"Relax," Fey told him. "I know you didn't mean anything by what you said, but just because you're right doesn't mean I have to like it. It's a tough time for me right now. I'm learning there are a number of areas I should be doing better in. It's discouraging. I thought I was all grown up."

"I don't think you should be discouraged. Be encouraged that you're still growing. It means you're alive."

"Thank you, Dr. Lawson. When are you going to be leaving the department and going into private practice?"

"Ah, come on, boss. I'm just trying to help."

"The best way you can help me right now is by getting an ID on the damn sheriff's victim."

"All right, all right," Monk said. "You got it." He clambered out of Fey's chair and walked away with the first teletype in his hand.

Fey felt weary. She sat down and fumbled in her purse for her makeup bag. She took out a couple of Midol and swallowed them dry. Before she put the makeup bag back, she freshened her lipstick and powdered her nose with the aid of the mirror in the top of her compact.

She checked her watch. Five o'clock. It had been a long shift. As she got older, she didn't seem to have the stamina she did when she first came on the job.

She could remember pulling all-night stakeouts, working through the next shift, and then going out to party. Those days were long gone. Now, if she wasn't in bed by ten, she dragged through the next day as if she had five-pound weights on her eyelids. And a shift like this one was guaranteed to screw her metabolism up for the rest of the week. Getting old was hell.

She rubbed her eyes before making a few notes on a yellow legal pad. She wanted to stay on this case, but she also knew that she wouldn't be any good to anybody if she didn't get some rest.

It had been an emotional rollercoaster of a day. From the high of the successful interrogation of Darcy Wyatt, to the low of the discovery of the murder victim. The high of the sparks she felt after meeting Ash, to the lows of dealing with her shrink and her brother.

If she could work it right, she'd brief Mike Cahill on the unit's progress, check with her people that there was nothing else that could be done before morning, and then get clear for some dinner and shut-eye.

It wasn't just getting old that was hell. Living until you died wasn't that easy either.

◄◘► CHAPTER TWENTY

FEY FELT WEARY. EVEN HER HAIR ACHED. SHE'D FINALLY escaped from the office shortly before eight o'clock—much later than she'd intended. Mike Cahill knew that Fey did not like dealing with the press, so he often stood in for her. The gesture had a lot to do with the fact that Cahill enjoyed seeing himself on the eleven o'clock sound bites. Everyone knew that if a TV camera showed up at the station it wouldn't be long before Cahill found a way to get himself in front of it.

Today, however, Cahill had forced Fey to step into the spotlights as part of her punishment for arguing with him about keeping the case. Cahill also had damage control in mind. If this case suddenly went sideways, he wanted to be able to hang Fey out as the scapegoat.

Unlike Cahill, Fey hated watching herself on television, and there was no way she was going to watch herself tonight on the local broadcast. She'd been having a bad hair day to begin with, and by the time she was shoved in front of the cameras to say her piece, she knew the wear and tear of the day had deepened the dark circles under her eyes. All in all, she figured she probably looked to all the viewing world like the Wicked Witch of the West.

She'd driven home in an exhausted slump. When she finally pulled into her driveway, she sat for a few minutes with her head back against the headrest and her eyes closed.

"Are you all right?" a young voice asked.

Slightly startled, Fey sat up, looking out the driver's side window at a teenage girl with long blond hair pulled back into a ponytail. She was wearing worn jeans, well-used rough-outs, and a man's plaid shirt.

Fey opened the car door. "Good grief, Lori. You scared the daylights out of me."

"Oh, I'm real sorry." The girl put a hand up to her mouth in apparent worry.

"Relax," Fey said with a laugh, seeing the girl's concern. "I'm not mad at you." She put her hand on her chest, feeling her pulse pounding. "I've just got to pull back on the reins of my heart."

Lori giggled and then smiled, revealing a mouth full of braces. "That sounds like the catch phrase of a bad country-western song."

Fey broke into a twangy falsetto and sang, "You threw me over for a honky-tonk tramp, so now I've just got to pull back on the reins of my heart."

"You've got it," Lori said, and both of them laughed together.

"What are you doing here so late?" Fey asked. Lori and her family had recently moved into the neighborhood a few houses up the street from Fey.

"I had a dentist appointment this afternoon, and then Mom made me do all my homework before she'd let me come over and take care of the horses. I've got this dumb term paper due for history."

Fey and Lori had struck up a friendship over Constable and Thieftaker, the two horses Fey stabled in her backyard. Lori loved horses, having figured out instinctively that they were smarter, more reliable, better friends, less problems, and more fun than boys. In return for caring for Fey's horses, Lori could ride them whenever she wanted and also picked up good spending money.

Fey had often relied on one of her immediate neighbors—Peter, a freelance journalist with horses of his own—to take care of feeding and mucking out when the press of work made it impossible for Fey to do it herself. Recently, however, Peter had been unavailable and both he and Fey had needed somebody to help them out. At a responsible fifteen years old, Lori had been the answer to that need.

Fey still rode on a regular basis, but the day-to-day slog of feed and care for the animals, on top of the escalating and stress-filled workload of the homicide unit, was taking its toll. Increasingly, Fey was getting Lori to take care of her horses even if she herself was available. It was an indulgence, but one that she found definitely worthwhile.

"How's the gang?" Fey asked, referring to the horses.

"As ornery as ever, but eating well as usual."

"Well, I hope they appreciate you as much as I do."

"Uhmm . . ."

"Yes?" Fey prompted.

"There was this guy hanging around outside the house about an hour ago. I saw him when I first came over."

Fey was instantly very wary. "What did he look like?"

Lori shrugged. "Geeky, I guess. He was short and skinny and his face was full of acne craters."

"How old?"

"I don't know . . . older guy . . . in his forties maybe."

"Long hair?"

"Yeah. Black. Pulled back into a frizzy ponytail."

Tommy, Fey thought to herself. He was the only forty-year-old geek she knew that would be hanging around her house.

"You speak to him?" she asked.

"Yeah. He was ringing your front doorbell. I told him you weren't home yet. He asked me when you'd be coming back. I told him I didn't know."

"Then what happened?"

Lori gave her all-purpose teenage shrug again. "He got on his motorcycle and split."

It was Tommy all right. Obviously, he'd been released from the hospital. But what, Fey thought, would propel him to come to her house? Especially in light of their confrontation earlier in the day.

She didn't want him around her house. She'd sent him to jail for breaking into it and ransacking the contents to feed his drug habit. It had been the last of the last straws.

While she still wanted to help Tommy, Fey didn't need him invading her life or her castle.

"Do you know the guy?" Lori asked.

"Sounds like my brother," Fey said.

"Oh," said Lori, picking up on Fey's tone.

"Yeah, oh," Fey said, with raised eyebrows. "Steer clear of him if you ever see him again. He won't hurt you, but you don't need the hassle of confronting him."

"Okay."

"It's been a long day," Fey said. "I'm going to go in and crash. Are you done with the horses?"

"Yeah. They're put up for the night."

"Thanks."

With a wave, Lori turned and headed off toward home. Fey returned the wave and walked to her front door. Her mind had kicked into an even higher whirl. She felt as if her head was spinning. She needed to be concentrating on the homicide—she brought home with her a copy of the file on the sheriff's homicide to sift through—but her personal life kept intruding. First her shrink telling her she should be writing letters to her dead father—no way that was ever going to happen in this lifetime—and now her brother was beginning to play mind games with her all over again. Tommy should be able to take care of himself by now, but he was over forty years old and still thought the world revolved around the rock n' roll lifestyle.

Personally, Fey didn't need the grief.

As she let herself in through the front door a white blur of fur and claws darted in to attack her shoes. Expecting the assault, Fey bent down and scooped her cat up into her arms. As she did so, the file she had been carrying spilled onto the tiled entryway.

"Hello, darling," Fey said, nuzzling her pet. "How is my little Brentwood today? Did you miss me?"

The cat yowled.

"Oh, I see," Fey said. "As usual, all you're interested in is being fed. If I didn't know better, I would swear you were a male. Of course, then all you would be interested in was being fed and getting laid."

She set Brentwood on the floor and walked through to the kitchen to open a can of food. The cat followed her, running through and around Fey's legs while keeping up a constant chatter of yowls.

The house was a long, ranch-style floor plan that had been constructed to Fey's design with the proceeds from the disaster of her second marriage. It was the only positive and enduring entity to come out of that relationship. There was a small pool and Jacuzzi in the backyard, and beyond that, separated by a six-foot-high slump stone wall, was the stable and corral area for Thieftaker and Constable.

Fey had been forced to rebuild the stables after they had been destroyed by an arson fire a year earlier. The fire had been devastating at first, but in the long run she was now happier with the new, more modern stable building.

After feeding Brentwood and checking on the horses—Lori had done her usual fine job—Fey showered and changed into a set of sweats. She drank an iced vodka and 7Up as she threw together a prepackaged Caesar salad and cut up a boneless, grilled chicken breast to sprinkle across the top. Turning on the small TV she kept in the kitchen, she tuned the channel to CNN—more for the noise of human voices than for the entertainment value.

She ate while standing up, leafing through the day's collection of junk mail and feeding bites of chicken to Brentwood, who sat attentively on the kitchen counter next to her. When she was done, she cleaned up and poured another drink. She took her glass through to the front door and bent down to pick up the scattered file.

Shuffling the papers together, she noticed an advertising circular of the type usually left by real estate agents on the front doorstep. This one had been folded in half and actually shoved halfway under the front door. She picked it up and unfolded it, noticing that there were block letters inscribed on the blank back side of the advertisement. She'd seen enough of Tommy's hate letters to recognize his writing.

This one was different, however.

It simply said, "I'm sorry."

Fey put a hand to her forehead. She was already crouched down, and now she let herself the rest of the way down to sit on the floor.

For the first time since she was thirteen, she began to cry.

❦

CHAPTER TWENTY-ONE

"EXPLAIN TO ME WHY YOU'RE BUSTING YOUR BALLS ON this, Brindle. Exactly what's in it for you?"

Seeing as she was tired, and seeing as the request came from the innocuous Alphabet, Brindle did not take offense. In actuality, it was a pretty fair question. One to which Brindle didn't have a ready answer.

"Call it professional pride," she said, leaning back against a brick wall and feeling the thumping vibration of the music from the Doppelganger nightclub on the other side. It was muggy out on the street, night bringing no relief from the heat of the day.

"Get outta here," Alphabet said. "I'll grant that you have a certain amount of professional pride, but it has nothing to do with solving cases."

"Okay, okay, so the bitch is getting to me. She acts as if the only way I can get a promotion is by wearing out a pair of knee pads."

"Why are you pissed at Fey? It's not her fault that you behave that way."

Brindle shot Alphabet a look hard enough to blast him into the next postal zone. "Screw you, Alphabet."

"Do you kiss your mother with that mouth?"

"In spades, Jew boy."

"Now that's funny," Alphabet said, unfazed.

Brindle covered her eyes and chuckled. "Yeah, I guess it is. But she pisses me off. I want to be the one to break this case open. Rub her nose in it."

"You had your hostility levels checked lately? All Fey is doing is pushing you to live up to what she thinks is your potential."

"Now who's bullshitting who?"

"No, I'm serious. You could be a hell of a detective if you dropped all this seduction crap and got on with the job."

Brindle didn't know why she let Alphabet get away with talking to her like this. There was something about him, however, that made her think he was more than just some guy who wanted to get into her shorts. If she gave him the chance she figured he probably would jump her bones, but if she didn't he'd still be her friend anyway.

Brindle had gone home shortly after Fey had left the station. She'd done her full eight-hour shift and then some, but she knew that Monk and Fey had put in even more overtime. They'd had to handle the early morning call-in on the rape suspect.

While still at work, she had spent time on the telephone with Alice Long—poor dead Ricky's mother. Alice had been called in from the scene of a traffic accident, where she'd been taking a report. Her watch commander had softened her up for the shock, but Brindle was still surprised at how calmly the woman had taken the news. It was as if Alice had been expecting something like this to happen to Ricky, and now she was relieved that she could stop worrying about it.

Brindle's interview with the woman had covered the basics. Ricky was the oldest of Alice's four children and had always been a problem. Alice had been a cop for six years, seeing it as a way to support her family without a husband in the home. The father of her three other children had also been a cop, but he was out of the picture now. Alice was never really sure who Ricky's father had been. When she had been younger, she'd never claimed to be a model of abstinence. Now, her own mother took care of the kids while Alice worked to keep them all in Cheerios and underwear.

Ricky was eight when he ran away for the first time. He ran away three more times before Alice had discovered that Ricky was being molested by an uncle who had been happily acting as a babysitter. During the prosecution, Ricky had run away again to avoid testifying.

Every time he came home or was brought home after running away, Ricky appeared to be more and more withdrawn. Alice didn't know how to reach him. Family intervention, counseling, nothing seemed to work. When he'd been picked up three weeks earlier by the West Hollywood sheriffs for prostitution, Alice had finally known that there would never be a happy ending for Ricky. And now he was dead.

Alice herself felt dead inside. Six years of being a cop, however, had taught her to kill any outward display of emotion. She took the news that Brindle broke to her without tears or hysterics. Later that night, she would perhaps consider eating a bullet from her service revolver, but until then she would handle the situation with icy calm.

Brindle had tried to elicit as much information as she could from Alice Long, but she knew she would have to do a more in-depth follow-up when Alice came to LA to claim the body. It appeared, though, that Alice would be able to give the LA detectives little to go on. Ricky's story was pathetic, but not unusual. The fact that his mother was a cop simply proved that carrying a badge didn't make you immune, it didn't make you a god, and it sure as hell didn't protect you from being personally touched by the horrors of the world.

After leaving work for the day, Brindle had thought about Ricky Long. She also thought about the John Doe victim from the sheriff's murder. From talking with the vice unit at the West Hollywood sheriff's station, she knew the name of the nightclub where Ricky had been busted for prostitution. It didn't take a genius to figure out that perhaps the John Doe had operated in the same area.

She called Alphabet at home, catching him in the middle of his daily Nordic-Trac workout. Monk had asked them to concentrate on getting a positive make on the John Doe. The identity could help establish a connection between the two victims and give them a clear lead to the killer.

Alphabet had been surprised when Brindle called. She never paid him much attention at work. He figured this was probably because he couldn't do anything for her, couldn't smooth out the fast track to a promotion or a cushy assignment. Still, it didn't take much persuading on her part to get him to meet her in West Hollywood with pictures of the two victims taken from the murder books.

Brindle and Alphabet started their quest at the West Hollywood sheriff's station, a squat building on the corner of San Vincente and Santa Monica Boulevard. The city of West Hollywood butts up against the northeast end of the LAPD's West Los Angeles area. It is a small municipality, known as a predominantly gay enclave. For cost and resource reasons, the city contracted its law enforcement needs through the Los Angeles sheriff's department.

Checking in with the deputies assigned to the sheriff's vice detail, the LA detectives flashed around pictures of Ricky Long and the John Doe. The deputy who'd arrested Ricky happened to be at the station. The young boy had been caught up in a sweep of male prostitutes who ply their trade outside the area nightclubs. There was nothing special about the arrest, except perhaps for Ricky's age, but even that wasn't unusual enough to elicit more than passing comment.

"Street kids," Deputy Hogan said. He was a big man, ex-football player type with a heavy mustache. "They're the same here as everywhere else. They close ranks for their own protection. I don't think you're going to get anywhere showing them the photo of your John Doe. They won't tell you a thing."

"I agree," Brindle said, although she didn't. "But we've got to cover all the bases to satisfy our boss."

Hogan shrugged. "Good luck to you then, but I still say you're spinning your wheels."

"The overtime money is too good to pass up," Alphabet said. "If the city wants to pay us to spin our wheels, who are we to complain?" He gave Hogan a knowing wink. He wanted to give the deputy the feeling they weren't going to be looking too hard. If the deputies began to think LAPD might ace them out of a good murder case lead, they'd become less cooperative—hoping to grab any brownie points for themselves.

Alphabet knew that, in actuality, the deputy was probably right—they were spitting into the wind trying to get a lead on their John Doe by talking to the street kids. But there was always a chance he and Brindle could get lucky.

Hogan and the other vice deputies gave Brindle and Alphabet a rundown on the local club scene and the most active areas for chickens and rabbits—juvenile male prostitutes. Armed with this information and their photos, the two LAPD detectives hit the streets.

They started at the One On One Club on Santa Monica Boulevard, and then made their way through the maze of gay discos, leather bars, and more upscale watering holes that populated the area. It was boring, tiring, unforgiving work. They talked to bartenders, bouncers, and patrons, all without success. The didn't try to hide the fact that they were cops, and as such they were strangers, outsiders to this closed world.

"We should have brought Fegerson with us," Brindle said, referring to one of several known gay LAPD officers who worked out of West LA. "He might have been able to give us an in with some of these people."

Alphabet shook his head. "Fegerson may be gay, but he's still The Man as far as the people we're talking to are concerned. He'd get the same stonewall."

In front of the clubs, they watched as the mostly male prostitutes plied their trade along the boulevard. Transvestites, in outfits that left little to the imagination, added a sleazy splash of color to the scene. The youngsters, mostly runaways, hung back, lining the outside walls of the clubs, kept in check by the older pros who didn't need the competition.

After a couple of hours on the street, Alphabet was not just tired from the long day, he was weary from the sleaze of the cesspool around them. West Hollywood was actually a nice upscale town, but the despair on the faces of the street people was made even more poignant with the specter of AIDS lurking around every corner—an unspoken threat more deadly than any human killer.

AIDS not only scared Alphabet, but also touched something inside of him. He wasn't gay, but neither was he a gay basher. He also knew that the gay community as a whole was not represented by what he and Brindle saw around them on the street. However, he still found it hard to imagine living in a world where so many of your friends were dying around you at an age when life should be just beginning for them.

"Why did you come on this job?" he asked Brindle. It was more for something to say than anything else.

"Why did you?" she countered.

"The department offered excitement and security. It seemed like a good idea at the time."

"I rest my case," said Brindle.

Alphabet turned toward her. Even dressed in jeans, hiking boots, a plaid lumberjack shirt, and bomber jacket hiding the gun at her waist, Brindle looked like she'd just stepped out of a fashion magazine. "There has to be something more?"

Brindle bent over and rubbed the backs of her legs. "I don't know. I guess I had something to prove. I've got three older brothers. One went to 'Nam and became some big deal hero. He's now an army colonel bucking for general. One became a priest and thinks he's on the fast track to becoming a bishop. The other started out with IBM and now runs his own corporation making advanced computer shit for wireheads." She straightened up and leaned back against the Doppelganger's wall again. "They have all given me shit over the years about how easy things must be for me because I'm a good-looking woman. I became a cop because I thought it was a job where being a woman didn't matter . . ." She trailed off.

"And . . ." Alphabet prompted.

Brindle's shoulders rose and fell. "And I was wrong. Any time a woman gets ahead on this job everyone says it's not because she's good, but because she has two lumps of fat on her chest and doesn't have an appendage between her legs."

"So you decided, since everyone was ready to accuse you of using those factors to get ahead, you might as well use them?"

"Damn right. Not only that, but it's fun as well. If you men only knew how pathetic you act when a woman bats her eyelashes at you or rubs up against you."

"You better be careful," Alphabet said.

"What do you mean?"

"Well, that's a hell of an axe you're grinding. If you're not careful you might just cut yourself off at the grindstone."

Outside of the Doppelganger, a young boy no older than thirteen hopped out of a black Mercedes that had pulled over to the curb. One eye was swelling and there was blood flowing from his nose. Brindle and Alphabet exchanged glances.

The kid looked back into the car and gave the occupant the finger. "Eat shit, asshole!" the kid yelled as the car drove away.

"I hope he got his money up front," Alphabet said.

Brindle made a mental note of the car license plate. "What a hell of a way to make a living," she said. Somewhere down the line she'd get a printout on the registered owner of the vehicle and see if she could make his life miserable in some way.

A little further down the wall from where Brindle was leaning, two large shapes peeled themselves out of the shadows and it was clear the kid's problems weren't over. One of the shapes was tall and slender, a ballet dancer wrapped in denim and attitude. The other shape was a muscular fireplug. Point and counterpoint. Either one could have eaten the kid for an hors d'oeuvre and not even noticed.

The ballet dancer grabbed the kid by the right ear and twisted hard. The kid screamed.

"Shut it!" the ballet dancer screamed back into the kid's face. He dragged the kid away from the curb and toward an alley entrance. Fireplug had taken up the position of rear guard, defying anybody to object to ballet dancer's treatment of the kid. He followed into the shadows of the alley.

The sound of a sharp slap and another yelp from the kid reached back to the street. The other prostitutes and club patrons continued about their business as if everything was normal.

"You guys are cops. Can't you do something?" a voice next to Alphabet spoke up. "They're gonna kill him."

Alphabet turned around to see the eyes of a young girl staring at him out of a dirty heart-shaped face. Long strands of unwashed blond hair flopped everywhere.

Alphabet had shown her the pictures of Ricky Long and the John Doe a few minutes earlier. She'd barely looked at both photos before saying she didn't know anything.

"Who's he to you?" Alphabet asked.

The gamin squirmed inside her oversized army fatigue jacket. "He's just another rabbit who's gonna get gutted if you don't stop Bomber."

"Bomber?"

"Yeah. The tall guy."

"Who's the muscle?"

"Mace. He likes to hit people."

"Bomber a pimp?"

"What do you think?"

"You and your rabbit boyfriend been holding out on him?"

The gamine fidgeted with her hair and continued squirming as if she had to go to the bathroom real bad. Another yelp reached the street from the alley mouth. She looked over that way. "Come on, man. Do something. Please." Her voice was pleading.

"You got somewhere to go?"

"Yeah. There's a shelter."

Brindle had walked over to stand next to Alphabet. "What about our photos?" she asked, shoving the two glossies under the gamin's nose.

The girl was silent.

Brindle waited a few beats. "Your choice," she said to the girl.

More silence.

Brindle took Alphabet's arm. "Let's go," she said, beginning to move away.

The girl's squirming increased. "Shit. Ain't nothing free?"

"Not in this life," Brindle said, stopping. "I'd thought you'd have learned that by now."

"And I suppose you want a free head job," the gamine said to Alphabet.

"All I want is for you to tell me about the photos," he said, feeling the color of embarrassment rise up in his face.

The girl grabbed the two photos from Brindle's hands and stared at them. "Never seen this guy," she said, handing back the photo of Ricky Long. She looked back again at the photo of the John Doe for a few seconds before turning to talk to Alphabet. "This guy calls himself Rush. He's a raver. Makes all the regular scenes. Haven't seen him for a couple of weeks."

"Do you know his real name?"

"Down here nobody has a real name anymore."

"Was he a rabbit?"

"Shit, man. What do you think? Everybody on the street does sex for money." She looked back toward the alley mouth, grabbed Alphabet's sleeve, and began tugging him toward it. "I swear that's all I know, man. Now, come on, you gotta do something."

Alphabet shrugged off the girl's hand as he sensed Brindle moving up beside him. Together they entered the alley. Mace had the kid by the arms, bending him backward over a trash can. Bomber, the ballet dancer, was standing in front of the kid. He had a knife out and was tearing open the pockets of the kid's thin jacket. A wad of money fell out onto the ground. None of the three noticed Brindle and Alphabet enter the alley.

When Bomber bent down to pick up the kid's stash, Alphabet took advantage of the appealing target that was presented. With purposeful accuracy, he drove the toe of his cowboy boot deep into Bomber's groin. An explosion of breath and a high-pitched scream preceded Bomber dropping to the ground. Alphabet put his right boot down on Bomber's neck.

"Who the hell are you?" Mace asked.

"Avon lady," Alphabet said.

Mace pulled the kid across the trash can and whipped out a knife of his own. He held the point of the knife to the kid's throat.

Brindle drew her 9 millimeter and aimed it at Mace's head. "How very melodramatic." She took a step forward. "Go ahead," she told Mace. "Slice him open. Give me the excuse I need to justify splattering your brains all over the wall behind you."

"What do you want?" Mace asked. His voice was raspy with fear. He might be a bully with those weaker than him, but he was a coward in the face of resistance.

"I want to kill you," Brindle said. "I don't think you deserve to live. So, you've got one chance. Throw the knife down, let the kid go, and get the hell out of here."

"What about him?" Mace gestured toward Bomber with his chin.

"What do you care?" Brindle asked.

Mace looked down the barrel of Brindle's unwavering pistol and made up his mind. He pushed the kid hard toward Brindle, turned, and ran for the other end of the alley.

"He didn't drop the knife," Alphabet said.

"So we'll give him an F in following instructions."

"He doesn't play well with others either."

The kid had staggered forward and then dropped to his knees. With speed born of desperation he grabbed the wad of notes that was still on the ground and blasted past Alphabet like a sprinter coming out of the blocks.

"You're welcome," Brindle called after him.

Alphabet reached down and grabbed a healthy wad of Bomber's greasy hair. He pulled back and dragged Bomber over to a sitting position against the alley wall. The pimp still had his hands between his legs and was whimpering.

Alphabet crouched down in front of his captive and used the curve between his left thumb and index finger to C-clamp Bomber's neck back against the wall. He figured they'd gone this far so he may as well take advantage of the situation. In for a penny, in for a pound.

"If you ever want your balls to drop back down to their normal position," he said in a conversational tone, taking out his photos of Ricky and Rush, "then you're going to tell me everything you know about these two kids."

✡

CHAPTER TWENTY-TWO

RHONDA LAWLESS RAN THE FLAT OF HER HAND SLOWLY and caressingly across Arch Hammersmith's bare chest. Even in sleep Hammersmith was catlike—appearing to be fully relaxed, yet with a constant tension of wariness. It seemed as if at any second, he could instantly leap from the bed and into action. It was a trait that fascinated Rhonda as much if not more than the curves and knots of the corded musculature she was touching.

In his younger days Hammersmith had been a world-class swimmer. He'd gone to the 1976 Olympics in the 1,500 meter freestyle and missed a medal by two-tenths of a second. His shoulders, already genetically broad from the Welsh mining stock on his father's side, had been enlarged by the years of pool workouts. They still maintained an impressive breadth and tapered down to a thirty-two-inch waist. Rhonda had once teased him about his lack of a butt by making out a theft report for it and processing it through the station's record unit.

It had been a long day. Knowing that Fey was tied up with the new homicide, the duo had handled the brunt of the day's new MAC reports with their usual quick efficiency. There had also been four bodies taken into custody during the course of the day. Two had been spousal abuse arrests, another for ADW, and the last for indecent exposure—all crimes covered by the newly formed MAC unit. The processing of the bodies had been fairly straightforward, but was still time consuming.

They had also read through Darcy Wyatt's rape arrest report and seen the need for somebody to jump on the follow-up immediately. With the more pressing homicide case taking precedence, it would be easy for the rape case to possibly fall through the cracks. With Hop-Along away on vacation, there was no sex crimes specialist to assign to the case, so they had decided to tell Fey they would handle it.

Taking another crack at Devon Wyatt also appealed to them. Darcy Wyatt's lawyer father had once put Hammer and Nails through the ringer while they were working internal affairs. Devon Wyatt had been representing a police officer accused of child molest, and the possibility of conviction had been touch and go for a while before finally dropping down in Hammer and Nails's favor. Neither one had forgotten what a tough opponent Wyatt could be, and they were damn sure Wyatt hadn't forgotten them. He was a man who carried a long grudge.

The work had stretched into a couple of hours overtime before they were able to get to the gym for one of their four weekly workouts. Afterward, they had grabbed a quick Caesar salad at a small restaurant in Santa Monica and then had driven to Rhonda's for the evening and eventually bed.

Rhonda loved watching Hammersmith sleep. It was the one time when she felt completely in charge of his well-being. They had been partners for three years and emotionally attached from the very beginning. It had been a year, however, before they had physically consummated their relationship. This was not from lack of desire, but due to an intense, teasing courtship they had developed that had been too much fun to rush through.

From their first day assigned together at internal affairs they both knew it was a foregone conclusion that they would end up in bed together, so there was no rush to get there. Sex was only sex, after all, and there were far more fascinating aspects of their relationship to explore first.

There were times, however, before their relationship had become physical, that Rhonda had lain alone in bed with a stone-ache of desire for the man who was her partner.

The beginnings of their lovemaking provided all of the electricity and fire that their relationship had promised. It bothered Rhonda a lot, however, that Hammersmith would never spend the complete night in bed with her—never sleep. But she was smart enough to give him time and space, and now, occasionally, he would allow himself to fall asleep in her arms. The first time he did this, she knew that at last his trust in her was as complete as hers was in him.

Rhonda's initial contact with Hammersmith had been ten years earlier. She'd been fresh out of the academy working morning watch patrol in Shootin' Newton, one of the hottest areas in the south end of the city. Even back then, Newton division was a war zone—a jungle of crime, vice, and violence—that earned its nickname by consistently having the highest rate of officer-involved shootings in the city.

Rhonda had been working with Murray Olbretch, a grizzled veteran training officer who had grown to despise working with rookies and hated working with women even more. Murray's idea of class was farting after a meal instead of burping, and chain smoking dog-turd cigars instead of cigarettes. He was crass, lazy, hyena-sly, and brutal. It was the last of these attributes, however, that led to his biggest problem.

Olbretch was hated by the citizens who populated the Newton area. He was quick with his nightstick, and even quicker to apply the bar arm—the infamous choke hold employed as the standard method to render uncooperative suspects unconscious. It was officers such as Olbretch, whose idea of uncooperative extended to somebody looking at them funny, that eventually caused the department to outlaw the bar-arm. The department also moved all other upper body control holds up the "escalation of force" scale to the same step as using a gun—deadly force.

Olbretch certainly wasn't afraid of using his gun either. In his time in Newton division, he'd been part of five officer-involved shooting situations. Three of those situations had resulted in the deaths of the suspects. All of the situations were reviewed by a police shooting board and found to be officially "in policy." Unofficially, everyone knew that Olbretch had stretched circumstances to the point of provoking the shootings.

Olbretch didn't give a damn. He liked to brag about his "kills" and had even gone as far as to notch his gun butt as if he was a western gunslinger. There was no doubting Olbretch had watermelon-size balls, but he was also a sadistic bastard.

All of this made Olbretch a target with an underground price on his head. He'd laughed when a snitch told him about the street contract. However, he wasn't laughing when he and Rhonda rolled on an "unknown trouble" call in the projects and found themselves in the middle of a deadly ambush.

Olbretch hadn't even let Rhonda answer the call when it came in over the radio. Olbretch was driving, but he still snaked out a hand to beat Rhonda to the radio microphone.

"14A21, roger," Olbretch said, pressing the send button and verbally acknowledging receipt of the call. He hung the mike back on its hook.

As far as he was concerned, Rhonda was simply there to keep the log and take reports like a good little secretary.

Anything else resembling police work was to be left to him.

"Unknown trouble, my ass," he said, making an illegal U-turn in front of traffic to head toward the call. "Damn niggers are too stupid even to tell communications why they need the police."

The citizens of Newton division weren't the only people that hated Olbretch. Rhonda hated him as well. She hated his racist attitude, his chauvinism, his smug belief that Olbretch's Law was the law of the land.

"Olbretch's Law," he'd told her when they first started working together. "Courts ain't got nothing to do with justice," he said, and then held up his wooden nightstick and pointed the scarred end toward her. "This is justice. And when some scumbag's brains and blood are flowing down the gutter because they've just been introduced to Mr. Hickory, that's justice in action."

Rhonda just figured Mr. Hickory was an extension of Olbretch's dinky dick and tried to ignore him as best she could. As a rookie, she had no standing. If she complained or asked for another partner, she'd be instantly branded as a troublemaker, someone not to be trusted, and she'd be damned if she was going to let an asshole like Olbretch hang that kind of jacket on her. Somehow, someway, she had to put up with Olbretch until a natural partner rotation came around.

On the night of the unknown trouble call, Olbretch had been particularly obnoxious. He was nursing a bad cold and kept hacking up phlegm and spitting it out the window. It was the spitting action, however, that probably saved his life when the first bullet whizzed over his head as he bent forward to hawk a lugee. The bullet hit the door post and ricochetted around the car before burying itself in the rear seat cushion.

"Holy shit!" Olbretch yelled. He floored the accelerator, bullying the ten-year-old patrol car into sluggish action. He reached for the microphone, but this time Rhonda was faster.

More bullets riddled the vehicle as she reported the ambush and gave their location to communications. She was surprised at the lack of panic she felt in the situation. It was as if her entire body had leapt into a time/space continuum in which everything moved in slow motion except for her own actions.

A fusillade of bullets poured through the front windshield of the patrol car, shattering glass and buzzing around the car's interior like angry bees. Two of them simultaneously tore into Olbretch. He gasped in pain, turning the steering wheel involuntarily.

The car flew up over the curb and smashed headfirst into a power pole in front of a brick wall. Wires flashed as the transformer above exploded, showering sparks in every direction. The street was plunged into full darkness except for the patrol car's headlights.

As Rhonda turned to pull Olbretch back from the steering wheel, another bullet hit her in the back. The bullet was stopped by her Second Chance Kevlar vest, but the dissipated force made her feel as if she'd been hit by a sledgehammer. She fell forward against Olbretch and saw another bullet tear into his shoulder not two inches from her nose. Desperately, she hit the release on her lap belt, reached across Olbretch, and opened the driver's side door.

Using strength she didn't realize she possessed, she pushed Olbretch out the door ahead of her. He flopped to the ground, either unconscious, dying, or dead, and Rhonda crawled out on top of him. She had her .38 in her hand and fired three blind shots back down the street.

There seemed to be a momentary lull in the firing, and Rhonda took advantage of that factor to shove Olbretch under the car and out of the line of fire. With her left hand, she pulled Olbretch's gun from his holster and moved to the front of the crashed police car. Once there, with the brick wall to her back, she smashed the car's headlights with the butt of Olbretch's gun, and then squatted down to quickly reload her own gun with a speedy loader from her belt.

She picked up the three unspent cartridges she had dumped out from her first load and shoved them into her pocket. She now had six shots in her own gun, six in Olbretch's, six in another speedy loader on her belt, and the three in her pocket. She prayed they would be enough and cursed herself for not grabbing Olbretch's speedy loaders as well as his gun.

The firing started again and a bullet ricochetted off of the hood of the car to tear a bone-deep graze in her right cheek. She fired two shots back in blind anger and then held her fire. She realized she still didn't know where the shots were coming from, and couldn't even remember if communications had acknowledged her help call. She was pinned down in front of the patrol car with no way to get back inside to the radio. Sirens sounded in the distance, and she could only hope they were on the way to her location.

Movement off to her right caught her eye as a figure bent over a rifle scurried across the street. As far as Rhonda was concerned there were no friendly bodies in the area. She capped off a round and heard the body grunt as her shot hit home. The figure stumbled and fell.

"Take that, you puke!" she screamed. "Anybody else wants some of this, they can come and get it."

A flurry of bullets again put her head down behind the patrol car's grill.

Shit, I'm going to die. The thought invaded her senses, her own mortality hitting home for the first time. She'd known the job was dangerous when she'd hired on, but she didn't expect to get killed before her first year was finished. Then again, nobody did.

"Damn it, I'm *not* going to die," she said out loud in defiance. "Come on, you dickless pukes!" she yelled, capping off two more rounds. "Come and get me if you think you're good enough. Come out in the open and let's rock n' roll, assholes." *If I do die*, she thought, *I'm taking as many with me as I can.*

And then she heard it: a screeching of tires, the full-throated roar of a Chevy engine running flat out, and a screaming maniac blasting a shotgun indiscriminately into the shadows. Arch Hammersmith had arrived out of the darkness like hell on wheels.

Hammersmith had just over eight years on the job at the time. He was a newly promoted detective assigned to work the K-car out of detective headquarters division—DHD. His job was to roll on all the South Bureau homicide scenes. The PM watch K-car was a two-man unit, but the morning watch car was only a one-man assignment, and that was the way Hammersmith liked it. He'd never found a partner who was willing to work as hard as he did. There were a number of cops Hammersmith respected and had learned from, but for the most part he considered partners more of a hindrance than a help.

Hammersmith had found that most cops talked about three things: cars, guns, and sex. Two of the three Hammersmith had no real interest in, and the other he didn't talk about in public.

The first time he had verbalized that view to Rhonda, she had asked him why he didn't like to talk about cars in public. It was one of many times that she had blindsided him with humor—an idiosyncrasy that he would come to love in her.

When he'd heard the ''officer needs help'' call come out that evening, Hammersmith had been three blocks away. It had been a slow night and he was simply cruising the streets, waiting to see if something would happen before he had to go out and make it happen. Most K-car detectives were happy simply to roll from homicide scene to homicide scene and list the incidents for the chief's log. Hammersmith, however, used the down time between catching calls to catch crooks. In the past month, he'd already nailed three GTA suspects and two 211 artists wanted for a string of supermarket robberies.

Putting the pedal to the metal, he'd roared toward the location communications had put out for the help call. With his right hand, he unlocked the Ithica twelve-gauge shotgun and took it from the rack parallel to the front seat. He pushed the safety off and jacked a round into the chamber.

As he rounded the final corner, he saw the police car crashed into the power pole. He saw the silhouette of an officer pop up from behind the front of the car and fire a round at a running figure. The figure stumbled and fell.

Flashes of rifle fire came from open windows on both sides of the street.

"Hot damn!" Hammersmith yelled. "Hang on, pal. Help's comin'."

Hammersmith flew down the roadway, barely feeling the hits as rounds tore into the car's body work. A tire blew, but Hammersmith was damned if that was going to stop him. He fired a round from the shotgun at a window showing rifle flash. He knew there was no chance of hitting anything, but maybe it would keep a few heads down.

"Heeeeee-haaaa!" he yelled out his window, a cowboy on a runaway bronco.

Standing on the brakes, he turned the car into a power slide and brought the rear end around to barely kiss the trunk of Rhonda's disabled patrol car. He slid his body up through the driver's side window, jacked a round into the shotgun and fired back up the street.

Rhonda had been moving fast. Taking advantage of the shooters' concentration on the entry of Hammersmith's stripped-down detective Chevy, Rhonda had scrambled around to drag Olbretch out from under the car. For some inexplicable reason, she felt she knew exactly what the guy driving the rescue car was going to do, and she had to be prepared for it.

Before Hammersmith's car was even stopped, Rhonda was dragging Olbretch toward it. She yanked open the back door as Hammersmith fired another round down the street. Heaving and dragging, she backed herself into the car pulling Olbretch along with her.

"Hit it!" she yelled, even before Olbretch's legs were completely in the car.

She rolled Olbretch onto the floor. Without thinking about it, she reached over the seat to take the shotgun from Hammersmith as he slid back into the driving seat. Later they would recognize this action as the first time their

minds had linked together to work as one. They didn't
need to communicate vocally. Hammersmith had wanted
and needed Rhonda to grab the shotgun, and she had already done it before he verbalized the thought.

Hammersmith floored the car again as Rhonda reloaded
the Ithica and began blasting away out the back window.

Another tire was blown out from under them, but it
didn't slow them down. Hammersmith powered around the
first corner on rims, and ran directly into the cavalry.

Patrol cars were flooding into the area, three of them
forming a protective cordon around Hammersmith's car as
it limped forward to safety. When the car stopped, eager
hands helped to ease Olbretch into the back of another
patrol car and sped him away to the closest emergency
room.

When all was said and done three suspects were in custody, and Hammersmith and Rhonda found themselves
nominated for the police star for bravery. Olbretch survived his wounds, but was never able to return to full duty.
The three suspects were eventually convicted of attempted
murder.

Olbretch was also unable to ever acknowledge Rhonda
for saving his life.

But she knew and Hammersmith knew. And that was
enough.

Now, after having worked as partners for over three
years, the pair had developed an extraordinary efficiency
that was almost telepathic. They were an inseparable team.
Working internal affairs had cemented both their relationship and their somewhat legendary reputation as Hammer
and Nails. It had also given them enough dirt on both high-
ranking city and police personnel to insure their continued
partnership. It wasn't quite a case of getting whatever they
wanted, but it was damn close.

As Rhonda's hand wandered from Hammer's chest to
his abdomen, he roused and reached a hand down to capture hers before she became carried away.

"I was thinking," he said clearly, an indication that his

eyes may have been closed, but sleep hadn't overtaken him. "This Darcy Wyatt caper—"

"You're not happy about it," Rhonda said, knowing what was coming.

"It's too damn trite. There's something else there."

"I agree. So, tomorrow we go back to square one."

"Yeah. Reinterview all the victims. See if Wyatt will talk to us. Find out who else from the pizza joints may have had access."

Rhonda freed her hand from Hammer's grasp and moved it down to caress him. He was already hard.

Rhonda wanted him. Needed him. Not just anyone. Him.

"But that's tomorrow," she whispered into his ear, her own pulse an increasing drumbeat in her head.

"Tomorrow," he agreed, rolling toward her.

"And this is still tonight," she said.

Opening her legs, her hands guided him to her. She arched her back, raising her buttocks to expose herself fully to him.

As she always did, she gasped when he entered her.

❖
CHAPTER TWENTY-THREE

JOHN BASSETT FOUGHT TO KEEP HIS EYES OPEN AND THE patrol car between the white lines. His training officer Dick Morrison had to be tired as well, but you couldn't tell it from looking at him.

Not only had they worked almost ten hours overtime the night before, dealing with the pizza delivery rapist, but while Bassett had gone home to collapse in bed, Morrison had gone to court and testified in a "last day" case. Bassett figured his older partner couldn't have achieved more than three or four hours sleep before being due back on duty.

Any of the other older cops Bassett had worked with would have been curled up against the passenger door with their eyes closed, but not Morrison. Morrison was not just The Man, he was THE MAN. A real cop's cop. A cop to make Jack Webb proud. Over twenty-five years on the job, the majority of it working uniformed patrol, and never a sick day taken or a court date missed.

Morrison was all the more amazing because he'd also managed to keep his personal life intact. Married to the same woman for thirty years, two sons—one a doctor, the other an airline pilot—and a daughter, who was now an LAPD rookie, much to her dad's disgust.

Morrison pressed the glow button on his watch and checked the time. It had been a relatively slow tour: three reports, two tickets, a community meeting, and three false alarms.

"Why don't we take a swing down along the coast to kill some time?" he said to his partner. "Then we can call it a shift and head for the barn."

"You got it," Bassett replied. He'd be glad to be done for the night, get off on time for a change. It seemed that when you worked with Morrison something always came up. Morrison was one of those cops who had the knack of always being in the right place at the right time. It sure made life exciting, and you sure learned a lot, but some nights you just wanted to go home and crash—or possibly grab a beer somewhere before closing time and maybe get lucky.

Bassett turned out of an upscale residential area onto Sunset Boulevard. The wide street took them westbound toward the ocean. Within a mile they were passing the entrance to Will Rogers State Park where the body of Ricky Long had been discovered the previous morning.

It was almost midnight and Sunset was quiet. The side turnings into the residential areas appeared deserted. There was one car in front of Bassett and he watched as its wheels touched the center line. Was the driver drunk or tired, Bassett wondered. He watched the car through the next curve, but the driver seemed to have his act together.

"A little toasted, perhaps," Morrison said, as if interpreting Bassett's thought process. "But I don't think he'd blow enough to book."

Bassett had learned to rely on Morrison's judgment. He'd seen his training officer accurately predict, time and again, exactly where a drunk driver's alcohol level would register on a GCI breathalizer machine.

Sunset eventually brought the patrol car to the T-intersection with the Pacific Coast Highway. Beyond the wide highway were parking lots, a stretch of dirty sand, and the vast reaches of the Pacific Ocean.

Stopping for the light at the T-intersection, Bassett looked across PCH at the upscale Gladstone's 4 Fish restaurant. The parking lot was full and most of the outside tables were occupied in the warm night air. The warm glow of the lighting expressed an invitation that everyone there was having a good time.

The restaurant was a California dream: trendy nautical interior, an impressive, immediate ocean view, and food and drink priced accordingly. You could fill your gullet with beer and seafood in an atmosphere conducive to conversation or seduction, but you paid the price when you turned over your plastic money card. It would be far cheaper to stack your old fishing tackle in your kitchen, turn on the water tap, light a hurricane lamp, throw some fish fingers in the oven, and open a bottle of the supermarket's vintage vino. Who knows, you might get points for ingenuity and get laid anyway.

Bassett thought about returning to Gladstone's after work for a beer. Expensive it might be, but there was always a babe or two hanging around waiting to be impressed and taken home by a reasonable-looking guy.

"Go home and get some sleep," Morrison said.

"How the hell do you do that?" Bassett scowled in frustration. "How do you know what I'm thinking all the time?"

Morrison tapped his temple with a long forefinger. "It's not been such a long time since I was a young buck. I still remember what it's like to have a sperm count higher than my IQ, and a thirst that could cut through leather."

The tri-light changed and Bassett turned the patrol car left onto PCH. "So, you're telling me you used to have those things and still went home to the little woman?" Bassett figured to stay on PCH until it changed into the beginning of the Santa Monica Freeway, which would zip them back to the station.

"No, I'm telling you I used to have those things and didn't go home to the little woman. Not only did it almost cost me a marriage that's been the best thing that ever happened to me, but it almost cost me my life."

"You're kidding?" This was a side of Morrison that Bassett was not familiar with.

"There was more than one occasion when I came to work still half-cut." Morrison paused, as was his wont, to see if Bassett was really listening. "There was one time in particular that, if I'd have gotten behind the wheel of the patrol car, I'd have been bookable for DUI."

"Your partner know?"

"Absolutely. He'd been the one I'd been drinking with. He was only slightly less drunk than I was." Morrison shifted in his seat, looking out the passenger window at the sand and sea beyond. "We decided to play it cool, grab a cup of coffee at the local Winchell's, and lay low—ride the shift out, not go looking for trouble." Morrison paused again.

"So, what happened?" Bassett prompted.

"So, trouble came looking for us. There we are standing at the counter of the doughnut shop, in full uniform, when this stupid hop-head strolls through the door with his head down. My partner and I clocked him, but didn't read it right. We thought he was just another transient looking to bum some carbohydrates and a cup of Joe, but he suddenly pulls out some damn cowboy six-shooter—probably ripped it off during his last burglary—and starts capping off rounds."

"Man, I bet you about crapped," Bassett said with a laugh.

"To say the least."

"Did you blow him up?"

"Yeah, but not before he'd shot the owner and me. I was just too damn slow. If I hadn't been running on fumes from the previous night's drinking, I would have seen the whole situation developing. I could have taken action earlier, maybe the poor hop-head wouldn't have had to die because he was stupid."

"Sounds to me like he got what he deserved."

"He didn't deserve to die in a squalid little crumb shop trying to get money to feed a monkey that was so deep into him that he had no real idea what he was doing."

"Yeah, but he shot you."

"And it was my fault. If I'd have been sharp, the damn junkie would never have had the chance to clear leather. I'd have seen the situation developing and shut it down before it went too far."

"You don't know that."

Morrison didn't turn his head from the window, but his voice suddenly filled with ice and steel. "I do know that. And every day when I come to work, I live with the fact that some poor bastard died because I had too much party inside me."

Bassett snorted. "Are you telling me not to drink?"

Morrison did turn his head now to look at his young partner. "No. I'm not telling you not to drink. I'm telling you to know your limits. I'm telling you to go home tonight and get some sleep. You've been dragging your ass all shift. You're not sharp."

"That's because we worked so long yesterday." Bassett was defensive.

"And did you go straight home after you got off yesterday?"

Bassett was silent for a moment. "No," he said eventually, quietly. "I grabbed a few beers with the morning watch guys."

Morrison was back staring out to sea. "That spell it out enough for you?"

Bassett felt put out. Who did Morrison think he was to be telling him how to act? He already had one mother, he didn't need another.

"I'm not your mother, kid," Morrison said, as if on cue. "I'm your partner and your friend. Now, do me a favor and turn this heap around and head back the other way."

"What?" Bassett was caught off-guard by the change in subject. "What do you got?"

"I don't know. Maybe nothing."

"Come on, man. Let's go back to the barn."

Morrison's voice filled with ice and steel again. "Turn this car around. Now. We go back to the barn when I'm ready. You got that? When you've got twenty-five years on this job and I'm molding in my grave, you can be car commander. Until then we play things my way."

Bassett was seething mad. He didn't need this crap. He made a wide U-turn in front of oncoming traffic.

"Don't get your shorts in a wedgie, kid. Hate me if you want, but if you're going to be a good cop then learn to develop your instincts. While you're still wet behind the ears learn to put your money on mine."

"Where we going?" Bassett asked.

"Cut the lights and pull in over there," Morrison said, pointing to a parking lot on the beach side of the highway. "Don't pull all the way in. Park blocking the entrance."

Bassett did as his partner asked. He could feel butterflies taking off in his stomach. There was something happening. He couldn't see anything, but Morrison's second sight seemed to be rubbing off. Bassett felt the hairs on the back of his neck prickling.

"What do you see?" he asked Morrison.

"Well, the first thing I see is that brand new Jeep Cherokee over there." Morrison gestured with his chin toward the vehicle in question. It was the only vehicle in the otherwise deserted parking lot. With quick fingers he typed the vehicle license plate number into the MDT unit attached to the patrol car dash. The license was a personalized plate: SLMDUNK.

"Okay. So I see the Jeep. So what?" Beyond the Jeep a ribbon of sidewalk separated the parking lot from the edge of the sand. The sand stretched out in a dark mass past a lifeguard station with the number three on the side. The luminescence of the whitecaps tumbled gently down to mark the line between shore and water.

"Use your eyes," Morrison told his partner.

Bassett stared out into the darkness. "You must be eating a lot of carrots, partner, 'cause I can't even see the license plate on the Jeep."

"Don't just look straight ahead. Use all of your sight. The best way to see movement is by using your peripheral vision." Morrison checked the MDT screen for a DMV return on the Jeep. He read the information and then swiveled the screen toward Bassett.

"JoJo Cullen?" Bassett asked in surprise. "JoJo 'Jammer' Cullen?"

"How many other JoJo Cullens have you ever heard about?"

"None, but you never know."

"If there are other JoJo Cullens," Morrison said, "what are the odds they'd have SLAM DUNK as a personalized license plate?"

JoJo Cullen had made a lot of headlines in Los Angeles over the past seven years. First in leading the UCLA Bruins back to the top of the national rankings, and then by signing a huge contract as a first-round draft choice with the San Diego Sails—a first-year NBA expansion team. His endorsement deals had become the stuff of legend.

In three years, with Cullen playing at center, the Sails had exploded from expansion team pushovers to an NBA powerhouse. Cullen was the San Diego franchise. Without Cullen, the San Diego Sails were just another expansion team. With Cullen, the Sails were putting butts in the bleachers and were a major playoff force. Every kid playing street ball now wanted to be the next JoJo "Jammer" Cullen. Way cool, man.

"I still don't understand what you're getting so excited about," Bassett said. "You've never struck me as a celebrity hound."

Morrison reached over and hit the cut-off switch that deactivated all of a patrol car's interior and exterior lighting. "I don't understand what's going on yet either, but I can feel it in my bones. Something's not right. Get out of the car, and don't close the door."

Both officers slipped out of the car and made their way to the Jeep. Bassett brought his flashlight up to light the interior of the Jeep. Morrison put a hand out to restrain him.

"No lights," he said. "Don't ruin your night vision." Morrison was not looking into the Jeep. Instead he was staring out toward the lifeguard station.

The station was a wooden, roofed box supported on thick stilts about eight feet off the sand. On the water side of the station, a wooden stairway led from the sand to the platform.

Bassett squinted his eyes and stared out in the same direction as Morrison. He tried not focusing on looking straight ahead, but on using his peripheral vision as Morrison had told him. After a second or two, he finally saw the same slight movement in the shadows under the lifeguard station that had drawn Morrison's attention.

"You must be half-eagle," he said to Morrison.

"Maybe," Morrison told him, watching. "But it probably has more to do with years of learning what to look for and how to look for it."

"But just because it's JoJo's Jeep doesn't mean he was driving it. Maybe he lent it to somebody."

"I don't care who was in the Jeep. I just have a feeling something isn't right."

"How can you tell?" Bassett was sounding exasperated, as if Morrison was expounding on a concept that Bassett just couldn't grasp. "I mean it's probably just some guy who brought his girl to the beach to play park the dolphin."

"I don't know how I know. It's a gut feeling, instinct,

experience," Morrison said patiently. "It's midnight. The beach is officially closed at ten o'clock. There's only one car in the parking lot. There's no young couple snogging down near the water's edge trying to reenact *From Here To Eternity*. Instead, whatever activity is going on is taking place in the shadows under the lifeguard station. It just doesn't set right." He turned to face his young partner. "Are you willing to walk away, or do you want to find out for sure?"

Bassett raised his eyebrows up and down in the dark. He heard the challenge in Morrison's voice. He wanted to walk away. He wanted to get off on time. But he knew that if he did, he'd lose Morrison's respect.

"Okay, let's find out," he said. "If it is somebody getting their rocks off maybe the girl will have big tits."

"Ah, to be young and still able to get a chubby over such things," Morrison said, a happy anticipation in his voice. He moved forward, running his hand over the hood of the Jeep and feeling its heat. "Jeep's been here ten minutes. Fifteen tops," he judged.

Moving onto the sand, the two officers fell silent. Using hand signals, Morrison shooed Bassett off to the left, both of them now circling and approaching the lifeguard station from different sides.

Morrison had his powerful, six-cell Kelite in his left hand. Silently, he eased his Manadnock baton out of its ring with his right hand. He gripped the Yawara handle and felt the long end of the aluminum nightstick nestle comfortably along his forearm, the short end extended out beyond his grip ready to jab.

Gradually, making little noise in the sand, Morrison moved into position near one of the lifeguard station's supporting stilts. He could clearly hear grunting and heavy breathing coming from the dark shape in the shadows under the platform. Maybe his younger partner was right. Perhaps all they had was a pair of lovers rutting in the sand for all they were worth.

Judging that Bassett should be in position, Morrison brought up his flashlight and turned on the powerful beam.

The tall black man kneeling on the sand yelled out in surprise and instantly brought up a hand to cover his eyes.

Beside him was a shallow hump of sand with a human arm sticking out of it.

✢

CHAPTER TWENTY-FOUR

THE BLACK MAN ON THE SAND WAS THE FIRST TO RE-cover. Coming out of his crouch like a surface-to-air missile, he launched himself at Morrison.

Still stunned by the scene before him, Morrison took the full brunt of the black man's shoulders at belt level. The remains of an undigested chili cheeseburger and fries made an instant return trip from his gullet, sprayed out of his mouth by the blast of air driven from the depths of his lungs. The Kelite spun free from his hand, dropping into the sand and leaving the scene in darkness.

From the other side of the lifeguard station, Bassett turned on his own flashlight. Being careful not to get sand in his shoes, he'd been slower moving into position than Morrison had anticipated. When Morrison had illuminated the scene, Bassett had only been able to see the blur of a body tackling Morrison and then the scene had gone dark again.

Hearing his partner's animalistic grunt, Bassett's adrenaline kicked into high gear. The beam from his flashlight bounced like a demented firefly as he sprinted to where he had seen Morrison's body fall. Concentrating on nothing more than reaching his partner's side, the young officer didn't see the shallow grave in the sand and stumbled over it as he passed under the middle of the lifeguard stand.

Down on his knees, having lost his own flashlight in his fall, he crawled forward. Morrison was facedown in the sand.

"Dick! Dick!" Bassett yelled, as he rolled his partner over.

Morrison groaned, spitting bile and sand. He croaked, more a choking sound than anything else.

"Are you okay? Did he stab you?"

"Just get after him!" Morrison gasped, his voice barely audible. "Get after him!"

"But—"

Morrison shoved Bassett away from him. "Now! Go!"

Bassett had fallen back onto his butt. Disoriented, almost more in shock than Morrison was, he rolled slowly onto his knees and pushed himself to his feet. His night vision, destroyed by the beams of the flashlights, was returning and he could see a tall form running across the beach toward the parking lot.

Morrison had pushed himself up into a sitting position. "Get after that asshole," he croaked louder, air returning to his lungs. He threw sand at Bassett to get him started.

When he saw his younger partner begin to slowly run after the fleeing form, Morrison pulled his rover from his utility belt. He brought the hand-held radio to his mouth and pressed the send button. "Eight Adam Fifty-six. Officers need help. Sunset and PCH. Beach-side parking lot." He released the button, but nothing happened. There was no instant verbal response from the RTO.

"Shit," Morrison said, loudly, and hit the rover to knock sand out of it. He tried his broadcast again. Still no response. With fingers that felt like fat sausages, he pushed the emergency switch on the top of the rover.

In the communications command center, a light came on indicating a rover emergency switch had been activated. The RTO immediately checked to see to which unit the rover number was assigned.

The RTO hit her broadcast switch. "All units. Rover 5480 has been activated. Eight Adam Fifty-six come in."

The husky, feminine voice was alert but calm as she attempted to get a response.

"Stupid bitch," Morrison said. "If I could come in," he yelled at the radio's voice box, "I wouldn't have hit the emergency switch!" Morrison knew his frustration was unfounded. The RTO was only trying to establish if the emergency switch had been activated by accident.

When there was no response from Morrison, the RTO broadcast again. "All units. Rover 5480 has been activated. Unknown location at this time." It was the best the RTO could do; advise all the other patrol units that one of their buddies was in deep shit somewhere and there was nothing they could do about it but wait. "Eight Adam Fifty-six come in." The RTO again tried to raise Morrison, frustration tinging the edges of her calm voice.

"Hell!" Morrison said, and jammed the rover back into its belt holder. He dragged himself to his feet and staggered after his partner. Inwardly he cursed himself. He'd made a rookie mistake. He knew he should have given communications their Code 6 location before getting out of the car to investigate the movement under the lifeguard station. He was getting sloppy in his old age.

Even if Morrison had been able to give his location now, he knew it would take forever before any units were able to reach them. Sunset and PCH was at the furthest, most inaccessible corner of the division. It was also time for change of watch, and almost everybody would be circling the station waiting to turn over their cars and equipment. If their suspect was not going to escape, it was strictly down to Morrison and Bassett to stop him.

John Bassett put on a burst of speed as he cleared the last patch of sand and began running along the concrete sidewalk. He had regained most of his composure, realizing that this was the type of action he'd joined the department to engage in.

Ahead of him, Bassett saw the fleeing shape stop at the door to the Jeep and begin fumbling with keys. "Freeze!" Bassett yelled, and then realized he was wasting his breath. The figure got the Jeep door open and slid inside.

Bassett shot a look over his shoulder, confirming that the patrol car was effectively blocking the exit to the parking lot—another clever gimmick out of Morrison's bag of tricks. Escape by jumping the curb was nixed by the inch-and-a-half cable that ran parallel to the curb at a height of three feet. The cable was supported every six feet by an iron pole.

The Jeep's engine caught and the rear wheels spun as the driver backed up. Bassett cut for the middle of the parking lot. Drawing his 9 millimeter, he brought the pistol up in a two-hand grip and settled into a stance. The Jeep accelerated toward him.

Standing his ground, Bassett took a deep breath and squeezed the trigger. The Jeep's windshield shattered, and Bassett fired a second and third time. The Jeep kept coming straight for him.

Bassett felt as if he was trapped in a nightmare, unable to move, his feet rooted to the ground. The Jeep became a snarling, hideous monster raging toward him with intent to devour.

A heavy weight hit him from the side and drove him out of the path of the mechanical monster. Bassett hit the ground hard with Morrison on top of him. Pain brought back reality.

"What do you think you are? A deer caught in the headlights? Get up!" Morrison was already on his feet again, dragging Bassett up by one shoulder.

There was a loud crash as the Jeep smashed into the rear quarter panel of the patrol car. The trunk of the car swung away but jammed against one of the iron posts supporting the restraining cable. There wasn't enough room for the Jeep to squeeze through. The driver backed the Jeep up and then rammed forward again. The patrol car buckled, but didn't budge.

"Call for help," Morrison said, shaking his partner. He literally took Bassett's hand and wrapped it around the rover on Bassett's belt. "Call for help," he said again. "Remember to tell them we're at Sunset and PCH in the beach parking lot." So far Morrison hadn't been too impressed by Bassett's reactions. If he had to treat him like a five-year-old—tell him everything—then he would. He left Bassett fumbling with the rover and started for the Jeep.

As Morrison approached, the Jeep's door opened and the driver spilled out onto the asphalt of the parking lot. When the driver climbed to his feet, Morrison had no doubt he was dealing with JoJo "Jammer" Cullen in the flesh. He recognized the broad features of the game face that had made JoJo the terror of the professional basketball courts. At six foot ten inches, with two hundred and fifty pounds plus of professional muscle set on a pair of size seventeens, JoJo had personalized the smash-mouth, in-your-face brand of basketball in the NBA. Other players of the same style had preceded him, but JoJo was the current spearhead of the movement.

"Give it up, JoJo," Morrison said. He had his gun extended in the standard two-handed grip. "Put your hands in the air. Do it!"

JoJo began walking forward.

"Don't be an idiot!" Morrison yelled. "Give it up."

JoJo kept coming. He held his hands out to the side, his fingers spread. He wasn't carrying a weapon. "Come on, man, kill me," he said, his voice a low growl. "Kill me!"

Morrison backed up a step, then two. "Don't screw with me, JoJo. Put your hands up. Now!"

"I want you to kill me. I'm guilty. It's a sin." JoJo moved forward again. "Come on, shoot me. You know you want to do it. I'm just another nigger. Come on, shoot me!"

"Only if you make me," Morrison said. Both men's voices were clear in the night air.

"Then I'll make you." JoJo began to run toward Morrison.

Morrison scooted backwards in a half-shuffle. He didn't want to shoot an unarmed man. He waited a half a second as JoJo closed on him and then swung the butt of his gun with both hands.

The impact on the big man's jaw was devastating. He

lurched to the right and dropped to one knee. He had expected Morrison to shoot, not to fight. Morrison moved in fast, pressing his advantage. He kicked out with his right foot, the toe of his steel-capped combat boot making contact with JoJo's temple. The big man tottered and then fell all the way over.

Morrison stood back, his gun extended again. Sound came back to his ears and he could hear the *whumf-whumf* of the police helicopter coming in from the distance. Somewhere there were sirens.

He looked for Bassett, who suddenly appeared beside him.

"Roll him over and cuff him," Morrison ordered.

"Why didn't you shoot him?" Bassett asked, moving to do as he was told.

Morrison could feel his heart pounding in his chest. He gasped for air before speaking.

"Because I didn't have to," he said finally.

❁❁❁

CHAPTER TWENTY-FIVE

FEY OFTEN FOUND THAT WHEN SHE WAS UNDER STRESS her dreams seemed to be of an erotic nature. She didn't know what that meant, but perhaps it was something to talk with her shrink about at the next session.

When the phone rang at 1 a.m., she was in the middle of a particularly breathtaking sequence that had something to do with muscles, 501 button-fly Levi's, and the vague smell of musk mixed with fresh-cut leather and sweat. The image was shattered by the insistent ringing, and Fey unwillingly clambered to wakefulness with her heart pounding and an itch she knew wouldn't be taken care of soon.

"What?" she grunted into the phone.

"Fey? It's Terry Gillette."

"Oh, for hell's sake, Terry. I need my beauty sleep."

"But you're going to love this," Gillette said. He was calling from the watch commander's office at West LA. "They've got him."

"Got who?" Fey asked.

"The guy who's putting the kids in the graves."

"What are you talking about, Terry?" Fey sat up in bed, turned on a lamp, and looked at her clock.

"Morrison and Bassett," he said. "They caught the guy burying another body down on the beach at Sunset and PCH."

"In the act?"

"Absolutely, but that's not all. The guy they caught is JoJo Cullen." Gillette sounded excited, triumphant.

"Who?" Fey's brain was fogged.

"JoJo Cullen! Come on, Fey. He's only the hottest basketball player in the NBA. He's just signed a three-million-dollar contract to promote Nike shoes, but I guess he can kiss that goodbye."

"I only follow hockey," Fey said. Her third ex-husband was still an assistant coach with the Chicago Blackhawks. "But the name rings some bells."

"You've got to get in here and control this thing, Fey," Gillette implored. "The press are going to be all over us."

Fey began to pull her thoughts together. "Have you called Cahill yet?"

"I called his house and spoke to his wife. She says he was called out a couple of hours ago and should be in here already. Nobody has seen him though. I tried his beeper, but there was no response to that either."

Fey laughed. "Well, you probably dumped him right in the shit. I bet he stiffed in a phoney call-out to get away from his wife and knock off a piece on the side."

"His own fault then for not letting me know he was going code X."

"Amen to that," Fey said. Code X was the unofficial

designation when a cop needed to be covered for some kind of extracurricular activity. "Keep trying his beeper until you get hold of him."

"Right. Anything else?"

"Yeah." Fey flung back the bed covers and swung her feet to the floor. "This happened down on the beach?"

"Yeah."

"Okay, I want the whole beach area down there taped off, not just the main crime scene. Nobody gets in, and I mean nobody, Terry. No press, no brass, no stray dogs, nobody. Go it?"

"I've already got all of the mid-p.m. shift down there."

"Great. Have them rope off a separate holding area for a command post. Where's the suspect, this JoJo character?"

"He's getting MT'd over at Santa Monica Hospital. Apparently, he tried to get Morrison to shoot him, but Morrison kicked the shit out of him instead. He hasn't regained consciousness yet."

"Were there any shots fired?"

"Yeah. The kid, Bassett, capped off some rounds at the suspect's Jeep as it was trying to run him down."

Fey started pulling clothes out of her closet: black slacks, low-heeled shoes, a white blouse, and a black suede blazer. "What are you operating down there, Terry? A frigging three-ring circus? Get the officer-involved shooting team rolling from DHD, but keep them on a leash until I get there." She pulled underwear out of a drawer. "Hang on," she said, and held the phone away from her ear as she pulled her nightshirt over her head. She put the receiver back to her ear. "Also relieve Morrison and Bassett," she said. "Keep them separated from everybody. Feed them and make them as comfortable as possible. It sounds like they're in for a bumpy ride. Nobody talks to them until I do. Got it?"

"No problem," Gillette said. He was busily writing out a list. "Anything else?"

Fey thought for a second. "I want everyone in on this," she said. "Start with Monk Lawson and then get Brindle

Jones and Alphabet rolling. I'll call Hammer and Nails. Have everyone meet at the station code two.'' Fey gave the code two direction so everyone would know the urgency. ''Tell them to clear the decks and stand by for a long haul.''

''You got it,'' Gillette said, glad to have somebody taking charge and taking the responsibility off of his shoulders.

''Get the coroner rolling as well, Terry, like usual. I want a criminalist and a photographer from SID. Wait. Make sure they send Eddie Mack to take the photos. Insist on it.''

''Okay. I'll do what I can.''

''All right, I'll be there in forty-five minutes. Thanks, Terry.''

''*De nada.*''

Fey hung up. She reached into the drawer in her bedside cabinet and pulled out her phone book to look up the home numbers for Arch Hammersmith and Rhonda Lawless. As she dialed, she walked through her house turning on lights. In the kitchen, she displaced an unhappy Brentwood who was sleeping on top of the sheriff's murder file.

From inside the file she pulled out the card Ash had given her with his home number. If she had to be up and miserable, there was no reason why everyone else shouldn't be—including the FBI.

What a zoo, she thought wryly.

As Fey turned her car, a black Datsun 280Z of older vintage but in prime condition, onto the freeway on ramp, she checked her watch. She'd have to put her foot down if she was going to get to the station in the forty-five minutes she'd promised Terry Gillette.

She took the car up to seventy-five on the almost-empty freeway and set the speed control. Steering with one hand, she wedged her mug of instant coffee between her thighs, the warmth flowing through her crotch and bringing back a fragment of the dream she'd been torn from. With her free hand, she fumbled in her purse on the passenger seat and pulled out her cellular phone.

It sounded as if this case was going to get hairy right from the start. She had taken a quick glance at her sports page from the previous day's newspaper, and sure enough there was a photo of JoJo Cullen jamming home a two-handed slam dunk as the San Diego Sails put away the LA Clippers. As high profile as the situation was going to get, Fey decided she wanted legal counsel with her right from the get-go.

She pressed one of the memory buttons on the cellular phone and waited for Jake Travers to rouse himself from sleep and answer the phone. Their personal relationship may need patching up, but Jake was still one of the best deputy district attorneys she knew. He'd also jump at the chance to get out to a crime scene, especially one where there would be a lot of cameras.

"Hello." The voice that answered the phone was young, feminine, sultry, and sleepy.

Fey held the phone away from her ear and stared at it. The correct number for Jake's residence was prominent in the lighted digital display. She put the phone back to her ear.

"Hello?" the feminine voice said again, this time as a question.

Before Fey could answer, she heard Jake's voice in the background saying, "Give me that."

"Hello." Jake's voice came on the line thick with sleep.

Fey felt anger rising up inside of her. She didn't give a damn if the feeling was rational or irrational, it was still there bubbling away.

"Hello, Jake," she said.

"Fey—"

"Let's not try to think up any excuses on the fly," she interrupted. "I know damn well that wasn't your mother who answered the phone."

"My sister—"

"Nice try, pal, but you don't have a sister. Let's just accept the fact that you're a philandering asshole who can't keep his dick in his pants and go from there.''

''That's not fair, Fey—''

''The hell it isn't!'' Fey yelled into the phone. ''I couldn't go to your flashy little fund-raiser, so you had to go out and find yourself some little trophy slut to hang on your arm. Bet you couldn't wait to get her home and bed her down. Another notch on your bed post.''

''I'm not like that and you know it!''

''I don't know anything anymore,'' Fey said, anger, hurt, and exasperation all fighting for the upper hand in her voice. ''Hell, Jake, I don't have time to deal with this now—''

''—What else is new,'' Jake said, interrupting and fighting back.

''Screw you, Jake, and the horse you rode in on!'' Fey hit the disconnect button, threw the phone back on the passenger seat, and used both hands to swerve around a mini-van who thought going sixty-five in the fast lane was fast enough.

With clear road ahead, Fey slammed her right palm into the steering wheel. The pain felt good. Coffee from the mug between her legs slopped over onto the seat. She picked up the mug and threw it onto the floor on the passenger side of the car.

''Shit!''

She took a deep breath. She had to shut this down. Keep the emotion under control. That was something at which she was very good. She'd had a lot of practice over the years, one way or the other. Had to compartmentalize every segment of her life—keep them separate, don't let one segment bleed into another. She kept the deep breathing going until she felt things were under control again.

What was she so pissed off about anyway? She knew whatever she and Jake had between them was over. She'd known that for months. Then why did it hurt so damn much?

If she was honest with herself, she knew why. It all came down to ego. She wanted to be the one to do the leaving. She wanted to do it when it suited her. But Jake had beaten her to the punch, had taken up with some floozie, and now her feelings were hurt. *How pathetic*, she thought.

And then she turned off all thoughts about Jake. Had to do it. She had a job to do, and she couldn't be falling all apart when she got to the station like some love-sick teenager.

She couldn't have anyone think she was falling apart "like a woman." When you were a woman, you weren't allowed to be human.

She picked up the phone again and dialed another number. Jake Travers wasn't the only fish in the sea. She knew several other DAs who would bust a gut to be in on a case like this. And now that she thought about it, one in particular might be the best choice of all.

You had to think ahead in a case like this. Two white officers beating up one poor black man out gathering his thoughts on the beach—their word against his, no independent witnesses—she could see the racial overtones of the defense forming already. In these days, race was the issue even when it wasn't.

From information, Fey got the number for Winston Groom. She'd done a couple of cases with Groom. The district attorney's office was only a start for him. He'd be a top-flight private practice lawyer within a few years, demanding fees that were high enough to cause nosebleeds. He was sharp and aggressive.

He was also very, very black.

CHAPTER TWENTY-SIX

FEY SET HER COMMAND POST UP IN THE BEACH PARKING lot where JoJo's Jeep still had its nose buried in the rear quarter panel of Bassett and Morrison's patrol car. Both vehicles had been pulled far enough out of the entrance to allow other police vehicles to enter and exit. SID had brought a brace of klieg lights with them, elevating them on spindly poles set in tripod bases. The lights spread an eerie glow over the scene, and the noise of the power generator provided an irritating background hum.

Arch Hammersmith had brought his personal war wagon with him. It was a black 70's Chevy van, with custom rims and wide tires. Inside, it was completely carpeted and had been adapted to provide Hammersmith with anything he may need in his somewhat obsessive pursuit of justice.

Both he and Rhonda had been awakened by Fey's call to Rhonda's house. Rhonda had answered and told Fey that she would call Hammersmith. Fey didn't question the offer. She knew better.

Driving a gray BMW, Winston Groom had appeared on the scene within thirty minutes of Fey's arrival. He cut an impressive figure. Tall and rapier thin, his body was draped in a rich, chocolate-brown suit below which protruded highly polished shoes. A cream-colored shirt and yellow tie set off the ensemble. He was bald, and the black skin of his scalp glistened in the artificial lighting. He'd adjusted the wire-rim glasses that rested on his long, patrician nose, and looked around as if trying to absorb everything at once.

"Have you called in robbery-homicide?" he asked when he found Fey.

"This is my investigation, Winston. If I can keep robbery-homicide out of it, I will," she answered. "If you want in, then you play on my team."

Groom shrugged. "No skin off my nose." He turned around in a full circle. "Where's the suspect?"

"Last I heard, he was off to County USC jail ward."

"He recover consciousness yet?"

"Morrison apparently kicks like a mule. Mr. Basketball is still trying out for the real dream team."

"You got anybody there in case he wakes up and makes spontaneous statements?"

"Give me some credit," Fey said. "This isn't my first homicide."

"Don't get on your high horse," Groom replied, his glasses glinting as he turned them full on Fey. "If you want me on your team, I've got to be able to speak my mind."

"Touché," Fey said.

There was another flock of klieg lights set up around the lifeguard station. Lily Sheridan and her crew from the coroner's office were back sifting through the sand. Eddie Mack had been roused from a sound sleep, but was happily standing by Lily's side popping flash shots.

A fire department rescue unit had just departed the scene. Morrison had called them on the slight chance the victim had been still alive. After Bassett handcuffed JoJo—whose arms had been so muscular two sets of cuffs had to be linked together to accomplish the job—Morrison had rushed back to the lifeguard station. Once there, he had dug madly with his hands to uncover the victim whose arm he had seen sticking out of the shallow grave.

At the beginning of watch, Morrison had read through the murder book on Ricky Long and remembered the conclusion that Ricky had been buried alive.

The victim in the sand was another teenager, trussed with the same manner of strangling rope around his neck as the others. Morrison had used his pocket knife to cut the rope, and started artificial respiration—knowing all the while that it was to no avail. When the paramedics arrived, they took over from Morrison, but quickly declared the victim dead.

Fey understood Morrison's actions, but the crime scene had been virtually destroyed in the process. However, it was a factor they had to live with. If the victim had still been alive and Morrison hadn't taken any kind of action, the consequences were almost unthinkable.

Fey had sent Brindle to County USC to be present if and when JoJo regained his senses. There was no doubt that sending Brindle was a calculated move. Waking up to a pretty woman could work to their advantage if JoJo was inclined to spill his guts. Fey was also playing to the strengths of her team. Brindle was a master at manipulating men. Having her at JoJo's bedside made much more sense than having her out digging around in the sand.

Before Brindle had gone, however, she and Alphabet had given Fey the information that they had dug up on Ricky Long and the boy known as Rush, the victim of the sheriff's homicide.

Bomber, whose real name was Jackson Carter, stated that Rush had been working the local scene as a party boy for about three months. He was a runaway from either Kansas City, Seattle, or Denver, depending on what mood Rush was in when he told you. He'd started out working the streets, but soon found a safer niche immersing himself in the underground rave culture. He was still tricking, but it was a step up the ladder.

Bomber had given Brindle and Alphabet a location for where Rush had been living, but they hadn't had the chance to follow up on the lead. As far as a complete identification was concerned, Bomber had been a wash. Rush was the only handle he knew for the boy, and not even Alphabet's kindly, persuasive manner could coax out anything further.

Fey had been both surprised and appreciative of the effort of the two detectives, and told them so. She wasn't ready to completely reassess her judgment of Brindle, but it was a start. Alphabet had always been reliable, but his willingness to help Brindle—who was a difficult personality—raised him a notch in Fey's estimation.

Monk Lawson was running the scene underneath the lifeguard station with Alphabet working with him. Hammer and Nails were in Hammersmith's van pounding out reports and playing with the computers.

Fey and Groom walked over to the open side door of the van. Inside, Rhonda was crouched over a laptop computer that had a cellular phone hooked into the modem attachment. The whole system was plugged into a small generator.

"I've got two addresses for Cullen," Rhonda said when she saw Fey walk up. "One fairly close by—a townhouse in the Palisades—and the other is a house in San Diego."

"Can we get warrants immediately?" Fey asked Groom.

"I'll get telephonic approval from the on-call judge for the local one. The San Diego warrant may take a bit longer because of the jurisdictional difficulties, but by the time we get someone down there to execute the warrant we should have approval. Who's going to type the warrants up?"

Hammersmith, who was working on another laptop computer, scooped a sheaf of papers off of the laser printer sitting on the desk next to him. He handed the whole wad to Groom. "Done and done," he said. Hammersmith had only been in West LA for a few months, but Fey had never known him not to have needed paperwork at his fingertips.

Hammersmith explained. "Those are search warrants for both residence locations, Cullen's Jeep, and one to get blood, hair, and pubic combings from Cullen himself."

"Why one for the Jeep?" Fey asked. "We can get anything we need from the Jeep during impound."

"Why take any chances?" Hammersmith stated.

Groom grunted assent. "He's probably right, Fey. Everyone is going to be second-guessing us on this. How did you get the descriptions of the locations to be searched?" Groom asked.

"I called down to San Diego PD and had one of their units do a drive by and call me back with a description," Hammersmith told him. "The local address is about a mile from here, so I took a plainclothes unit and drove by it myself."

"You work fast," Groom said as he looked through the pages of the warrants. "If you work too fast you can make mistakes."

"If you don't work fast enough you can lose evidence, if not the whole damn case." This came from Nails.

Still reading, Groom asked, "Your only probable cause for the warrants is that Cullen was at this most recent crime scene?"

"Not just at the crime scene, counselor," Hammersmith said, "but caught in the act of burying the body."

"How do we know he wasn't just out for a stroll on the beach and happened to stumble across the grave?"

"Right," said Rhonda. "And instead of being ecstatic to see the police arrive, he tries to kill both officers."

"Maybe he panicked. Maybe he thought he was going to be blamed." Groom was playing devil's advocate.

"Maybe," said Rhonda. "His defense attorney can come up with a whole courtroom full of maybes for a jury. Right now we're only talking about establishing probable cause for a search warrant." She held up her hand, her index finger extended. "One, Cullen is the only person on the beach. Two," a second digit popped up, "Morrison stated Cullen was burying the body, not digging it up. Morrison said that in the time it took him and Bassett to get out to the lifeguard station, Cullen could have had the body exhumed—if that's what he was trying to do." She popped up another finger. "Three, Cullen ran when he was discovered. Okay, maybe he panicked, but he also tried to run Bassett over, and then tries to get Morrison to kill him. And four," another digit, "Cullen makes a spontaneous statement that he's guilty."

Groom nodded. "I think I can get a judge to buy it," he said. He looked up from the warrants and stared into the interior of the van. It was filled with more gimmicks than a Japanese electronics store.

"Where did you get all this stuff?" he asked. "It sure isn't city issue."

"I have friends in low places," Hammersmith told him. Groom smiled and went back to reviewing the warrants.

"No sign of Cahill?" Hammersmith asked Fey.

"Not yet."

"You going to call Captain Strachman?"

"That's Cahill's job."

"They're going to take the case away and give it to robbery-homicide," Hammersmith said. "It's inevitable."

"Maybe so," Fey replied. "But if they do take it, I want to give it to them gift-wrapped."

"Okay, you're the boss," Hammersmith said. He turned to a chart drawn on a whiteboard that was propped up on one side of the van. The chart had a listing of all aspects of the investigation and what personnel had been assigned to handle which assignments.

"What about notifying somebody from the San Diego Sails?" Rhonda asked. "I checked the schedules. They played the Clippers in town last night, and they're set to play the Lakers tomorrow night."

"Let's not start complicating things yet," Fey replied. "There'll be plenty of time for everyone to start getting their fingers in the pie later. Right now we have enough on our plate."

A commotion from the entrance to the parking lot drew everyone's attention. A white Ford Taurus had been let into the lot and a news van had tried to follow it through. Patrol officers had stopped the van and were arguing with the occupants.

"How the hell do they always find out?" Fey asked nobody in particular in reference to the press. She turned back to Nails. "Make some calls, would you?" she asked. "I should have known better than to try and keep this low profile. I don't want Strachman or downtown to find out about the crime scene over their breakfast Wheaties. Make whatever notifications you can, but hang up before they can start giving us directions.''

Nails nodded and reached for the phone in the computer modem.

Special Agent Ash parked the Taurus and levered himself out. A lumberjack flannel shirt and 501 Levi's over hiking boots put him in complete contrast to Winston Groom. He spotted Fey standing by the van and walked over. Fey introduced him to Groom and brought him up to speed.

''Who's going to handle the warrants?'' he asked.

''When we're clear from here,'' Hammersmith volunteered, ''Rhonda and I will head for San Diego, if that's what you want. That will leave Monk and Alphabet to stay with the body and handle the scene.''

''Brindle Jones is with Cullen at the hospital,'' Fey informed Groom and Ash. ''So, that would leave the three of us to take on the local search.''

''It's the most likely spot to yield evidence considering the location of the body,'' Groom said.

Ash looked out to the lifeguard station. ''Do you mind if I take a closer look?'' he asked Fey.

''Be my guest,'' she answered with a sweeping arm gesture.

''I'll go, too,'' Groom said, and the two men walked off together.

''Boss?'' Rhonda called gently for Fey's attention.

Fey turned back to the van and found both Hammer and Nails watching her.

''What do you two have on your mind?''

''Are you sure you want to run with this thing?'' Hammersmith asked. His tone was neutral.

''Why?''

Hammersmith shrugged. ''Don't make out you don't see the storm coming. This case could eat you alive. With JoJo Cullen as a suspect, every move made in this investigation is going to be second-guessed, and you personally are going to get dragged ass-backwards through the shredder.''

Fey wanted a cigarette badly. ''This department has

been here before. We've survived high-profile cases in the
past and we'll survive them again in the future. This case
is just another in a long line of explosive cases. Would
either of you walk away if you were running the show?''

Rhonda and Hammersmith exchanged slightly twisted
smiles.

''No,'' they said in unison.

''Just make sure you don't drop the ball with Darcy
Wyatt,'' Fey said, remembering that there was always
more than one important case going on at a time.

''We won't,'' Rhonda said.

''As soon as you guys get back from San Diego, I want
you back on the rape cases. And I'm going to need you
now more than ever to keep the rest of the MAC cases
flowing.''

''No problem.''

Fey started to walk away, but stopped and turned back.

''One other thing,'' she said.

''What?'' Rhonda asked.

''Be there when I need you,'' she said softly.

Hammersmith gave her assurance in the same tone.
''Count on it.''

CHAPTER TWENTY-SEVEN

AT THE STATION, MORRISON AND BASSETT SAT IN THE
small interrogation room where Fey had questioned Darcy
Wyatt the morning before.

''You all right, kid?'' Morrison asked his young partner.

Bassett nodded, but didn't say anything. He was sitting
hunched forward on the hard chair. His elbows were on

his knees, his hands together as if he were praying, his head resting on the tips of his steepled fingers. He was rocking slightly.

Morrison had told the story of the night's events several times already. Once to Terry Gillette, again to Fey, and another time to the other detectives arriving at the station. He knew at some point he would have to go over the story several more times, probably innumerable times. The next interview would be with detectives from the OIS—officer-involved shooting team.

Morrison had started penciling out his statement on a continuation sheet. Because shots had been fired, somebody else would be detailed to take care of booking Cullen and handle most of the paperwork. Still, Morrison knew he would have to get his statement down on paper to be included in the arrest report.

He wanted Bassett to write out a statement as well. It was important they got their stories straight, and that they didn't contradict one another. They had done nothing wrong out there in the field. Sure, things had gone to shit on them, but that was the nature of police work.

Bassett hadn't done as well as a more experienced officer might have, but he'd still done okay. Morrison had to find a way to get that across to Bassett, because it looked like the kid was getting real shaky on him.

"This was your first shooting, right, kid?"

"Yeah." Bassett started to rock a little harder in his seat.

"I've been through five of them," Morrison said. He scraped his chair clear, leaned it back on two legs, and propped his feet up on a corner of the scarred table. "It's never easy." He took out a cigarette and set it alight. "After it's over with, you always ask yourself if you could ever go through it again."

Morrison watched Bassett's body language change. The rocking stopped, and the younger officer turned his face toward his mentor.

"You thought that?"

Morrison puffed on his cigarette. "Of course. Do you

think you're the first officer to ever get the shakes after a shooting? It happens to everyone. Hell, my first two shootings I had brown stains in my shorts and I couldn't even remember shitting.''

"I don't know, man.''

"Why'd you come on this job?'' Morrison asked, taking a different tack. "And don't be giving me no bullshit about public service.''

Bassett shrugged.

"I'll tell you why you came on this job,'' Morrison said. "You came on for nights just like tonight. Nights when you're pushed to the limit of your abilities. When you have the piss scared out of you and you live to tell about it.''

Morrison took a hard drag on his cigarette. He dropped his feet off the table and brought his chair back to an even keel. "You did all right out there, kid. You survived. I survived. The bad guy got captured. Tomorrow night, you'll be telling drunken Paul Bunyon tales about our exploits and I'll be backing you up. We'll have our fifteen minutes of fame, and then some other poor bastards will get into a shooting situation, or a knock-down, drag-out bar fight, and it will be their turn to tell war stories.''

"But, I felt like I froze out there. I felt like I let you down. I don't know if I could go through something like that again.''

Morrison let some silence settle. He took a couple of slow drags on his cigarette and crushed it out before speaking again. "You're lucky that you're young enough to have missed Viet Nam,'' he told Bassett. "But one thing I did learn over there is that with every fire-fight you respond quicker and with more cool. Every fire-fight is a panic, but if you survive, then you stand a better chance of surviving the next one. If you survived that one, you got better again. They called it seeing the elephant.''

"What does that mean?''

Morrison was pleased Bassett was asking questions. It meant he was listening and maybe Morrison's line of bullshit was getting through.

"Before the Civil War, the circus coming to town was

about the biggest deal around. It was a rite of childhood to go to a circus and see the elephant. When the Civil War broke out, seeing the elephant became a term to indicate you'd been through a battle—another rite of passage. Every time you 'saw the elephant,' a little of the luster wore off, it became a little more commonplace, you weren't in as much awe as that first time you saw a pachyderm.''

''You're saying I'll do better next time?''

''I'm not saying you did bad this time. You hung in there. You took shots at the Jeep. You did what you had to do—''

''But if it hadn't been for you, I'd have been run over! I couldn't get out of the way.''

''And if it had been me doing the shooting, I'd have been run over.'' Morrison figured if you were going to tell a lie you might as well tell a big one. The kid had made some mistakes, but he wasn't a bad copper, and Morrison knew he was the only one who could build up his confidence again. A little humility on Morrison's part could go a long way toward accomplishing that goal. ''But you'd have been there to knock me out of the way, just like I was there for you. It's what partners are for.''

''You ain't bullshitting me?''

''Next time you see the elephant, you'll do just fine. Trust me.'' Morrison held up three fingers in the scout sign. ''Scout's honor.''

A goofy grin slowly spread across Bassett's face. ''Shit, man. Cullen's a big mutha, isn't he?''

Morrison kicked back in his chair again and lighted another cigarette. He was pleased with himself.

''He sure is, kid,'' he replied. ''He sure is.''

CHAPTER TWENTY-EIGHT

THE ROOM'S FOUR-POSTER BED WAS A GENUINE VICTOrian antique. The wide-screen television built into the wall facing the foot of the bed, however, was an intrusive modernistic monster. When the television was turned off, a large damask tapestry rolled immediately across the screen and returned the room to its elegant atmosphere.

Devon Wyatt was a man who appreciated elegance in all things. This was especially true of the women he chose as bed mates, although he treated them with the same regard he reserved for the other items of beauty with which he surrounded himself.

The young lady with the warm and able mouth, who was currently ministering to Wyatt's early morning sexual demands, was no exception. She was long of limb and lean of hip, with flawless skin the color of eggplant. Her hair was lengthy and full-bodied, covering her face as she buried it in Wyatt's crotch. She made soft noises as she worked, as if to emphasize her performance.

Wyatt sat propped up against the bed's headboard with three goose-down pillows behind him. It was only 8 a.m., but he'd already finished his thirty-minute routine of stretches, isometrics, and Stair Master exercise that kept him in reasonable shape. He'd drank his juice, scanned the paper, made several phone calls to the East Coast, and set out his clothes for the day. All that remained before showering was his daily head job.

Wyatt wasn't exactly sure where his wife was today—Aspen or somewhere equally as banal—and he didn't much care. Anyway, the last time he'd gotten a head job from her was before they were married. He'd made her his bride for reasons of money, not sex.

Going back to his bedroom, all moss greens and salmon pinks, he'd roused his latest concubine into action. He wasn't exactly sure what her name was—Shirley, Shirell, Sheila, or something close—but he had found her to be reasonably competent. Maybe she couldn't suck a tennis ball down a garden hose, but she was enthusiastic.

While Shirley, Shirell, Sheila, or something close worked her magic, Wyatt reached out a hand and picked up the television remote control. He pushed the power button and the damask tapestry rolled to one side to reveal the wide screen.

Images flickered past his eyes as he grazed the channels. CNN held his interest for a few moments, but he quickly surfed by looking for a more local report.

Briefly, he turned his thoughts back to the woman between his legs. He could feel his sap rising and knew her work for the day would be done soon, or at least until he returned home later in the evening.

He put his hands on the woman's head and began to move his hips in time to her efforts and felt a quickening of his pulse. His eyes glanced up to the television screen for the briefest second and caught Fey Croaker's flickering video image. He immediately picked up the remote control again and turned up the volume.

Sensing she was about to lose Wyatt's concentration, the woman between his legs began to increase her efforts—bouncing up and down on the mattress and raising the volume of her moaning.

''Get off of me, you stupid bitch,'' Wyatt said. He roughly pushed her mouth off of him. When she tried to reengage her mouth and his manhood, misunderstanding Wyatt's intentions, he threw her right off the bed.

''Hey!'' she said, landing in a tangle of limbs. ''What are you doing?''

''Shut up.''

''But—''

Wyatt turned an angry expression on her. Deep in his eyes she could see the danger that rested there. ''If you don't shut up, I will kick your ass out of here and you can go suck off some other sugar daddy to get your nose candy.''

The woman immediately went silent and subservient. Grabbing a thin robe, she slipped as quietly as possible out of the room.

Wyatt didn't see her go. He was glued to the local newscast. It was a stand-up filmed earlier at the beach parking lot at Sunset and PCH. Fey had agreed to make a quick statement regarding the arrest in order to get the press off her back.

She'd known she had to give the press something. If you ignored them there were so many ways that reporters could make life miserable. They had a job to do, and were under many of the same kinds of pressures that cops were. Cops had to solve the case—reporters had to bring back a story. Fey had learned a long time ago that if you didn't work with the press, then the press would turn on you like a pack of wild dogs.

Somebody from the press corps had seen the crashed Jeep and used connections to find out it belonged to JoJo Cullen. Fey knew she couldn't lie about the situation. If she did, the press would crucify her later, so she made a brief statement regarding the body discovered on the beach and the fact of JoJo Cullen being taken into custody for further investigation.

''What's JoJo's current physical condition?'' one of the reporters asked. There were three local news teams that had found their way to the beach.

''Mr. Cullen is currently being held at County USC jail ward. There is no further comment on his condition.''

Another voice. ''Did he resist arrest?''

''Yes.''

''Were the arresting officers injured?''

''They sustained minor bruises and abrasions.''

''Were shots fired?''

''Yes.''

"How many?"

"That has yet to be determined."

"Was JoJo hit?"

"There is no current comment on Mr. Cullen's condition."

"Did he have a weapon?"

"I think we can consider the Jeep to be a weapon." Fey waved a hand vaguely in the direction of the crashed vehicles.

"What charge is JoJo being held on?"

"Currently, Mr. Cullen is being treated for injuries sustained during the arrest. There have been no formal charges made at this time."

"Are you going to charge him?"

Fey smiled slightly. "That's all I have for you right now. You'll be told more when I know more. Now, if you'll excuse me, I have an investigation to run."

The camera cut to an in-studio talking head explaining that the interview with Detective Croaker had been taped in the early hours of the morning and that no further developments had been forthcoming.

Devon Wyatt hit the mute button on the remote control. He rolled back over the bed and picked up the ornate phone receiver from its cradle resting on the bedside cabinet. He quickly dialed a number, cursing the delay as the phone rang on the other end.

"Hello," a female voice answered.

"Mary, the cops have arrested JoJo Cullen—"

"The basketball player?" Mary Tolliver was Wyatt's personal assistant. She was used to his brusque manner, and also to jumping when Wyatt said jump. She couldn't say she liked her boss, even though she'd been with him for over eight years because he paid so damn well, but she did admire him.

"Of course the basketball player. Peter Rayne is his agent. Get a number for Rayne and get me through to him as soon as possible. Also find out who owns the San Diego Sails and set up a conference call ASAP." Wyatt hung up without saying goodbye.

He turned his attention back to the television screen, but the story had changed to shots of an earthquake in Columbia.

He felt a smug satisfaction. "Look out, Croaker. Here I come," he said.

There was nobody in the room to hear him.

✠
CHAPTER TWENTY-NINE

THE WESTSIDE YMCA'S HARDWOOD BASKETBALL FLOOR had recently been replaced. It was so full of spring that Kenny imagined he could feel the energy from the floor flowing through his legs. It was as if the court was a living entity and Kenny an integral part of the whole. He was in the zone—a state of mind where an athlete feels completely at one with his chosen game, he is unbeatable, unstoppable, and completely alive.

It was only a morning pickup game—a motley crew of locals against a solid team of off-duty cops from the West LA station. Normally, Kenny wouldn't have anything to do with a game that didn't have money on the line. His normal day consisted of hustling hundred-dollar one-on-one games across the inner city. But he liked playing against the cops. It gave him an edge, a thrill.

He only worked at places like Fratelli Pizza just so he could have something to put down on a tax form. He'd learned early in life that you had to make the straights think you were one of them. If you paid your taxes, filled out paperwork—even if it was phony information—it kept the government and the world of the straights from paying attention to you. Of course, every once in a while he'd hook up with somebody like Darcy Wyatt and have fun pushing their buttons. He figured the bonus kicks were his due.

Kenny snaked out a plate-sized hand on the end of an orangutan arm and slapped the basketball away from a tall black cop. Kenny picked up the free ball on the second bounce and flew down the court. All his joints were sweat oiled and he was flowing like lightning. Five long strides and he launched himself into the air and jammed the ball with a vengeance through the hoop.

"Whoooo-wheeee!" he yelled when he touched down. "I coulda been a contender!" It was his usual rallying cry after a great play. He'd never made the NBA—blamed it on them already having their quota of white boys.

His mission in life some days appeared to be trying to beat every black court hustler in the inner city at their own game—Kenny called it mind-sucking them—and still get out of the ghetto alive. It was a game within a game for Kenny. Blast them, snatch their money, run for his blue van, and blow before they could recover enough to organize a threat to him.

Whenever he burned one section of town, he'd move on to another. Hustling with the b-ball. Pushing his luck. Practice. Practice. Practice. Livin' the life.

Sometimes, he had to take jobs like the one at Fratelli Pizza to make ends meet. He was a pretty good short-order cook and bartender. If he had a bad day and got burned on an unfamiliar court, he could use those mainstream skills to build up his poke again and get back on the jam.

Every once in a while he came into contact with somebody like Darcy Wyatt. Somebody with whom he could share a portion of his personal perversions—not the whole plan mind you, but enough to put an edge to the whole thing. It was a way of teasing himself, keeping things interesting. How far could he push them before they caught on to him and he had to kill them too?

Darcy had been fun. Getting him tied up with the cops had been a blast. In a small corner of Kenny's mind, though, there was the thought that maybe Darcy knew too much, but then again, he couldn't say anything without dumping himself in the shit. Kenny reassured himself it would be okay. After all, he was smarter than the cops. He knew they'd never catch him.

Time was called on the pickup game after Kenny's spectacular play. A couple of the cops came over and gave him a high-five. They were a pretty friendly group. They didn't like losing, but they took it well. The other guys on Kenny's team weren't as enthusiastic. They figured him for a ball hog and a one-man show. Kenny figured they could go screw themselves. If they couldn't take the heat, then they should get off the court. He didn't need them.

"Hey, you hear what happened to JoJo Cullen," one of the cops asked as they all walked toward the showers.

"Nope," said Kenny, his heart rate skyrocketing.

"He was arrested for killing some street kid. Picked him up, butt plugged him, and then buried him alive down on the beach. Kinky stuff, man," the cop said. "Apparently, it may be tied in to two other similar murders."

"No way," Kenny said.

"Don't you listen to the radio or watch TV?"

"Maybe you should hustle your butt down to the San Diego Sails head office," another of the cops said to Kenny. "It looks like they're gonna be needing a new star forward. You just might fill the bill."

Kenny smiled at the thought. Yeah, that would be sweet. He laughed inside at the thought of it. Hell, he'd never even thought of that scenario. He knew it would never happen, though. They'd never let a white boy replace JoJo "Jammer" Cullen, the Great Black Hope, but it would be the icing on the cake.

"I ain't heard nothing about it. What's the story, man?" Kenny asked. He already knew all about it, but he wanted to hear all the details again. He needed the inside scoop from the cops, needed to see what they had right and what they had wrong.

✠
CHAPTER THIRTY

PACIFIC PALISADES WAS THE MOST UPSCALE OF ALL THE upscale areas in West LA. Brentwood and Westwood each housed their share of actors, musicians, doctors, lawyers, prominent businessmen, and the ilk, but they all would have traded their eyeteeth for a Palisades address.

The most prestigious addresses in the Palisades were those that overlooked the ocean from atop cliffs that wouldn't disintegrate in bad weather or earthquakes. The Malibu area a few miles further north was perhaps better known, but didn't provide the security against nature that the Palisades enjoyed. The biggest annoyance attached to living in the Palisades was that the slightest amount of rain had neighboring Malibu sliding down to the sea and blocking the Pacific Coast Highway. That made it difficult to get out to the espresso bars and boutiques.

Pacific Palisades blessed the northwestern tip of the West LA area. Residences in the Palisades spoke the language of old money, new money, laundered money, and still-dirty money. But even "Palisades hovels," such as Cullen's million-dollar townhouse, had very little in common with the true hovels that occupied The Hood in the eastern tip of West LA.

In The Hood, apartments were crammed together like impacted teeth. A patch of grass in The Hood was as rare as a whore with a heart of gold. In The Hood, you knew your neighbors well. You knew when they flushed the toilet, watched television, argued, hit their kids, made love, burped, and farted.

By contrast, the complex that included Cullen's Palisades townhouse was Nirvana—as remote from The Hood as heaven was from earth. The Palisades Cliffs townhouse complex was a collection of miniature mansions surrounded by greenbelts in a gated and patrolled environment. Each townhouse had four or five bedrooms and a view—either of the ocean or the golf course. Each grouping of three townhouses within the complex was separated from neighbors by manicured trees and cultivated gardens. There were two-car garages for the Mercedeses and the Volvos. Extra parking for gauche RVs and *de rigueur* speedboats was provided in another, hidden, portion of the complex.

Unlike in The Hood, evenings in the Palisades were not spent out on the stoop buying drugs or drinking beer, scamming food stamps, or worrying where your next meal was coming from. Evenings in the Palisades were spent on private nine-hole golf courses, or at the clubhouse with wine and cheese, or scamming tax shelters and junk bonds.

Fey believed, however, that the biggest difference between the Palisades and The Hood was that the Palisades had more criminals. The crimes of the Palisades crooks may be as white collar as their jobs—but money didn't make a person good, just as lack of money didn't make a person bad.

If confronted, Fey would never deny that she was prejudiced. Her prejudices, though, were determined by a person's actions, not their skin color or religion. If you were a scumbag who preyed on those weaker than you, Fey didn't give a damn about anything else. If you were a predator, you deserved to be put in jail. If JoJo Cullen was indeed the murderer they sought, then it didn't matter to Fey who he was, where he lived, or whether he was black, white, or purple. If JoJo Cullen had done the dirty deeds then he deserved to rot in hell, and Fey would do everything she could to help him on his way.

The security guards at the gated front entrance to the Palisades Cliffs complex attempted a token resistance to admitting Fey and her crew. Their objections were quickly overridden, though, when Fey marched into the tiny security office and pushed the open button for the gates herself.

"You boys want to go for your guns?" she asked. Her commanding presence filled the small hut like a positive energy that radiated from inside of her. Her control of the situation was unquestionable. It wasn't a matter of force, but of attitude.

The two private security guards had started out full of their own importance, but quickly backed down. Fey figured their combined IQ was somewhere about two above a Nerf ball. One of them reached for the cellular phone on his belt.

"What are you going to do?" Fey asked. "Call the police?" She gave the guard a hard stare. "Why don't you just turn on the Bat Signal instead?" She winked and walked out of the office. Ash drove Fey's detective sedan through the gates and then stopped. Fey got back in on the passenger side.

"You've got style," Winston Groom said from the back seat.

"Not style, *chutzpa*," Fey said.

Groom and Ash both snickered.

"Drive on, Jeeves," Fey commanded, and Ash put the car in gear.

"Yes'm, Miss Daisy," he said.

Groom had obtained a judge's telephonic approval for the warrant to search Cullen's townhouse. He was also pleased to be included in the search. He didn't often get out into the field, and he already had visions of what this case could do for his career. If things were as dead-bang as they looked, nailing JoJo Cullen could put him at the front of the fast track.

He was, however, somewhat daunted by the opulence of the complex they were driving through. Doubts began to niggle at his mind. Doubts that whispered to him that maybe he was getting himself out on a very long limb. He tried to push the quiet voices aside, but he couldn't ignore them completely.

Cullen's townhouse was like a page out of *California Living* magazine. The exterior was designed to resemble a miniature hacienda with inlaid mosaic tiles, sand-colored stucco walls, carved oak doors, and mission roof tiles. Black wrought iron added highlights along with terracotta wall sconces.

After receiving no response to his knock and bell ringing, Ash used his elbow to smash a small window next to the front door to gain entrance. Fey took Polaroid photos to record the damage. She also planned to take photos before the search and after the search as a nod to civil liability.

As the trio entered the townhouse they quickly saw that the interior reflected the same precise taste and decorating as the exterior.

"Does anybody really live here?" Fey asked, turning on lights as she moved through the residence. "Everything looks too perfect."

"Maids?" queried Groom.

Fey turned on her heels to face him. "Probably, but come on, everything here has been shipped in wholesale. There's nothing that jumps out at you and says 'JoJo Cullen lives here!'" Fey remembered another investigation that had started out in a house with a similar feel—nothing personal in the rooms, nothing to give personality to the owner.

"Here's a room that screams, 'Somebody lives here!'" Ash said, his voice coming from down a narrow hallway.

Fey and Groom moved down to meet him. The room he was looking in was a den. A big picture window was open to a million-dollar view of the ocean that was barely visible in the false dawn. The room was filled with leather couches, modern lamps, stereo equipment, and a huge console television.

"I bet the maid has orders to stay clear of here," Groom said.

"No kidding," Fey agreed, moving into the room.

Every surface in the room was covered with beer cans,

dirty glasses, and the detritus of fast-food restaurants and junk food junkies. Partially eaten Twinkies sat on top of cold pizza in an open box. Containers of Chinese food lay open near bowls of peanuts and Cheerios.

The walls displayed hundreds of photos of Cullen in action. Some were framed posters, others were simply torn from magazines and newspapers and pinned up at random.

"Not too impressed with ourself, are we?" Fey's question was rhetorical.

"When you're good, you're good," said Groom. He looked closely at several of the pictures.

"Are you a fan?" Fey asked.

"Boy and man," Groom told her. "Been playing round-ball since I could crawl."

"College?"

"Absolutely. University of Las Vegas, Nevada, Running Rebels. Full scholarship."

"I'm impressed. What about the pros?"

"It was always the dream."

"So what happened?"

"Bad knees."

"Really?"

Groom didn't answer for a second. "You knew I was lying?"

Fey shrugged.

"Truth is," Groom admitted, "I was too slow and not aggressive enough for the pros. I got cut in camp. Twice. Decided I better try another line of work."

Ash called their attention to the smeared remains of cocaine lines on the glass-top coffee table. In an ashtray was a pile of marijuana debris. A small refrigerator held more beer and wine. Behind the bottles and cans was a collection of vials.

"Steroids?" Groom inquired, looking over Ash's shoulder.

"Cullen may be at the top of his game, but he's hardly the All-American boy," Ash commented.

"In this day and age," Groom corrected him, "he probably is. However, does eating Twinkies, snorting coke, and popping steroids make him a killer?''

''Hard to tell,'' Ash said.

Moving through the townhouse, not yet overturning everything in sight, not yet starting a methodical search of every nook and cranny, the three investigators found a bedroom that was obviously used by Cullen. The bed was unmade and the room unkempt, but there was no sign of struggle or murder being done.

Fey moved through to the garage. One side was obviously where Cullen parked his Jeep, but the other half was turned over to exercise machines and free weights.

''Look at that,'' Fey said in amazement.

Ash and Cullen tracked where her finger was pointing. On the padded exercise bench was a roll of silver duct tape. Under the bench, loops of white, quarter-inch rope lay innocently coiled next to a pile of clothing.

''Bingo,'' Groom said, his voice deep and troubled.

Several hours of fruitless searching later, Fey agreed with both Ash and Groom that there was nothing more to be found. The clothing under the exercise bench had consisted of a t-shirt, a pair of jeans, white socks, and a pair of size nine Reeboks. In the back pocket of the jeans was a slim wallet containing three dollar bills and an ID card in the name of Wallace Hillman. The picture on the ID card matched the face of the young victim buried at the beach. The date of birth on the ID card had been obviously altered to show that Wallace was nineteen. Fey figured that sixteen was easily closer to the truth.

The rest of the house was a blank. Other than the two rooms where Cullen appeared to live, the rest of the residence was a showplace. Fey figured the place was one of the complex's model homes and Cullen had bought it outright, furniture and all. It had that kind of feel.

Fey even went so far as to run pencil lead over a blank notepad by the den phone, but raised no lettering. Taking a Swiss Army knife from her pocket, Fey used the screwdriver blade to jimmy the locked, center drawer of a large oak desk. The knife had been a gift from an old partner, and Fey always carried it in an accessible pocket as it constantly proved handy. The desk drawer was empty except for several pens and a stack of blank writing paper.

So much for tips from the *Hardy Boys' Detective Handbook*, she thought. Maybe next time she could come up with something using a *Dick Tracy Crime Stopper*.

She picked up the phone and hit the redial button. Seven beeps and two rings later the other end was answered by the China Gardens restaurant.

"Do you deliver?" Fey asked.

"Thirty minutes," came the reply.

Fey thanked the other party and hung up. She looked at the phone's memory buttons. There were five of them. Fey pushed the first one. China Gardens answered again. Fey hung up.

She pressed the second memory button.

A harried male voice answered, "Boffo Burgers, what can I get you?"

"Do you deliver?"

"You bet. What do you want?"

"A million dollars, peace on earth, and a date with Mel Gibson," Fey said and then hung up.

Memory buttons three, four, and five were also fast food delivery services: Palisades Deli, Fratelli Pizza, and the Shoreline Market.

"A man of varied tastes," Fey told the others when she related the information.

"A junk-food junkie," Ash said. "How the hell does he manage to stay in shape eating all that crap?"

"Some people are lucky that way," Groom said.

"Yeah, but if he keeps putting that shit in his body, along with all the dope and other stuff, his system is going to turn traitor at some point or another."

"Who knows?" Fey said. "Maybe his diet is a blessing in disguise. Prison food will be a step up."

She looked around at the room's disarray again—the photos on the wall, the piled-up garbage. It was as if Cullen was some kind of big kid. Fey thought immediately of the three dead victims. Cullen maybe was a big kid, but he was also a bad one.

"What do you think?" she asked Ash.

"I don't know what to make of it."

"What do you mean?" Groom asked, unbelievingly. "Talk about your slam dunk. We capture the suspect at the crime scene. We've got spontaneous statements. Rope and tape, matching those used on the victims, are recovered in the suspect's residence along with the clothes and identification of the last victim."

Before Fey or Ash could find a valid argument, Fey's cellular phone rang. She pulled it out of her purse and answered it. Brindle Jones was on the other end.

"Cullen has rejoined the land of the living," she reported. "The doctor is checking him over right now."

"Sit tight, we're on our way," Fey said. Excitement began to brew in the pit of her stomach. "Don't let anyone near Cullen but the doctor. If Cullen talks to you fine, but don't ask him any questions or tell him anything."

"No problem."

Fey closed the phone.

"Let's travel, boys. It's time for tip-off."

EXE

CHAPTER THIRTY-ONE

THE TRIP TO COUNTY USC HOSPITAL JAIL WARD WAS AN obstacle course of heavy morning commuter traffic, jack-knifed trucks, stalled passenger vehicles, fender benders, and a wrong-way driver who went up an off ramp and didn't notice anything was wrong until he'd run seven on-coming cars off of the road.

Fey drove the detective car with a lead foot and a total disregard for traffic conditions. The plain brown sedan sported blackwalls and more antennas than a bushel of martians. The vehicle was considered dual purpose and was equipped with emergency lights and siren capabilities.

When the traffic on the freeway ground to a halt, Fey pulled down the hinged red light so that it showed through the windshield. With a flip of a switch, she activated the car's light system and pulled onto the emergency shoulder.

Scooting sideways to brace himself, Ash put a hand on the dashboard. "Hi-ho, Silver, away," he said under his breath.

"Don't give me a bad time," Fey said, hearing the comment, but not taking her eyes off the road. "Time is getting too short to be stranded on a temporary parking lot."

There was a tension in the car that was more than the mix of anticipation and exhilaration that usually accompanied a major ongoing investigation. Fey knew her time on the case was getting short. With a suspect as high profile as JoJo Cullen there was no way Fey would be able to keep the case within her unit.

Fey knew that there was no shame attached to robbery-homicide division taking over a case. RHD had the manpower to assign detectives to the case for the long term, personnel that geographic divisions couldn't afford. When the next murder went down in West Los Angeles, Fey's unit had to be available to handle it. They couldn't all be tied up proving that JoJo Cullen was a serial murderer. Just handling the press on this one was going to be a full-time job for some detective.

There was still something inside Fey, however, that drove her to complete as much of the case as she could before she had to turn it loose. If she was honest, it had nothing to do with being a woman in a man's world. It had to do with professional pride—an attribute that was more often a curse than a blessing. There was a reason God declared pride as one of the seven deadly sins.

Finally breaking free of the freeway logjam, Fey used every surface street shortcut she knew to get to the hospital. Once there, Fey parked in an empty ambulance zone and quickly hung the radio mike over the rearview mirror. Despite her acrobatics with the mike and having to grab her purse, she was still the first one out of the car. Quick strides propelled her toward the automatic glass doors of the entrance, and left Ash and Groom floundering in her wake.

"Is she always this wired?" Ash asked Groom.

"This is only second gear, man. You should see her when she really kicks in." Groom followed Ash through the entrance. "I saw her in court once with a novice prosecutor. The case was going to shit in a big way. Fey was the investigating officer on the case and she was getting pissed."

"I can't imagine she was pleased," Ash said.

"Not in the least. It was a sexual battery case. The defendant had a prior record for numerous indecent exposure arrests, but the evidence against him had always been too weak to get a filing. This time he'd actually put his hands under a victim's blouse and grabbed her breasts. The identification was good and it looked as if it was a dead-bang case. The district attorney, however, was dropping the ball big time, and Fey could see the jury wasn't going to buy off on the case."

"What did she do?"

"She had a coughing fit in the middle of the courtroom—damn near prostrated herself across the prosecution table. The judge was forced to call a recess." Still following Fey, Groom took off his glasses and rubbed them with a cotton handkerchief. "As soon as the judge's gavel declared the recess, Fey's coughing disappears as if she's undergone a laying on of hands at a revival meeting."

Ash snickered at the image.

Groom's lips thinned. "She stood up, grabbed the DA by his tie and drags him out of the courtroom. In the lobby, she pulls him out of sight around a corner—as if he were a suspect she was going to let practice falling down."

"She must have exploded."

"It was unreal. She read this DA the riot act up one

side and down the other. You would have thought the case was a gang rape instead of a simple 'come and run.' She had a legal pad covered with questions that the DA should have been asking and instructions on how to plead the rest of the case. She jams it in the DA's chest and tells him if he doesn't pull his finger out of his butt and win the case, she's going to shove a nightstick so far up his ass he won't make noise when he farts.''

''Colorful. What did the DA do?''

Groom replaced his glasses. ''I pulled my finger out and went back in and won the case.''

Ash laughed out loud. ''You're kidding? You?''

''Yep. She also left a lasting impression on the jury. Part of the evidence in the case was the defendant's trousers. When he was arrested, the trousers were covered with semen from the orgasm he'd had when he touched the victim.''

''Euuuu,'' Ash made a disgusted sound and wrinkled his nose.

''Exactly,'' said Groom. ''So, while I'm introducing them into evidence, the male bailiff's holding the semen-covered trousers by two fingers at arm's length. The semen is dry, of course, but the bailiff is still treating the trousers as if they were radioactive.'' Groom held out his own arm in imitation. ''Watching this reaction, Fey leans back in her chair and says—just loud enough for the women on the jury to hear—'Typical man. They won't even touch the stuff, but they expect us to swallow it.' ''

Several nurses turned to look as Ash laughed out loud.

JoJo Cullen might be awake, but whether he would talk or not was another question.

There had been a collection of news mavens in the jail ward's lobby located on the floor above the county hospital. Fey and her companions had plowed through the reporters and camera people in a flying wedge with Fey leading the way. They made no comments and relied on the uniformed sheriffs, who staffed the ward, to time their entry through the security doors to keep the press from following them through.

Once inside, the trio identified themselves to the jail ward watch commander and to Dr. Amos Fallon, the MD who had been treating JoJo.

Fey knew Fallon from previous encounters in the jail ward. He wore thick glasses and a spotless white smock. He was also so short that when Fey looked down at him, she felt she was looking at an aerial photo of a human being.

"Cullen has a mild concussion, but nothing that will do him any permanent damage," Fallon told her when she inquired. "He also has a collection of superficial bruises and abrasions, but nothing worse than he'd pick up in an NBA game."

"Nothing to indicate the officers used excessive force?" Groom asked the question, trying to anticipate future problems.

"Not as far as I can tell. The injuries are consistent with what I was told happened."

More concerned about losing valuable evidence, Fey asked, "Did you take blood, hair combings—"

"—fingernail scrapings, and everything else. A full work-up," Fallon interrupted her. "You know me, Fey. I could do a work-up like this in my sleep."

"I know," Fey told him. "But this one is going to have everyone jumping through hoops."

"I figured that out when you had the court order faxed over almost before the body got here. We've had stars down here before—"

"—And we've been burned before," Fey said. "I don't want that to happen this time around."

"I understand," Fallon said. "Do you want to talk to him on the ward or in an interview room?"

"If he's up to it, let's do it in an interview room. The ward has too many interested ears."

Fallon pushed his thick glasses up his nose and scurried away.

"How do you want to play this?" Groom asked Fey as

the watch commander unlocked the door of an interview room for them.

"It's hard to tell," Fey said, entering the small room followed by Groom and Ash. There was a small table surrounded by four chairs. Fey sat down and faced Ash. "You've interviewed serial killers before," she said to him. "What do you think?"

Ash remained standing as Groom took the seat next to Fey. "You're going to have to remain flexible until you get a feel for this character. If he is the killer of these young boys, he won't feel remorse or guilt. It's not like interviewing your regular run-of-the-mill murderer. A serial killer with a sociopathic personality is not going to react in the same way as somebody who has acted in the heat of passion, or even somebody who has killed for more routine motivations such as revenge or greed."

Before they could discuss the situation further, the interview room door opened and Dr. Fallon pushed JoJo through in a wheelchair. Brindle Jones followed in behind. The small room was suddenly overcrowded.

Fallon took his leave, and Fey introduced herself to JoJo. The clothing he had been wearing at the beach had been taken for evidence and he was left wearing a hospital smock. Even sitting down and draped in the unflattering gown, JoJo was a huge muscular presence. He seemed to fill the room all by himself.

Recognizing that there were too many people in the room to do an effective interview, Brindle excused herself and slipped out. Ash remained silent, standing to one side of JoJo. His eyes were hooded, almost as if he was about to fall asleep, and he had crossed his arms over his chest. Leaning back into the corner, he seemed to fade into the paint work.

Fey and Groom sat across from JoJo who watched them both through large, spaniel's eyes. His face was moon shaped, with full lips emphasizing a wide mouth. His black, curly hair was close cropped, and his skin color was a blend of light browns and yellows.

Fey let a silence fall as she mentally searched for the

first key to twist. She felt slightly unbalanced. JoJo was an intimidating presence, combining both size and star power—charisma.

Before she could say anything further the magnetic presence in front of her suddenly crumbled. Tears flooded from JoJo's eyes as if driven by a monsoon. The big man slid out of the wheelchair onto the floor, curling up into a fetal position, crying and wailing.

"JoJo—" Fey said, standing up.

A pitiful wail came from the form on the floor. "I just want to play ball again."

CHAPTER THIRTY-TWO

IT TOOK DR. FALLON AND THREE BURLY SHERIFF'S DEP-uties to manhandle JoJo into the wheelchair and maneuver him back to bed in the main jail ward. JoJo didn't fight them, but he didn't help them either. In essence, he was a limp Baby Huey; a ton of Jell-O constantly sliding away from whatever was used to support him or prop him up.

The only cohesive statement JoJo made was the one about playing ball again. Everything after that was a mish-mash of babbling and blubbering. Fey picked up the repeated words "brother" and "love," but could make no sense of the context. When asked, Dr. Fallon denied giving any kind of drugs to JoJo that would promote the kind of psychotic reaction they were all observing.

"Shock," Fallon said, as if that explained everything. He had a sedative-filled syringe in his tiny hand. With no ceremony, he pulled back JoJo's gown and jabbed it in the exposed portion of buttocks.

"Well," said Fey when JoJo was eventually wheeled from the room. "That wasn't quite what I expected. How the hell the man we just saw became an athletic legend is beyond me. He's freaked out."

"Do you buy it?" Groom asked.

"Beats me," Fey said. "How about you, Ash?"

Ash peeled himself away from the corner of the room as if he were an Egyptian mummy coming back to life. "I don't know enough yet to form an opinion."

"Now there's a good cop-out," Fey said. "Just give me your gut instinct."

"Okay. I don't like it," Ash said. The tic under his eye was suddenly more pronounced, and Ash put a finger up to touch it. The tic continued.

Observing the effort to control the involuntary action gave Fey the feeling that the tic was something new to Ash, something he wanted to hide.

"You think he's faking it?" Groom inquired, bringing Ash's attention back to the issue at hand.

"I didn't say that." Ash's eyes hooded over again, as if he were doing an internal examination. "I said I didn't like JoJo's reaction, and I don't. I'm just not sure what it is that I don't like. The man is being hailed as the next Magic Johnson. He's won almost every conceivable athletic award basketball has to offer. He's brilliant on the court, but the question really lies in what he's like off the court."

"I agree," said Fey. "The whole scenario is uncomfortable."

"What do you mean?" Groom looked puzzled. "I would have thought you'd be over the moon. You can't honestly believe there's a conspiracy in all this?"

Neither Fey nor Ash responded.

Groom shook his head in frustration. "Come on. This isn't an episode of 'Murder, She Wrote.' Angela Lansbury isn't going to come rushing in at the last second and prove somebody else did this."

Fey shrugged. "You're right. Ninety-nine-point-nine percent of the time in police work, the easy answer is the correct one. But I don't know. Maybe this time it's the point-one percent.''

"How can it be?" Groom was getting frustrated. He needed support on this if he was going to get a solid conviction. ''I know I gave your people a bad time when we discussed the probable cause for the search warrants, but I wasn't doing anything more than making sure we were all on the same page of music. And since then the case has become even tighter. We've recovered the victim's clothing and ID at JoJo's residence. We've also got rope and tape from JoJo's garage that will more than likely match that from the victim. I've filed and won murder cases on far less evidence.''

Fey spread her hand out on the table in front of her. ''There's also the biological evidence. If we can match JoJo's DNA to the semen recovered from the victims—''

''—Exactly,'' Groom interjected. His original doubts had begun to wash away, replaced by visions of glory and credit for getting a major conviction from the case. His ambition had taken over from his gratitude to Fey for bringing him in on the case. Now, if she wasn't going to back him on the case then maybe the sooner robbery-homicide became involved the better.

Fey and Ash made eye contact. Groom didn't notice. Fey intuitively knew she was reading Ash's wavelength. The FBI agent was bothered by the situation, and Fey was trusting that instinct.

A case like this should grip you in the thrall of its unfolding excitement. In a cop's career there were thousands of cases that required nothing more than going through the motions. Depending on the cop there was a fair share of cases that made a splash and caused a few ripples. If a cop wasn't careful there were also a few investigations where personal involvement could tear you apart. And then there were the big cases—maybe one, maybe two, rarely three—that became career landmarks.

Arresting and convicting JoJo ''Jammer'' Cullen as a serial killer was going to be a landmark, career-making case. The evidence was all there. The pieces of the puzzle, with a smattering of luck and a dollop of good police work, had all fallen into place. JoJo "Jammer" Cullen was as guilty as the day is long.

But.

The big *but.*

It hung in the air between Ash and Fey like a hawk riding an updraft—circling and circling, but not coming to roost. There was nothing to do or say. They had to go with what the evidence indicated, until they could put a finger on what was touching off all of their experienced warning systems.

Suddenly, Fey wanted to be done with the whole investigation. Since the discovery of Ricky Long's body, she'd been running from the specter of RHD taking over the case. Now she wanted nothing more than to dump the entire situation in their lap.

Ash's presence had twiddled her emotional and physical knobs. Fey's earthy nature was responding to the man, and she'd been around enough to know that Ash wasn't immune to the same reactions. Pheromones and receptors were working overtime in the age-old ritual that draws male to female and female to male. Fey could acknowledge to herself what was happening, but she was also aware of something else beyond lust.

It was a connection on a professional level. They were in sync. The experience gave Fey a flash of insight into the essence of Hammer and Nails's relationship.

The thoughts racing through Fey's mind came back full circle to JoJo. He was as guilty as sin. *But* . . . And at that immediate moment, Fey and Ash were the only two intimately involved in the case who were going to believe in the *but.*

A deputy stuck his head through the interview room doorway. "Excuse me . . . Detective Croaker?" He looked askance at all three of the room's occupants.

"Yes," Fey spoke up.

"Cullen's lawyer is here and wants to talk to you."

"Who called Cullen a lawyer?" Fey asked sharply.

The deputy shrugged his meaty shoulders. "Beats me. Nobody here did as far as I know."

A man stepped around the deputy and into the interview room.

"Wait a minute," the deputy said. He put a hand out to stop the man.

Devon Wyatt looked down at the hand on the sleeve of his handmade suit and almost snarled. The deputy stepped forward to meet the challenge.

"Leave it," Fey said, as if calling off an attack dog.

"Go chew a bone somewhere," Wyatt said.

The deputy was caught with his macho hanging out.

"I said, leave it," Fey repeated.

Reluctantly, the deputy released Wyatt's sleeve and stepped back.

"It's okay," Fey said.

Giving Wyatt a glare, the deputy turned and walked away. As he exited, two other men filled the doorway. Fey didn't recognize them.

"You don't appear surprised to see me," Wyatt said to Fey.

"I wouldn't give you the satisfaction," Fey said.

Wyatt almost smiled. "No. You wouldn't," he said. Without further prologue, he pushed his point. "I want access to my client." His tone was neutral, not challenging.

"I always thought you were a good lawyer," Fey said. She felt claustrophobic with too many people in the small room.

"I am a good lawyer."

"Then why are you trying to demand things you know you can't have right now?"

"Are you denying me access?"

Fey changed the subject. "Who are these gentlemen?" She pushed her chin out in the direction of the doorway.

Wyatt turned for the introductions. "This is Martin DeVries. He owns the San Diego Sails."

DeVries stepped forward and extended his hand toward Fey. She shook it and in turn introduced Ash and Groom.

DeVries was in his late sixties, portly in the way of successful men who can hire tailors to hide their bulk. His full head of salt and pepper, razor-cut hair gave him a distinguished presence.

"Ozzie Balzac," said the other man, sliding past DeVries to shake hands with Fey. "I'm the Sails's head coach." He was tall with high cheekbones, a crooked nose, and massive hands.

Fey figured Wyatt must have picked up the early morning news broadcast about JoJo's arrest. He'd obviously been damn busy since then. She wondered if Wyatt had a tame helicopter pilot on call to shuttle in his clients, or if he'd had to hustle to dig one up.

"You're the ambulance chaser to beat all ambulance chasers," Fey served the ball to Wyatt. There was a hint of admiration in her voice.

"You want to match testosterone levels?" Wyatt asked, returning easily.

"How's your son?" Fey asked, casually. Spike and point.

"Now, Detective Croaker—" DeVries started, his voice sonorous. Fey gave him her attention.

"—I know what you're going to say," she interrupted. Standing, she picked up her purse and moved through into the hallway, continuing to talk. The small room had been getting to her. "You're going to tell me that there must be some mistake. That JoJo Cullen couldn't possibly have killed anyone. That you will bring all of your considerable influence and resources to bear on this case to free JoJo."

DeVries wasn't used to having underlings mock him. His expression clearly displayed his distaste.

Fey continued. "Though I'm loath to admit it, Mr. DeVries, you've hired yourself a top lawyer. If anyone can embarrass the police department, Mr. Wyatt can. But nobody is going to get in to see JoJo until the doctor gives the okay."

Balzac stepped forward. "What's happened to him? Is he injured?" It was clear to see where his priorities lay.

DeVries put a hand out and pushed Balzac back. "I want to speak to your superior."

"I have no superiors," Fey said. Playing semantics had always been a favorite pastime for her. "But if you want to talk to my supervisor, all you need to do is turn around." Fey pointed down the hallway and everyone turned to look.

Mike Cahill, accompanied by Captain Strachman, was walking toward the group looking like thunder. Behind them were two other men. Fey recognized them.

Derek Keegan and Andy Hale. Robbery-homicide had sent out their big guns.

The balloon was about to go up.

⚏

CHAPTER THIRTY-THREE

"I FEEL LIKE I'VE BEEN SHOT AT AND MISSED, AND SHIT and hit," Fey said. She was back at West LA station with her feet up on the corner of her desk, and the rest of her slumped back in her chair. A mug of overbrewed coffee sat close at hand on her blotter.

Her sentiment was shared by the rest of her crew. Having the Cullen investigation taken over by robbery-homicide was a major letdown. Even though they knew it would happen eventually, the feeling was akin to being a quarterback in the Super Bowl, only to find yourself replaced before calling the first play.

The desultory talk amongst the unit was about how relieved they were that they weren't going to get caught in the middle of the brouhaha the Cullen case would create; how they could now get on with their other cases; how nice it was going to be to go home on time for a change; how glad they were that robbery-homicide was stuck dealing with the press and the pressure that this case would generate. But it was all a crock. Deep down, everyone in Fey's unit yearned to be a part of the investigation. Each believed, in their heart of hearts, that they could do a better job than the prima donnas from robbery-homicide.

It was arrogance and detective ego speaking, but no homicide dick worth anything was lacking in either arrogance or ego. Those traits, as much as any other skills, set them apart from other mainstream detectives and contributed to the unique mindset of the death romancers.

Ego made a homicide detective stay with a case until it was solved. Arrogance helped homicide dicks deal with facing the daily specter of their own mortality. The combination of the two created a greater whole than the sum of the parts. Nonhomicide detectives often figured the combination created an ass "whole."

Working homicide was the most demanding of all investigative assignments. Detectives who had never worked homicide were looked on by dicks who had as merely being "play detectives." Popular sentiment among homicide detectives ran that if you weren't working homicide then you weren't worth shit.

Homicide was king of the hill, the ultimate assignment. You could take the worst that the human condition threw at you, the more depraved the better, and beat it down. If you didn't develop the twin shields of arrogance and ego, however, then working homicide would eat you up and spit you out in broken, whining, thumb-sucking little pieces.

There were two commandments when you worked homicide: Never lose your cookies; and never, never let anyone see you cry.

To work homicide successfully, you had to learn to commit murder—because, over and over again, you had to kill the part of yourself that feels pity and empathy. If you worked homicide long enough, your emotions became diamond-hard, and you lived as if you were already in your own grave. You drank to remember life. You drank to forget death. And you drank because it beat all hell out of trying to deal with the horror of either one.

As other detectives begrudged the attitude of the area homicide detectives, the area homicide detectives begrudged the attitude of the robbery-homicide dicks. Robbery-homicide division was the most exclusive club in the world, a tough, tight-knit fraternity that acknowledged nobody outside of their own sphere. Divorce, chauvinism, and alcoholism were rampant. A team of dicks from RHD could take pride in drinking a bar dry, then being called out to solve a who-dun-it murder, and have it wrapped up with a suspect in the can before the sun was over the yard-arm again.

The majority of murders are sordid, miserable, sickening affairs involving petty and pathetic lives. These were the cases that RHD would turn their nose up at working. It was a mindset that claimed these types of cases were beneath them. But the Cullen case was different. This was a limelight case—something big enough to get fat RHD asses off of bar stools and out to fight crime.

But RHD hadn't solved the Cullen case. Fey's unit had laid the groundwork, and luck and good coppering by a West LA uniform had broken the investigation wide open. But now RHD was stepping in to claim all the kudos on the way back to their bar stools.

The situation left a bad taste in the mouth of Fey's unit. There was still a lot of investigating to be done on this case, investigation that they felt they were entitled to carry out. But they had been usurped, left standing at the altar, screwed without being kissed. It was the stuff of which grudges were made.

The squad room was a hive of activity as other detectives buzzed about their duties, but none of the activity touched the repressed mood of the Homicide/MAC Unit. Alphabet had his rump perched on Brindle's desk, with Brindle herself in a chair near him. Sitting opposite them, Monk's posture imitated Fey's, while Hammersmith and Rhonda Lawless had pulled their chairs close to Fey's desk. It was as if the unit had spun in on itself, circled the wagons, and was preparing to repel boarders.

Hammer and Nails had returned from San Diego half an hour earlier to discover the change of command.

"I knew it," Hammersmith had said. He set a brown envelope down on a desk before stretching and yawning.

"Can we do something about it?" Rhonda asked. Fey was struck by the fact that the question was directed specifically at Hammersmith and not at the unit in general. It was as if Hammer and Nails may have had something in their bag of tricks to reverse the order of things.

Hammersmith shrugged. "I think that's a bit of a stretch, even for us."

Fey decided to put in her two cents' worth. "It's a done deal. A moot point. We couldn't get the case back if we wanted it. And even though we're all sitting around here as if we've had our teddy bears stolen, I'm not sure we would want it back."

The declaration brought some thoughtful nods from the assembled detectives. They had almost convinced themselves she was right.

"How did the San Diego search go?" Fey asked.

"It was an experience," Nails said. "The guy lives in an orphanage."

Fey looked taken aback. "An orphanage? What are you talking about?"

"Apparently, if any of us knew anything about basketball, we would have known the JoJo Cullen story," Hammersmith said. "He grew up in an orphanage in San Diego. The pride and joy of the nuns and priests. A sweet child with the physical skills of a god."

"They never found a family to adopted him?" Monk asked.

Hammersmith bounced his eyebrows. "He went into foster homes a couple of times, but they didn't work out for one reason or another. That was until he was fourteen, when a high school coach saw him playing basketball in the local park with a bunch of high school team members. JoJo was blowing them off the court. The coach and his wife had two sons of their own, but the guy convinced his wife to adopt JoJo. From that point on, JoJo's basketball career took off. When he became rich and famous, he donated big bucks to the orphanage, had a dormitory converted for his own use, and moved back in.''

"Weird," Fey said. "What about the coach and his adopted family?"

Hammersmith shrugged. "Don't know. I didn't think we were writing a biography. I'm sure, though, that we'll all be able to read about it real soon once the press starts digging for sound bites."

"You're right about that," Fey agreed. "Anyway, did you turn up anything from the search?" Pointedly, she looked at the envelope Hammersmith had brought in with him.

Nails had slid on a pair of latex gloves. She picked up the envelope and opened it before carefully sliding the contents out onto the desk. "JoJo appeared to live like a monk at the orphanage—"

"A sloppy monk perhaps," Hammersmith interjected.

"—so there wasn't really anything of interest," Nails continued, ignoring her partner. "Nothing, anyway that appeared to connect JoJo to any of the murders. Then we found these." With long, latex-enclosed fingers she spread a series of Polaroid photos and a cassette tape across the desktop.

Everyone gathered around to examine the booty.

"Oh, sweet Mary," Brindle Jones said with her first glance.

Her impression was justified. There were four Polaroids—two each of Ricky Long and the boy known as Rush. In all the photos the boys were naked and bound and gagged elaborately.

"Where did you find these?" Fey asked.

"In JoJo's bedroom between the mattress and the box spring."

"That's original," Fey said.

"Well, the guy is obviously no rocket scientist," Hammersmith said.

"Yeah, but how smart does a killer need to be?" Brindle asked.

"Fortunately, or unfortunately, that's not going to be a question we have to answer this time around," Fey said. She shuffled the photos together with a pencil and pushed them toward Rhonda. "Call Keegan and Hale down at RHD," she said. "This case is their baby now, let them change its dirty diapers."

Monk pointed to the cassette. "What's on the tape?"

Hammersmith produced a small tape recorder from his jacket pocket. He handed it to Rhonda, who used her gloved hands to place the tape inside. She pressed the play button.

The squad room filled with a pathetic wail.

"Come on, man. Let me go. Please. I'll do anything you want. I'll do you like you've never been done before." The young male voice was filled with fear as it gasped for breath. *"I can't breathe. This rope is choking me. Please, don't let me die."*

Hammersmith hit the stop button. The silence that followed was deadly still. Nobody wanted to move.

"A voice from the grave," Hammersmith said grimly.

CHAPTER THIRTY-FOUR

ASH WAS ALSO FEELING LET DOWN OVER THE CASE. HE had no illusions about robbery-homicide. They would freeze him out completely. The cooperation between the bureau and the LAPD was tenuous at best. With a high-profile suspect successfully in custody, LAPD was not going to let the FBI anywhere near the case. Credit was not going to be shared.

But that wasn't the only reason Ash was unsettled. The case stuck in his craw. It didn't wash. He still wasn't sure what it was about the setup that he didn't like, but there were elements that didn't ring true for him.

Maybe he was losing his touch, he thought. Maybe his reactions to the Croaker woman were clouding his judgment. After everything he had been through in the past year, how could he possibly allow himself to be attracted to a woman—a woman who, with any luck, was going to be around a year or so from now.

He was bothered because his attraction to Fey hadn't been of the one-night stand variety. He'd never followed that path anyway. Even with Holly, the commitment had been his even if it wasn't hers. Sure he was attracted to Fey sexually, but Ash was well aware that for him to be interested in a woman physically, there also had to be an emotional connection. Fey had beguiled him from the start, and he sensed that he was having the same effect on her.

The big problem was that he didn't have time anymore for those types of feelings. The doctors told him that his body would betray him very soon now, and he'd made a pact with himself to not allow that to happen. It made him confused and angry. Two days ago he'd started out simply wanting enough time to take one more monster scalp. After that, he would have been happy to embrace his ending. Now, however, passions and emotional sensations he thought long repressed were wreaking havoc with the acceptance of his plight.

He'd never set out to become a monster hunter. It was a vocation that had chosen him, not the other way around, but now it had become almost an obsession. If his life was to have meaning in the short time left, he needed to find personal closure by plying his skills in a final coup d'etat. What energy he possessed needed to be channeled in that one direction; there wasn't enough for anything else.

The investigation that culminated in the arrest of JoJo Cullen was exactly the kind of case that he'd been waiting for. But he'd been cheated of the resolution, and had made no significant contribution. The case appeared to be a done deal, but somehow it didn't sit right.

Ash tried to examine his restlessness with the situation. Was he simply fooling himself? Was he so desperate for one last success that he was grasping at any straw? Or was there some substance behind the tenuous unease that was taunting him?

It was clear the case and the suspect didn't match with all of the behavioral science bells and whistles that set the standards in the investigation of serial killers. But who knew with killers?

There were principles that could be applied in most cases. On the surface, however, they did not appear to fit in this one, and Ash didn't have enough information to determine if further investigation would show the genesis of the violence to run true.

Ash was bothered—bothered to the point of knowing he couldn't leave the investigation alone. Somehow, he would have to find a way to take a closer look at everything that had occurred. He would also need to take a closer look at Cullen's history. Only then would he be able to see if all the ducks lined up.

His thoughts came back to Fey again, but the ringing of his phone cut his reverie short.

"Ash," he said into the receiver.

"Hey, hey, Monster Man. How's it hanging?"

Ash knew the voice. "What do you want, Tucker?"

Around the edges of his consciousness he could sense the hovering weight of blackness creeping in. Depression. Where Ash was concerned, Tucker could bring it on faster than a day without Prozac. It made no sense for Ash to ask how Tucker found out his unlisted home phone number. As the *American Inquirer*'s top reporter, Tucker had more sources than a priest had confessions.

"Hey, come on, now. Don't be that way." Tucker's voice was a nasally whine. "I'm the man who made you what you are today, superstar." Tucker's true crime books featuring Ash's cases had both been on the best-seller list for weeks.

"Don't do me any more favors, Tucker. I need you like a snake needs a skateboard."

"You need me more than that, my man."

"You think so?"

"Absolutely. I know you. This JoJo Cullen thing must be eating you up."

Damn the man. "What makes you say that?" Ash tried to keep his voice steady.

"It stinks. I've researched enough about what you do, and watched you in action enough times to know that this whole setup is out in left field somewhere. It makes about as much sense as a bad Ed Wood film."

"You don't know what you're talking about."

"Yeah, right." Tucker was sarcastic. "I've been watching you, man. I know every move you make. This thing has you wound tighter than a Catholic school girl in heat. You'd sell your soul for another notch on your gunbelt before your Lou Gehrig impersonation gets out of control."

"What are you babbling about, Tucker?" Ash felt as if there was a rod of ice through his heart. Outside of his bosses at the bureau and his doctors, nobody knew. Damn it, nobody knew.

"You can't keep secrets from me, man. Don't you know better by now? You may be the best monster hunter alive, but I'm the best muckraking hack journalist around.

"Just like the mounties, you always get your man, and I always get my story. Your life is an open book to me. I know more about you than even you do. I've seen your medical files, buddy. They don't tell a pretty story. You're gonna be whacking out big time real soon. You know it and I know it.

"What do you say? Let's work together for once. People love this true crime shit. They eat it up. You and your cases are enough of a cash cow to keep both of us in buffalo chips. Come on, say we're a team. Accept it."

"Tucker, you are the scum-sucking bottom feeder to beat all scum-sucking bottom feeders."

"How nice of you to say so. Thanks. I thought for a while there that you didn't care."

"I'm not like you, Tucker. I don't make my living from other people's misery."

Tucker laughed. "Of course you do. Without monsters in the world making people miserable, you'd have no reason for your existence. I admire you, man. You're the best at what you do, but you live off bad news just like me."

Ash was silent. Thinking. He hated Tucker. He loathed the exposure that Tucker's books had brought into his life. He despised the thought that Tucker might be right in his assessments.

But most of all he hated the fact that there was so little time left for him that he might have to use Tucker to get what he wanted.

Tucker's voice crackled down the phone wires. "Talk to me, big guy. Give me an exclusive before you bite the big weenie. Make me rich and famous."

"I'll make you a deal, Tucker."

"I knew it. I knew you'd come around. I knew you wouldn't buy off on this JoJo thing." Tucker sounded excited.

Ash gritted his teeth. "Shut up, Tucker."

"Whatever you say, boss."

Ash took a deep breath. "I'll grant you that you can find out more shit than a whole platoon of flatfeet. Get on this JoJo caper. Bring me something concrete, something I can use to break it open, and we'll talk."

"You must be joking. What do I need you for if I find something to break the case open?"

"Don't push your luck, Tucker. If you can't bring me something, then I sure don't need you. And if you do bring me something, then you need me to catch the real bad guy."

◆

CHAPTER THIRTY-FIVE

THE NEXT SIX WEEKS FLEW BY FOR FEY IN A BLUR OF activity. Keegan and Hale, the two heavyweights from robbery-homicide division's "homicide special" unit, may have taken over the case of *People vs Cullen*, but Fey and her people were still swept up in the middle of the hyperbole.

The press were in a feeding frenzy of gargantuan proportion. Each aspect of the three murders that was unearthed, no matter how minor, was hashed over and dissected in the minutest detail. The brilliance of JoJo Cullen's basketball career was replayed time and again on television screens across the nation. In the off-camera words of a well-known television news anchor, "If it bleeds, it leads," and JoJo Cullen's case was bleeding all over the landscape.

JoJo's private life, or more particularly the lack of it, was scrutinized under the harsh glare of John Q. Public's insatiable need to know. The fact that JoJo did not have a string of thousands of feminine conquests came as a letdown.

Where was the spice in a flashy sports figure who didn't screw everything that moved? It made him look guilty—as if by lack of obvious sexual excess, he was capable of anything. An All-American boy screwed women by the dozens, didn't he? It was what made a man a man, wasn't it? It was what made America great, by gum. What was the matter with this JoJo guy? He certainly didn't seem to fit the white man's fear of a black man's sexuality, so he must be a pervert and a sex killer. He must be guilty.

Even Fey had to admit that JoJo's apparent total lack of feminine company, coupled with his lack of off-court antics, made him an oddity. Here was a man who was rapidly becoming one of the leading pro basketball players of his generation, but he seemed to have no life outside of the game.

A per-game average of thirty-two points, twelve rebounds, and twelve assists were killer on-court numbers that could slaughter the opposition, but did they translate into off-court murder? JoJo appeared to live for only one thing—the game. His every breathing moment since he'd first picked up a roundball seemed to have been aimed at becoming the perfect basketball machine.

JoJo had cruised through school on his athletic talent alone. His grades were passing, but in reality he was little more than a functional illiterate. The tongue-in-cheek coalition of the legal system's rumor control declared that in looking for twelve jurors who had never been exposed to JoJo, the best source would be his university professors.

In a game that demanded aggressive, outrageous, on-court conduct, coupled with fluid skill and pantherlike quickness, JoJo ''Jammer'' Cullen was the heir apparent to the vacated throne of Magic Johnson.

Every prep basketball player over six feet, six inches who could dribble a basketball between his legs has been touted as the ''next Magic,'' but none came close until JoJo. The comparison, however, only applied to JoJo's on-court skills. Away from the hoops, he didn't hold a candle to Magic's personality and outrageous lifestyle.

He was a robot that turned up for tip-off, played like a man possessed for four quarters, and then put himself away in a closet until it was time for the next game.

Turn on. Turn off.

JoJo's on-court demeanor—the in-your-face, smash-mouth, slick-as-whale-snot, slam-dunking, backboard-shattering maniac—was Mr. Hyde compared to the almost childlike Dr. Jekyll he became when the final buzzer sounded. Michael Jordan one moment, Michael Jackson the next.

He was an enigma that was now being torn apart by public opinion and condemnation.

But while the public reveled in vicarious blood lust, San Diego Sails players all made personal statements of support for JoJo. Other players from around the NBA rallied to his defense. JoJo's UCLA coach and university teammates all took a stance that JoJo was a man who, despite his game demeanor, would never consider the violence of which he was accused.

Leaders of the black community and clergy backlashed against redneck I-told-you-sos. A rumble of racial hatred that had been quiet since the summer of '92 in LA began to echo. Battle lines were being drawn.

Moderates of all ethnic backgrounds within the city stepped forward and spoke of tolerance, of allowing the courts to do their duty, of letting justice run its course. But the world still waited with jaded breath to see what the spark would ignite.

Dead kids, fallen superstar athletes, and the taint of kinky sex weren't enough. The world wanted more. The world wanted to watch Armageddon while they sipped their morning java, or watched the late evening news—that is as long as it didn't involve them in any way.

At the center of the controversy, Devon Wyatt stood like a sentinel in the raging storm. A mad Machiavelli determined to leave no pot unstirred.

From his early days as a district attorney, through his transition to private practice and the early defense cases that had brought his name to prominence, Wyatt had always gone in for the drama of the moment. He gave juries what they wanted—entertainment.

The Wyatt approach to juries was that they consisted of twelve people too stupid to get out of jury duty. "I'm a salesman," Wyatt was apt to say after a bottle or two of Dom Perignon. "I sell bullshit to juries!" And he sold it by the ton.

In one of his greatest triumphs, his researchers uncovered a minor fact about a detective who had obtained a taped confession from Wyatt's client. The detective, Dan Rivers, was well known in the squad room for his dead-ringer impersonations of various captains and deputy chiefs. No promotion party was complete without Rivers doing his Rich Little routine for the never-ending amusement of his drunken colleagues.

In court, Wyatt put Rivers on the stand, disarmed him with the professional charm of a snake oil salesman, and drew him into doing an impersonation of Wyatt himself. The DA objected to the irrelevance of the action, but Wyatt successfully argued that he would shortly show the court how amazingly relevant his actions were. The judge overruled the objection and Wyatt continued.

Rivers was reluctant to comply at first, but gradually gaining confidence, he displayed his mimicking talents and had the jury in stitches. This was entertainment.

With consummate skill, Wyatt gave Rivers—a frustrated performer at heart—a stage on which to play to the audience in the jury box. Rivers became sucked in by Wyatt's tactics and, despite the DA's frantic pleading, worked himself through impersonations of Bill Clinton, John Wayne, Marlon Brando, and a classic Richard Nixon. The jury loved it.

But Wyatt, who'd been doing his own impersonation of Ed Sullivan up to this point, suddenly became serious. Like a Doberman going for the throat of an intruder, Wyatt pinned Rivers with an icy stare. "Now, Detective Rivers," he started, using his voice as a tool, "would you please impersonate my client for the jury the same way you did on this taped confession?"

Rivers looked shocked and confused. "But, I didn't impersonate—"

Wyatt jumped in before Rivers could finish. "Isn't it true, Detective Rivers, that my client never made any statements to you during the interrogation?"

"No—"

"Isn't it true that you impersonated my client while making this tape of a false confession?"

"No—"

Wyatt kept his hammering style going, never giving Rivers a second to breathe or finish a statement. "Isn't it true that you desperately needed a good arrest to put yourself in line for your recent promotion, and framing my client was the best way you could think of to do that?"

Rivers knew he hadn't impersonated Wyatt's client. Wyatt knew that he hadn't. The DA and the judge knew that he hadn't. But the jury were another kettle of fish.

Reasonable doubt reared its ugly head. The client walked and Wyatt pocketed a huge fee and added another notch to his proverbial gun butt.

In Wyatt's assessment, juries weren't interested in guilt or innocence. Instead they were concerned only with their own prurient interests and creature comforts. If your dog and pony show held more smoke and mirrors than the prosecution, then nine times out of ten the jury was going to come back in your favor. A little sleight of hand, bring something unexpected in from left field, make up for the jurors missing their daily soap operas, and bingo, you had yourself an acquittal.

The big splashy defenses that had established Wyatt as an icon in the legal world began far before the case saw the inside of a courtroom. His maneuvering began with the press and with the tangled web of political strings that he was a maestro at conducting.

It was Wyatt who tapped into Reverend Aloishious Brown's sphere of influence. Nobody could say exactly what the reverend did for a living. Over the years, however, Aloishious Brown had become first a local and then a national spokesman for the black cause—whatever that cause might be. Brown was always first off the mark whenever the tentacles of racism lashed out. And if the tentacles of racism were quiet, then the right Reverend Aloishious Brown would whip some up just for the hell of it. Brown needed racism the way cops needed crime—job security.

Brown owed Wyatt for getting him off on an embezzling charge when he'd been rising through the ranks of the LA power scene. Brown had seen himself as mayor of

LA until the question of his honesty came into play. Now that everyone knew he was dirty, even if unconvicted, mayor wasn't good enough. Now, the reverend's ambition was heading him toward governor, or maybe even a democratic vice-presidential tag.

Brown's LA power base was the congregation of the First Black American Evangelical Church, an organization of good-minded folks being led to glory by hucksters, conmen, and the gleaming, angelical countenance of Aloishious Brown himself.

The church was a powerful political entity that could stir up a demonstration at the drop of a politically incorrect statement—or the jailing of a black role model. The press loved the church and Reverend Brown. Either one was good for any number of inflammatory quotes and inches of column copy.

At Wyatt's request, the church and Reverend Brown mounted their high horses and rode to JoJo's defense. What had been a "simple" case of serial murder with a high-profile suspect, was suddenly turned into a racially charged issue that was on the verge of forcing sides to be chosen.

Every action the police had taken in the case was suddenly suspect, and the most outrageous statements of nonfact were given feasibility strictly by being said, repeated, and published by the media in its never-ending quest for the public's right to know.

Wyatt outdid even himself when the DA's office leaked news about the DNA evidence that tied JoJo directly to all three of the murdered boys.

Wyatt called a press conference immediately. He had a trump card to play and he wasn't going to play it quietly.

CHAPTER THIRTY-SIX

"CAN YOU BELIEVE THIS CRAP?" FEY ASKED IN EXASPER-
ation. She spread the front page of the newspaper on her
desk and turned to an inside page to continue the story she
was reading.

"What particular crap is that?" Monk asked. "That's
the *Los Angeles Times* you're reading, which means there's
an awful lot of crap to pick from."

"Yeah," chipped in Alphabet. "I can't even use the
Times to line my parakeet's cage because there's already
crap on most of the pages."

"Ha, ha," said Fey, not laughing. "I'm serious. This
crap that Devon Wyatt is putting out about the DNA evidence results—it has got to be total bullshit."

DNA matching, or genetic fingerprinting, was the current evidence *du jour*. Just as nobody has the same traditional fingerprints, everybody's genetic DNA makeup is
different—with one exception. Using blood, semen, or
other biological samples, scientists can read the DNA
strips and match them to the individual who produced
them.

Semen had been found and recovered from the rectal
cavities of the three buried boys. The DNA readings from
the semen had all matched with each other. Further, the
DNA readings from the semen had been matched with the
DNA readings worked up from samples of JoJo Cullen's
blood.

The one exception to individual DNA readings is identical twins. Identical twins, split from the same female egg,

would have different traditional fingerprints, but matching DNA readings.

"I heard this coming in to work today on the news," Brindle said from her desk next to Alphabet. "Wyatt is standing up and saying that the reason JoJo's DNA matches that found in the bodies is because JoJo is an identical twin who was separated at birth from his sibling. Wyatt's making a big deal that the police aren't searching for this missing twin."

"Give me a break," Monk said. "Does he expect anybody to buy off on that baloney? That's about the most stupid thing I've ever heard."

Alphabet put his coffee mug down after taking a long swallow. "The old 'my evil twin did it' defense." He snickered.

"Where the hell is his proof regarding this twin?" Brindle asked. Her exasperation with the justice system was obvious in her tone.

Cop work had worked its way into Brindle's psyche. Despite her best efforts not to be swayed by it, Brindle was finding herself rapidly becoming attached to a job that she had once seen as strictly a temporary career move until something better turned up—something better in the shape of a man with a lot of money. Along the way, however, Brindle had been infected by the work and was beginning to find a depth of intestinal fortitude that she hadn't figured on. She still didn't see herself becoming like Fey, but neither did she any longer see her career goal as letting a man keep her.

Max Cassiday had returned from vacation and immediately tripped down one of the station's stairways, breaking a leg and throwing his back out of whack. With Max long-term "injured on duty," Hammer and Nails were still carrying the sex crimes case load.

Chip Hernandez hadn't even bothered to come back from vacation—just mailed in his badge and gun. With ten years invested in the LAPD, he'd pulled the pin and moved on to help his brother run their father's construction business. Even though Chip's position still hadn't been filled,

Fey wished him the best of luck. She had seen the signs of discontent running through Hernandez for several years. She figured he was better off out of police work.

The uproar over JoJo Cullen's arrest seemed to have put a damper on major criminal activity in West L.A. There had only been one other murder since JoJo became big time news for something besides throwing up three-pointers. It had been a smoking gun scenario that Monk and Alphabet had cleared up without raising a sweat.

Fey and her crew had been called out earlier in the morning on an unusual suicide. Normally, the whole unit didn't roll on suicides, but this one was distinct enough to get everyone's attention.

The victim was a twenty-eight-year-old coroner's deputy—a co-worker of Lily Sheridan named Dan Potter. Fey had worked several murder scenes with Potter, but mostly he had been assigned to other areas. He'd been tall and skinny with bad acne scars and a bad haircut. Fey had once likened him to a number-two pencil with a chewed end and a worn eraser.

Potter had kept to himself and was considered more than a little odd, which was not unusual for somebody working out of the coroner's office—not everybody down there had Lily Sheridan's outlook on life. Potter had been an inoffensive, overpolite fellow who did his job—nothing more perhaps, but nothing less. Nobody had been aware of his depression and despair.

As a coroner's deputy, Potter had known all of the procedures and reports that responding officers and coroner's personnel would go through at the scene of a suicide. When the pressures of life finally became too much for him, Potter still didn't want to be impolite.

As a result, before killing himself, Potter took pains to ensure nobody would be inconvenienced. He strung crime scene tape around the outside of the small two-bedroom house that he shared with his recently deceased mother. He laid the two hunting rifles that had belonged to his deceased father on the bed in his room. To save authorities the effort of searching for other weapons, he laid a printed note alongside the guns stating that they were the only firearms in the house other than the handgun he was to use on himself.

Another printed sign was taped next to a wall phone, providing the information that he had used that particular phone to dial 911 emergency. On the kitchen table, completely filled out, were all the necessary coroner's forms. Next to the forms was a Mr. Coffee with a fresh-brewed pot of java and a box of doughnuts. Yet another printed note informed that the coffee and doughnuts were for the responding paramedics and cops.

Polite to the end, Potter had dialed 911, gave his address and stated he was going to kill himself, hung up, pushed Mr. Coffee's brew button, and walked casually into his bathroom. Inside the bathroom, he'd taken off his clothes, tied a completed corpse identification tag to his toe, climbed into a black body bag, worked his way into his bathtub, and closed the shower door.

Dan Potter had laid waiting. He heard the sirens coming, heard the patrol cars and the paramedic's ambulance pulling into his driveway. Still waiting, he heard the crunch of heavy boots on his front porch. He heard the knock on his front door, heard the ringing of the doorbell. He heard somebody call his name.

And then he put the barrel of his father's Army-issue .45 in his mouth and pulled the trigger.

The Mr. Coffee finished brewing as a cop the size of Mount Rushmore shouldered down the front door.

Fey and her unit had all been at the sad little scene. There wasn't much they could do. It wasn't a homicide. There was nothing to investigate. The coroner's office would handle all the follow-up and only a couple of uniforms were needed to keep the place secure. Still, the setup was out of the ordinary enough for them all to put in an appearance. It was more attention at one time than Potter had ever received when he'd been breathing.

Returning to the station, Fey had taken a break with the

paper only to be bowled over by Devon Wyatt's astounding allegations.

"This guy Wyatt is a piece of work," she said, continuing to read the article.

"Who does he think is going to believe him?" Brindle asked again.

Fey turned back to the front page. "It says right here that Reverend Aloishious Brown and the First Black American Evangelical Church will again be making statements of support for JoJo. They will also be making demands for law enforcement to begin a reinvestigation of the case in order to bring the true suspect to justice."

Monk had stood up to move over behind Fey. Looking at the article he read a quote out loud. "Reverend Brown denounced law enforcement efforts in this case as reactionary and shoddy. 'How can we sleep safe in our beds with a mad killer still on the loose?'"

"Yeah, like he fits the victim profile," said Alphabet. "I bet the old reverend is quaking in his boots."

"Whether we like it or not, it makes good copy," said Fey. "Wyatt's smart. People will believe Brown simply because he is a power base within the black community."

"I don't get it," Brindle said. "They want us to believe that JoJo couldn't do it because he is black. But his twin brother would be black also."

"It doesn't matter," Fey said. "He's already got you accepting, if not believing, the bullshit about an identical twin."

"Get out of here."

"No, I'm serious. People out there are going to believe this simply because it's a way to attack the police. You know the world we live in. How can you underestimate the stupidity of the masses. Look how many copies of tabloid newspapers sell each week—all with 'news' made up out of thin air."

"Check out Geraldo's ratings," said Monk.

Alphabet nodded. "There are people who still think professional wrestling is real."

"You mean it isn't?" asked Brindle.

•   •   •

Everyone from the unit except Fey had either gone to
lunch or was out doing follow-ups. Fey stuffed the last of
a dry bagel in her mouth and then threw her signature
down on the last piece from a pile of paperwork. As she
shuffled the stack together, the front page of the *Times*
caught her eye again. She set the stack of paperwork down
and picked up the newspaper.

An evil twin, she thought. *Nah, no way*. She read the
article again. Not a shred of truth there, she was sure.

But she still harbored instincts about the case. Earlier
she'd called down to RHD and talked to Keegan. He'd
told her what she'd known all along—Wyatt was full of
shit. No way was there a twin. Keegan had checked it out
himself. JoJo was an only child whose poverty-level
mother had died in childbirth. There had been no other
relatives. JoJo had been born an orphan.

Maybe JoJo did have a brother somewhere, Keegan had
said, but it wouldn't be a twin and no way would the DNA
match, and would Fey please stop wasting his time.

Fey agreed. Didn't she? Didn't she? She didn't know.
Not an evil twin, perhaps, but something else. What? She
didn't know.

Fey set the newspaper down. She knew if she hesitated
she'd never do what she had in mind. She picked up her
phone. With her other hand, she dug in her purse for a
business card. When she came up with it, she punched the
number on it into the phone.

She had to be out of her mind.

Her heart was thumping around in her chest.

Ash answered on the third ring. "Hello."

"Hi, this is Fey Croaker. I'm sorry to bother you—"

"What took you so long to call?" Ash asked, interrupting her flow of words.

"What do you mean?"

"I've been waiting for you to call for over six weeks.
You don't buy any of this stuff with JoJo, do you?"

Fey didn't reply at first, and then committed herself.

"No I don't. Haven't done from the start." Her voice held a strong determination.

"Neither do I," Ash said.

"Then what are we going to do about it?" Fey asked.

"I don't know, but it could get messy," Ash said. "I can feel it."

"I'm not known for backing down when things get tough," Fey told him.

Fey remembered seeing Ash for the first time. Something fluttered in her stomach. A hell of a thing to base a career decision on. She wondered fleetingly what Ash's hand would feel like as it touched the back of her neck. She remembered how he seemed to look into her.

"Okay, I'll fix it," Ash said into the phone.

"That's it? You'll fix it?"

"This won't be the last time you'll have to trust me."

Fey heard the phone disconnect as Ash put down the receiver on his end. She wanted a cigarette. She wanted a drink. Leaving her desk, she walked out of the squad bay to go to the bathroom.

Before finishing in the bathroom she freshened her eye makeup and brushed her hair through. Looking in the mirror she was aware of her slate-blue eyes questioning her. She noticed the crow's feet and other lines making themselves into permanent fixtures on her countenance. *I'm too old to be wearing my emotions on my sleeve*, she thought as she examined herself. *What the hell do I think I'm doing? Isn't my life complicated enough? What the hell do I expect from Ash after such brief contact? Sex? Love? The instant solution to a murder? Am I reacting to him out of instinct or lust, or is there a difference?*

Oh, well, she thought. *Nobody ever said I was smart. Just stubborn.*

CHAPTER THIRTY-SEVEN

THE FEDERAL BUILDING AT THE CORNER OF WILSHIRE AND Sepulveda played home to numerous government agencies, including the LA office of the FBI. On the sixteenth through eighteenth floors, the FBI had laid out a rat warren of partitions to supplement the already complex maze of standard corridors and offices. White-collar crimes, bank robberies, fugitive, antiterrorism, narcotics, and numerous other investigative details all fought for space. The hierarchy pecking order determined how large, how plush, and how many windows with which your office was equipped.

The largest and most plush office was reserved for Freddie Mackerbee, the special agent in charge—SAC—of the FBI's Los Angeles branch. The room was fifteen by fifteen and dominated by a huge mahogany desk and a high-backed leather chair. There was also the standard American flag, and a portrait of the current FBI director. If you took a close look at the portrait, you could see several dart holes between the director's steely eyes.

Two picture windows gave the office a wonderfully open feel. The view beyond them was of the beautiful green and white expanse of the veteran's cemetery across the street. It was a peaceful view, and one that Mackerbee appreciated after his last assignment in DC.

The office, however, was impersonal. There were no private mementoes of any kind. Mackerbee had been the Los Angeles SAC for three years, but he knew he could be moved on at any time. That was simply a fact of life in the bureau.

Mackerbee sat behind his desk, studying a man he not only considered a top resource, but also a friend—if the man could be said to have any friends. "This is an unusual request coming from you, Ash."

"Are you telling me I can't have her, sir?"

Mackerbee held up a placating hand in Ash's direction. "No. All I'm saying is that for as long as I've known you, you've been fanatical about working alone. Now you're asking for a partner. It's like the pope asking to get married."

Mackerbee was a short man built like a throw pillow on legs. He had a happy but florid face that spoke of too many late-night stakeouts, too many murder scenes, and too many fingers of Jamesons.

For some reason, women were attracted to Mackerbee like bees to honey. Something about him made women want to cuddle him and take him home. Ash had seen the reaction time and again at office parties and even during professional or official meetings. Mackerbee, however, never appeared to take advantage of this knack. He had a beautiful, devoted wife—a tall, blond, statuesque Amazon—and never strayed. Mackerbee knew when he was well off. He also knew that if he was ever caught fooling around, his wife would tear him in half and throw his stuffings everywhere.

Ash stared at Mackerbee in silence. Waiting.

Mackerbee finally shook his head. "You're a weird one, Ash. I swear to Buddha, the bureau ain't never seen the likes of you before."

"You have a complaint about my clearance rate?"

"Hell, no!" Mackerbee held up both hands in Ash's direction this time. "As far as I'm concerned, I wish I had another dozen like you."

"Then what's the problem?"

Mackerbee shook his head. "Same old stuff. The other guys see you as some kind of prima donna. They don't like to see you get the long leash all the time."

"That's their problem. I'm retired, remember?"

"That was just a wheeze to buy you some time," Mackerbee said. "This special consultant business is wearing thin for some of the other agents. Call it professional jealousy or anything else you like, but it's a fact of life. You'll never live to be retired, and you know it."

Mackerbee was one of the few people who actually knew the truth about Ash's physical condition.

"The problem is that some of the brass are also starting to ask questions," Mackerbee continued. "They're hearing the rumblings of discontent from the troops and wonder if I'm not giving you too much leash. It's a case of what have you done for us lately."

"The brass is your problem."

Mackerbee looked at Ash through lidded eyes.

"Do you want this monster caught or not?" Ash asked.

Mackerbee leaned back in his chair. "LAPD is telling the world they've already caught the monster. JoJo 'Jammer' Cullen, homosexual basketball player and sadistic murderer."

"They're wrong," Ash said simply.

Mackerbee picked up a letter opener and spun it around between his hands. "If LAPD has indeed got the wrong man and you catch the real killer, the brass from the director on down will get on their hands and knees and lick your ass."

"Then get me Croaker."

"As easy as that? I get you Croaker, and you get me the real killer?"

"It's never that easy. You get me Croaker, and somewhere along the line she and I will bring you the real killer. Maybe tomorrow, maybe next week, maybe sometime in the afterlife."

"I didn't know you believed in the afterlife, Ash."

"Everybody has to believe in something."

"Yeah? Well, I believe you better bring me the real killer sooner than later."

"Are you trying to tell me I don't have a lot of time left?"

Mackerbee didn't flinch from it. "I saw your last medical report. We both know you don't have a lot of time left.''

Ash shrugged. "You itchin' to ask me why I'm not spending my waning days sunning on some beach in Tahiti, drinking fruit vodkas with umbrellas in them, and chasing grass skirts?"

"No," said Mackerbee. "I know that answer. What I want to know is why one more monster is so important to you."

Ash looked out the window over the veterans' cemetery. "I think you've known me long enough to also answer that one for yourself."

Mackerbee waited a beat.

Ash waited with him.

"I know Croaker," Mackerbee said eventually. "She may be wound a bit tight, but she's a heck of a detective. Rumor has it she's so tough she rolls her own tampons."

"She does have a razor-sharp tongue," Ash agreed, and then let silence fall again, waiting his boss out.

Finally, Mackerbee gave in. "I'll get you Croaker."

A wry grin crossed Ash's mouth. It was there for a second and then gone. "And we'll bring you the real monster."

"Okay, it's a deal," said Mackerbee. He put his hands flat on his desk top. "Well, what are you waiting for? Go catch me a killer."

Ash stood up and moved away.

"Ash," Mackerbee said, stopping the agent at the door.

Ash turned to look at him. Mackerbee had a puzzled expression on his face. It was as if he was struggling to grasp a concept beyond his capacity.

"What else do you believe in?" he asked.

Ash shrugged. "An apple a day, a stitch in time, death as an adventure, suicide as an answer, happy endings, Democrats saving the country—all the usual fairy tales."

"How about love at first sight?" Mackerbee asked. He thought he saw something slide across Ash's dark eyes like a shark swimming in shadows.

"Only in the movies," Ash said, not wanting to give Mackerbee any satisfaction.

"Never at murder scenes?" Mackerbee pressed.

"Never."

Mackerbee shrugged. "If you say so."

Ash nodded. "And what do you believe, sir?" he asked, feeding Mackerbee the straight line he knew his boss and friend was waiting for.

Mackerbee started reaching for his bottom drawer. "I believe I'll have another drink."

✠

CHAPTER THIRTY-EIGHT

THE VERBAL EXPLOSION IN MIKE CAHILL'S OFFICE PRACtically rattled the old-fashioned Venetian blinds that covered the windows. Two seconds later, Cahill was at his open office door bellowing into the squad room.

"Croaker! Get in here!"

Cahill turned and strode back into his office without waiting to see if Fey was coming.

"Whoa," said Hammersmith, pausing while filling out an arrest packet for a spousal abuse suspect. "He sounds pissed. What have you done, boss?"

Fey had been in the middle of shuffling her own paperwork when Cahill had yelled at her. The bellow had startled her so much, she'd shot out of her chair like a fifth-grader caught cheating on a pop quiz.

"I think he just got news that I'm going to be loaned to the FBI for a while. I don't think he's too happy about it."

Rhonda Lawless was in her accustomed position, across

from Hammersmith, working her way through a stack of MAC reports. Like every other detective in the squad room, she had turned her head to look at Fey. Rhonda's brain was racing to analyze the situation. "You cook something up with that Ash character?"

"Maybe," Fey said. "But I think I might have cooked my goose instead."

"Does this have something to do with JoJo Cullen?" Hammersmith asked, already knowing the answer.

"Maybe," Fey said again, adding, "I better get in there."

"Wait a minute," said Hammersmith. "I take it this is something you really want to do?"

Fey sighed. "Yeah. This whole thing doesn't sit well with me. We wrapped everything up in such a pretty package that nobody seems willing to untie the ribbon and find out if the truth is actually inside."

Hammer and Nails exchanged glances. Fey found their habit of nonverbal communication disconcerting. They appeared to function on a different plane than everyone else.

"Do you think Cahill is going to nix your party?" Hammersmith asked.

"It sure sounds like it," Fey said.

"Then you better let us talk to him first."

"What do you mean?"

"He means that we're with you on this thing," Rhonda said as she stood up. "We can smooth the way for you to hang out with Ash, but if what you're doing pans out, we want in on the kill."

"Are you guys sure you know what you're doing?" Fey wasn't sure herself. She wasn't used to putting her faith in others.

"Trust us," Hammersmith said, his smile was sardonic. He twirled an imaginary mustache. "We didn't earn the nicknames Hammer and Nails for being soft. Give us a couple of minutes with Cahill and I think we can cool him down."

Hammersmith stood up and walked with Rhonda to

Cahill's office. They entered without knocking, and Rhonda closed the door behind them.

"Where's Croaker?" Cahill barked as he glared up at the pair from behind his desk. "I don't have time for you two right now."

"Oh, I think you do," Hammersmith said. He planted himself on the top of a credenza that ran along one wall. He put the sole of one cowboy boot on the edge of Cahill's desk. Cahill looked pointedly at the boot, but didn't say anything.

Rhonda sat in the visitor's chair closest to Cahill's desk and crossed her long legs. Cahill spared her a three-second appraisal to see if she was purposely Sharon Stone-ing him, and decided that if it ever came down to it, she was probably the more deadly of the duo.

"Well?" Cahill said. He had a high voice to begin with, but under stress he sounded like a ferret on helium.

Hammersmith took the lead. "By any chance did your little temper tantrum just now have anything to do with Fey and the FBI?"

"That's none of your business." Cahill was feeling mightily pissed off, and he wasn't going to be shoved around by a couple of subordinates. "I'm not sure who you two think you are, but you're getting awful close to stepping over your boundaries. You may think you're Batman and Robin, but don't push your luck."

"I forget," Rhonda said to Hammersmith, ignoring Cahill completely, "which one of us is Batman?"

"You are," replied Hammersmith. "I don't have the legs for the part."

Rhonda brought her attention back to Cahill. "Whatever Fey has arranged with the FBI, we think you should go along with it."

"Where do you get off?" Cahill couldn't believe his ears. "Just because you come here from internal affairs and can pull enough strings to stay together as partners doesn't mean you run my detective division."

"Actually, we're not string-pullers," Hammersmith said.

Cahill's head swivelled back to the lanky cowboy.

"We're blackmailers," Rhonda said.

Cahill's head swung back to her. He felt as if he were a spectator in a tennis match. He realized the two detectives were keeping him off-balance on purpose, but he couldn't do much about it.

"Blackmailers?" Cahill asked when neither of the detectives said anything further.

"Yeah," said Rhonda in a slightly breathy voice. She had a sexual edge working and was enjoying this almost a little too much. "Such an old-fashioned word, isn't it?"

"I don't understand," said Cahill. "Are you threatening to blackmail me?" He snorted. "I haven't done anything to be blackmailed for."

Both Hammer and Nails looked at the lieutenant silently.

"This is ridiculous," Cahill said after a bit.

"Then how come you're not telling us to get out of your office anymore?" Hammersmith asked.

"Okay," said Cahill. "Get out of my office." Sweat had popped out on his forehead, and it was clear he was trying to bluster his way through the situation.

"Nice bluff, Lieutenant, but come on. Do we have to spell it out for you?" Hammersmith asked.

"Spell what out? Damn it."

"S-E-C," Rhonda spelled softly in a sing-song voice.

"See you kissing her in the parking lot," said Hammersmith.

"R-E-T-A-R-Y." Rhonda forced the letters to fit the well-known rhyme.

"Why? Because you're poking her." Hammersmith leaned forward.

"A-M-B-E-RRRRRRRR . . ." the two detectives sang together, finishing their Mickey Mouse Club imitation by naming Cahill's secretary.

Cahill looked big-time uncomfortable. If he'd been an ostrich, he would have stuck his head in the sand. "You don't know what you're talking about," he said.

"You're not even convincing yourself," Hammersmith told him.

"What would Mrs. Lieutenant say if she found out that instead of being called out to roll on police calls twice a week, Amber has been hauling your ashes?" Rhonda asked coyly.

"What would Mrs. Lieutenant say," Hammersmith chipped in, "if she knew your overtime balance was almost down to zero from all that code-X time you take to coincide with your secretary's sick days?"

"You guys can't be serious." Cahill looked ill. "My wife would never believe you."

Hammer and Nails laughed. It wasn't a nice sound.

Hammersmith took his boot down and leaned forward with his palms flat on Cahill's desk. He brought his face in close to his supervisor's. "Shit, Lieutenant," he said, his voice low and full of menace. "We've got videos. Can't be letting those internal affairs surveillance techniques get rusty, you know."

Cahill's coloring had gone from pale white to green. He was sweating bullets. "What do you want?"

Hammersmith leaned back to his original position and smiled. "We're easy," he said. "Back off of Fey and let her go and do her thing. We'll cover for her while she's gone. We won't let you down."

"That's it?" Cahill asked.

"Hey," Rhonda said. "We just want to make things run smoothly around here and put villains in jail. You don't screw with us, and we'll take good care of you."

"You two are too much. I curse the day I ever signed your transfer acceptance forms. Not that I had much choice when the pressure came down. How much stuff do you have on other people in this department?"

"Now don't be that way, Lieutenant," Rhonda said, trying to placate. "That would be telling. We can all get along here. Stand by us, stand by Fey, and we'll make you look good."

"Trust us," said Hammersmith, his sardonic smile in place.

• • •

"Videos?" questioned Rhonda as the pair made their way back to their desks.

Hammersmith shrugged. "Hey, so I ran a little bluff. Worked, didn't it?"

"Yeah, but you almost gave the poor guy a heart attack. I'll be surprised if he'll even be able to get it up the next time he's with Amber. He'll be paranoid about being filmed."

Hammersmith laughed. "Amber will be disappointed, that's for sure."

"What are you two laughing about?" Fey asked. She'd been regretting her decision ever since agreeing to let Hammer and Nails talk to the lieutenant. What if Cahill had wanted to talk to her about something else?

"It's cool," Rhonda said. "Your FBI gig is on. Cahill will tell you himself when you go in."

"Just go easy with him," Hammersmith said. "The poor guy has had a bit of a shock."

"Remind me not to get on your bad side," Fey said to them both. "By the way," she said, pausing on her way to Cahill's office. "What's new with Darcy Wyatt?"

Rhonda sat down again at her desk. "The prelim was delayed again last week. His father has hired and fired three different lawyers on the case and they keep getting continuances so they can become familiar with the case. Devon Wyatt is, of course, playing the puppet master where the defense of his son is concerned. I think he's hoping our best victim will die before we get to court."

"From the injuries sustained from Darcy?"

"No. The old gal has recovered very well and she's got all her marbles. But she wasn't in the best of health to begin with, and it is possible she could pass away at any time."

"Is Darcy still in custody?"

Hammersmith answered up. "Yeah, and it's really hacking off Devon Wyatt. The defense has asked for three separate bail hearings, but each time we've managed to shoot them down. Between Darcy and JoJo,

Devon Wyatt is not having much luck getting his clients out of jail.''

"Don't let him fool you," Fey said. "Devon Wyatt isn't concerned about getting either of them out of jail. He probably figures he's better off with both of them in jail. He knows where they are and they can't get into any more trouble. Wyatt is like a magician, he'll use smoke and mirrors to misdirect you and then blindside you when you least expect it."

"Devon Wyatt," Hammersmith said, "is living proof that snakes fornicate with cockroaches."

"How about the other victims?" Fey asked. She still felt proprietorial about the case since she'd obtained Darcy's confession.

"Not much joy there, I'm afraid," Hammersmith said. The coffee room was right behind his desk and he'd poured a mug for both himself and Nails. "Most of them are scared out of their wits to testify. Their response to the trauma they suffered hasn't been as good as with our local victim. The pizza delivery thread and MO ties them all together, but beyond that we don't have much to prove Wyatt was involved in all of them."

"There's something else as well," Rhonda said. "Two of the victims report they thought there was a second suspect at the crime scene."

"They were raped by two suspects?"

"No. They just felt that there was someone else in the room along with the suspect who raped them. Somebody watching."

"You think Darcy had a running mate?"

"Hard to say. We're still checking employees from the pizza chain to see if we can come up with a connection. Nothing yet, however."

"Okay. Stay on it and let me know what happens."

"We'll do that," Hammer said. "So, when you go off to play footsies with the feds, make sure we have some way to stay in touch."

"Yeah," said Rhonda. "And don't hurt the feds' feelings. Let them think they were the ones who arranged

for you to get kicked free. We prefer to keep a low profile.''

Fey gave a mock salute and headed for Cahill's office.
Low profile, she thought. *Those two are about as low profile as a couple of sharks in a goldfish bowl.*

CHAPTER THIRTY-NINE

ASH OPENED THE IMPOSING CARVED WOOD FRONT DOORS
of his unusual residence. Fey was leaning against a low
railing at the top of a flight of six stone steps.

As soon as she saw Ash, Fey knew she wanted him. It
was ridiculous. She was supposed to be here on a professional basis, but her hormones kept getting in the way.
Calm down, she told herself. *You're not sixteen, for heav-
en's sake. Sure, he's lean and attractive, but so are hundreds of other guys in this profession who you wouldn't
touch with a ten-foot pole.*

Ash was not unaware of Fey's reaction. Unwanted emotions of his own had immediately resurfaced, and he didn't
understand them. Fey would not be considered knock-
your-eyes-out beautiful, but there was something attractive
about her that grabbed him. There was something more
that held him—something underneath the surface beauty.
Something intangible, yet very real.

"Pretty impressive string-pulling," Fey said without
moving from the railing. "Four hours after talking to you,
my boss gets a call telling him I've been reassigned to
robbery-homicide as LAPD's liaison with the FBI. I call
down to RHD and they tell me to meet you here." She
didn't say anything about Hammer and Nails's role in the

affair. Ash may be a sexy fed, but he was still a fed. And she'd never met a fed that didn't like an ego stroke. It was a need that was handed out along with the Cracker Jack prizes the feds called badges.

Ash smiled. "Don't tell me, let me guess. Your boss, and both Keegan and Hale down at RHD, are ranting and raving like nuns in a whorehouse."

Fey agreed. "I think they want to tear your head off and spit in the hole. My boss certainly didn't want to let me go, and Keegan and Hale don't want the FBI anywhere near this case." She trailed off with a laugh and Ash felt his heart lurch.

This is silly, he thought, trying to shake himself emotionally. He stood in the open door looking at her without saying anything.

"Can I come in?" Fey asked eventually. She pushed off the railing to a standing position. "Or are we on the way out?"

"No. No. Come in," Ash said, stepping back out of the way and holding the door open for her. He felt like he'd just hit puberty and needed to check in the mirror for new pimples.

Fey moved inside. Under a pinch-waist black jacket decorated with black brocade piping, she was wearing a burgundy jumpsuit. A wide black belt cinched it tight to her waist. Around the belt were distributed a 9 millimeter in a black holster, a black ammo pouch, a black plastic beeper, and a pair of handcuffs. Her shoes were fashionable, but modest black heels—high enough to give a hint of sexual understatement, but low enough to be practical in a police situation. It was a more fashion-conscious look than what Ash had seen her wearing before, and he allowed himself the thought that she may have worn it for his benefit.

Fey looked around with interest. "An interesting choice of homes for a cop. I've never known anyone who actually lived in a church before."

"A converted church," Ash emphasized.

"Okay. If you say so." Fey did a slow three-sixty

turn, taking in the chapel around her. There were no pews or altar, just a huge open room with a two-story ceiling decorated in warm colors and fabrics. "I understand that not many people get invited to visit you here. I'm honored."

Ash didn't know what to say to that, so as usual, he kept his mouth shut.

Fey turned to look at him and gave a self-conscious chuckle. "I didn't mean to sound sarcastic," she said, misinterpreting his silence. "I truly am honored."

"I'm glad you're here," he said. It wasn't much, but it was something.

Sexual tension was catching them both in its undertow, but before it could be acknowledged, a spitting explosion of fury attacked Fey's feet.

The large sphere of frenzied black fur somewhat resembled a cat. It had no ears, one eye, a stub of a tail, and a long strip of fur down one side that had grown back over a long scar in the opposite direction to the rest of the fur.

Rather than pull away in surprise, Fey reached down and scooped the cat into her arms.

Ash let out a yelp and moved forward in order to grab a hissing, clawing ball of spit away from Fey's face. He was stopped short, however, by a strange noise.

The cat was purring.

"Well, I'll be damned," Ash said softly. The cat had hated Holly. Refused to even be in the same room with her.

"What did you say?" asked Fey.

"Nothing," he told her. "Nothing at all."

"What's her name?" Fey asked. "And don't tell me Lucky." The cat was obviously a veteran of many wars.

"You are holding the one and only Marvella," Ash said. "And getting to hold her is the true honor. She's the most antisocial animal I've ever come across."

"Oh, really? Then why do you keep her?" Fey was scratching the cat's head. Marvella appeared to be satisfied with the attention.

"I don't keep her. She keeps me."

"Ah, I see," Fey said. "I'm in the same situation with a lump of fur named Brentwood."

"Brentwood?"

"It's a long story," Fey said. She took a few steps forward. "How about showing me around?"

"Okay."

Ash moved away from the central portal, through the narthex, and into the nave.

"Is it odd living in a church?" Fey asked.

"In some ways perhaps. My father used to preach here."

"So you grew up in the church."

"No."

Fey shifted her eyes to Ash's face when he didn't say anything more. He'd never before told anyone the story behind the church. Certainly not Holly, who'd never even bothered to ask. He'd actually never felt the need to explain the story before, but for some reason he did now.

Some facet of Fey's personality was drawing the story out of him like a magnet attracting steel filings. Ash felt instinctively in tune with her, almost as if he'd known her all his life. He could feel his heart pounding in his chest and felt heat rising up from the base of his neck.

"My mother left my father before I was born. Before he started all this," he waved a hand in the air around him, "and filled it with fundamentalist, hellfire and brimstone preaching." Once he'd started the story, it seemed to flow effortlessly out of the inner recesses where he'd always kept it hidden.

"He loaded the pews with fervent, blind-faith followers willing to throw money at him day after day, week after week. The church services led to a radio show and, eventually, to a full-blown television ministry. He filled first this small church, and later another, larger monstrosity, with cameras and sound stages, and went from bilking a local congregation to bilking a worldwide ministry."

"Bilking?"

Ash nodded. "My father was a very crafty bastard. He

channeled almost every dollar donated into private accounts in Switzerland and the Grand Caymans. Millions of dollars. And the most brilliant move of the entire scam is he knew exactly when to quit. He timed his exit perfectly. The day before the IRS was about to fall on him like a ton of bricks, he did a runner into the sunset.''

"Never to be seen again? End of story?''

"Not quite.'' Ash paused.

"Well?''

"Well, he was able to outrun the IRS and the parishioners who were howling for his blood by escaping to Brazil. The way I understand the story, within a week of landing there he'd bought himself a mansion, hired an army of security guards, and had become Rio's latest overnight sensation.''

"Sounds like nice work if you can find it.''

"Ah, yes, but there was one small problem.''

"There always is.''

Ash nodded in agreement. "While still the toast of Rio society, my father became good friends with a powerful local business man. The man's business was drugs.''

"Oh, my.''

"Oh, my, indeed. My father's new friend may have been powerful within his own little world, but apparently he had even more powerful enemies—enemies that didn't care that my father was with him when they used a car bomb to blow them both to hell.''

"That's a harsh judgment.''

"No. That's justice.''

Ash held Fey's eyes for a second. She literally felt his consciousness trying to probe her thoughts, trying to match them with whatever judgments of character he had already passed. Eventually, Fey broke the eye contact and returned to inspecting her surroundings.

"How did you end up with the church?'' she asked.

"Simple. A bankruptcy sale. I was raised by my mother who worked damned hard to provide for our needs. Her only real talent was playing the guitar, and when she couldn't get work in the local coffee houses or clubs, she would sing for tips on the ferry-crossing circuit in Seattle where I grew up. It was one step up from begging, but she kept us together one way or the other.

"I never knew my father personally, and by all accounts, he never made any effort to know me. He'd swept my mother off her feet before he began his holy-roller routine. When he found out she was pregnant and wouldn't abort me, he walked out and didn't look back.

"My mother told me who he was, and I'd listened to him on the radio and seen him on television, but even at a young age I knew he was preaching a load of twaddle and I had no desire to be around him. When he died, however, I received a sealed letter from his firm of lawyers."

"A will?"

"After a fashion. The bottom line was that I now had sole access to all of the filthy lucre he'd stashed away in various and numerous bank accounts."

"You're kidding? We're talking millions of dollars here?"

Ash nodded. "Millions and millions. Years and years of taking the cream off the top of a nationwide, and finally worldwide, collection plate."

"Holy shit?"

"You could call it that."

"Were you with the bureau when all this happened?"

"Yeah. It was just after I'd caught Michael LeBeck."

"The Vermont Vampire?"

"Yeah."

"You didn't think about quitting?"

Ash shook his head. "Not really. The money may have been in my control, but it wasn't my money. It belonged to all the people who'd donated it over the years, believing they were giving it to a good cause."

"Did they try to get it back from you?"

"Not the individuals, no. The IRS had a crack at me for a while, but I was personally clean and there was no legal way for them to get to the money since it was all out of the country."

"What did you do?"

"I put all the money into a trust administered from Switzerland and the Grand Caymans. The trust invests the money and then uses the profits to back programs in third-world countries, respond to the needs of various children's hospitals, hospices, and the like, or any other disaster or philanthropic arena that the board deems worthy."

"Putting the money your father stole back to work in the areas it should have gone in the first place."

"Exactly. I like the irony."

"Perhaps he knew it is what you would do."

"No. He didn't know me."

"But he left you all the money."

"Only because there was nobody else."

"And I take it you bought the church?"

"My one indulgence. Even though I didn't like him, he was still my father and I wanted a piece of him. This church seemed appropriate since it was where everything began for him. From here he ran a fantastic fraud. And it is from here that I now chase down villains that make what my father did seem insignificant."

"It's a hell of a story."

"Aye, it is, but . . ."

"But," she finished for him, "it's not getting us any closer to the killer of three young boys."

Ash nodded. "Okay, so let's make a start," he said, leading the way into the heart of the church and the working center of his life.

CHAPTER FORTY

THE CONVERTED CHURCH WAS A SIMPLE TWO-STORY REC-
tangle. The middle of the ceiling was vaulted through the
second story over the chapel, which took up the majority
of the first floor. A series of stained glass windows added
drama to the vaulted sides of the ceiling. There were large
tapestries on the walls depicting medieval hunting scenes,
and several well-upholstered couches surrounded a wide-
screen television and a mediocre stereo system. A Nautilus
weight machine stood on a raised platform that had once
held the altar.

A small kitchen, a bathroom, and two other rooms that
had once been used for more intimate meetings were located along one side. One of the meeting rooms had been
turned into a library filled with floor-to-ceiling book-
shelves. The books that lined the walls were an eclectic
gathering of reference tomes, philosophy, true crime, and
oddly, a collection of children's books. The other room
had been made over into a rarely used but comfortable
guest bedroom.

The stained glass in the vaulted ceiling was a testament
to subdued religious craftsmanship. It was beautiful without being overwhelming. It settled for muted splendor
without reaching for magnificence. There were a number
of other stained glass windows throughout the converted
church. The depicted scenes in the windows were of innocuous landscapes, clouds and sun rays, doves with olive
branches, and Celtic designs.

One scene, dominating the large window behind where

the Nautilus weight machine had replaced the altar, did not fit the motif of the others. It couldn't help but catch Fey's eye.

It was a brutal scene of a winged, sword-wielding figure dressed in white robes and sandals. Sun rays parted the clouds of the heavens to fall like beacons of almighty power across the figure's powerful shoulders. One of the figure's sandal-shod feet pinned a red-winged, horned-and-tailed Satan firmly to the ground. Satan's hands were raised in false supplication. The sword in the figure's hand was pressed to Satan's throat, pausing before the final stab that would rend the adversary asunder.

"St. Michael," Ash said, answering Fey's unasked question. "The patron saint of police officers."

Fey studied the stained glass scene. It held incredible power. More than all the other windows combined. "It doesn't appear to be something your father would have erected."

Ash allowed himself a small smile. "I put it in myself."

"Irony?"

"Perhaps," he said. "All that stuff about vengeance is mine, sayeth the Lord."

Fey felt she understood. "And he can have it back as soon as you're done with it," she said.

"As soon as we're done with it," Ash said.

A stairway ran up from one end of the chapel to the second story. At the top of the stairs were two large rooms and a bathroom with a ball-clawed porcelain tub. The rooms ran directly above the other meeting rooms, kitchen, and bathroom below. A balcony walkway looked down into the chapel/living area below.

Ash had converted one of the rooms, the one with a small outside balcony, into his own bedroom. Japanese prints hung on the wall, complimenting the wicker furniture and futon bed on a high pedestal. Ash's upright piano stood against the inside wall.

"Do you play?" Fey asked, indicating the piano. She set the cat in her arms down on the floor where it began rubbing around her legs.

Ash shrugged. "I play *at* the piano," he said. With one hand he tinkled the exposed ivories in a short riff. "I can hold my own doing boogie or jazz, but as a classicist I'm a total loss." What he didn't say was that he was playing far less as the weakness in the muscles of his hands became greater. He felt the nausea rise up inside him as he again became aware of the sand quickly running out of his own personal hourglass.

The room next door was Ash's work space. It was filled with flat work surfaces and several file cabinets. Two computers sat on separate desks, both hooked to a laser printer. Bulletin boards covered the walls.

There were two chairs in the room. Both were well padded, swiveled and tilted, and were on rollers for easy movement across the expensive but low pile carpeting. Fey sat in the chair closest to the door and took in her surroundings.

Ash had been busy. Separate cork bulletin boards were plastered with crime scene photos from each of the murder victim's shallow burial sites. Another bulletin board was dedicated to photos from all three crime scenes that showed common denominators: arms sticking out of graves, the position of the bodies, the knots and design to the bonds, the condition of the victims.

On another wall, across a large whiteboard, Ash had indexed the three victims. A list under each victim denoted individual characteristics. A fourth list denoted common characteristics among the three victims.

Another whiteboard on the opposite side of the room was labeled "killer." Below the title was another list of characteristics.

A third whiteboard was broken down into three categories: clues, leads, and strategies.

"The profiler at work," Fey said.

Ash grunted.

Fey swivelled around in her chair, looking at all of the bulletin board collections. Not studying them, simply trying to assess their scope. "I've heard about all this profiling and analysis stuff. We spoke about it before, but I've never had cause to use it.''

''Chasing a one-off murderer is a lot different than pursuing a serial killer,'' Ash said. ''The mindset, motivations, and psychological profile are completely different. In a regular homicide the motivations behind the killing quickly become clear. There is always a reason—many times a ridiculous reason, but still a reason exists. There is usually a clear suspect—usually someone the victim knows. Sometimes there are several suspects. The trick is to find enough evidence for an arrest and a conviction. In many cases the murderer will never murder again, especially in the cases of family disputes and domestic violence. This doesn't make the murder any less important, but it does make the detection of the murderer different.''

''And in a case like this one?'' Fey asked, waving her hand in a motion that took in all the photos and bulletin boards in the room.

Ash sat down in the second chair and swiveled it toward Fey. ''We're dealing with a serial killer, obviously. The reasoning behind the crimes is not something that a normal person can easily comprehend—madness and chaos are at work. There is still a reason, but that reason is usually so obscure that it only makes sense to the killer. The murderer's connection to his victims is so tenuous that establishing a suspect is extremely difficult.''

Fey stood and walked over to the bulletin board holding the common crime scene photos. She ran her finger over the glossy pictures of sordid violence. ''It's like art in a way, isn't it?''

''What do you mean?'' Ash wasn't following her.

Fey turned back toward him. ''Well, to really understand an artist, you have to understand their paintings. And to really understand the psyche of a serial killer you have to understand what their crime scene is telling you. In a perverse way, the crime scene is the serial killer's canvas—his art. And to be a serial killer is, by definition, to be a successful killer.''

''Absolutely. The first thing that can be told from a

crime scene is if the killer is of an organized or disorganized type. Though still difficult to catch, tracking a disorganized serial killer is the easier of the two types. A disorganized killer has an almost nonexistent self-esteem and feels inferior to everyone around them. They are low-IQ loners whose mental illness has manifested itself over long periods of time before exploding in the violence of a series of murders. A disorganized crime scene indicates spontaneity and a more frenzied assault. The scene itself is most likely the location of the victim-suspect encounter.'' Ash reached out and picked up a pile of duplicate crime scene photos from one of the desks.

"An organized serial killer," he continued, "such as the one we're dealing with here, feels superior to almost everyone—especially the police. They belittle police and psychiatrists as too stupid to catch them. Other than the monstrousness of their crimes, they may only be moderately bright, but they still consider themselves the smartest and cleverest individuals around.'' Ash spread the photos in his hand out on the floor.

"Some of them are," Fey said.

"Yes, but in the end it is their ego more than any other factor that leads to their downfall. They come to believe they are invincible and begin taking greater and greater risks. Sooner or later it catches up with them and the police get lucky.''

"Okay, so we have an organized crime scene," Fey said. "What does that tell us?''

"An organized crime scene indicates planning and premeditation on the part of the offender. The killer often chooses the crime scene and lures the victim there. Or, as I think it is in this case, the victim is killed in one location and transported to another.''

Fey examined the photos. "Our victims were still alive, though, when they were buried.''

"Yes, but I think that they were assaulted at another location and trussed up before being brought to the burial scene.''

"Makes sense," Fey said thoughtfully. "There were no

signs of a struggle at the crime scenes. That would indicate that the killer would have to be strong enough to carry the victim to the burial site.''

"Sounds like JoJo again, doesn't it?"

"Don't start trying to confuse me. Didn't we agree that JoJo didn't do these killings?"

Ash nodded. "Yes. But we have to look at the reasons behind why we are eliminating JoJo as a suspect."

That gave Fey pause. "Gut instinct."

"Yes," Ash said. "But what is sparking that gut instinct?"

Fey mulled the question over in her mind. "First off, I would say JoJo's reaction when he was confronted by Dick Morrison. He was scared—petrified in fact—not at all in control of his emotions or his responses. He was overwhelmed by the situation to the point where he tried to get Dick to kill him—virtually trying to commit suicide."

"I agree," said Ash. "None of the organized serial killers I've studied or pursued have ever reacted in that manner when confronted with exposure. They remain cocksure of their ability to fool the police and get away."

"I also don't like the way the evidence of the tape and the victim's clothing turned up at JoJo's townhome."

"I agree, but why?" asked Ash. "Isn't the easy answer usually the correct answer in police work?"

Fey realized Ash was playing devil's advocate. "Yes, but this time the answer was too easy. Everything was laid out for us to find, as if the pieces of evidence were gifts around a Christmas tree."

"Kind of like the photos and the cassette tape that your people found down in San Diego."

"The thing that bothers me most about that scenario is there were no pictures of the third victim—not in San Diego and not in the townhouse here. Nor was there a Polaroid camera in either location."

"I agree," Ash said. "Ritual killers, like what we're dealing with here, don't change their m.o."

"I don't think the killer did," Fey said. "When we find the killer, I'm betting we find more photos of the first two victims and photos of the third. Also more cassette tapes.''

"There's another thing," Ash said. "When we saw JoJo in the hospital jail ward, he was falling apart mentally—anguished to the point of mental breakdown. His background reveals that, other than on the basketball court, he's a loner with no social skills. If JoJo had become a serial killer, his crimes would be of a disorganized nature. Not plotted and planned and laid out as in the crimes of which he is being accused."

Fey sat back down and spun around in the swivel chair. "Still, objectively everything points to JoJo," Fey said. "And that's why Keegan and Hale at robbery-homicide, Winston Groom at the DA's office, and everyone else is convinced JoJo did it."

Ash grunted his agreement and then asked, "And what does that tell you?"

Fey thought for a minute before answering. "That the killer, whoever he is, has some kind of a connection to JoJo. An obsession, or an axe to grind."

"Exactly," Ash said. "The ritual of the killings doesn't end with the death of the victims. It goes beyond that to include the torment of JoJo, and finally the framing of JoJo for the crimes."

"Are you saying that the crimes will stop if JoJo is convicted?"

"Absolutely not. But the killer may change his focus and method once his goal of framing JoJo has been achieved."

"How many celebrities does the killer think he can frame?"

"I don't think it's JoJo's celebrity status alone that caused the killer to focus on him. I believe the motivation has a deeper connection. I think there is a closer tie between JoJo and the killer."

"Don't tell me you're buying off on Devon Wyatt's evil twin theory?"

"Not completely, but maybe there is some kind of similar connection between the killer and JoJo."

"But what about the DNA? How do we explain that away?"

Ash stood up and began to pace the room. "I'm not sure we can at the moment, but there has to be an explanation. This evil twin stuff isn't going to cut it with a jury."

Fey waved a hand back and forth. "That's just a curveball thrown up by Devon Wyatt. It's bullshit, pure and simple. The semen recovered from the victims belongs to JoJo. Some time before the victims were killed, JoJo had sex with them. If we assume JoJo is innocent, then we have to assume that the killer took each victim shortly after their encounter with JoJo."

Ash was nodding his head, showing Fey that she was confirming his own thought process. "Which indicates," he said, "that the killer was watching JoJo and waiting for his chance."

"Stalking him."

"Absolutely."

Fey looked thoughtful. "Perhaps having a stalker after JoJo would explain the items Hammer and Nails recovered in San Diego."

"Are you saying the killer sent the photos and tape to JoJo?"

"It would fit traditional stalker behavior—taunting his victim."

"Either that, or the tape and the photos were planted by the killer. They weren't hidden very well. And that might explain why there wasn't a photo of the third victim."

"Possibly. Maybe the killer didn't have time to get down to San Diego and plant the photos of the third victim."

"Hard to tell at this point, but it's something that needs thinking about. It might lead to a break."

"So, what's our next move?" Fey asked. Marvella had followed them into the room and had jumped into Fey's lap. She stroked the cat absently. "You've obviously been making charts and collecting photos for six weeks now. Isn't it time for some field work?"

"You betchum, Red Rider. There are two ways to approach the situation. Dig deeper into JoJo's personal background—find out who he has connections with and who might want him to take this kind of fall—and take a harder look at the victims. Both JoJo and the killer had contact with each of the victims. It's the one area we know JoJo and the killer overlap."

Fey cocked her head like the RCA dog. "Unless there really is an evil twin who's doing the killing," she said. "Then JoJo wouldn't need to have had contact with the victims."

Ash gave her a glare of mock disgust. "Now it's my turn to ask you if you believe Devon Wyatt's dog and pony show?"

"Only kidding," Fey said, straightening up her head. "All three of the victims were street chickens. JoJo's sexual fetish must kink that way. From all the publicity on this case, it's clear he wasn't into women. And I know somebody who might be able to give us a handle on victim number one."

<hr/>

CHAPTER FORTY-ONE

"Hɪ, Sʜᴀʀᴏɴ. Hᴏᴡ'ʀᴇ ʏᴏᴜ ᴅᴏɪɴɢ?"

"Could be better. How about you?"

"Pretty good," Fey told the receptionist in Dr. Winters's office.

After discussing their game plan, Fey had agreed to meet with Ash again much later in the evening when they could put the first part of their plan into action.

Fey had hoped that Ash would suggest getting together

for dinner before going out. She sensed that it was in the forefront of his mind, but when he didn't come out and say anything, Fey suggested it herself.

She was pleased when Ash immediately agreed, but was still a little unsure as to why she'd had to push the issue. She knew she was reading the vibrations she was getting from him right, but also perceived something holding him back.

Ash had suggested an Indian restaurant in Santa Monica, near where they intended to start their investigation. When Fey agreed, she hoped it would be the beginning of solving two riddles—the mystery surrounding JoJo Cullen, and the enigma of Special Agent Ash.

Leaving Ash's converted church, Fey had driven home and changed. The last few weeks had been so busy that she had only gone to one other session with Dr. Winters. It had been an interesting fencing match with the psychiatrist trying to draw more of Fey's childhood abuses into the open, and Fey fighting to keep them bottled up where she believed they couldn't hurt her.

She had thought about cancelling her current session, but when her afternoon freed up, she decided to follow through and keep the appointment.

Sharon, the receptionist, was a slightly obnoxious anorexic who looked as if she'd had more plastic surgery than Michael Jackson. Fey was suspicious that Sharon's breasts, nose, eyes, chin, and tummy had all become familiar with the surgeon's scalpel. A bad Dolly Parton wig, along with makeup by Tammy Faye Baker, capped an ensemble of sixties fashion rejects. Fey had to wonder if the woman didn't work for Dr. Winters in return for therapy to deal with apparently rock-bottom self-esteem. How much more of herself could the woman change on the outside, before she'd be forced to deal with what was on the inside?

That was a question Fey was reluctantly being compelled to also ask herself.

Fey didn't quite know why Dr. Winters kept Sharon in the front office. She never had a good word to say about anything. The woman was one of the most depressed individuals Fey had ever come across. Perhaps Sharon was there so that Dr. Winters's patients could be around somebody who was worse off than they were.

"So, do you really think JoJo 'Jammer' did those murders?" Sharon asked. Fey had never mentioned to Sharon that she was a police detective. However, Fey realized Sharon must have recognized her from the number of times she'd been on television recently in connection with the case.

"It's hard to tell," Fey said. "I guess we'll have to see what happens when the preliminary hearing starts in a couple of weeks." She was actually getting tired of answering questions about JoJo's case. Everyone she knew assumed she had inside information because she'd been part of the original arrest.

Not being able to escape the case anywhere she went was getting to be a real pain. Every time Devon Wyatt pulled another rabbit out of the defense hat, Fey found herself in for a fresh round of questioning from her friends. It was bad enough with people discussing the case all day at work, but the constant bombardment from the checker in her local supermarket to her hairdresser was really getting tiresome.

Fey sat in the front lobby for a few minutes before Dr. Winters came out of her office.

"Hello, Fey. I'll be right with you." Dr. Winters handed a cassette tape to Sharon. "Put this with Mr. Hawkins's file," she said, taking a fresh cassette from a stack on a credenza.

"Come on in," she said to Fey, leading the way back into her office.

Fey gave Sharon a nod of her head, which the receptionist ignored, and followed Dr. Winters. She waited for the doctor to go behind her desk and install the fresh cassette for Fey's session.

In the beginning, Fey had been reluctant about having her sessions taped. Dr. Winters had explained, however, that as a patient progressed through therapy, sometimes it was necessary to listen again to a particular session for something that could lead to further progress.

Once Dr. Winters had the tape functioning, she started her fifty-minute alarm running and turned her attention to Fey. "How's the woman responsible for JoJo Cullen doing?" she asked.

Fey shook her head. The damned case was at the forefront of everyone's mind. It was the last thing that Fey needed to talk about when the session was costing her a hundred dollars an hour. She'd almost rather talk about her father. Almost.

"I know it's probably the last thing you want to discuss," Dr. Winters said intuitively. "You must constantly be asked about the case."

Fey sat down in one of the easy chairs and rubbed the back of her neck. She blew out a deep breath. "There certainly is a lot of attention from the media," Fey responded.

Dr. Winters sat down in the chair next to Fey's. "Your friends and neighbors as well, I should expect."

Fey shrugged. "I understand it, but it's hard when you can't escape it. Not even here," she said pointedly.

Dr. Winters laughed. "But that's the whole reason why I brought it up. It must be driving you crazy."

"It is."

"How are you holding up?"

"Not bad, but if I'm right, the worst is yet to come."

"Really, why do you think so?"

"Because I don't think JoJo did it." Fey felt as if she was dropping a bomb, but she knew Dr. Winters was ethically bound to keep what was said in the sessions a secret.

"Wow," Dr. Winters said. "I thought the whole case was almost a foregone conclusion."

"Not according to the defense."

"Nonsense," Dr. Winters said, waving a hand in the air. "Anyone with any common sense can see that this Devon Wyatt person is strictly using chewing gum to put together a defense. But now you come along and say he might be right?"

"I'm not saying that Devon Wyatt is right," Fey said.

"I just think there's more to this case than meets the eye."

"Are you alone in this thinking?"

"Almost," Fey said. She went on to explain about Ash and their assumptions about the case. It felt good to go through the whole process with an objective outsider. It gave Fey a clearer view of her purpose. Perhaps it was worth the hundred dollars an hour.

"And you say you are going to start off by asking your brother about the first victim, this Rush character?"

"There's a chance Tommy can tell us something more about the kid. We need to figure out how the killer came into contact with his victims. Rush was supposed to be into the rave scene, and Tommy is making a living from staging raves. They could have had contact. It's a small culture."

"How do you feel about that?" Dr. Winters asked. She stood up and walked to a sideboard where a coffee pot stood. She poured two cups.

"Tommy staging raves, or asking him for help?"

"Both."

Fey took a sip of the coffee Dr. Winters had set on the low table next to her. "I don't much like Tommy being into the rave scene. First of all it's only quasilegal. And with all the drugs that are supposedly done at these things, I think it will be very hard for Tommy not to backslide."

"Is that your responsibility?"

Fey had touched on her relationship with Tommy in an earlier session. "You tell me it isn't, but it's still hard for me to genuinely feel that way."

"You had him sent him to jail."

"No, he sent himself to jail. All I did was stop being his victim."

Dr. Winters clapped her hand. "Very, very good," she said. "I think you're beginning to understand." She took a sip from her own coffee cup. "Now, are you sure that going to Tommy for help with Rush is not simply an attempt to check up on him?"

Fey shrugged and answered, "Maybe a little of both."

''Well, that's a start,'' Dr. Winters said. ''At least you're not deceiving yourself about it.''

''Do you think I shouldn't go?''

''No, I think you should. Your brother is the only close relative you still have, and you need to resolve your issues with him. It will help you when it comes to resolving your feelings toward your deceased parents.''

''What good does picking at scabs do?'' Fey asked.

''Believe it or not it helps the healing process by cleaning the pus out of the wound.''

Fey and Dr. Winters continued their discussion until the fifty-minute alarm bonged softly. They both stood.

''I'm not quite sure what we accomplished this time,'' Fey said.

Dr. Winters laid a hand on Fey's arm. ''Not every session is going to lead to a breakthrough. Therapy takes time.''

Fey thanked the doctor and took herself out through the office's secondary exit door. The separate entry and exit assured patient privacy.

After Fey left, Dr. Winters finished her coffee while making notes at her desk. She turned off the tape of the session and took it out of the machine. She stretched and walked back to her reception area. Her next patient was already waiting.

''I'll be right with you,'' Dr. Winters told him. She handed the cassette to Sharon.

''For the Croaker file?'' Sharon asked.

''Of course,'' Dr. Winters said with a smile. She picked up a fresh cassette.

''This way, Mr. Napier,'' she said, taking her next client back with her.

Sharon tapped the tape on one thumb. One of the things that she enjoyed most about her job with Dr. Winters was being able to eavesdrop on the patient sessions. She didn't do it all the time, and certain patients interested her more than others.

When Sharon wanted to listen in to a session, she put

the office phones on hold and went into the suite's small cubicle bathroom. The bathroom and Dr. Winters's office had a common wall with a shared heating vent.

On one occasion when she had been in the toilet, Sharon heard a patient shouting and crying. When the patient calmed down, Sharon found that if she stood on the toilet lid she could continue to listen through the vent. Since then she had made a practice of listening in whenever she thought something might be of interest. Dr. Winters was totally unaware of Sharon's habit, and the receptionist revelled in her knowledge of other people's secrets. It made her feel special, superior to the people who tromped through the office on a daily basis.

Sharon hadn't been interested in Fey to begin with, until Fey paid for her sessions in cash. That was unusual and made Sharon suspicious. When she recognized Fey as one of the detectives involved in the JoJo Cullen case, she made sure she eavesdropped.

This last session that Dr. Winters had with Fey, however, was of particular interest. She'd never done it before, but this time Sharon wondered how best to use what she'd learned—corroborated by the tape in her hand—and, more importantly, how much money she could make from it.

✥

CHAPTER FORTY-TWO

"DETECTIVE JONES, THERE'S SOMEBODY AT THE FRONT desk to see you." The volunteer's voice droned over the speaker system into the squad room.

"What now?" Brindle asked of nobody in particular. She was by herself on the MAC table, and between answering the MAC calls on the phone and at the desk, she was having trouble getting any real work done.

Hammer and Nails were in the field, and Alphabet was down in the jail interviewing a Persian who'd been arrested for making a "terrorist threat" directed toward his business partner—"I will kill you! It is a blood feud!" As far as Brindle was concerned it was bad movie dialogue and simply the way Persians did business. She just wished they wouldn't keep getting the police involved in all their nonsense. The city attorney's office was never going to file, so it was all a waste of time.

Dropping her pen on top of her paperwork, Brindle headed for the detective desk. Entering the reception area, she saw a waiflike girl sitting in one of the visitor's chairs against the wall. The girl stood when she spotted Brindle.

Brindle felt she should recognize the girl, but couldn't immediately place her.

"Do you remember me?" the girl asked. There was almost a cry for recognition in her voice. Self-consciously, she pushed a strand of lank blond hair out of her face, and the penny dropped for Brindle.

"You were with the boy being rousted by the pimps down in West Hollywood. You told us about Rush."

The girl nodded, and Brindle felt she'd passed some kind of test.

"What can I do for you?" she asked.

The girl looked around her, as if she felt exposed in the lobby. There were several other people there dealing with vehicle releases and other problems.

"Do you want to go somewhere to talk?"

"Yeah," the girl said.

Brindle led the girl to an interview room. The girl was skittish, like a kitten placed in a threatening environment.

"Don't worry, I won't bite you," Brindle said, sensing the girl's reluctance.

Under a fatigue jacket the girl wore a t-shirt with the phrase, "What are you looking at, Dick Nose?" emblazoned across the front. Torn jeans and combat boots made up the rest of her attitude clothing. An outward defense worn like armor against a cruel world.

"What's your name?" Brindle asked.

"Do I have to tell you?"

Brindle sat down in the chair opposite the girl. She pushed it back from the table, giving the girl breathing space. This was an interview, not an interrogation. "Look," Brindle said. "I'm not stupid. I know you must be a runaway from somewhere. And it has to be somewhere pretty bad for you to choose life on the streets over returning home."

The girl didn't say anything, so Brindle continued. "I'm not going to send you home if you don't want to go. You came to me, remember? You can leave any time you want. I won't stop you. I will help you, though, if that's what you want."

The girl still didn't say anything.

"Are you hungry?" Brindle asked.

The girl nodded.

"Let me see if I can rustle something up." Brindle stood and started for the door to the room.

"My name's Lake," the girl said suddenly.

Brindle half-turned. "Nice to meet you, Lake. I'll be back in a minute. Okay?"

"Yeah," Lake said, seeming to relax in the hardback chair.

Brindle left the door to the room open, not wanting to put any stress on the fragile truce she had established.

Taking the station's back stairs two at a time, she made her way to the jail. Once there, she located Alphabet as he was finishing up with his terrorist threat suspect. She filled him in on the girl upstairs.

"You going to take her a couple of jailhouse burritos?" Alphabet asked.

"Yeah. They're in the microwave."

"Sounds like cruel and unusual punishment to me. If you fed me that stuff I wouldn't tell you squat."

Back in the interview room, Brindle half-expected to find Lake missing. She was still there, however, puffing on a cigarette in defiance of the No Smoking sign on the wall. Brindle didn't care. She wasn't going to start picking nits at this point.

Alphabet entered behind Brindle and set two burritos and a can of Pepsi in front of Lake. "Remember me?" he asked.

"Yeah," Lake said with a genuine smile. "You're the guy who tore Bomber a new asshole that night."

"And a pleasure it was," said Alphabet. He watched as Lake tore open one of the burritos and chomped into it as if it were her first meal in a week.

"I know you didn't come here for the cuisine," Alphabet said.

"The cu-what?" Lake said, her mouth still half-full.

"The food," Alphabet cleared up his meaning. "What can we do for you?"

"You guys were kind of hard to track down," Lake said. "I finally had to ask that prick Hogan over at sheriff's vice if he knew who you were."

"I'm sure anything he told you about us wouldn't be flattering."

"Yeah. He never has anything good to say about anyone. He's an asshole."

"Okay, so you worked hard to find us. So what's it all about?" Alphabet hardened his stance, and Brindle laid a hand on his shoulder.

"Easy boy," she said, not wanting to lose Lake's cooperation.

"It's cool," Lake said. "He's right. It's no big deal."

"You came here for a reason other than a free meal?" Alphabet continued to push.

"Shit, man. Back down already," Lake said. "I'm getting to it. You got a cab waiting or something?"

Alphabet laughed. "Now that's more like it," he said.

The banter had eased Lake's emotions. She casually lighted another cigarette and blew the first puff of smoke toward the ceiling. "The kid you saved from Bomber and Mace. His name was Terry Macklin."

"Was?" Brindle said, picking up on the past tense.

"Yeah," Lake said. A tear suddenly appeared in the

corner of her left eye and ran down her cheek. Lake didn't make a move to wipe it away.

"Did Bomber and Mace do it?" Alphabet felt his anger rising.

"No. He squared with them—ripped off some rich fag's cocaine stash and gave it to Bomber to recycle. Terry OD'd. Got some spiked crank."

"I'm sorry," Brindle said.

Tears were freely flowing down Lake's cheeks now. She didn't appear to be embarrassed by them. "He was just a kid."

The two detectives considered that to be an odd statement. Lake couldn't have been over fourteen or fifteen herself.

"I felt like his mother or something," Lake explained.

The two detectives were silent. Waiting.

"When he was alive, he didn't want to come to you guys with this. He said you wouldn't care. He said you'd arrest us. Make us go home." She was crying hard now, almost shouting.

"It's all right," Brindle told the girl. She stepped around the desk and took Lake into her arms.

The girl clung there for a second, but then pushed Brindle away. She wiped her face on her sleeve. "Hey, no big deal, right? One less rabbit on the street." Street tough was making a comeback.

"No," Alphabet said softly. "It's always a big deal. But sometimes there just isn't anything that can be done. He was lucky he had a friend like you."

"Terry! Terry! He had a name, damn it!"

"Whoa, girl," Brindle said. "We aren't the ones to be angry with. We want to help you."

"Where were you when Terry needed help?"

"We were there the night he needed help with Bomber," Alphabet said. "He didn't seem to want any more help. There's shelters, group homes, children's services. It may not have been the perfect answer, but we would have done something if he'd asked. Not everyone is a predator."

The assertion had a cooling effect on Lake. She got hold of herself, slipping back into her hardened emotional defenses. "Yeah. You're right," she said.

"What didn't Terry want to come to us about?"

"JoJo Cullen."

Brindle and Alphabet looked at each other. If Lake had wanted to achieve an effect, she'd done so. The atmosphere in the room was suddenly charged.

Ever since JoJo had been arrested, cranks had been coming out of the woodwork looking for their fifteen minutes of fame. This was different, however. Lake hadn't gone to the tabloids, or the six o'clock news—wanting to get her face on national television. It had been hard for her to come to the station, and she'd come looking specifically for two detectives who she felt she could trust.

"What about JoJo?"

"JoJo cruised by one night and picked Terry up."

Alphabet and Brindle both felt as if they were holding their breath.

"He didn't do nothing kinky. Just an alternate around the world."

Homosexual anal sex was kinky as far as Alphabet was concerned, but he didn't want to argue the point. "How did Terry know it was JoJo?"

"Shit, man. Where have you been? The street knows these things. The guy was pretty hard to miss. Anyway, everybody knew the Jeep with the Slamdunk license plate."

"Where did JoJo take Terry?"

"Back to his pad. They did the dirty deed, and then JoJo brought him back and dropped him off."

"Had Terry been with JoJo before?"

"Once or twice. It was a no sweat, easy deal."

"So JoJo was a homosexual who liked street rabbits. How does that change anything? Maybe Terry was just lucky he didn't end up like Rush and the others."

"That's not the point," Lake said.

"No? What is?"

"It's what happened after JoJo dropped Terry off."

"Yeah?" Alphabet ran a hand across the back of his neck in exasperation. This was getting to be a bit too much like pulling teeth.

"When JoJo dropped him off, the next john to pull in was this guy in a blue van. He called Terry over, but JoJo had tipped big and Terry figured he didn't need to work again. Terry blew him off and we started walking away, but the guy didn't want to take no for an answer. As we walked past the van, the guy tried to grab Terry."

"Physically tried to grab him?"

"Yeah, but Terry was fast. He poked the guy in the eye with his thumb and we took off running."

"Did the guy chase you?"

"Yeah, but he didn't stand a chance. We laughed about it later. After JoJo got arrested, though, I thought about it some more. Terry said it didn't mean nothing, but it didn't feel right. I mean JoJo treated Terry cool. No weird shit. He liked a little booty, but that was it. No hassles. But the guy in the van—he'd cut you up in a heartbeat."

"You get a good look at this guy?"

Lake shrugged. "Just a flash when he grabbed at Terry."

"Black guy? White guy?"

"White guy with bad acne scars."

"Hair?"

"Yeah, he had hair. Why? Are you jealous?"

"You're not funny," Alphabet said.

"Black hair," Lake said, serious again. "Buzzed close. He was tall—about the same size as JoJo."

"You ever see him again?"

"Yeah. He was around for a while. Cruising, mostly. A looky-loo."

"Any word on the street about him?"

Lake took her time answering. "The other kid—Ricky Long—I asked around. Like Terry, he'd done JoJo a couple of times." She paused, picked up the second burrito and put it in the pocket of her fatigue jacket. "But the noise on the street is that his last gig was the guy in the blue van."

CHAPTER FORTY-THREE

DARCY WYATT LAY ON HIS CELL BUNK LISTENING TO HIS heart pound. His cell mate was a buffed-up Aryan Alliance member who was awaiting trial on ten counts of armed robbery. Bubba Jack Henderson was built like an ape and had more tattoos than a warehouse full of topless dancers. His IQ, like his personality, had a lot in common with a fence post.

Darcy's previous cell mate had been a Jamaican check-kiter who'd been afraid of his own shadow. The check-kiter had been given his day in court, however, and was now on his way to doing a county lid at Wayside Honor Rancho.

The check-kiter had been little company, but he'd posed no threat. Bubba Jack Henderson, on the other hand, scared Darcy to death. He'd been moved into the cell earlier in the day, and his eyes had lit up when he'd seen Darcy. It was brutal lust at first sight.

"You hearing me, sweet cheeks?" Bubba Jack asked from the upper bunk. "You and me gonna be real good friends once the lights go down. I do hope you're a screamer. I love a good screamer."

The cells had just been locked down for the night and Darcy felt as if his heart was going to burst through his rib cage.

"Gonna be just like in that movie *Deliverance*. Gonna make you squeal like a pig."

Icy sweat beaded on Darcy's forehead and his stomach churned in fear and anticipation.

''You better not tell nobody, sweet cheeks,'' Bubba Jack said, his voice filled with soft menace. ''And you better not try to get away. If I don't nail you here, I'll nail you somewhere else later. And if I have to wait, I ain't gonna be gentle.''

Darcy thought he was going to suffocate. He knew his father had pulled numerous strings to get him released, but a couple of detectives, Hammersmith and Lawless, had been in court at the arraignment and had fought to keep Darcy in custody. The judge, who happened to have an eighty-year-old mother of his own at home, had agreed with the detectives and refused bail.

A preliminary hearing had been held two weeks later. Hammersmith and Lawless had been in court again testifying, under proposition 115, in place of the victims. They had made Darcy sound like a mass murderer. Darcy's lawyer, Harley Bryson—a high-priced contemporary of his father's, had only been able to do limited damage control.

Without being able to pick apart the elderly victims themselves, Bryson had been faced with trying to crack the steel reserves of the two detectives. Between their testimony and Darcy's confession—which Bryson had been unable to get suppressed for the preliminary hearing—Darcy had been easily held to answer and sent back to county jail to await trial. Bail had been denied again.

Darcy had tried talking to his father, pleading with him to get a different lawyer, or to find a way himself to get Darcy out on bail. Devon Wyatt, however, simply told Darcy to grow up. Things couldn't be as bad as he was making out. Didn't Darcy know how busy he was representing JoJo Cullen?

The other factor was that with Darcy in jail, Devon Wyatt didn't have to worry about what further excesses Darcy might commit.

Darcy tried to accept the situation. He still believed his father would get him out sooner or later. And his father was right, it wasn't too bad.

But then Bubba Jack Henderson entered the frame.

"You're gonna love it, sweet cheeks, when I make you my woman. It's gonna be a butt-busting party." Bubba Jack gave a bit of a sigh. "I surely do love popping cherries."

Darcy was trying to think, trying to figure his way clear. He knew some things, some things that may just buy him a ticket out of this threatened hell. He knew he should have used this ace earlier, but he'd thought he wouldn't need it. Even though he'd wanted to get at his father, he'd believed his father would somehow get him out. But that wasn't going to happen fast enough.

Darcy knew what he'd done was bad, but he also knew about what somebody else had done. And what that person had done made Darcy's transgressions pale by comparison. As he lay agonizing on his bunk, he tried to make himself believe he could work a trade off—his knowledge for a "Get out of jail free" card, or at least an escape from Bubba Jack.

He began to pray. Darcy prayed for access to a phone. And he prayed for those two damn detectives to believe him. That his sins had brought him closer to the devil than the Lord didn't bother him. He knew God forgave all sins—even grave ones.

He kept his eyes closed, and tried not to concentrate on the rumbling in his bowels. His sphincter itched.

His lips moved in silent supplication.

He knew he needed a miracle.

And suddenly, he heard one walking down the row of cells.

CHAPTER FORTY-FOUR

RHONDA LAWLESS PUT DOWN THE PHONE RECEIVER AND gave a cat-that-ate-the-canary grin to her partner across the table.

"Surprise, surprise," she said. "Darcy Wyatt wants to talk to us, and he wants to talk to us right now."

"Without his lawyer?" Hammersmith asked. There was mock amazement in his voice.

"Without his lawyer," Rhonda confirmed. "And since Darcy called us, we don't have to advise his lawyer that we're going to talk to him."

"No fuss, no muss, no Miranda problems," Hammer said. He stood up. "Maybe we'll get to the bottom of this thing yet."

The two detectives had been working late at the station, catching up on a stack of minor cases that had been piling up. Darcy's off-hours call had come at a good time.

"Darcy's lucky he caught us," Rhonda said.

"You know what they say about the Lord working in mysterious ways," replied Hammer, buckling on his gun and handcuffs. "So, let's not look a gift horse in the mouth."

"We're going to have to work on getting you a new set of metaphors."

"Can I also get one of those metaphor racks that hang on the wall? I've always wanted to be able to alphabetize my metaphors."

"I swear, Hammer, you spew so much bullshit around,

I'm beginning to think you're anal-expulsive instead of anal-retentive.''

The trip to county jail took thirty minutes through the evening traffic. Another twenty minutes was spent checking in at the front desk and arranging for an interview room. A further fifteen ticked by as Darcy was brought down from his cell.

When he entered the interview room, Darcy looked even worse than normal. His long, dirty blond hair was pulled back in a ponytail, giving full exposure to his weasel face and weak chin. His generally anemic countenance was further intensified by the pale and clammy pallor of his skin.

"Sit down," Hammersmith said. He pointed to a chair on the other side of a small wooden table where he and Rhonda were sitting.

Darcy almost scurried to the indicated seat.

"Thanks," Rhonda said to the deputy who had brought Darcy in. The deputy tipped his finger to his head in a caricature of a salute, and left them alone. He closed the door behind him.

Darcy had his hands clasped on the table in front of him to stop them from trembling. "Hey, how you guys doing?" he asked.

"Don't try and ingratiate yourself," Hammer said. "We didn't drive all the way down here to make small talk. You got something worth talking about then say it."

Darcy felt sick. This wasn't going to work.

He thought of Bubba Jack waiting for him back in the cell.

He swallowed.

Somehow, it had to work.

Hammer set a small tape recorder in the middle of the table and turned it on. He spoke the date and time and named those present in the room.

"Does your father know you called us?" Rhonda asked.

"No."

"How about your lawyer?"

"No." There's no way either of them would have agreed to let me talk to you."

"But you still called us?" Rhonda asked. It was important to get the legalities straight.

"Yeah. I called you." Darcy knew how the game was played.

"Why?" Hammer took over the interrogation. He and Rhonda were one of the few teams of detectives that could split the responsibilities of an interrogation.

The days of the good cop/bad cop routines had gone the way of bright lights and rubber hoses. The good cop/bad cop technique of intimidation had been so successful that liberal defense lawyers had found a way to make it against the law.

Current standard procedure was to let only one detective do the talking. The single lead detective technique ensured that only one line of questioning was pursued—two detectives asking questions often tore an interrogation into separate tangents, often destroying the fragile bond established between interviewee and interviewer.

Hammer and Nails didn't have that problem. They were so in tune that each knew instinctively where the other was going during questioning. They preferred to respond to the interrogation as it progressed, controlling it by trading off the questioning and keeping a suspect off-balance.

"I want to trade," Darcy said, plunging into the deep end.

"Trade?" Hammer asked. Rhonda was sitting next to him, and he suddenly felt her toes making their way under his pants leg. He twisted his head to look at her, but she was ignoring him. She was sitting up close to the table, her hands beneath it.

"Yeah. You know," Darcy said, not picking up on the seduction that was happening on the other side of the table. "I give you something, and you give me something in return."

"What could you possibly give us that we'd be interested in?" Rhonda asked. She knew it was her turn to do the talking. Hammer was slightly flustered. Her hand was in his lap.

"What I can give you is big. Bigger than big. So big it will make you famous."

"What if we don't want to be famous?"

"Come on," Darcy said. "Everyone wants to be famous."

"And just what do you expect to get in return?" Hammer asked. He was back in control of himself, but Rhonda was doing her best to distract him again. Underneath the table, he could feel her trying to pull his zipper down.

"I want out of here. I want the charges against me dropped in return for me turning state's evidence."

Hammer laughed. "Let's get out of here," he said to Rhonda. He would have stood up to leave, but she had her hand inside his pants, her fingers wrapped around his quickly hardening member.

"You must either think we're crazy, or you really do have something to trade," Rhonda said to Darcy. Her visible demeanor gave nothing away concerning her under-the-table manipulations.

"I do! I do!" said Darcy. He'd always had trouble with women, but this one seemed to understand him. Funny enough, so did the first female cop who'd talk to him when he'd been arrested. Croaker. That was her name. She seemed to understand him also. Maybe it was something to do with being a female cop. Maybe it gave you an understanding of outsiders. "Just get me outta here."

Hammer leaned across the table. The tips of his ears were turning red. "You're full of shit," he said. "You claim you've got some hot scoop, and we're just supposed to roll over and release you on eighteen counts of rape, ADW, and attempted murder—release you so you can go out and do it all over again? I don't think so."

Darcy looked askance at Rhonda. "I'm not lying here."

"You must be," Hammer said. "Your lips are moving." He suddenly backed off as he felt Rhonda squeeze him tightly under the table. He relaxed slightly and pushed back in his chair. Rhonda's hand loosened its grip slightly and went back to a more stimulating movement.

"The man is right," Rhonda told Darcy. "It doesn't matter how big your information is, there's no way you're walking on the charges."

"Not even if it has to do with JoJo Cullen?"

Both Hammer and Nails were silent for a few seconds after that bomb dropped.

"What are you saying?" Hammer asked eventually.

"I'm saying that you got the wrong guy, and I know who the right guy is."

"Bullshit."

"No way, man," Darcy said. He was feeling a little more sure of himself. "I'm not crazy either. I wouldn't try to make a trade like this without being able to deliver the goods."

Rhonda's hand had slipped back out of Hammer's pants. The situation had become far more serious than they had imagined. Hammer squirmed in his chair, putting himself back together again.

"Saying yes or no won't be up to us," Hammer said. As independent as the pair liked to think they were, everybody had their limits.

"I'm only dealing with you. Nobody else."

"That's cutting your options down."

"I'll take that chance. I've seen how you two have taken on my father. You ain't scared of nothing. If anybody can make this fly, it's you."

"I'm not so sure we want to make it fly," Hammer said. "You're one bad dude. It doesn't seem to make sense to let one major asshole go just to catch another one. If you were a small fish giving up a big fish it might be different. As it is . . ." Hammer shrugged.

"You've already got me," Darcy said. "I don't expect to walk away clean. I can do time, but it's got to be country club time. I'll do whatever therapy you want. When I get out, I'll have to register. You'll know where I am. I can be monitored. I can be stopped from doing it again."

"Bullshit," Hammer said again.

Darcy shook his head. "It's better than what you've got."

"And what's that?" Rhonda asked.

Darcy leaned forward. "Those kids in the graves.... There's gonna be more. The guy got JoJo just like he wanted, but he won't be able to stop forever. When that feeling comes over him maybe he can fight it, subdue it, but he can't stop it. I know how that works. He has the taste. He'll kill again. And again."

Rhonda felt her heart pounding. "You've got to give us something more," she said.

"What's in it for me?"

"What do you want?"

"Get me away from Bubba Jack Henderson."

"Who?"

"My current cellmate. Either get me away from him, or get him away from me. I want to be safe in here. If you leave me in a cell with him, I won't be around to give you the information you want."

"All right," Hammer said. "We'll go that far. No other promises."

Darcy's relief was so great he felt light-headed.

"What are you giving us in return?" Rhonda pressed.

Darcy thought of the best clue he could give them with the minimum of information. He didn't want to lose his edge.

"There's a blue van involved," he said.

"There's a lot of blue vans out there," Hammer said. "Give us more."

Darcy sat back with his arms across his chest. This was the moment of truth. "That's it," he said. "I can't afford to give you more."

"Get your stuff together, Bubba Jack," the deputy said from outside the cell. "You're moving on."

Bubba Jack swung his feet off his bunk and hopped to the floor. "You got something for me?" he asked.

The deputy held up three cartons of Marlboro cigarettes.

"Compliments of Detective Hammersmith. He threw in an extra carton."

Bubba Jack smiled. "I knew the Hammer was a man of his word." Using economical movements, learned from long years of incarceration, he began to gather his few belongings. "You tell him that if he ever needs Bubba Jack to do him a favor again all he's got to do is ask."

"Easiest smokes you ever earned—scaring fish like Wyatt."

Bubba Jack gave the deputy his patented hard scowl. "I give good value. All the Hammer man has to do is get me put in a cell with his target, and he knows I'll do the rest. Works every time."

Almost wilting under Bubba Jack's stare, the deputy was sure the con was right.

Bubba Jack's features suddenly lightened. "You ever see that lady partner of his?" he asked.

The deputy gave a low wolf whistle in reply.

"Damn right," said Bubba Jack. "Now that's what I call a real woman—capable of kicking your butt or screwing your brains out, depending on how the fancy takes her."

"I think we bit off almost more than we can chew," Hammer said. They were back on the freeway in their plain detective sedan.

"I certainly know we ended up with more than we bargained for when you reached out and touched Bubba Jack." Rhonda felt excitement move inside of her. It was tied to a sexual urge. She delighted in turning Hammer on when there was nothing he could do about it. She loved to watch him fight to stay in control.

"We both agreed there was something more to this case than meets the eye. All I expected was to put enough pressure on Darcy to get him to tell us about it," Hammer said. "I never expected to be faced with this kind of proposition."

"Be careful what you wish for," Rhonda said. "You might get it."

"And speaking of touching," Hammer said.

Rhonda laughed. She reached out and placed her hand in his lap again. "You should have seen your face."

"Yeah. Well, what did you expect?"

Rhonda's hand began to wander. "A blue van," she said, thinking out loud. "What can we do with that clue? How could a slimeball like Darcy know anything about the JoJo Cullen case?"

"Slime attracts slime. If we can figure it out, we won't even have to consider doing a deal with him."

"I'll do a deal with you," Rhonda said.

"What do you propose?"

She had his zipper down and her favorite playmate exposed. "You drive, and I'll take care of everything else." In the dark interior of the car she leaned over and brought her mouth down to meet her hand.

A short time later, she asked, "Does Mr. Happy like this?"

"Silly question," Hammer said, fighting hard to keep his concentration on the road.

Rhonda continued to stroke him with her hand. She loved the way he felt. "Do you know why men always name their penises?" she asked.

"I have no idea." Hammer's voice was hoarse.

"It's because they don't want a stranger making all their decisions for them." Laughing again, she took him back into her mouth to finish what she'd started.

CHAPTER FORTY-FIVE

THE MUSIC COMING FROM THE WAREHOUSE COULD BE heard from a block away. It was after midnight and almost pitch black. All of the street lights in the area had been broken out at one time or another and not replaced. Venice Beach had been undergoing urban redevelopment for years. The Bohemian, eclectic culture that defined the area, however, was not going down without a fight. Yuppie developers may rule the daylight hours with mobile phones and Range Rovers, but the night still belonged to a beat generation born forty years too late.

The glow from the loading bay of the condemned warehouse acted like a wrecker's beacon in the fog, luring ships to destruction on a hostile shore. From inside, the pounding beat of a generic, angry anthem poured out into the night.

"We're a bit overdressed for this aren't we?" Ash said as he took in the rag-tag clothing of the kids walking the cracked sidewalk toward the warehouse entrance.

Fey was still wearing the burgundy jumpsuit, her gun and equipment hidden under the black brocade jacket. Ash was in cowboy boots, Wranglers, and a faded denim work shirt with the sleeves rolled up. He carried a five-shot Smith & Wesson .38 with a two-inch barrel in his boot, and a two-shot derringer tucked down by his scrotum. The derringer was of minor discomfort, but on two occasions it had saved his life. Ash figured discomfort was a small price to pay.

Fey had the scent of blood in her nostrils. She could

feel the pulse of the case quickening, and it had her in its grip. "My mamma always taught me," she said, "that if you ever found you were underdressed, you copped an attitude and made out as if everyone else was overdressed. We just need to reverse the psychology."

A trio of girls in combat boots, heavy tights, plaid skirts and camisoles with holes cut out over their nipples, half-skipped and half-ran past Fey and Ash. Their hair was a punked out mish-mash of unnatural colors. They were obviously high.

"Cute butt," one of them said, and patted Ash on his posterior as she cruised by. "For an old guy."

"Charming," Ash said.

"Actually, I thought she was pretty observant." Fey waggled her eyebrows.

"You're embarrassing me," Ash said.

"You're about as embarrassed as a peacock in a petting zoo."

Fey watched the girls enter the warehouse. Actually, their appearance had somewhat startled her. "I didn't realize body piercing and tattoos were still the rage," she said.

"I'm sure we can get you hip in a hurry," Ash said.

"No thanks. I think I'll pass. Being plain old white bread might be boring, but at least it isn't painful."

Two back-lit bodies took up a defensive position in the warehouse doorway.

"I think we've been made," Ash said.

"Now that's the height of cool," Fey said. "Using female body builders as bouncers. This could end up being more fun than we figured."

Ash could feel his pulse quicken. A year ago, he'd have been ready for any physical confrontation. Now, he was having trouble simply keeping up with Fey as she stepped up her stride. He mentally girded himself for the effort ahead. Getting into a tussle with a pair of female steroid freaks was not particularly high on his agenda, but Fey was already taking the lead.

"Hello, girls," Fey said, as she stepped onto the loading dock.

The women stood with their muscular arms crossed over t-shirts that fit as tight as second skins. Above the right breast the t-shirts bore their wearer's names. The taller and wider of the two was Alice. The other, a smaller-scale model of the first, was Trixie.

"I don't think this is quite your scene, Grandma," Alice said. She had stepped forward to bar the warehouse entrance. Behind her, Ash and Fey could see a line of kids waiting to pay the entrance fee that would get them past a line of oil drums. The music emanating from inside was louder in the entrance. It sounded like the wail of a screeching cat laid down over a jackhammer back-beat.

"Grandma is it?" Fey was immediately getting her dander up. "You just had to use the G word up front and piss me off."

Alice looked a little surprised at Fey's aggressive attitude. Ash doubted the female bouncer got much back talk from anyone who wasn't drunk or high.

Trixie stepped up into the space next to her partner. "If you're here to look for a runaway kid, you're out of your depth." Her tone was matter of fact. The roles of the two bodybuilders was clear—the intimidator and the peacemaker.

"Let me get this right," Fey said. "You're running a quasilegal, movable nightclub in a condemned building with no liquor license, no business license, no health department permits, and more designer drugs than a Timothy Leary reunion, and to top things off you call me grandma. I know somebody is out of their depth here, but it sure isn't me."

Alice unfolded her arms and took a step forward. Fey shuffled her feet into a balanced stance. Trixie moved wide to flank the action.

"Ladies, ladies, please," Ash said, sliding between the potential combatants. "Your testosterone is showing. The next thing you know, all of you will be sprouting mustaches and Elvis sideburns." With Fey behind him, he had his hands held out palm up. ''There's no need for any of this.''

''Yes there is,'' Fey said. ''She called me grandma.''

Ash didn't need this. ''Cool your jets, will ya, Fey? I'm trying to make nice here.''

''I tell you what, Grandma,'' Alice said to reassert herself. ''Any time you want to rock n' roll, you just let me know.''

Ash looked at Trixie who smiled at him and shrugged. ''Sounds as if they're auditioning for the World Wrestling Federation, doesn't it?'' she said.

''Pay per view,'' Ash agreed. ''I guess there's just no reasoning with some people.''

''Shall we let them duke it out?''

''I have this feeling,'' Ash said, ''that you are expecting trouble tonight, but not from someone like us.''

As Ash and Trixie conversed, the tension between Fey and Alice had eased.

''Could be,'' Trixie said.

''Want to tell us about it?''

''You're cops?''

''Even grandmas have to make a living,'' Fey said.

There was movement in the entrance.

''What are you doing here?'' a voice asked, somewhat amazed.

''Hello, Tommy,'' Fey said to her brother.

Tommy Croaker wore torn jeans over combat boots, and a sweatshirt with the sleeves cut off. His thinning hair was tied back in a ponytail with a leather thong, and a shower of decorative moons and stars hung from the earring in his right lobe. He looked older than Fey remembered, his face weathered from years of substance abuse and physical neglect. He had put on weight, however, since Fey had last seen him, and she took that as a good sign.

But even though he was her younger brother, he looked older. A lot older. And a lot more shopworn. Fey had been around the block once or twice, but Tommy's odometer was turning over for at least the third time. He was over forty and still living on the edge of society. Drugs and rock n' roll were all he knew. Fey felt an ache in her heart for him, but knew she couldn't let it show in her face or her attitude. Tommy had to make it on his own. Fey couldn't help him anymore—unless he asked her.

Behind Tommy were two more bouncers, a Mutt and Jeff male team this time.

"I thought the whole idea of a rave was that if the guests got rowdy and tore the joint apart it didn't matter," Fey said. She almost had to shout to overcome the sound of the band that had enthusiastically ripped into a new sequence.

Tommy glanced at his collection of bouncers. "There are other problems, but you wouldn't understand."

"Let's not get off on the wrong foot," Fey told her brother. "Of course I understand. Anytime there is money to be made from a venture there are going to be sharks in the water who want to take a bite. You're being muscled, aren't you?"

Tommy looked uncomfortable.

"That's how you ended up in the hospital a few weeks ago." Fey knew she was winging it, but all of the pieces seemed to be fitting into place. "All that stuff with the PCP being squirted over the ravers was intimidation. Protection is an age-old racket. It started right after the invention of prostitutes and lawyers."

Tommy grinned at Fey's verbal expression. "You always shoot from the lip, don't you?"

"I need your help, Tommy."

"Whoa," Tommy said. "You need my help? That's a first." He turned to the bouncers who were still hovering in anticipation. "My sister, the cop," he said to Alice. "You're lucky I came along. From what I hear on the street, she's capable of biting your head off and peeing in the hole."

Alice looked disgruntled.

"Don't take it personally," Fey told her. "Just because I'm old enough to be a G word, doesn't mean I can't still kick butt." She put her hand on Tommy's arm. When he didn't pull away, she asked, "Is there somewhere we can talk?"

"Come on," Tommy said. He turned and headed into the warehouse with Fey and Ash following. "Keep your eyes open," he said to his bouncers. "Sooner or later, Ottoman's crew will come."

Tommy led them past the barrier of oil drums. Two more bouncers took money from the line of punked-out patrons at a gap in the barrier. The kids in the line wore identical sneers under spaced-out eyes. Black and leather garb predominated, decorated with rips and metal.

"The generation of hate and violence," Tommy said.

"Don't tell me you're getting philosophical in your old age, Tommy," Fey said to him, surprised. She had never known him to express an insight before.

"Jail does bring some changes," he said.

For the first time, Fey noticed there was no bitterness in the words.

"Who's Ottoman?" she asked.

"It's like you said. He wants a part of the action. Raves make money. Look around." They were walking through a crush of tightly packed bodies bouncing and crashing against one another. The inside of the warehouse was a wide open space with sagging ceiling beams supporting temporary spot and laser lights that burned into the crowd below. There was a crude bar set up to one side—three planks laid across two oil drums. Three bouncer-sized bartenders pulled beer from iced tubs and hard liquor from boxes on the floor behind them. The band—four skinheads who could scream and play bar chords—performed on a raised platform in the middle of the floor, their music drowning out even the hum of the generators that supplied the electricity. "The overhead is nonexistent," Tommy continued his soliloquy. "The booze fell off the back of a truck. The bands are cheap. There's no taxes, no licenses, no insurance, and nobody to sue. It's an entrepreneurial heaven."

"It's also illegal," Fey said.

"Well, you can't have everything." Tommy stopped

walking. They were at the far end of the warehouse. The noise was still loud, but bearable. He turned to face his sister. There was a challenge in his eyes. "Is that what you want to talk about? Have you come to show me the error of my ways? I thought you said you needed my help, but now I get the feeling you're here to arrest me."

"Not me," Fey said. "I'm not working vice. What you do is your choice." She paused and then said, "What's Ottoman's tie to all this?"

"He wants a cut. If he doesn't get it, he sends out a group of heavies to disrupt the gig."

"How does that affect you? I thought these gigs were all staged at different places."

"Yeah, but the customers know who's running them. Word on the street is a powerful thing. If you can't keep the danger at an acceptable level, even the burn-outs won't come. They may be fried, but they ain't stupid."

"So you're going to keep him out with your hired muscle."

Tommy shrugged. "Gotta try."

"Why not pay?"

"Would you?"

"No. But since when did you start making the same decisions that I would?"

"My brains might be fried like everyone else's around here, but I'm still a Croaker."

"I didn't realize that was something that made you proud."

"Just because you're a tough act to follow," Tommy said, "doesn't mean I'm going to be a screw-up forever."

There was another pause as the two siblings eyeballed each other. "You wanted help?" Tommy asked finally.

Fey drew a photo out of her pocket and extended it to Tommy. "This character was supposed to make the rave scene on a regular basis. All we know about him is that his name was Rush, and he was probably a street chicken."

"You're using past tense. Is he dead?"

"If he wasn't, I wouldn't be here. Dead is what I do."

"Yeah," Tommy said. "Silly question." He took the picture. "I know Rush," he said, taking a quick glance. "He was a location scout for me. Helped find a good rave site. His real name was Michael Rushmore. He was a runaway from Kansas or somewhere. Turned tricks over in West Hollywood to keep him in Twinkies. He was a freak for Ecstasy, or any other designer drug that turned up at a rave. Couldn't get enough of the stuff."

"Anything else?"

Tommy shrugged and handed the photo back. "He was a star-fucker. Always bragging on how he'd screwed this movie star or that band member. I always figured he was only running off at the mouth."

"He ever talk about JoJo Cullen?" Ash asked.

Tommy's eyes widened. "Is that what this is about?"

"He was the first victim."

"Holy shit. Rush said he was doing JoJo. Everybody just blew him off."

"When was the last time you saw him?"

"It was right after he said he'd done JoJo again. Said Jammer had come looking for him on the boulevard. He was flashing a wad, playing Mr. Cool. He made the scene for a while and then I remember him splitting with some guy. It looked like a love-business thing. They got in a blue van and split. Any of this a help to you?"

"Hard to tell at this point, but at least we have more information than when we came in."

"How do you know he got in a blue van?" Ash asked. There was something there that bothered him.

"It was when we first started having trouble with Ottoman. I was hanging outside, eyeing the action on the street to see if I could spot trouble coming."

"Trouble sounds as if it's still coming," Fey said.

Tommy looked at her. "Life ain't nothing but trouble. You know that. It's just one damned soul after another."

"You can work this out?" she asked him.

"If not, I know where to turn for help."

"You've changed," she said. This new Tommy confused her. She still didn't approve of him, but somewhere he seemed to have discovered a trace of backbone. "I don't understand."

"Maybe it was time," he said. And then he shocked her by kissing her on the cheek.

"Let's get out of here," she said to Ash, turning quickly to hide the moisture in the corner of her eyes.

⊷⊷⊷
CHAPTER FORTY-SIX

OUTSIDE OF THE WAREHOUSE, ON THE DARKENED SIDE-walk again, Fey and Ash walked back toward Fey's detective sedan.

"Interesting," Ash said. "But where does it lead us?"

"I'm not sure," Fey said. "Perhaps nowhere. On the other hand, we probably have enough information now to make a positive identification on the first victim. Perhaps there's something there that will give us a clue as to what set the killer off."

"Maybe," Ash said, his brain tumbling possibilities around. "But I'm really getting vibes now that the answer lies in JoJo's past."

"Vibes? Who do you think you are? Shirley MacLaine?"

"Nah. My past lives haven't been that interesting."

"Well, I don't know about this vibes stuff, Shirley, but visiting the orphanage in San Diego where JoJo lives sounds like the next logical step."

The pair walked on for a few strides before Ash spoke up again, changing the topic. "I have a feeling there's a lot more going on between you and your brother than most people know about."

"More vibes?"

"Like ringing a bell."

"It's a classic love-hate relationship," Fey said. "I've felt the need to protect Tommy all his life, and he's resented me for doing so. I've tried leaving him to his own devices, but when he crashes into walls he somehow still sees it as my fault. I've never been able to win with him."

"Sounds as if he's controlling you instead of the other way around."

"You going to send me a bill for the psychoanalysis?"

"Easy, there, girl. I'm not passing judgment—simply making an observation."

"Sorry," Fey said with a sigh. "Actually, you're more right than you know. It's one of my more sensitive buttons."

A primered Chevy Camaro with its windows down cruised past them on the street. Four punks sat in the blacked-out interior, heavy metal pounding from cracked speakers.

Ash stopped and watched them pass.

"You can't even see their eyes, but you can still tell their purpose," Fey said. She had also stopped as the car drove by.

"Maybe they're just out looking for a good time," Ash said.

"And maybe the pope's getting a blow job right now."

Ash laughed. "You really have a way with words." He watched as the car cruised past the warehouse loading dock. "Ottoman's heavies?"

"Probably. Rent-a-thugs nineties style."

The Camaro turned around and drove past the warehouse loading bay again. It headed back toward Fey and Ash.

"Checking the lay of the land and building up their courage," Fey said.

"Hitting that one last line of coke," Ash agreed. In a softer voice he asked, "Are you going to let Tommy handle this one on his own?"

"And let him have all the fun? I don't think so."

"It's his fight."

"Yeah, but he owes me a good outlet to vent my frustrations. Four low-lifes in a bandit-mobile could be exactly what the doctor ordered."

"So we're going to roust these guys for you, not Tommy?"

"Sounds good."

"Hell of a piece of rationalization."

"I think so."

Ash watched the car slowly make its way back towards them. He'd never backed down from a fight in his life. Recently, because of his physical complications, he'd stopped looking for trouble. This was Fey's play, however, and he had to back her up. He bent over and removed the five-shot. He stood up and, holding it casually down by his side, swallowed it in his left hand. In a mock sonorous voice he quoted, "Once more into the breach, dear friends."

Danny Olson had started working for Ottoman while he was still in high school. He'd pushed drugs, broken heads, stolen cars, and hijacked trucks, anything and everything that Ottoman had asked him to do. He was now a trusted lieutenant in Ottoman's growing organization.

Tonight his job was to disrupt the rave being put on by Tommy Croaker. Ottoman wanted a piece of the rave action. There was a lot of fast money floating around in the underground parties, and they could also act as great laundries for dirty money from other ventures. Croaker didn't want to play ball, however, which meant he had to be taught a lesson.

Olson had been behind the PCP squirt gun attacks from a few weeks earlier. Croaker hadn't been brought into line, but he had folded his parties for a while. He was now operating again and Ottoman didn't want competition that wasn't paying its way.

Rumor had it that Croaker's sister was a cop, but that didn't cut much mustard with Olson. He'd done time inside, and he knew he'd do time again. Inside or out didn't make much difference to him. Either way, it was survival of the fittest.

Sitting beside Olson was Jaime Baca, a weasel-faced youth who would do anything to get into a fight. He rolled a Louisville Slugger between hands graced with knife fighter's fingers.

In the back seat were the Anderson twins, Denny and Gary, looking like tag-team rejects from the World Wrestling Foundation. They loved to hit things, people, cars, walls—it didn't matter. If it tried to hit back, all the better. Chunky metal rings adorned all of their fingers under initials that spelled out the traditional "hate" and "love."

"Waddya think?" Baca asked, as the Camaro drove past the warehouse for the second time.

"Croaker's beefed up security, but it don't look like anything we can't handle," Olson said. "You guys ain't scared of women with muscles are you?" he asked the twins sitting behind him.

Denny Anderson giggled. "Me and Gary will handle 'em," he said and giggled again. "Grab 'em by their tits and toss 'em around like swinging a cat by the tail."

Denny elbowed Gary sitting next to him. Gary giggled, and butted heads with Denny.

"You guys are screwed up," Olson said, watching the pair in the rearview mirror.

"Hey, man," Baca said suddenly. "What's that?"

Olson brought his eyes back to the road and saw a decent-looking woman staggering down the middle of the roadway.

"Now, would you look at that," Olson said. "Anybody in the mood for a bit of over-the-hill pussy?"

"What about Croaker's rave?" Baca asked.

Olson slowed the Camaro down to walking pace. "It ain't even in full swing yet. We got time. Screw first, fight later."

"My kinda party," Denny said from the back seat.

"Can we thump her when we're done?" Gary asked.

"Why not?" Olson replied. "She's so drunk, she'll never notice."

• • •

Fey tried not to overdo the drunken gait as she stumbled down the middle of the street. Her hair was mussed, and her clothes were artfully dishevelled. She could hear the Camaro coming up behind her, but she didn't want to turn and look at it just yet.

She heard the car slowing.

"Hey, Mama," Olson said through his lowered window.

Fey stopped walking and turned to look at him with glassy eyes. "What?" she asked through a slur.

This is too easy, Olson thought, sensing something wasn't quite right as he stopped the car next to her. His little head, however, had taken over the thinking process for his big head. His misgivings were chased away by thoughts of playing hide the salami with this woman who had dropped into their laps.

Fey leaned over on the car door. Her blouse was un-buttoned to the point where Olson got a full view of her creamy breasts. Her arm slid off the door and she slithered awkwardly down to the ground beside the stopped car.

"Man, is she out of it," Baca said, his voice excited. He opened his door and started to move around the back of the car. "We gonna do her good."

Olson opened the driver's side door. He put one foot on the ground and began to lever himself out of the vehicle.

From the ground, Fey waited for the moment when Olson's body weight was moving forward and his balance in transition. Hoping her timing was right she flashed out a hand and grabbed Olson by his exposed crotch. She squeezed hard, digging her nails in, and pulled. Olson screamed.

Moving like a wraith, Ash flowed out of the shadows on the other side of the street. Knowing he didn't have the strength for an extended fight, he was fully concentrated on doing things right the first time.

As Baca rounded the trunk of the Camaro, distracted by Olson's scream, Ash slid into position behind him. With precision born of desperation, he drove the point of his cowboy boot into the back of Baca's knee.

Baca's head snapped back as his knee gave out. Ash grabbed a fistful of long, greasy hair and bounced Baca's face off the Camaro's trunk. The Louisville Slugger clattered to the ground as Baca's senseless fingers lost their grip.

Taking advantage of Olson's off-balance weight, Fey hung on to the young thug's scrotum and pulled him to the ground. Maintaining her grip, she rolled over on top of him and drove the business end of her .38 into the soft flesh below his ear and behind his jawbone.

In the back seat of the car, Denny and Gary didn't know exactly what was happening. Denny pushed the driver's seat forward and started to clamber out.

From her position on top of Olson, Fey kicked the Camaro's driver's door hard as she saw Denny's foot touch the ground. The heavy door flew back and crushed Denny's knee in the jam. He howled and fell back into the car's interior.

On the other side, Gary tried to lever himself out from behind the passenger seat. He pulled up short when Ash slammed the flat side of his five-shot Smith & Wesson into Gary's forehead. The big thug grunted and dropped back.

Ash slammed the passenger door closed, and holding the five-shot in a two-handed grip, rested it on the door through the open window. "I want to see hands, now!" he yelled. His voice was deep and commanding, easily penetrating the music blasting from the car stereo.

Denny and Gary had been this route before and immediately placed their hands flat on the headrests of the seats in front of them. Blood ran freely into Gary's eyes from the gash on his forehead. The pain from Denny's crushed knee screamed along his nerve endings. Neither brother, however, whimpered or complained. Trapped in the back of the Camaro, they were in a no-win situation, and they had both been around long enough to know when to cut their losses.

Ash took one hand off his gun long enough to reach in and hit the power button on the car stereo, killing the tape in the deck. "You boys must have serious hearing impairments," he said in wonder to his docile captives.

Leaving her gun jammed into Olson's neck, Fey released her grip on his groin. Getting her feet under her, she moved to a crouch, grabbed Olson by the front of his t-shirt, and dragged him the rest of the way up with her. He was scrawny enough not to give her much trouble.

Shock, more than anything else, was keeping Olson from thinking straight. He moved when Fey dragged him around the back of the car and pushed him across the trunk from the passenger side. On the way there, they passed Baca, who was just beginning to moan from his crumpled position in the roadway.

Another group of kids and two other cars had passed by the action. There had been no comments made as everyone looked out for their own skin by staying clear. The kids, however, must have alerted the bouncers at the warehouse because Fey could see Alice and Trixie jogging toward their position.

"Who the hell are you?" Olson asked, as Fey quickly searched him for weapons.

"Your worst nightmare," Fey said. "A woman with more *cajones* than you." She threw a switchblade into the gutter after first snapping it in half.

"Do you know who you're screwing with?"

"Well, let's see. We've got the Pillsbury Doughboy twins in the back seat. We've got Jose Jimenez impersonating a big leaguer on the ground behind the car. And you're Rotarian of the Year. Am I close?"

Alice and Trixie pulled up next to Fey.

"Forget I ever mentioned the word grandma," Alice said, watching Fey finish dealing with Olson.

"There's a few tricks still left in this old broad," Fey told her.

"You've been real stupid," Olson said. "Whoever you are, Ottoman will get even with you."

"No, he won't," Fey said. "Ottoman is smart. He's a mean bastard, but he isn't psychotic. He's a businessman. When he finds out who I am, he'll know that if he retaliates I'll make life so hot for him it'll singe the hair on his balls.

He'll weigh the odds and realize that there are easier ways of making money." She leaned forward and whispered into Olson's ear. "And if I ever see you again, I'll pull your cock off and shove it so far up your ass you'll be peeing out your ear."

"There's a nice cache of cocaine sitting in plain sight on the front seat," Ash said. It had actually been in the glove box, but there was nobody around who wanted to quibble over technicalities. "The ignition is also hot-wired, so it's a lock that we have ourselves a stolen ride here."

"How terrible," Fey said. "All this crime in the streets. Sounds as if the local police should be called."

The other Mutt and Jeff duo of bouncers from the rave jogged up behind Alice and Trixie.

"You kids think you can handle this from here?" Fey asked.

"Yeah," Trixie said. "We'll move everything a couple of streets over so the rave can run, but you can rely on the local cops getting this bunch as a 'gimme' tonight."

Alice picked up the Louisville Slugger from where Baca had dropped it. With the other hand, she easily picked up the groggy Hispanic and threw him over the trunk on top of Olson.

"Watch out for these two Baby Huey look-a-likes," Ash said, backing away from the car window. "Given the chance, they still have some fight left in them."

"No problem," Alice said, flexing her muscles and slamming the bat down on the car roof to punctuate her statement.

"Give my compliments to Tommy," Fey said, before stepping back to join Ash and move away. "Tell him we're square on favors tonight."

CHAPTER FORTY-SEVEN

"I HAVE GOOD NEWS AND BAD NEWS," ASH TOLD FEY the following morning as they set off for San Diego.

"Everything in life is a trade-off," Fey replied. "What's the good news?"

"We may have a break in the case from an outside source."

"I don't see a down side to that news."

"The source is Zelman Tucker."

"As in Tucker the Sucker? *American Inquirer*'s top-selling sleaze artist? That Zelman Tucker?"

"Don't rub it in."

"How did he get involved?"

"I made him a deal."

Ash was driving Fey's detective sedan. Fey turned and rested her back against the passenger door to look at him. "Let me get this straight," she said. "You made a deal with a man you hate and despise? How does that work?"

"I did it to get him off my back. I never dreamed he'd come through."

"You said he wasn't stupid—that he knew what sells. A man like that has to have his sources."

Ash scowled. "And apparently they're better than ours."

"What kind of deal did you make with the devil?"

Ash kept his eyes on the lanes of the 405 freeway as he steered the car through the thickening morning traffic. "I told Tucker that if he came up with a clue to crack this case, I'd collaborate on a book with him."

Fey had to laugh. "Talk about selling your soul."

"We'll see," Ash said. He took a cup of too-hot McDonald's coffee from between his thighs and sipped at it tentatively.

After leaving the rave and dealing with Ottoman's thugs the night before, the pair had been too wired to call it a night. Surprising himself, Ash had suggested a small after-hours jazz club. Fey had agreed, not knowing exactly where the night was leading, but willing to go along for the ride.

The Blue Cat was buried in a darkened side street near San Vincente and Bundy. A small blue light and a simple cutout of a blue cat were the only indication of the club's location. Word of mouth among true jazz fans was what kept the club alive, not reliance on trends or high-profile advertising.

From their reception, it was clear to Fey that Ash was an appreciated club regular. It wasn't long after their arrival before he was coaxed up onstage to jam with the band.

After two numbers, Ash was given the lead. Moving from reluctance to passionate intensity, Ash caressed the piano through half a set. The notes were pure and clear, ringing with the hidden pain that is true blues. Finally, finishing on a sweet riff, Ash shook hands with the other musicians and moved offstage to a solid round of applause. He waved to the crowd, who were mostly ignoring the *"no smoking"* laws, and moved back to where Fey was making her way through a second designer coffee.

"Maudlin crap," Ash cynically called his choice of music. Fey, however, picked up the change in the man. The music had cost him physically. He was sweating, almost shaking, and his mood had turned bleak.

A short while later they left the club and Fey returned Ash to his somehow lonely residence. Her heart ached for what she sensed in him, but she refused to pressure him about it.

Outside the car, he had turned to her window, stopping her from driving away. "There are things you don't know about,'' he said. The reference would have been cryptic if both of them hadn't been able to clearly read what was in the other's mind.

"I won't let you hide it from me forever," Fey said. She reached a hand through her window and caressed his face as he leaned forward against the car door.

Ash pivoted his head and kissed her hand gently. He then turned and walked away to the front door of the converted church without looking back.

Fey had waited until Ash was inside before taking a deep breath and driving away. Somehow, some way, she was determined to break through to Ash. It had become very important to her.

Now, on the road with the morning sun glaring in their eyes, Ash's mood appeared to have pulled itself out of the dumps. Despite his chagrin at having to deal with Zelman Tucker, he seemed more at ease.

"When did you hear from Tucker?"

"Last night. He'd been calling every thirty minutes until I answered."

"At least we kept him up late," Fey said, as if offering some kind of solace. "What kind of break are we talking about? It must be something pretty hot if Tucker was that bent on getting through to you."

"I'm not sure what he's got," Ash said. He changed lanes to let an old Pontiac, held together by rust and prayer, fly past at thirty miles over the speed limit. "He wants us to meet him for lunch in San Diego after we finish at the orphanage."

"I can't wait," Fey said. "Anybody who can get your goat like this guy has got to be worth his weight in gold."

The orphanage that JoJo had called home as a child, and had returned to as a man, was in an older area of San Diego on Adams Boulevard. Diagonally across the road was a large children's bookstore named after a Mark Twain story. On either side were businesses either giving up their dying breath, or being born from the hope that renovation was bringing to the area.

"Hardly looks like a good place to raise kids," Ash said. The orphanage building was a tattered brownstone that appeared to have seen better days.

"Hammersmith and Lawless said the exterior was misleading. Apparently, JoJo funded the refurbishing of the interior."

There was a chain-link fence around the back of the property. Inside the perimeter, behind the main building, there was a small patch of grass along with several basketball courts that looked in decent shape.

"That figures," Fey said, referring to the good condition of the basketball hoops, nets, and courts.

"Well, why not?" Ash asked. "Basketball was what JoJo was all about. Living here, he must have been a larger-than-life hero to the kids."

"Let's not lose track of the fact that the man is accused of being a serial killer. I know this makes me a cynic, but what is a grown man doing living and hanging out with a bunch of kids?"

"Just because he was homosexual doesn't mean he's a pedophile."

"I didn't say JoJo was a homosexual," Fey said. "I'm well aware that there's a big difference between being homosexual and being a pedophile who preys on young boys. Just like there's a huge difference between being heterosexual and pedophiles who prey on young girls. That doesn't change the fact that all of the street chickens JoJo picked up were barely into puberty. I don't know if he was preying on any kids from the orphanage, but I'll bet he was fighting the urge big time."

Ash had parked the detective sedan against the curb in front of a hydrant. He hung the radio microphone over the rearview mirror. "You have a point," he said with a sigh. "But does that mean we stop trying to clear him of the murder charges?"

"No way," Fey said. "Because if we do, then whoever the real killer is will just keep on killing. We're already agreed on that point."

"There will always be more victims," Ash said. "Even

if we clear JoJo and catch the real killer. There'll always be killers and consequently there'll always be victims.'' Ash didn't catch the scathing look Fey sent his way.

"That's depression talking," she said, unknowingly hitting Ash where he lived. "Yes, there will always be victims, but that doesn't mean we stop trying to save or help as many as we can."

Ash took the keys out of the ignition and rubbed a hand over his face. "You're right," he said. "And the simple fact is that you and I have to keep believing in what we do, otherwise our own lives have been meaningless."

"Whoa, slow down, big boy," Fey said. "It sounds as if you better come with me to my next therapy session." The words were out of her mouth before she could stop them. Nobody knew she was in therapy. "Just joking," she said, trying to recover when Ash turned his head toward her.

"So we both have our secrets," Ash said, hearing the lie in her voice.

"I said I was just joking."

"Bullshit." Ash knew the stigma law enforcement attached to therapy.

"How about we call a truce and go inside and do this interview?" Fey opened her door and slid out of the car.

"Truce," Ash said, and followed Fey up the walkway toward the orphanage.

Inside the main entrance to the Sacred Heart orphanage was a small carpeted lobby with a receptionist's desk at one end. There were several padded chairs and a low table with scattered magazines. Behind the desk was an open door that appeared to lead into the rest of the building. A slender woman in a complete nun's habit came through the door and slid into position at the desk.

"Can I help you?" she asked. She had a long nose on which a pair of wire-rim glasses perched tentatively.

"We're here to see Sister Ruth, the Mother Superior," Fey said. "She's expecting us."

"Your names?" the nun asked, standing up.

"Detective Croaker and Special Agent Ash."

The nun gave them a look that could have fried the devil, but only said, "Wait here." She turned and went out through the doorway.

"I don't think we rate real high on their Christmas card list," Ash said.

"What do you expect?" Fey asked. "JoJo must be a real hero to these people. They're caught between not wanting to believe JoJo is guilty, and their own guilt at perhaps not recognizing a killer within their midst." Fey waved a hand around the small reception room. "I'll bet this setup wasn't necessary before the news media descended on this place after JoJo was arrested."

The slender nun returned trailing behind an older woman in a black business suit with a startlingly white blouse. A modified coronet sat on coarse black hair piled into a high bun. Over the years, the sun had not been kind to the skin of the matronly woman. It had wrinkled her face with hundreds of tiny lines like the cracked bottom of a mud-dried river bed.

"I'm Sister Ruth," she said in a voice used to being obeyed. Her eyes through heavy lenses were cold steel. She held out her hand to shake first with Fey and then with Ash. "Please come through to my office." She spun on her heels, not waiting to see if she would be obeyed, and stalked away.

Fey and Ash followed Sister Ruth through the open doorway and into an office a short way down the corridor. The office was carpeted in the same fashion as the lobby, and contained a desk with two padded chairs in front of it. A graphic rendition of Christ on the cross wearing a wicked crown of thorns and painfully impaled hung on one wall.

Sister Ruth gestured for Fey and Ash to sit.

"Coffee?" she asked.

"Please," both detectives replied at the same time.

Sister Ruth turned to a countertop that was part of the built-in shelving behind her desk, and poured into three mugs that had been arranged around a stoppered coffee flask.

Sister Ruth handed out the mugs and then sat down behind her desk. "Father Peter, who is our head administrator, is sorry that he couldn't see you today, but he has business with the Los Angeles archdiocese."

"JoJo Cullen business?" Ash asked.

"When isn't it these days?" Sister Ruth replied. "However, I had thought that by this time we would have been done with law enforcement types. Mr. Cullen's room has been searched so many times that I'm surprised the carpet hasn't been worn out." It was clear from the Mother Superior's tone that she would be hospitable to a point, but no further. "And I'm afraid I don't understand where both of you fit in with the grand scheme."

Fey took a chance. "Sister Ruth, do you believe JoJo is guilty?"

Sister Ruth suddenly reached out to touch the simple cross that hung against the hidden shape of her bosom. "I'm not sure I understand what you mean."

"It's a simple question, Sister. Do you believe JoJo is guilty of having sex with three young male prostitutes, and then burying them alive?"

"Are you trying to be brutal on purpose?"

"No, Sister. I'm just trying to cut to the chase."

Sister Ruth continued to fondle her cross. She was somewhere between fifty and seventy—an impression that in some women seems to last forever.

"I have been with the Sacred Heart Orphanage since its inception, which happened to coincide with my own induction into the Sacred Heart Order. Many years have passed since then, along with many children." She paused, self-consciously dropping her hand from her cross. "I am not naive. Though I am a nun, I have not sheltered myself from the outside world. When you have had a hand in as many lives as I have, that would be an impossibility. Therefore, I can conceive that a child could pass through this home, grow up—even become spectacularly successful—and later be found guilty of the most heinous of crimes. But, in my heart of hearts—despite of all the evidence we keep hearing about—I cannot accept that JoJo Cullen is guilty.'' Her face had taken on a stonelike expression of defiance.

"Good,'' Fey said, smiling. "Because we don't believe it either.''

Sister Ruth looked stunned. "What? I don't understand.''

"We're well aware of what you, the other members of your order, and the kids who live here must have gone through in the last few weeks. Every official entourage or media maven has come here with one mission in mind— to pound more nails into JoJo Cullen's coffin.''

Sister Ruth nodded her head, still cautious. "It has not been easy. JoJo has been very good to the orphanage. His arrest has been a tremendous blow to many of the children here to whom he was more than just a big brother. As much as I hate to admit it, JoJo is much more real to them than God himself. But what is JoJo to you?'' she asked, almost angrily—as if she didn't want anyone else to share her martyred belief in JoJo. "Why would you believe he is not guilty?''

Fey sipped from her coffee cup before replying. "There are a lot of pieces that don't fit this particular puzzle,'' she said. "I'm not sure that JoJo is the epitome of clean living that his work here at the orphanage may suggest, but we don't think he killed those boys.''

"And if he didn't,'' Ash entered the conversation for the first time, "then somebody else did. Somebody else who is still out there, maybe getting ready to kill again.''

"So what do you want from me?'' Sister Ruth asked.

"We believe the real killer has some personal connection to JoJo. We want you to tell us about JoJo, give us a feel for his life here—both as a child and as a man. Not the impressive stone wall you've maintained with the media, but the unvarnished truth.''

Sister Ruth sat quietly, then turned and refilled her coffee mug. The fact that she did not offer a refill to Fey and Ash was an indication of her inner turmoil. "The unvarnished truth can often do more damage than good," she said eventually.

Fey ran another gamble. "Have you been saying your prayers for JoJo, Sister?"

"Of course."

"Well, God has sent two boats and a helicopter," Fey said.

Both Ash and Sister Ruth gave her a strange look.

Fey caught their expressions and explained. "A preacher said his prayers and refused to leave his church when the local river overflowed its banks during a heavy rainstorm. Pretty soon the water had flooded through the first level of the church.

"The preacher again said his prayers and moved up to the second story. A passing boat spotted him through a window and asked him if he wanted a ride. The preacher said no because God would provide for him. The rains continued and the preacher was forced to move up to the roof of his church. Again he said his prayers.

"A second boat came by and offered him a ride to safety. The preacher again refused, saying God would provide for him. The rains continued and the preacher was forced to climb the church steeple where he continued to pray.

"A helicopter came and hovered over the preacher. They extended a rope ladder down. The preacher refused to climb the ladder, again saying that God would provide for him. The rains continued and eventually the preacher was swept away and drowned." Fey paused.

"And your point?" Sister Ruth asked.

Fey drained her coffee cup. "When the preacher got to heaven he angrily confronted St. Peter. 'After all my prayers, why did God abandon me?' he asked. 'God didn't abandon you,' St. Peter told him. 'He sent two boats and a helicopter.'" Fey paused again for effect. "Well, Sister, we're your helicopter."

✠ CHAPTER FORTY-EIGHT

"IT'S NOT A PARTICULARLY LONG STORY," SISTER RUTH had said after coffee cups had been refilled and homemade sweet rolls had been provided as a peace offering. "And I'm sure you already know most of it from everything that the press has dug up." The lines in the Mother Superior's face seemed to have deepened since she first greeted the detectives. It was as if she only had so much reserve energy to draw on to deal with JoJo's situation, and that reserve was running dangerously low.

"The press has a way of giving a distorted spin to most stories," Fey said. "It's one of the first things you learn when you become a police officer."

Sister Ruth set her cup down on the desk in front of her. "I have to agree," she said. "I've never read a story I've been connected with that had all the facts right."

"That's exactly the point, Sister. We want you to tell us what you know, not just what the press and the instant biography books have churned out."

"And this will help JoJo? Not just make things worse?"

"We can't give you any guarantees one way or the other," Fey said. "But I believe we're on the same side here. And if we're going to help JoJo, then we need help from the people who knew him best."

"Sister Ruth," Ash crossed his legs and spoke up. "I don't understand your reluctance to talk to us. We're the police. We're supposed to be the good guys. We want to help, but we can't if you won't help us first."

Sister Ruth picked up a pencil and began to fidget with

it. "Mr. Wyatt, JoJo's defense lawyer, came to see Father Peter and I when all this started. He told us not to speak to the police. He told us if we did we would be jeopardizing the case that was being built to defend JoJo."

Fey felt herself start to lose her temper. "Sister, we're not Romans out to crucify Christ." She didn't make any effort to hide the exasperation in her voice. "It doesn't matter to Devon Wyatt whether JoJo is innocent or as guilty as original sin—his only interest is in getting JoJo off. As far as I'm concerned, if JoJo is guilty, then he deserves to rot in hell. If he isn't guilty, then it's our job to find out who is. You're going to have to decide what side of the fence you're on. If you're not going to help then say so, and we'll get out of your hair and find somebody who will."

Sister Ruth put the pencil in her hand back down on the desk. "You're not shy about speaking your mind are you, Detective Croaker?"

"I haven't been accused of being shy since my first high school dance, Sister. And that's more than a few years ago."

Touching her crucifix again, Sister Ruth sat back in her chair and seemed to come to a decision. "JoJo's mother died in the hospital while giving birth," she said. "She was a prostitute and a drug addict—an illiterate, indigent woman with no family and no idea who the father of the child might be."

Ash caught Fey's eyes and winked. He knew she'd taken a chance on Sister Ruth clamming up, but it was clear Fey had judged the situation right.

"Sacred Heart has always been a nursing order," Sister Ruth continued, unaware of the byplay between the two detectives. "We have a number of orphanages all over the world. This one in San Diego is one of three in America. We are one of the few facilities able to provide extended care for orphan infants born addicted to drugs. JoJo was born addicted to heroin." She paused for a second. "Have you ever seen a drug baby, Detective?"

"It's not a pretty sight," Fey replied.

"But one that is seen all too often," Sister Ruth said. "Especially since the explosion of crack cocaine."

Sister Ruth found herself on the receiving end of inquiring looks from both Fey and Ash.

The nun's lips parted in a sardonic smile. "I told you I am not naive to the ills of the world. Everyone has the idea that nuns live a cloistered, untouched life—and some do—but the majority of us toil in the realms of the world where there can be no illusions."

"I take it that JoJo came to Sacred Heart from the hospital," Fey said, bringing the conversation back onto point.

"Yes," Sister Ruth said, nodding her head. "He had an especially difficult time, but he made it through. The problems, of course, came when we tried to find an adoptive home for him. Most people are not prepared to give the extra care that a drug baby needs. They have visions in their head of perfect children and there is no room for a child that already has challenges.

"It is no different now. We still have many drug babies that come to Sacred Heart. We try to find homes for as many of them as we can, but it is difficult. Most of those we don't find adoptive homes for move on to other institutions, but a few—like JoJo—continue to grow up here."

"How many children do you have at Sacred Heart?" Fey asked.

"Currently we provide care for seventeen infants, four toddlers, eight intermediates, and seven teens."

"Quite a responsibility," Ash said.

"We do more than just provide a home and raise children here," Sister Ruth said, looking as if she'd been insulted. "We do a lot of work within the community and—"

"I'm sorry, Sister," Fey interrupted. "I'm sure you do far more than your share of good works, but it's JoJo we're interested in here."

"Yes, of course," Sister Ruth said.

"We understand that JoJo was placed in homes on several occasions," Fey prompted.

"Yes. When he was four and six—and of course his

final placement when he was fourteen with the Kingston family.''

''Why the early returns?'' Fey asked.

''There are often many reasons for the failure of a child to assimilate into a foster or adoptive family.''

''Don't be coy, Sister. I thought we'd gone beyond that point.''

Sister Ruth reached up and slightly adjusted her coronet. ''The first choice turned out badly. There were other natural siblings in the family, one of which took a dislike to JoJo. The dislike resulted in two broken bones. The police took a hard look at the parents, but JoJo was old enough to explain what happened. The parents refused to believe JoJo and he was sent back to us. A blessing in the long run, I'm sure.''

''And the second time?'' Fey asked.

Sister Ruth shifted from shrugging to sighing. ''I'm afraid that even at a young age, JoJo showed a predilection for what you now know is his homosexual nature. Later he learned to hide that part of himself from the world, but at the time he was far too young to know better. The family he was with were not at all accepting of the situation. It was very much a mess.''

''So, JoJo stayed and grew up at Sacred Heart?''

''Yes. He was an extremely sweet child. To most people he was a withdrawn loner, but to those of us who knew him well he was a quiet delight.'' This last was said with a certain amount of satisfaction. ''He was a slow learner in school, but he discovered his physical skills with a basketball and spent hour after hour watching games and practicing by himself with an old backboard and hoop that Father Peter installed for him.''

''It must have been quite a shock to you then when the Kingston family offered to take him in when he was fourteen.''

''Yes, but a wonderful shock. Richard Kingston was renowned as a championship high school basketball coach. Many of his players went on to star in college and have professional careers.''

"You sound like a fan yourself, Sister," Ash said.

"But, of course," Sister Ruth said with a laugh. "Wouldn't you be if one of your children became a star like JoJo?" The motherly pride in her voice was obvious. "And JoJo has long been a part of our Sacred Heart family."

"Didn't Richard Kingston have children of his own?" Fey asked.

"Yes. He had two boys. Both of them were excellent basketball players, but they didn't have the drive or the skills that JoJo possessed. They were only slightly older than JoJo, and at one point all three played together for their father on their high school championship team. A tremendous accomplishment."

"I'll just bet you were in the bleachers for the finals," Ash said.

"Wouldn't have missed it for the pope's blessing," Sister Ruth said, and then put a hand over her mouth in guilt.

"When did JoJo come back to the orphanage to live?" Fey asked.

Sister Ruth's mood suddenly turned somber. "After his graduation from UCLA and he was drafted by the San Diego Sails."

"I don't mean to be insensitive," Fey said, "but what was his motivation for returning to Sacred Heart. I mean, if he wanted to move home, why didn't he move back with the Kingston family?"

"He couldn't," Sister Ruth said bluntly.

"I don't understand," Fey said.

"You said you wanted something that the papers haven't got hold of yet."

Ash and Fey both sat forward on their chairs. "Go on," Fey said.

Sister Ruth looked squarely at both detectives. "It was covered up at the time, but Richard Kingston committed suicide in JoJo's senior year on the night when UCLA was eliminated in the quarter finals of the Final Four competition."

"Suicide?"

"Yes."

"How?"

"He hung himself."

⚏

CHAPTER FORTY-NINE

DEVON WYATT EASED HIMSELF BACK IN THE RED leather chair behind his desk and allowed himself a small, self-satisfied smile. He reached out with the manicured fingers of one hand and opened the humidor that sat along one edge of the huge Empire table that acted as his desk. He removed a La Gaza from the stock inside and then closed the lid.

Taking a cigar guillotine from the pocket of his gold brocade waistcoat, he clipped the end of the cigar into a brass wastepaper basket. He rolled the expensive tobacco back and forth between his fingers and then ran it under his nose. He never knew what that accomplished, but he recognized it was as much of a ritual as inhaling the odor from a glass of wine before taking the first sip. Only a few rare individuals could truly judge anything from such actions, but everyone wanted to be recognized for their class even if the only person they were impressing was themselves.

Wyatt's Beverly Hills offices occupied the top floor of the Esterman Building—a square-domed edifice that ran twenty-six stories high. From a distance, the phallic symbolism of the building was obvious, and Wyatt liked to think of himself as a steroid-injected sperm whenever he pressed the penthouse button and ejaculated up the internal elevator.

His corner office overlooked Sunset Boulevard where the famous street literally turned from the class of 90210 to the crassness of Hollywood. Wyatt enjoyed looking out of both picture windows and seeing the change in the street. He saw the transition as representing the both sides of his own personality—the smooth dandy covering the remorseless shark.

Once Wyatt had lighted his cigar evenly and blown a long stream of smoke into the air, he picked up the remote control perched on his desktop. He pointed it at the elaborate entertainment system across the room and pressed one of the soft buttons. There was a click as the tape player activated.

"Because I don't think JoJo did it." Fey Croaker's voice abruptly spat from strategically placed Bose speakers.

Devon Wyatt smiled and turned up the volume.

"Wow," the voice Wyatt knew belonged to Dr. Emma Winters stated. "I thought the whole case was almost a foregone conclusion."

"Not according to the defense." Fey again.

"Nonsense," from Dr. Winters. "Anyone with any common sense can see that this Devon Wyatt person is strictly using chewing gum to put together a defense. But now you come along and say he might be right?"

Wyatt puffed at his cigar and then grinned so wide his gold-capped molars showed. *Chewing gum maybe, but damned good chewing gum,* he thought.

The tape continued to whirl.

"I'm not saying that Devon Wyatt is right." Fey's disembodied voice filled the room.

Of course you wouldn't, Wyatt thought, almost getting aroused.

"I just think there's more to this case than meets the eye."

Fey's voice continued, explaining to her psychiatrist the theories she and Ash had developed regarding JoJo's innocence. Devon Wyatt drank it all in. He listened to the tape all the way through, hearing for the fourth time Fey speaking about her brother and her innermost feelings regarding him. When it was over, he rewound the cassette and turned off the tape player.

He had been skeptical when one of his toadies had been approached by Sharon Barnes—Dr. Winters's receptionist—but he quickly came to see that Sharon's motives were pure and simple greed. Now that was something Wyatt could understand.

He'd bartered for the tape, paying a third of what Sharon had started out asking, but it had turned out to be worth a hundred times the price and then some.

The tape put not only Fey Croaker in the palm of his hand, it put the whole damned LAPD there. And Devon Wyatt could make a fist and crush them all anytime he wanted.

He reached out and plucked a portable phone from his desk. He pressed an automatic number. Waiting for the number to dial, he adjusted his brocade vest that stood out in vivid contrast to the piercing white of his starched, French-cuffed dress shirt.

A voice answered the phone on the third ring. "Empowerment to all people."

"This is Devon Wyatt. Put me through to Reverend Brown."

There was a click on the line.

Ten seconds later another voice came on.

"This is Reverend Brown."

"Aloishious, how are you?"

"A pleasure to hear from you, Brother Wyatt." Aloishious Brown, political and racial shaker and mover, knew Wyatt hated to be called brother. However, it was one of the few liberties Brown allowed himself to perpetrate against a man he knew was a powerful ally. Mutual manipulation had often paid off for both of them. "Is your call business or pleasure, brother?"

"It's always a pleasure to do business with you, Aloishious." Wyatt paused to puff on the stub of his cigar. "How would you like to whip up a little demonstration for me?"

"Racial, political, or environmental? Women's rights, antiabortion, or proabortion? Animal activists, gay rights, or—"

"—Slow down, Aloishious, you're beginning to sound like a Chinese menu." Wyatt chuckled. "You truly don't give a damn one way or the other, do you?"

"I never tried to hide the truth from one of my own kind."

Wyatt wasn't sure if he liked that, but perhaps objectively it might be true. "You're going to make a great governor one day," he said, knowing Brown's political aspirations went far beyond. "But how do you know I'm not taping this conversation?"

"Because I have the latest in anti–phone taping equipment placed on this line and I'm not getting the slightest reading on the dial."

Wyatt allowed himself a full chuckle. "You have a style, Aloishious. You surely do."

"So what's it going to be, and can you pay my fee?"

"Have I ever not been able to cover your fee?" The question was rhetorical and Wyatt didn't wait for an answer. "I need a little mix of racial attitude and cop baiting."

"The specialty of the house," Brown said. "When and where?"

"Why don't we decide together? I have a tape I'd like you to listen to first."

"Send a limo for me," Brown said.

"Like I said, you have a style, Aloishious." Wyatt hung up.

Placing the remains of his cigar in a chunky glass ashtray, Wyatt intercommed his secretary to send a car for Brown. He then stood up and began to pace the office as he listened to the tape of Fey's psychiatric session yet again.

The problem he had was that Croaker might be right. Her thought process made a warped sense.

And if Croaker was right, then Wyatt was wrong.

He'd thought JoJo was guilty as hell.

❁

CHAPTER FIFTY

"YOU SHOULD HAVE SEEN YOUR FACE," ASH SAID TO FEY as they drove away from the Sacred Heart Orphanage.

"My face?" Fey questioned. "What about your face? I thought we were going to have to peel your chin off the floor."

"I think old Sister Ruth got a kick out of dropping that bomb on us."

Ash steered the detective sedan up a freeway on-ramp.

Fey was again turned with her back against the passenger door, her left leg bent at the knee and resting on the bench seat. As usual, she was breaking the law by not having her seatbelt fastened. She smoothed the creases of her black slacks between two fingers. "Do you think it means anything?"

"You mean the fact that Richard Kingston committed suicide by hanging himself?" Ash slid a pair of Ray Bans on to combat the sun. He checked his mirrors, looked over his left shoulder, and changed lanes.

"Yeah—coupled with the fact that the murder victims were tied in such a way that they literally hung themselves."

Ash gave what passed for a shrug. "There could be a connection there, but it doesn't appear that anyone has put the two scenarios together yet. You would have thought the press would have been all over it.''

''Maybe not,'' Fey said. ''Sister Ruth said it was something the press didn't know. I wonder why.''

Ash checked his watch. ''We've got time before meeting Tucker. Let's see what the local PD can tell us.''

The main San Diego police station, headquartered at 1401 Broadway, was an unassuming building almost lost within the surrounds of downtown San Diego. Fey and Ash parked in a red zone along the front curb. They knew the radio microphone looped over the rearview mirror would keep them safe from tickets.

At the front desk, Fey asked to see Gerard Montegue, a San Diego homicide dick she'd met several times while networking at different homicide conventions. Five minutes later Montegue hustled into the lobby to greet them and take them back to his office.

''Coffee?'' Montegue offered as soon as they were inside. Both Fey and Ash accepted. Fey knew her daily coffee intake was far higher than was good, but you couldn't eliminate all vices. After all, coffee seemed to have replaced cigarettes as the drug of choice in the workplace. You couldn't escape it anywhere you went. Instead of offering around smokes anymore, everyone felt obligated to offer coffee in order to facilitate conversation and encourage hospitality.

Fey introduced Ash and the two men shook hands. Around them the buzz of activity in the San Diego homicide unit was like a soothing white noise—both familiar and reassuring. A cop could walk into any police station in the world and be at home.

''It's nice to see you again, Fey,'' Montegue said. He was a smallish, wiry man of Gallic extraction. His pencil-thin mustache and black, slicked back hair made him look even more French. ''They've certainly been putting you guys through your paces up there in LA.''

''That's why we came down here for a break,'' Fey said.

Montegue gave a soft chuckle. "Well, I've got a couple of cases you could take over."

Fey shook her head. "Thanks, but no thanks. That wasn't exactly what we had in mind."

"Then how can I help you?" Montegue hooked his buttocks on the corner of his desk.

"Richard Kingston," Fey said. "Does the name ring any bells?"

"Whoa," Montegue exclaimed, taken aback. "You didn't tell me we were going to be running into JoJo Cullen territory."

"Then you know who Kingston is?" Ash asked.

Montegue turned his head to look at the FBI agent. He shrugged. "I certainly do—and so would anybody else around here who is any kind of a basketball fan. He was the head basketball coach at Mission Bay High School for years. And everyone knows the story of how he discovered JoJo and adopted him. The year Kingston's two natural sons and JoJo all played together and took the high school state championship was incredible. It sure as hell won't be forgotten around here for a long time."

"Actually," Ash said, interrupting Montegue's verbal flow, "we're more interested in the story of Kingston's death."

The statement had the effect of throwing a bucket of cold water on the conversation.

Montegue placed a thin file on his desk. He had reluctantly retrieved it from a locked cabinet containing the unit's murder books—blue binders containing all the reports pertaining to an individual case. Fey realized something odd was going on. Suicide reports weren't routinely kept in with the murder books. As far as police investigations were concerned, suicide and murder had only death in common—otherwise, never the twain should meet.

"Richard Kingston was one of San Diego's lesser gods," Montegue said. He was sitting behind his desk now, three fingers perched on top of the suicide file. "His connection to JoJo Cullen elevates him even higher—JoJo being a major San Diego god."

"You have a point to make?" Fey asked. She wasn't sure where Montegue was headed. He had a reputation for being a straight shooter, and she could only hope that was true.

"This is still fairly recent history. It all happened less than two, three years ago."

"Okay," Fey said and waited.

"Nobody likes their closet skeletons brought out into the light of the sun," Montegue said.

Fey leaned forward in her chair. "Gerard," she said, intensifying the exchange. "If there is something in that file that has a bearing on JoJo Cullen's case, you can't sit on it."

Montegue still didn't lift his perched fingers off the file.

"Was there something questionable about Kingston's suicide?" Ash asked.

Montegue seemed to come to a decision. He moved his fingers from the file and sent them off to massage the nape of his neck. "Officially, Richard Kingston didn't commit suicide. Officially, he had an accident—a freak accident, but an accident."

Fey and Ash exchanged glances. Fey sat back and let Ash take the lead. "We were told he committed suicide by hanging himself," Ash said slowly.

"And where did you get that information?"

"A nun told us."

"Sister Ruth?"

Ash nodded silently.

Montegue sighed. "I knew she would let the cat out of the bag sooner or later. JoJo told her what he thought was the truth about his adopted father's death and it seemed to fester inside of her."

"I don't think nuns approve of lies," Ash said.

"That's the point," Montegue said. "Kingston didn't commit suicide either."

That got Fey's attention. "What—I don't understand."

Montegue turned the file toward Fey and Ash. "The

official story is that Kingston was home alone when he tripped down the stairs in his residence, became entangled with a drapery cord, was knocked unconscious when he hit the floor, and suffocated from the cord around his neck.''

"That's some freak accident," Ash said after a moment's silence.

"The home is a dangerous place," Montegue said. "And there were a lot of high rollers out there who wanted Richard Kingston to remain a hero. The full truth was even kept from JoJo."

"What is the full truth?" Fey asked.

Montegue opened the file and slid out a sheaf of color photos. He spread them out on the desk as Fey and Ash stood to look at them.

"John Q. Citizen probably wouldn't recognize what was going on here," Montegue said. "But I'd wager you will."

Fey picked up one of the pictures. The snap showed a man naked except for a leather mask that fit completely over his head. The mask snapped tightly under the chin and had closed zipper openings over the eyes and mouth. The man was kneeling on the floor, one hand limp at his side. His other hand was resting near his exposed genitals.

The man was slumped forward, suspended from falling to the floor by a thin cord wrapped around his neck and running back to the handle of the closed door behind him.

"Autoerotic death." Fey said.

"Nasty," said Ash as he looked at the other photos.

Autoerotica was the sexual act of shutting off the blood to the brain by the use of a ligature while masturbating. Leaning forward against the cord tied to the door handle, Richard Kingston would bring himself almost to the point of passing out as he manually brought himself to orgasm. The leather mask was an added way to intensify the claustrophobia of the act.

Kingston had probably committed the act hundreds, maybe thousands of times, successfully. But one time, on the night JoJo's UCLA team was eliminated from the Final Four championship, Kingston misjudged the process—he pushed the envelope too far and actually passed out. His body stayed slumped forward, supported by the cord around his neck, and Richard Kingston strangled himself.

"The coroner's finding of accidental death by strangulation wasn't a lie," Ash said. His tone was slightly flippant—dark humor being used to gloss over a horrifying situation.

"Exactly," Montegue said, understanding Ash's tone. "But it was thought best to keep the details to a minimum."

Fey was riffling through the pages of the death investigation. "There's something else, isn't there?"

Montegue gave her a sharp look. "What makes you say that?"

She tossed the report pages back on the desk. "Autoerotic death, It's unusual, but not uncommon. Most homicide dicks would recognize it when they see it. I can understand not wanting to make the details public. It's messy."

"Nobody would have benefited," Montegue said, almost defensively.

Fey waved a hand in dismissal. "I'm not criticizing. I've been there. I can even see burying the file—losing it somewhere in the great morass. But you kept the file close by. Locked up, but handy. You knew you could lay your hands on it at any time."

"I was the investigating detective on the case," Montegue said. "It was my first and only autoerotic death encounter—"

Fey cut in. "That's not it. There's something here you're not happy about—and it's more than initiating a scandal about Richard Kingston dying with his dick in his hand. I can sense it."

Ash moved over to stand beside Fey. Both detectives stared implacably at the third.

"I have no proof," Montegue said eventually.

"Of what?" Fey asked.

"There was some slight bruising on Kingston's shoul-

ders. It could have been caused from anything,'' Montegue
vacillated.

"But you think it was caused how?'' Fey asked, pushing
the San Diego detective.

"I think,'' Montegue started, stopped, and started again.
"I think Kingston took himself to the edge of consciousness, and then somebody put their hands on his shoulders
just long enough not to let him back off. The added pressure caused Kingston to lose consciousness and black
out . . .''

"And then he was left to strangle,'' Fey said, completing the scenario. Montegue nodded.

"Not accidental,'' Ash said.

"Not suicide,'' Fey said.

"No,'' Montegue agreed with a sigh. "Murder.''

✠

CHAPTER FIFTY-ONE

FEY AND ASH WERE BACK ON THE ROAD AGAIN. WHILE
Ash drove, Fey paged through the file on Richard Kingston's death. Montegue had been reluctant to part with it,
but in the end had given up any thoughts of damage control as a lost cause.

"This is getting uglier and uglier,'' Fey said. She fanned
out the photos of Richard Kingston as if they were a deck
of cards, and held them in one hand. "Montegue has a
feeling this was more than an accident. If that's true, the
culprit couldn't be JoJo. He was miles away in Indiana.''

"So who does that leave?''

Fey put the photos back in the file. "Beats me at this

point," she said. She looked at her watch. "What time are we supposed to meet Zelman Tucker?"

"Fifteen minutes ago," Ash replied.

"Will he wait?"

"Tucker? Are you kidding? The man would wait for hell to freeze over if he thought it would get him what he wanted."

Fey noticed that Ash was driving very aggressively— speeding to catch up to traffic, then reluctantly slowing down until he could break clear again. She put it down to his agitation over meeting Tucker.

"What is it about this guy that irritates you so much?"

"He's a schmoozer," Ash said without hesitation. "There isn't a sincere bone in his body. He makes money at the expense of other people's misery."

"Sort of like us," Fey said, echoing the words Tucker had once used against Ash.

"No. Not like us at all. Tucker revels in the prurience of the misery. He enjoys it. He loves sticking his finger in and stirring up the pot. His passion is exposing the vulgarities of life." Ash braked hard to avoid running up the tailpipe of a senior citizen in a ten-year-old Cadillac. "We don't do that. Our job is to seek the truth in the interest of justice—only that. Nothing more."

"Does the fact that we have a loftier purpose make it any different?"

"You're damn right it does. If it didn't, neither of us would be doing it." Ash cut his eyes at Fey for a second. "Wait a minute. You're pulling my chain, aren't you?"

Fey gave a short laugh. "Pushing your buttons is like shooting cows with a cannon. You're too easy."

"I resent that," Ash said lightly. "I may be easy, but I'm not cheap."

Ash steered the detective sedan across three lanes of traffic, cutting off two good citizens in the process, and exited the freeway off ramp leading to Mission Bay.

The Prince & The Pauper was an upscale restaurant with an outdoor eating patio and a view of the placid waters of the bay. The sun had burned off the mid-morning fog and put a soft warmth into the air.

Though she had never met him, Fey spotted Tucker the second she and Ash stepped into the eating patio.

"Good grief," she said, looking at the journalist's electric-yellow plaid sports jacket. "His horse must be freezing."

"He's too cheap to put a blanket on a horse," Ash told her.

Tucker spotted both detectives and stood up. Under the electric-yellow plaid was a canary-yellow polo shirt with the top button done up. The shirt was tucked into a pair of softer yellow slacks with a white belt and white tennis shoes. Tucker waved animatedly, getting the attention of every diner on the patio.

"What's the matter?" Fey asked. "Does he think we can't see him?"

Walking toward the table, Fey tried to see beyond the garish clothing. Tucker was younger than she had expected—early to mid-twenties. His carrot-red hair was brush-cut, and he had more freckles than Opie. His body, however, was lean, clearly muscular even under his clothing.

Ash had taken Fey's elbow in his hand and moved in close to her. "Don't play this guy for a fool," he said near her ear. "He's a piranha."

"Hey! Good to see you, Ash, my man," Tucker said. He reached out, grabbed Ash's reluctant hand, and shook it up and down like he was pumping for water.

"Tucker," Ash said. "If you don't cool it, it won't matter what you've got. I'm outta here."

Tucker held up both hands in mock surrender. "Okay, okay. I'll cut the shtick." He turned to Fey. "Detective Croaker, I presume?"

"You presume again and I'll have to pop you one," Fey said. She knew Ash hated the guy, but there was something that appealed to her about him. He acted the goofball, but Fey could read between the lines.

Tucker laughed at Fey's comeback. "Hey! You and I are gonna be pals. I can tell that already."

There were two other people sitting at the table behind Tucker. Such was the force of the journalist's personality that their presence had barely registered.

Tucker turned to introduce them. "This is Etta Carson," he said, indicating an older black woman. She was heavy, enveloping the chair straining beneath her. The mass of her body was covered by a blue and purple muu-muu. A small hat perched on her head, and her hands were grasped together in her lap. A pair of short white gloves sprouted from between her fingers. She smiled at Fey and Ash and shook hands limply.

"And this is Dr. Frank Logan," Tucker said, completing the introductions. The doctor was a big man. Older than Etta Carson, his broad shoulders would never be described as stooped. He wore a well-cut gray suit with a carnation pinned to the lapel. His full head of hair was the same color as his suit, and was sprayed into obedience. Three small skin tags clustered together under the right rim of his heavy, black-framed glasses.

Everyone sat down and busied themselves with ordering and arranging napkins and silverware.

"Okay, Tucker," Ash said when their waiter moved away. "What's this all about?"

"We had a deal," Tucker said. "You told me that if I came up with a break in the case, you'd—"

"—I know what I said," Ash interrupted. "Just tell me what you've got."

For a moment, Tucker's face lost its friendly, kid-next-door look. "We still have a deal, or do I go elsewhere with this?"

"Where else are you going to go?"

Tucker's mask of civility slipped back into place. "I can take what I've got to Devon Wyatt. And believe me, that's something you don't want me to do."

Ash sipped from his water glass. "All right."

"Deal?" Tucker asked.

"Yeah, yeah. Deal." Ash's frustration was clear.

The waiter chose that moment to return with salads and drinks.

"Etta Carson knew Hallie Cullen, JoJo's mother," Tucker said, when everyone was resettled.

"I was her social worker," Etta Carson said. Her voice was tinged with the South. "Thirty-five years with the department of social services," she continued. "Or whatever they're calling it these days. Knew a whole lot of Hallie Cullens in my time. Always onto them to use some form of birth control, but they never did."

"Was Hallie Cullen a prostitute?" Ash asked.

"She was a heroin addict. What do you think? I did what I could for her—kept her in a place to stay, food stamps. She wasn't stupid, but she was stubborn, and she did have the monkey on her back bad."

In the silence that followed that statement, Tucker pointed at his other guest. "Dr. Logan was the obstetrician who delivered JoJo."

Dr. Logan nodded. "It was a mess," he said. "It had to be or I wouldn't have remembered it all these years later. I'm retired now, but I've never seen another case like it—either before or after."

"What made the delivery unique?" Fey asked.

"It was almost two o'clock in the morning when they brought Hallie Cullen into the delivery room. She was screaming bloody murder. She was pregnant, her blood pressure was through the roof, and there was heavy vaginal hemorrhaging." The doctor's voice was low and deep. He spoke slowly while the fingers of his right hand fiddled with the tines of his salad fork. "The ambulance crew had picked her up in a tenement apartment. Her screaming had scared hell out of everyone else in the rat-trap building."

"The woman was scared to death herself, poor child," Etta Carson interjected. Her salad had disappeared while Dr. Logan had been talking and she was trying not to obviously eye the still-full plates in front of everyone else. "She'd never been to see the doctor during her entire pregnancy. She was illiterate, scared of hospitals. Scared that she would be locked up and kept away from her dope connection. I took a doctor with me when I went to see her once, but I couldn't locate her. She seemed fine, though. No problems with the pregnancy. Not even morning sickness according to Hallie herself.''

''I'm surprised she didn't abort the baby,'' Fey said.

Etta Carson looked at her with world-weary eyes. ''There's money in babies. She was looking for a big score.''

The waiter came and cleared the salad plates. Etta Carson looked sad to see most of the remaining rabbit food going to waste. Fey had the feeling the social worker would have stuffed it all in her oversized purse if nobody had been looking.

Etta Carson continued. ''I tried to get Hallie to agree to go to the hospital when the baby was due, but this was the seventies and somebody had convinced her that natural childbirth at home was the way to go.'' The woman paused for breath and emphasis. ''The day before she was taken by ambulance to the hospital, she bore her child at home with nary a blink of the eye.'' Etta Carson gave both Fey and Ash a stare as if she was telling a ghost story. ''It was a sorrowful sight, though. The baby was all there—fingers and toes—but he was itching for the monkey just like his momma. She'd tried to stay clean, but the wagon is there to be fallen off.''

''Wait a minute.'' Fey frowned, shaking her head. She looked at Dr. Logan. ''I thought you said she was pregnant when she was brought into the emergency room.''

''She was.''

''I don't understand.''

''I told you it was an extraordinary case,'' Dr. Logan said. ''Hallie Cullen had two uteruses. One was normal, but the other was blind except for a small opening connecting it with the normal uterus. When Hallie Cullen became pregnant, the ovum in the normal uterus appeared to have split—the first split developed in the normal uterus, but the second split was forced, through the connecting opening, into the blind uterus. A freak accident. Through the connecting opening, the placenta in both uteruses received nourishment from the umbilical cord.''

"You're saying she had twins? Only they weren't delivered at the same time because there was no exit from the second uterus?" Fey asked, riveted by the implications of the doctor's explanation.

"Exactly."

"Slow down," Ash requested. "Are we talking identical twins?"

"They could be if it was one egg that split. Or they could be fraternal twins if there were originally two eggs."

"So there's possibly another JoJo Cullen running around out there? How come he hasn't stepped forward?"

"He doesn't know he's JoJo Cullen's brother," Tucker said. Everyone turned to look at him. Tucker deferred to Etta Carson. "Tell them what you told me," he instructed her.

While everyone else had been either talking or listening, Etta Carson had been scarfing down her veal parmesan. She paused and wiped her chin.

She appeared to be reluctant to speak. Tucker took two long, white envelopes out of his inside jacket pocket. He handed one to Etta Carson and the other to Dr. Logan. "As we agreed," he said.

Fey saw a hungry look pass across the face of Dr. Logan when he accepted his envelope. It made her wonder just what vices Logan had that would make him susceptible to tabloid money. The three empty glasses next to his elbow gave her one clue.

"Hallie Cullen named her first child MoJo because she thought he was magic," Etta Carson said, once she had snaked her envelope into a fold in her muu-muu. "When she died in the hospital giving birth to JoJo, little MoJo was taken into protective custody. Hallie Cullen had no relatives that anybody could find, and the daddy could have been anybody." She paused to push the remaining veal around on her plate. She seemed to have lost her appetite. "Since Hallie had been one of my cases, it was my job to find a home for the children. I was lucky. Even with his addiction problem, MoJo went to an adoptive family almost immediately. They changed his name to Martin—Martin Morgan. JoJo had more problems and was placed with the Sacred Heart Orphanage who had the facilities to deal with him.''

Ash watched Etta Carson with a wary eye. "And all these years later you're the only one who remembers MoJo—or Martin—was JoJo Cullen's brother?"

"I didn't even remember until Mr. Tucker come around stirring up memories and helping me put two and two together."

"How much did two and two add up to, Tucker?" Ash asked. "What's the going rate for two and two these days?"

Fey put her hand on Ash's arm. She was seeing a little too much of herself in his attitude. Maybe she was rubbing off on him.

"What happened at the hospital?" she asked Dr. Logan.

"We couldn't save the mother, she was losing too much blood. But we did a c-section and saved the child. He was small, almost didn't make it, but eventually he did. Fought like a champ." He shrugged.

"Where did the name JoJo come from?"

"That was me," Etta Carson said. "Hallie had a girlfriend living with her who called me at work the day after Hallie was taken away by the ambulance. I went to the hospital. I knew the first child's name had been MoJo. JoJo seemed like a logical progression."

"Where is this Martin Morgan now? What's he doing?" Ash asked, cutting to the chase.

Zelman Tucker almost disappeared behind a Cheshire-cat grin. "I shoulda been a detective," he said.

Fey could feel her heart pounding in her chest. "Spill it, man," she demanded.

✦ CHAPTER FIFTY-TWO

DEL MAR RACE TRACK WAS BUSTLING IN THE AFTERNOON heat of the perfect Southern California day. The temperature was in the high seventies and the track was clear and fast. The two o'clock post time was rapidly approaching, and the regulars were watching the odds and checking their racing forms.

"Where the surf meets the turf at old Del Mar" was the tuneful refrain that caught the dazzle of the old race track's glory days. Once a playground for the rich and famous, Del Mar had played host to movie stars and business moguls alike. The exclusive enclaves of La Jolla provided monied shelter from the storm, but Del Mar had been where the action was.

Not located right on the surf, but close enough for government, publicity, and musical purposes, Del Mar was now an aging lady. Though no longer the jewel of the fast lane, it still maintained an aura of faded glamour. Without the celebrities that had once walked its pathways, however, the track's clientele had been reduced to hustlers, track mavens, gamblers, and the people whose lives revolved around the love of thoroughbreds.

Ash pulled through the gated entrance to the parking lot and followed the arm waving of an attendant to an appropriate spot. With Tucker expansively spread out across the back seat, Ash had been silent for most of the drive from the restaurant. He left the questions up to Fey, and listened to Tucker's answers with a jaundiced ear.

Taking their leave of Etta Carson and Dr. Logan, Ash

had almost duck-walked Tucker out of the restaurant. They paused only long enough for Tucker to settle the bill with a credit card that drew on his *American Inquirer* expense account. If MoJo Cullen, now Martin Morgan, truly existed, Ash and Fey wanted to get to him now.

"Why did you set up this little luncheon tête-á-tête, if you knew about Martin Morgan all along?" Fey had asked as they walked out of the restaurant and headed for their car.

"I only found out the personal details of Martin Morgan shortly before coming to lunch. I had Carson and Logan on the hook, but my sources still hadn't been able to trace Morgan himself. I thought you'd figure I was scamming you if I simply told you what I'd found out, so I set it up for you to meet the original sources of my information."

"You still might be scamming us," Ash said as they all climbed into the detective sedan. "Those two back there could have been playing very effective parts. If this is some elaborate plot on the part of *American Inquirer* to generate false headlines, I'll have your ass on a platter."

Tucker had moved forward on the back seat of the car and reached over to grab Ash by the shoulder. "Look," he said. All pretense was gone from his voice. "I know you think I'm a scum-sucking bottom-feeder, or worse, but I'm damn good at what I do. Nobody else—not you, not your buddy Croaker here, or any other big shot LAPD or FBI detectives—came up with the witnesses that I've found. I should have taken them straight to *American Inquirer*—after all they are the ones footing the tab for all this—but I didn't. I brought them to you." Fey saw Tucker's grip tighten on Ash's shoulder. "You're the monster hunter, man, and I know how much this one means to you. I don't care that you can't stand the sight of me—everybody has their shortcomings—but I respect the hell out of what you do, and it's about time you started respecting me."

There was a short pause before Ash reached forward and turned the vehicle ignition. "Nice speech," he said.

"Now get your hand off my shoulder." His words were tough, but there was no heart behind them.

From Mission Bay to Del Mar was a twenty-minute drive with another ten to get parked and gain entrance to the track. On the drive, Fey had continued to question Tucker.

"How did you find Etta Carson and Doctor Logan? And what made you look for them in the first place?"

"I wasn't looking specifically for them," Tucker said. He was sitting relaxed in the back seat now. "I was just looking for a lead, some kind of handle on this whole story that nobody else had come up with. I figured that the detectives working the case would be focusing on the victims. Nobody was looking for a killer anymore, because everybody—that is everybody except you two—believed the killer was in custody."

Fey was beginning to see how Tucker's mind had worked. "So, you went back to the beginning." She nodded her head in approval. "You were right when you said you should have been a detective. Going back to the beginning is always the right thing to do when a case gets stuck."

Tucker stretched and folded his arms behind his head. "I found Etta Carson through the social services records—"

"How the hell did you get into those?" Ash couldn't help asking.

"Come on, man," Tucker said. "*American Inquirer* may be tabloid sleaze, but it's still read more than any other publication in America except *Reader's Digest*. I wouldn't be their highest paid reporter if I didn't know how to work a source."

Ash started to object, but Tucker cut him off. "Don't go getting your panties in a bunch about ethics. If cops had the money to throw around that *American Inquirer* does, they'd also use it for payoffs. Everybody has their price and government workers are cheaper than most."

"Shit," was Ash's only comment.

"So you bought off Etta Carson," Fey said.

"It was cheaper than trying to get into the adoption files," Tucker said. "Now that takes bucks."

"And Dr. Logan?" Fey asked.

"And Sister Ruth as well," Tucker said without remorse. He caught the look Fey threw him. "Hey, nuns got a price too, you know. It's amazing how much those rug rats she supports cost to keep in undershorts and squashed bananas."

"If this is all about money," Fey said pointedly, "then why haven't you run back to your tabloid and spread this all over the checkout stands? It would be the scoop of the century."

"It is about money. That's the point," Tucker said. "Screw *American Inquirer*. They may be footing the bill for this, but they aren't paying me anything beyond my salary to dig this shit up. Now my salary ain't nothing to sneeze at, and maybe they give me a bonus and a pat on the back, but so what." He reached forward and again grabbed Ash's shoulder. "My man here, however, is going to make me richer than rich. Between us, we're gonna write a Pulitzer Prize winner and come up with all the 'screw you' money I'm ever gonna need." Tucker smiled when Ash's whole body seemed to cringe.

"All right," Fey said in resignation. "But what about Martin Morgan?"

"MoJo was a little tough even for me," Tucker admitted. "After I got over the shock of his existence, I got on it and tracked him like a randy hound dog looking for a French poodle." When neither Fey or Ash responded to his stab at humor, Tucker continued. "I won't bore you with all the details, but the fact is that he works at the track selling programs and tip sheets."

"What do you know about him?" Fey asked.

"I know he isn't the success story that his brother is," Tucker said. "Rap sheet a mile long including time for child molest and rape."

"Get outta here," Fey said. "Quit yanking us around."

Tucker looked suitably aggrieved. "If I'm lying, I'm dying," he said. He took a folded sheet of paper out of his jacket and handed it over the seat to Fey. She unfolded it and ran her eyes down it.

"He isn't dying," she said to Ash. "He was convicted in 1988 for rape. Did his time in San Quentin and was released in 1994."

The trio was now walking toward the track turnstiles. Ash pushed Tucker forward to pay for all of their admissions.

"This is total bullshit," he said. "No way is this evil twin crap going to cut it. If this guy is JoJo Cullen's identical twin, how come nobody has ever brought it up? JoJo Cullen is a celebrity. Everybody knows what he looks like." Ash was getting agitated. "I don't care if he is JoJo's identical twin," he said. "I don't care if he's the biggest pervert since Caligula. I don't care if he confesses and we find photos of the victims in his possession. I'm not going to believe it."

"Believe it, man," Tucker said with confidence. "Leave this one to the old T-man. We got it nailed."

"How will we recognize him?" Fey asked, and then realized how stupid she was being. "Sorry," she said. "I guess we just look for the tallest guy at the track who looks like JoJo Cullen."

The midweek crowd was fairly heavy. Almost everyone was stopping as they came through the turnstiles to buy a program from one of three hawkers scattered across the main walkway leading to the stands. All three hawkers were wizened old men, two white and one black, who bore no resemblance at all to JoJo.

Walking further, Fey saw several other men hawking tip sheets from behind small wooden tables. One of the men was slender and tall. His left side was exposed to the detectives, as his table was turned sideways to the walkway, and he was sitting on a beat-up bar stool. He took money from a customer and handed back a tip sheet all with his left hand.

"That's him," Fey said "Got to be."

"Easy, girl," Ash said. He pushed Tucker back behind him. "Let's not leap too quick."

• • •

As the two detectives approached their quarry, with Tucker close on their heels, they both geared up for a foot pursuit if their man took off.

"Martin Morgan?" Ash asked when they were close enough.

"Yeah." The man turned to face them.

The trio looked at him.

He looked enough like JoJo Cullen to be taken for his brother if they were in the same room together, but they'd never be mistaken for identical twins. But there was more.

"What do you want?" he asked. "You bill collectors or sumthin'?"

"We're shocked," Fey said bizarrely. But then the whole situation was bizarre.

MoJo Cullen, aka Martin Morgan, fraternal twin brother of JoJo Cullen and convicted sex offender, had only one arm and one leg.

"You are a stupid shit!" Ash said to Tucker through gritted teeth. "I should blister your ass up one side and down the other."

"Relax, man, relax!" Tucker was almost whimpering. "I had no idea."

They had moved away from the main walkway to a small concrete bench near the entrance to the main stands. Around them a swirl of humanity gave them a wide berth. Ash was clearly getting ready to jump in Tucker's face, and Fey wasn't far behind him.

"I thought that maybe I'd misjudged you," Ash said, his voice low. "And then I find you're screwing us around on a wild goose chase." Ash filled his fist with yellow polo shirt.

"Hey! Hey!" Tucker said. "Calm down. I bruise easy. I didn't know, man. I swear. I thought we were on it, man. I thought this was it."

"Bullshit." Ash suddenly dropped his hold. He took a deep breath. Looking around him, he sucked in more air.

"I have to find a bathroom," he said, and moved away without further explanation.

"Whew," Tucker said after a few moments.

"I don't think you're out of the woods yet," Fey told him.

"He'll chill," Tucker said. "But I don't know how much more he's got left in him."

Fey quizzed him with her eyes. "What do you mean?"

"I mean it's obvious. It's getting to him. He's running out of gas. He's a physical guy. A year ago he would have reached down my throat and pulled my lungs out."

"I don't understand what you mean by 'running out of gas.' "

Tucker turned to face her and saw that she really didn't understand what he was talking about. "Ash is sick," he said.

"Sick?" Fey felt her heart block her throat. She couldn't breathe.

"Dying," Tucker said. There was no emotion in his voice. "Didn't you know?"

Fey felt stunned. She swallowed. "No. I didn't know. What is it? Cancer?"

"I would venture to bet he wishes it was."

"What do you mean?" The world around Fey seemed to have faded to nothingness.

"He has Lou Gehrig's disease—amyotrophic lateral sclerosis."

"I've heard of it, but what the hell is it?" Fey fought to stop tears from coming. *Stop it*, she said internally. *He's just some guy you know.* She knew she was lying to herself.

"It's a motor neuron disease. The nerves that control muscular activity degenerate within the brain and spinal cord. That's why he's so gaunt—his muscles are wasting away."

"Oh, shit," Fey said, feeling despair.

"There's no cure and the end of things is real ugly. The mind remains clear, but your body slowly shuts down around you until you can't speak, swallow, move, or breathe.''

"How long does he have?'' Fey thought of Ash playing the piano at the Blue Cat. He'd only done a few songs, but she thought he'd looked pooped afterward. She had put it down to fatigue from the day.

Tucker shrugged. "Far as I can tell he should be dead by now. He was diagnosed over a year ago. In some people, though, it's slower moving. Sometimes it plateaus. Some people go two, maybe three years after being diagnosed, but it always gets them in the end. That's why this case is so important to Ash. It's his last monster hunt. I never would have jerked him around, if I'd have known about MoJo. I'll grant you that I'm an asshole, but even I draw the line at baiting the dying.''

"There's no cure?'' Fey asked. She knew the answer, but needed to hear it said aloud.

"Only death,'' Tucker said. "Only death.''

CHAPTER FIFTY-THREE

A HUNDRED AND FIFTY MILES AND THREE HOURS LATER, Fey and Ash had finally reached the point where they could laugh about the situation.

"It's been a long time since I've been that sucked in,'' Ash said. They were back in West LA eating fast food at an In-N-Out burger joint. Their burgers dripped with fried onions, cholesterol, and fat grams. A cop's delight.

"I kept saying it couldn't be true,'' Ash continued, "but there was a part of me that had really bought into the possibility.'' Ash bit, chewed, and swallowed. "Evil twin my ass.'' He shook his head and Fey laughed.

''I thought we were caught by surprise when Sister Ruth dropped her bomb,'' she said. ''But Martin Morgan was shock therapy by comparison. I've had a lot of strange days in this business, however, none like today.''

After returning from the race track bathroom, Ash hadn't argued when Fey said she'd drive back to LA. Tucker was more than happy to escape from under the proverbial gun by abandoning them and taking a cab back to his own car.

Half of the journey home, Ash had ridden in silence. His head had been tipped back on the headrest, his eyes closed. Fey couldn't figure if he was still seething with anger over the situation or simply exhausted.

Where the San Diego 405 Freeway and the Golden State 5 Freeway intersected, Fey stayed with the 405, and Ash had opened his eyes.

''He told you, didn't he?''

''Who told me what?'' Fey asked.

''Don't be coy,'' Ash told her. ''I don't have enough time left to be coy.''

''Okay, he told me.''

''That shit. He had no right.''

Fey didn't argue the point, even though she was glad Tucker had told her about Ash's battle with ALS. ''How did he find out?'' she asked.

''The same way he finds everything out—intuition and money. Because of the books he's written, he's been following my career closely. He sensed there was something strange about my early retirement from the bureau, and he bought himself a look at my medical files.''

Fey felt there was no sense beating around the bush. ''How much time do you have left?''

''Hard to say,'' Ash told her. ''Things seemed to have flattened out for the last six months, but recently my legs have been getting weaker and I can barely still play the piano. I'll never be able to do what I did last night at the Blue Cat again.''

"I'm sorry," Fey said.

"Yeah. Me, too."

They drove in silence again for a while. "I guess I don't understand why you're still working," Fey said eventually. "Shouldn't you be visiting friends and relatives, getting your papers in order, taking that trip to Europe you always planned on taking, going to Mexico to find a miracle cure? From what you told me about your father, it's not like you don't have the money."

Ash chuckled at that. "I have no relatives. For the most part I'd rather be alone than with friends. My papers have never been out of order. I've been to Europe. And there is no cure." He shifted to find a more comfortable position in the car. "This job is what I do," he said. "It defines what I am. So, I'm going to do it until I can't do it any more. Then I'm going to end it. I may be stuck with dying, but I'm never going to allow myself to become helpless."

"What does that mean?" Fey asked quietly.

"You're not naive. It means exactly what you think it does. I'm not going to have somebody carry me to the bathroom. I'm not going to wait until I'm too weak to even breathe."

"Suicide?"

"If it comes to that. But perhaps I'll get lucky and fall in front of a bus."

"That's a heavy burden to carry."

"Not really. Once you've moved past the 'why me' stage, the 'poor me' stage, the 'I hate God' stage, and the 'life sucks' stage, acceptance becomes a relief." Ash smiled, really smiled, in a way that lifted his whole face out of the shadows usually cast by his angular and deep-set features. "I'm okay with it. I really am. I just want to get this one last monster."

"We'll get him," Fey promised. "And when we do, we'll make sure he has his full complement of appendages."

At the In-N-Out, they tried to put all they had learned from the day in prospective. They kept coming back, however, to the shock of Martin "MoJo" Morgan's missing limbs.

"I felt we were in a lost episode of the 'Twilight Zone,'" Fey said.

"I know what you mean. It was like 'The X Files' or something."

After their initial shock, Fey and Ash had let Tucker step forward and ask just enough questions to establish that Martin Morgan had lost his arm and leg as the result of a prison fight. There was no way he was up in LA burying bodies and planting evidence. He was a convicted violent pervert, but he wasn't their violent pervert.

Martin Morgan had wanted to know what it was all about, but they had left him hanging—no pun intended—not wanting to give anything to the news media or anyone else to muddy the waters. The case was complicated enough without giving Devon Wyatt more ammunition.

Fey had only eaten half of her burger when she set it aside.

"What's the matter?" Ash asked her.

"Nothing's the matter." There was something different in her voice.

"Yes, there is," Ash said.

"No, there isn't," Fey insisted.

"Don't con a con," Ash told her. "We've both been ignoring the fact of our responses to each other, but we both know it's there. Don't tell me there's nothing wrong."

"But there isn't. You're reading the signal the wrong way."

"What do you mean?"

"I didn't think you were that stupid, Ash. I want you to take me home and make love to me."

"Holy shit," Ash said. "Wait a minute. Does this have anything to do with me dying?"

"You bet it does," Fey told him. "I don't want to miss my chance. I want you now, before it's too late."

•   •   •

They barely managed to get themselves onto Ash's bed. Their clothes went one way, their bodies another. The coupling was an explosion, a release of pent-up passions and frustrations. And when they fell over the edge together it was like dropping into a black hole of inner consciousness.

Coupled together, they lay with arms and legs wrapped tightly around each other's sweat-drenched torsos. Little by little they moved apart until they lay spooned and dozing.

Fey was eventually brought back to consciousness by the sound of water running. Around her red and white candles flickered in a slight breeze from an unknown source.

Naked and chilled, she moved lightly to the bathroom and found Ash filling the huge, claw-footed porcelain tub with steamy water. She came up behind him and wrapped her arms around his chest, pressing her breasts into his back.

"Hi," he said, turning to hold her and kiss her.

There were other candles in the bathroom providing the only source of light. Again they were a mixture of red and white and all shapes, tall, short, fat, slender.

When the water was ready, Ash slipped in first, his back resting against the curve of the tub, and Fey then slipped in to nestle into him. It was intimate in a way that went beyond the boundaries of usual first-time lovers.

They had both been lost in languid thought for a while when Fey asked, "Do you believe in fairy tales, Ash?" Her voice sounded strange in the interesting acoustics of the room.

He was sunk to his armpits in hot water, his legs extended the full length of the tub. Fey was in front of him, her back nestled into his chest. His arms were around her, hands resting gently on her breasts. Steam rose toward the ceiling, glinting on its way in the light of the flickering candles.

"You mean as in 'once upon a time,' or 'they lived happily ever after'?"

"Yeah."

Ash paused before answering, as if carefully considering his response. "Once upon a time? Maybe," he said eventually. "Happily ever after? I don't think so. I've never seen it happen."

"As a cynic, Ash, you're right up there with the best of them," Fey said. Her gentle tone took any sting out of the words, turning them from a criticism to an understanding.

"It's a hard-earned frame of mind."

"So I've heard."

His hands cupped her breasts with slightly more insistence, the tips of his long fingers tenderly urging her nipples to hardness. She sighed, feeling the physical center of his passion hardening against the small of her back.

He leaned his head forward and kissed the back of her neck. His teeth nipped at her shoulders, and his tongue flicked out to feather the short tail of hair that ran down the back of her neck.

Fey put her hands on either side of the tub and pulled herself up and out of the water.

"Hey," he said. "Where are you going?"

"I want to make love to you again right now," she said with determination. She stepped out of the tub and reached back to help pull Ash to his feet. "But not in the water."

"Why? Are you worried about scaring the fish?"

"Har, har," Fey gave a casual fake laugh as she pulled on Ash's hand again.

He followed her out of the tub and allowed her to lead him from the bathroom into the bedroom. The warmth of a Santa Ana breeze caressed them through what Fey now saw was an open window. The stained glass of the French doors filtered the moonlight and cast colored shadows across their wet, glistening skin.

The candles flickered in the bedroom as they had done in the bathroom. Here, tall, thick, white, dripless candles were grouped together in various stages of meltdown. Scattered by the touch of serendipity were lone, slender red candles standing proudly in their autonomy.

As she reached the bed, Fey dropped Ash's hand. She leaned forward, bending at the waist and placed her palms flat on the edge of the mattress. She spread her legs slightly and swayed her backside.

Ash stepped behind her and bent his chest down to touch her back. His hands reached around her to caress her breasts again, as they had done in the bath. She could feel his hardness pressing against the soft skin that covered the hard muscles of her buttocks.

"I want you inside me now," she said. Her voice was tinged with both demand and desire.

His hands moved back to grasp her hips as he stood up and pushed forward to enter the heart of her. They both gasped and Fey fell forward onto her forearms.

"Oh . . . Ash," she said, pushing back to take him all the way in. His hands on her hips felt like hot talons where they grasped her. She could feel each finger burning into her flesh, then he pulled back and pushed forward and she forgot about all sensations except for the one exploding inside of her.

Ash watched her move with him as if he were almost detached from the act. He followed her forward as she crawled onto the mattress on her knees. Inside his emotional heart he felt his emotions lurch. He wanted this woman more than he had wanted anything in his life. He wanted her more than life itself.

Right there in that room, inside of her, he could have died without regret, blessed and cleansed by the passion he felt for her. Feeling began to spread through his body as she moved back against him, urging him physically deeper into the center of her being. A bright light seemed to explode inside him and he felt electric as adrenaline injected into his blood. His heart was pounding and he felt sure she must hear it.

"I want you," her voice was a husky rasp. "Please, please."

He pulled her hips to him and held her tightly as she squirmed against him.

"Yes! Yes!" she said. Demanding. Insistent.

Feeling Ash thicken and heat inside of her, Fey lurched forward and pulled herself clear. Rolling over, she spread her legs wide and reached up for him. Her arms circled his neck and pulled his body down and into her. She wrapped her legs around his waist with her arms still holding firm around his neck. Bucking up against him, she buried her face in his shoulder, her teeth bared on his skin.

The pleasure, the love, and the lust that she felt for Ash flushed through her. His body was lean and hard, a musculature once won and held through hard work and sweat, now carved by the encroaching demon of his ALS.

She smelled his maleness and licked the moisture from his shoulders.

Inside, she felt her moment building. He seemed to be still growing, probing deeper and deeper, and then suddenly she was on the edge of her personal precipice. She waited one heartbeat—and then threw herself over the edge and dropped into forever.

Ash knew a second before that Fey was in her moment. He raised himself up, with her still clinging to him, wrapping his arms completely around her. Then he dropped back to the mattress and surrendered himself to her shudders.

He heard her whisper, "I love you," and they were the most liberating words he had ever heard.

"And I you," he whispered in return in a voice that seemed to come from somewhere out of the darkness—somewhere out of his dark Celtic past. It was the voice of an ancient ancestor running naked into battle, carrying only sword and stone, down the heather-covered hills of his green and sacred isle.

With the change of voice came the rushing of an incredible waterfall inside him. The rushing burst through him as if a dam had exploded. For an endless tick in time he lost himself. Died and was reborn.

She fell into the center of him and drowned in passion. He erupted into her inner being and found a sanctuary.

Finally, they lay together. Each was spent and yet fulfilled. Each was finding their way back to individuality, but still with a craving need for the other.

Both were thinking of the words they had said, and how impossible they were right here, right now. Ridiculous, yet not.

"Happily ever after?" Ash asked quietly, knowing that there was no ever after.

"Only in fairy tales," Fey responded, also knowing the truth.

Ash smiled in the night.

His voice was still tinged with the past when he whispered to her, "Once upon a time . . ."

✖ CHAPTER FIFTY-FOUR

FEY HAD SLEPT LATE AND FELT WONDERFUL FOR IT. BOTH she and Ash were realists. They were comfortable with each other. By not addressing the future and confronting the inevitability that it would bring, they were able to live in the moment and not allow the future to detract from immediate pleasure. Fey had always pigeon-holed her life in that manner, but all cops learn to do it—the higher the highs, the lower the lows. Keep them separated, don't let one affect the other.

After a quick breakfast of toast and coffee, however, it was time to get back to work. In Fey's eyes Ash looked more worn than the day before. She knew it was because her perception had changed through learning about his battle with ALS, but she still couldn't get the loud ticking of a clock out of her head.

The cellular phone in Fey's purse chirped. She had only just turned it back on after leaving it off the night before, not wanting to be disturbed. Brushing crumbs from her fingers, Fey reached in and pulled it out. Ash was across the kitchen from her buttering another slab of toast in preparation for slathering it with marmalade.

"Hello," Fey said, holding the instrument up to her ear.

"Fey? It's Jake."

Fey grimaced. Jake Travers's timing never used to be this bad. "I can't talk right now, Jake." Hadn't she made it clear that what they had was over?

"Wait! Don't hang up!" There was something in Jake's voice that set off alarms in Fey's brain. "This isn't about us."

"Then what is it about?" Fey asked, not really wanting to know. There hadn't been enough of the high yet. She wasn't ready for a low.

"Have you watched any television since last night?" Jake knew Fey rarely turned it on.

"No."

"I'm sorry, Fey. Really sorry."

Fey turned away from the kitchen counter. Ash studiously buttered his toast for a third time. "I thought you said this wasn't about us."

"It isn't," Jake said. "Turn on channel seven and brace yourself for everything to hit the fan."

"What's going on, Jake?"

"Just turn the television on."

Fey hung up and turned to Ash. "Television?" she asked.

Ash knew better than to ask why she wanted to turn the television on. Clearly there was something afoot—something not good.

Ash reached out a hand and twitched open a cupboard door. Mounted on a shelf inside was a thirteen-inch color portable with a built-in VCR. He pushed the power button.

"Any specific channel?" he asked.

"Seven," Fey told him succinctly.

Ash picked up the TV remote and punched in the appropriate number. The screen flashed and the face of Devon Wyatt sprung into view.

The setup was a press conference in front of the Los

Angeles downtown courthouse. A short set of stairs led down from the sidewalk of Temple Street to a leveled perimeter that surrounds the courthouse like a moat. The first-floor walls of the courthouse were smoked glass with matching doors. The effect added emphasis to any proclamation made in front of them.

"Where did you get the tape from?" An off-screen reporter shouted a question.

Surrounded by microphones and faceless bodies, Devon Wyatt's expression was particularly somber. "It doesn't matter where the tape came from," he said, speaking sonorously. "What matters is the fact that my client, Mr. JoJo Cullen, is being held without bail on murder charges that the police themselves do not believe are valid."

"What the hell is he talking about?" Fey asked without expecting an answer. "What tape?"

"Detective Fey Croaker was the homicide detective who was initially assigned to investigate the cases in which my client is accused. She was there when JoJo was arrested. She was the first detective to speak to JoJo—without reading him his rights, I might add—on the night he was arrested."

"I didn't have to read him his rights," Fey almost shouted. "I never got to the point of asking him any questions. He was a basket case."

"Calm down," Ash told her. "Listen."

"Detective Croaker was removed from the case when it was taken over by the heavy-handed thugs from the LAPD's robbery-homicide division, but she is currently working with the FBI in an effort to find the real killer and then cover up the mistakes she made in the investigation that led to JoJo's arrest."

"What!" Fey was beside herself.

"I am demanding a full investigation of this situation as well as the immediate release of JoJo Cullen, until the police can prove beyond a doubt that there has been no cover up of evidence."

The scene on the screen changed from the courthouse to the inside of a newsroom. Two morning news anchors, a man and a woman for political correctness, took over the dialogue.

The camera focused in on the male talking head. "That was Devon Wyatt, lawyer for JoJo Cullen, earlier today being asked about the significance of a tape he released to the news media last night."

"What do you think of the tape, Jim?" the female talking head asked as the camera pulled back to include her in the shot.

"Well, Linda," the male's tone was almost condescending. "I think that's up to our viewers to decide. And I think we're ready to play excerpts for them now."

Anchor Jim looked away from Anchor Linda and directly back into the camera. "What you are about to hear are excerpts of an alleged," good old Jim emphasized the word *alleged* in the interest of fairness, "taped conversation between LAPD detective Fey Croaker, the detective initially in charge of the JoJo Cullen case, and a psychiatrist. This station, of course, cannot vouch for the authenticity of this tape, nor for the dubious morality of it being distributed to the media if indeed it is authentic. However, we believe the public has a right to be kept fully up to date on this startling turn of events."

Fey felt herself go cold. Fey felt the blood drain away from her brain.

The screen changed again to be filled with a still drawing of an audio tape recorder with a microphone attached. Printed words scrolled across the center of the screen, so viewers could confirm what they were hearing by reading the words as well.

"Because I don't think JoJo did it." Fey's disembodied voice came through the television's speakers. "There's more to this case than meets the eye."

Listening to her voice go on to explain the various theories she and Ash were considering in the case, Fey almost passed out.

"Fey!" Ash cried out, catching her as she began to slump toward the floor.

He lowered her gently and then knelt beside her. Sitting on the floor, Fey drew her legs up to her chest and hugged them to her. She was crying—anger and pain flowing through her. She felt raped, violated.

"That prick," she said, her voice thick. "That prick!"

"I don't understand," Ash said.

"That tape." Fey waved an arm around in frustration. "That damned tape. It's from a session with my shrink. It's a privileged communication. How the hell can anybody do this?"

Fey's cellular phone chirped again. It continued to chirp until Ash reached over and answered it.

"Hello," he said.

"Who the hell is this?" The voice on the other end of the line was mightily agitated.

"Boo."

"Boo who?"

"Well, you don't have to cry about it."

"For shit's sake, quit screwing me around. Let me talk to Croaker."

Ash was about to tell the voice on the other end of the line to go to hell, but Fey reached out and took the phone from him.

"Mike?" she asked into the mouthpiece. She was pretty sure she recognized the voice of her lieutenant blasting out of the receiver.

"Fey?"

"Yeah.

"What the hell is going on?"

"I don't know, Mike. I swear."

"Get your ass down to the station, now!" Mike Cahill demanded. "We've got a shitload of trouble."

The situation outside West Los Angeles area station was bad. News trucks had been forced to use the westside courthouse plaza, a block away from the station, as a staging area as they couldn't get any closer.

The station was located on Butler Avenue, five hundred yards south of busy Santa Monica Boulevard and five blocks west of the 405 Freeway. As Fey and Ash pulled off the freeway and drove down Santa Monica Boulevard, they got the first inkling of the trouble Mike Cahill had been talking about. There were people everywhere. Most of the people were black, but there was a considerable number of younger white faces from the local university mixed in. Whether they were there as part of the protest, or just to observe and cause further trouble was hard to say.

There was a lot of unintelligible chanting going on and placards demanding the release of JoJo Cullen were sprinkled liberally through the crowd. Other placards were emblazoned with REMEMBER RODNEY KING! and the near-riot-related NO JUSTICE—NO PEACE!

Neither Fey nor Ash spoke. Fey was driving, and she took her right hand off the steering wheel for long enough to flip down the flashing red windshield light and activate the siren. Almost daring someone to step into their path, Fey drove forward toward the Butler Avenue turning.

A half-dozen young, uniformed cops manned a road-block at Butler and Santa Monica. Plastic fifty-gallon drums filled with water acted as a barrier between the cops and the demonstrating public. Two of the uniforms in full riot gear rolled barrels out of the way to let Fey and Ash drive through.

"Flashbacks to ninety-two," Ash said, referring to the days of rage in Los Angeles that had broken out in response to the "not guilty" verdict at the first trial of the officers accused of beating Rodney King.

"I hope not," Fey said. "This looks more staged than anything."

"It could still get out of hand," Ash said. "Become a flash point."

There were several news crews that had been allowed to set up in front of the station. Fey and Ash parked in the official lot and avoided the media by entering the station's back door.

Upstairs in the detective squad room, Fey and Ash went directly to Mike Cahill's office. Inside, there was a crush of top brass, including the chief of police—a man large enough to fill the office all by himself.

Everyone was staring at a television to one side of Mike Cahill's desk. Reverend Aloishious Brown was holding forth, surrounded by a flock of reporters in front and a gaggle of demonstrators behind him.

"We are calling for peaceful demonstration," Brown was saying. "But this blatantly racial action on the part of the police department cannot be allowed to go unchecked. JoJo Cullen is a black man falsely accused. If he was white he would never have been arrested in the first place. We are demanding he be allowed bail until these other avenues of investigation are completely brought out into the open."

"Is he trying to start the riots all over again?" Mike Cahill asked.

"I'm sure he'd be delighted if that happened," Fey said, and everyone in the office turned to look at her.

"Detective Croaker," the chief said, acknowledging her.

"This is Special Agent Ash from the FBI," Fey made introductions. Nobody shook hands.

"Where did this tape come from? Is it legitimate?" Mike Cahill cut directly to the heart of the matter.

Fey took a deep breath. "Yes, it is legitimate. It is a tape of a session with my psychiatrist. It's a privileged communication between doctor and patient."

"You didn't tell anybody you were seeing a shrink."

"I didn't think it was anybody's business," Fey said.

"Well, it sure as hell is now," Cahill said.

"What about all these theories that JoJo Cullen isn't guilty?" This question came from the chief.

"They are exactly that—theories—avenues of investigation to explore," Fey told him. "They were not for public consumption."

"What about the stuff about you and your brother?"

It took Fey a moment to realize what Mike Cahill was asking about. "You mean that's been released as well?" The impact on Fey was almost devastating.

"Is he involved in putting on raves?"

"His actions have nothing to do with me."

"He certainly does," Cahill said, "especially when you use him as a source."

Fey didn't respond.

The chief spoke up. "We have to defuse this problem before it gets out of hand. The easiest way will be to arrange for JoJo Cullen to be released on bail."

"You can't do that, Chief," Mike Cahill said. Other voices in the room agreed. "If we look like we're giving in, these people will be all over us again next time they want something."

"They will be all over us next time whether we give them what they want this time or not."

"JoJo Cullen is still the prime suspect in this case. The evidence is overwhelming." Mike Cullen was one step away from pulling his hair out. "If JoJo Cullen is released on bail, based on the delusions of one renegade detective, then we are betraying all of the detectives that have worked so hard to put this case together."

"Thanks, Lieutenant," Fey said sarcastically. "I appreciate your backing robbery-homicide over your own people."

"It's gone way beyond who I back," Cahill shot his mouth at her. "Our whole system is going to be on trial here. We will be seen as weak."

"Is JoJo Cullen innocent?" Everyone's eyes shifted back to the chief. He was standing with his legs spread wide, supporting his bulk. The small eyes in his full round face were filled with a politician's street smarts. It was clear his question was directed to Fey.

Fey didn't falter. "Yes." Batten down the hatches. Full speed ahead.

"Can you prove it?"

"Not yet."

"If Cullen isn't guilty, who is?"

"I don't know," Fey paused, "yet."

The chief was a man who had been brought in to do a job. He was looked at as a hired gun from outside the department—a stopgap measure to appease a racially in-

flamed public at the time he was hired. He might control
the LAPD, but . . .

Still, he'd been a cop for a long time. Somewhere in his
brain a cop's instincts moved like a panther in the night.

Sometimes you have to gamble. There was no way
around it. Sometimes you had to go out on a limb.

"Get me the district attorney," he said to his adjutant.
There was a flurry of activity as the man started dialing a
cellular phone and talking low and rapid.

The chief brought his focus back to Fey. "Twenty-four
hours, Detective Croaker," he told her. "Bring me a killer.
If you don't, I'm going to run your ass up the city hall
flagpole and let the hyenas tear you to pieces."

✠

CHAPTER FIFTY-FIVE

"TWENTY-FOUR HOURS?" BRINDLE JONES SCOFFED.
"The chief must be off his head. We thought Cahill was
crazy when he gave you a week to crack the case the first
time around."

"We beat the deadline the first time around, we'll beat
it this time around," Fey said more calmly than she felt.
She was well aware that she couldn't let her crew see she
felt like panicking.

The station had been in such an uproar with the demonstration outside, that there was no way to get any work
done. The department had been placed on a tactical alert
that appeared headed for a full-scale mobilization.

Once mobilized, all detectives would be trading in their
suits and ties for uniforms, and hitting the streets with the
regular patrol guys. Twelve-hour shifts would be initiated

and specially trained mobile field force units would be un-
leashed.

After the chief's ultimatum, Fey had walked out of the
lieutenant's office to find her regular crew waiting for her.
Their presence was enough to show their willingness to
help.

Fey looked around at all the hustle and bustle. "Let's
get out of here," she said, "before it really hits the fan."

Everyone had grabbed jackets and guns and trailed after
her. Following each other in cars, the unit exited through
the roadblock at the end of the intersection of Butler and
Ohio thinking it would be less problematic than exiting
through the busier Santa Monica Boulevard and Butler intersection. They were right, but several rocks and bottles
still bounced off their car roofs.

Once away from the station, Fey led the procession to
the Gunnery, a local cop watering hole. Once inside, the
unit pushed two back tables together and sat down for a
briefing session.

Hammer and Nails sat together at one end of the tables.
Next to them Fey could see that Brindle and Alphabet had
appeared to form an unlikely partnership. Monk Lawson
was on his own, but as he was running the unit in Fey's
absence, that was probably the correct thing.

"They're going to give JoJo bail," Hammersmith said.
"It's inevitable."

"No way," said Alphabet.

"Don't fool yourself," Hammersmith responded. "The
chief is going to bend over backwards on this thing. If he
was going to make a stand, he'd have done so by now."

"He's already shown his true colors," Brindle said.
"No pun intended. He should have made a major statement by now backing Fey and denouncing Devon Wyatt
for releasing that tape."

"I don't know what the hell this department is coming
to," Alphabet said. "The top brass has turned into a bunch
of wimps. We don't back our people anymore. We don't
stand up for what's right, just what's politically correct."

"It's okay," Fey said, wanting to calm everyone down

and get back on track. It wasn't okay, but the release of the tape was something she was going to have to learn to live with. Everyone would now know she was going to a shrink. Well, screw them if they couldn't handle it.

"We've got to do what we do best, and we've got to do it fast," Fey told her people.

Several noncop customers entered the Gunnery, but Harry Cross—the bartender, cook, owner—chased them out. A retired cop himself, he knew an important strategy session when he saw one.

"Let's clear the decks right away, and lay it out that JoJo is innocent," Fey said.

"If he's guilty, and I'm still not convinced he isn't," Monk Lawson said, "we're really up Shit Creek without a paddle."

"Let's not even consider it," Fey said. "If JoJo is innocent, then somebody set him up but good. Any ideas?"

"Rival team?" Alphabet suggested.

"Get real," Brindle told him, not unkindly. "Maybe a rival team sets him up for gambling on games, playing with the point spread. They wouldn't go around murdering kids."

"How about a crazy?" Monk put in. "A stalker. Somebody who is obsessed with JoJo's celebrity."

Ash turned a hard-backed chair around and straddled it. "I don't think so," he said. "Stalkers want something from their victims—love, understanding, adulation. They attack the victims of their obsession directly not indirectly."

"Doesn't leave much, does it?" Rhonda Lawless said.

Hammersmith had been thinking. "JoJo didn't seem to have any kind of a life outside of playing basketball and the orphanage where he lived. His sex life revolved around one-night stands with street kids, which would indicate he had no steady bedmate. His whole psychology appears to isolate him from relationships."

"What's your point?" Fey asked.

"I'm not sure," Hammersmith told her. "I'm just talking this through. What are the reasons for framing somebody?'' He looked over at his partner.

''Profit or revenge,'' Rhonda said, seeming to be on Hammer's wavelength as always.

''Okay,'' Fey said, also picking up on the thought. ''Let's take profit. Who would gain by having JoJo arrested for murder?''

''Every other team in the NBA.'' Alphabet said. ''Which was my original point.''

''The same argument holds,'' Brindle told him. ''If it was somebody in the league trying to get rid of him, there are easier ways of doing it.''

Alphabet shrugged, but didn't argue.

''Anybody else?'' Fey asked.

''Devon Wyatt is going to make a mint off of this case,'' Monk said.

Everyone laughed.

''He sure is,'' Fey said. ''But somehow I think his year-end profits would still be astronomical with or without this case.''

''I know,'' agreed Monk. ''If he wasn't defending JoJo, it would be some other high-profile celebrity footing his bill.''

Ash rested his arms across the back of the chair he was straddling. ''I'd love to put Zelman Tucker up as a suspect. He stands to make a fortune writing a book about this case. But I have to say the same argument holds true for him as with Wyatt. He's going to make a mint somehow whether it's writing about this case or the next spectacular one that comes along.''

''How about revenge?'' Hammersmith asked, moving along to the next topic. ''Is there somebody out there who could hate JoJo enough to not just kill him, but destroy him?''

''Some kid he was punking, maybe,'' Alphabet said.

''I doubt you'd find a street chicken sophisticated enough,'' Ash said. ''They might kill somebody up front and personal, but this has been planned. Street chickens are too busy simply staying alive.''

"It would have to be somebody close to JoJo," Fey said. "Somebody who knew about his predilection for young boys. I think that was almost as big a revelation in this case as the fact that JoJo could be a murderer."

"You know we may have something there," Brindle chipped in.

"What do you mean?" Fey asked.

Harry Cross interrupted the flow of conversation with food and drink. Nobody had ordered, but Harry knew what was needed to stimulate the think tank.

"Thanks, Harry," Fey said, giving him her best smile and then turned her attention back to Brindle.

Brindle was looking at Alphabet, who spoke up for both of them. "When we were working the street for a lead on the first victim, Rush . . . This isn't anything much," he said sounding dubious.

"Come on," Fey urged. "Let's hear it."

Alphabet shrugged. "Well, one of the kids we talked to came to see us at the station. We'd helped out a friend of hers that night so she came to return the favor."

Brindle picked up the thread of the story. "She told us about this guy that had tried to grab one of the kids after he'd been with JoJo, but the kid got away. Apparently, JoJo's secret life was well known on the street even if it wasn't public knowledge."

"This girl told us that the night Ricky Long was killed, he'd been with JoJo right before being picked up by the same guy in a blue van that had tried before to grab the other kid who'd been with JoJo."

"A blue van," Hammer and Nails both said together, both sitting upright.

"What is it?" Fey asked. The mention of a blue van had set her own adrenaline flowing.

Hammer looked at Nails. "I have no idea," he said and shrugged. "But we got the same info from another source."

"Who?" Fey demanded.

"Darcy Wyatt," Nails said. "He called us. Wanted to make a deal for information regarding JoJo. We got his cellmate changed, but he wants a deal on the whole rape case. He says that what he's got is that big.''

''Without making a deal,'' Hammer said, ''he would only tell us that there was a blue van involved.''

Ash spoke up. ''Your brother also mentioned a blue van—in connection with Rush.''

''I remember,'' Fey said. ''I didn't think anything of it at the time. It was too innocuous. But there is something else.'' She closed her eyes in thought. ''A blue van. A blue van,'' she muttered. ''Why is that ringing a bell?'' She opened her eyes and looked over at Monk.

''Beats me,'' he said. ''But I'm hearing the same ringing.''

''How would Darcy Wyatt have anything to trade that pertains to JoJo?''

''His father, maybe,'' Hammer said with a shrug.

''I don't think so,'' Fey said. ''If he was on the outside, I would say maybe he overheard something. But being locked up, I don't think he would have the chance to get anything out of his father.'' She stopped and thought for a second. ''Is he trying to pull some kind of a scam? Does he really expect us to trade off the rapes?''

''I don't think it's a scam,'' Rhonda spoke up. ''He does think he can cut some kind of a deal. And now that the lead of a blue van has been confirmed from another source, it gives it credence.''

Harry Cross came back over to the tables. ''I'm sorry to interrupt,'' he said. ''But I thought you should know. They've just announced it on the radio. JoJo's being given bail.''

A collective ''Shit!'' emanated from everyone around the table.

''Maybe not,'' said Fey. ''Maybe this is a good thing.''

''What do you mean?'' Ash asked.

''When JoJo was locked up, he was robbery-homicide's baby. We had no access to him. Now he's out, he's fair game.''

''You mean you're going to try and talk to him?'' Alphabet scoffed. "Devon Wyatt will laugh you right out of his office."

"Maybe not," Fey said. "Because I've got something he wants."

CHAPTER FIFTY-SIX

"TELL ME EXACTLY WHY I SHOULD LET YOU HAVE AC-cess to my client," Devon Wyatt said to Fey. He was savoring every moment of this unexpected pleasure.

Fey and Ash were in Wyatt's Beverly Hills office. Wyatt was ensconced behind his desk enjoying another expensive cigar. Ash was leaning against a wall next to a Chagall original. This was Fey's show right now. His turn would come later.

Fey stood in front of Wyatt's desk. He'd offered her a chair when she came in, but she had been too stubborn to accept. She didn't like what she was going to have to do here to get what she wanted, but she couldn't see any way around it.

"You're very good at what you do, Wyatt," Fey said. "I can't say as I like it, or admire it, but you're good at it."

"If you are talking about my ability to defend innocent clients—"

"Innocent clients have nothing to do with this," Fey said. She was fighting to keep a handle on her temper. Maybe her time with Dr. Winters had done some good after all, despite all the damage. "You had no idea JoJo Cullen was innocent. You took the case to do a smear campaign against both myself and the department—it was

personal—and you've done a hell of a job.'' Fey threw up
her hands. ''Well, you've got what you wanted. You've
won. You want me to capitulate, I will. But don't let your
anger with me over the arrest of your son allow a killer to
get away.''

Wyatt sat smoking his cigar.

''Impressive,'' he said. ''But I don't buy it.''

''Damn it,'' Fey said. Leaning forward, she put her
hands flat on Wyatt's Empire table desk. ''This city is
going to tear itself apart unless you back down. I know
you have connections to Aloishious Brown. I'm not stupid.
I know how the street structure works around here. I've
seen Brown on the television telling everyone to remain
calm out of one side of his mouth. It's what he's saying
out of the other side of his mouth that concerns me. The
tape of my shrink session wouldn't have been enough by
itself to get JoJo released on bail. You needed to couple
it with the type of pressure Brown could bring to bear on
the city.''

Wyatt's expression changed slightly. ''I'm a little more
impressed,'' he said. ''But again I ask, what's in it for
me?''

Fey had to give a little laugh at that statement. ''Not
what's in it for your client?''

Wyatt shrugged. ''We're both putting some of our cards
on the table.''

''I can't take back what your son did. He takes his
chances in court just like anyone else. I'll help the DA
prosecute him, but I won't persecute him. I wouldn't offer
him a deal—even if I could—but I won't fight a deal if
he cuts one with the DA.''

Wyatt looked at the tip of his smoldering cigar, but
didn't say anything.

''I need to talk to JoJo,'' Fey said.

Silence from Wyatt.

Fey gave it her last shot. ''You deal in favors, Wyatt.
At some time you're going to need one from somebody
like me. Let me talk to JoJo, and you've got a marker you
can call in.''

Wyatt shifted his gaze from his cigar to Fey and rear-ranged himself in his chair. "How big a marker?"

"We'll have to play that by ear when the time comes."

Wyatt stood up suddenly. "You know," he said. "I really think you mean what you say. People with principles never cease to amaze me." He walked around his desk. "Wait here."

Ash pushed himself off the wall. "You're going to pay for this," he said. "Wyatt will take what you owe him out in blood."

"I'll cross that bridge when I get to it. Right now I can hear a clock ticking and it has nothing to do with my biology."

Wyatt returned a few minutes later with JoJo in tow. JoJo was wearing a custom-made suit and didn't look physically any worse for his time in jail.

"JoJo Cullen," Wyatt said by way of introduction, "Detective Croaker."

Fey and Cullen sat in the two chairs in front of Wyatt's desk. Wyatt returned to his own chair, and Ash went back to supporting the wall.

JoJo sat with his hands in his lap. Fey didn't quite know where to start so she hopped in with both feet.

"I'm sure you're aware that the police now believe that somebody else may be behind the murders of which you are accused."

"I could have told you that," JoJo said. His tone wasn't aggressive, just conversational. "I kept asking Mr. Wyatt to let me tell you my side, but he told me it was best to remain silent until we got to court."

Fey felt anger rising inside of her and fought to keep it in check. Wyatt didn't care about his clients. If he did, he would have let JoJo make a statement.

"Well, none of us had the chance to let you tell us," Fey said. She felt like shooting a dirty look in Wyatt's direction, but knew it would have fallen on barren ground. "There are some questions that I want to ask you. Hope-fully, what you can tell us will give us some sort of lead to the real killer."

"I don't know who it is," JoJo said. He was becoming visibly upset.

"Relax," Fey said. "Relax. Nobody is saying you know who it is. But there are some things you can tell us."

JoJo watched Fey closely. "Okay," he said.

"When we searched your house, we found some Polaroid photos of two of the victims and some tapes of the victims screaming. Where did they come from?"

Tears welled up in JoJo's eyes. "They came in the mail one day. I didn't know what to do about them."

"Why didn't you go to the police?"

"How could I? I didn't want anybody to find out about ... what ... what ..."

"About the fact that you had sexual relations with young male prostitutes?" Fey said.

"Yes," JoJo said. "It was bad enough trying to fight those urges, let alone admit that I gave into them. I also didn't know if it was some kind of cruel joke. I didn't know those kids were actually dead. I didn't want to believe it."

Fey changed tack. "On the night you were arrested, why were you down at the beach?"

"I got a telephone call—a call telling me that another boy was going to die unless I went to the beach."

"Did you recognize the voice on the phone?"

"No, it was all muffled."

"Why didn't you call the police?"

JoJo shrugged. "I was scared. I figured that if the first two boys were actually dead, then the police might blame me if I told them the story since I hadn't come forward right away."

"What happened at the beach?"

"The voice on the phone had told me to wait under the lifeguard station. I went there, but there was nobody around. Then I saw the arm sticking out of the sand and I freaked out. And suddenly the cops were there and everything got crazy. I wanted to die. I wanted that cop to shoot me. I didn't want to let Sister Ruth and everybody down."

Tears were flowing down JoJo's face now, but he made no move to hide them.

"Who would want to do this to you, JoJo?" Fey asked.

"I don't know. I don't know. Don't you think I've asked myself that question a thousand times?"

"Do you know anybody who drives a blue van?"

"A blue van? Why?"

Fey picked up on JoJo's hesitation. She sat forward on her chair and took one of JoJo's hands. Even Wyatt had tensed.

"Come on, JoJo. Who do you know that drives a blue van?"

JoJo hesitated for another moment and then said softly, "My brother from the family that adopted me does."

■○■

CHAPTER FIFTY-SEVEN

"HERE WE GO," FEY HAD SAID TO ASH ON THEIR WAY back to the station.

Ash had known exactly what she meant. There was a time in every case when suddenly a solitary leak leads to the sudden crumpling of the whole dam. As long as there wasn't a little Dutch boy around to stick his finger in the dyke, the whole case suddenly opened up and started to speed away almost out of control.

This was the feeling that every detective lives for. The scent of blood is in the air and electricity flows through your veins. You feel as if you could swallow lightening and crap thunder. You are on the jazz and there ain't any way of getting off the bullet train.

Devon Wyatt had proven to be as good as his word. In

the short time it took for Fey and Ash to drive from
Wyatt's office back to West Los Angeles area station, the
crowds in the streets had dispersed into the rat holes they
had originally sprouted from.

The barricades were still up around the station, but the
city appeared to be well on the way back to its normal
state of chaos.

At her desk, Fey phoned San Diego PD and asked for
Montegue.

When he answered, Fey jumped right in the middle of
him.

"Montegue, you are an asshole."

"What? Who is this."

"This is Croaker. Why didn't you give us the lowdown
on the rest of the Kingston family?"

"What are you talking about?"

"We've just come from interviewing JoJo Cullen. He
said he's got two brothers from his adopted family. One
named Kenny and the other one named Jim."

"Yeah, so?"

Fey was pissed. "So, you give us this shuck and jive
about how you think JoJo's adopted old man might have
been murdered, but you don't say squat about the brother
who dropped off the face of the earth one day never to be
seen again."

"Hey, I was speculating enough already. I had no idea
there was any connection between the two. Can you prove
one?"

"I don't have to at this point. There's too much coin-
cidence in this whole mess for them not to be connected."

"So, what do you want from me?"

"First of all I want you to cut me some slack for being
a first-class bitch," Fey said, backing off. "I'm all wired
up with a good case of twenty-twenty hindsight, and I'm
taking it out on you."

Montegue's soft chuckle came down the line. "All is
forgiven, but I'm sure as hell glad you're not my boss.
What else do you need?"

"I need anything you've got on the other brother, Kenny

Kingston. JoJo said he's a drifter, but maybe you can come up with a line on him down there. We ran his driver's license and it shows a San Diego address.'' Fey picked up a printout and read off the address.

"That's no good," Montegue told her. "That's the address of his dad's house. It was sold ages ago. There's another family living there now."

"Okay. We also show a van registered to Kenny with the same address and a PO box number." Fey gave the PO box to Montegue.

"Sounds like a mail drop, not the post office," Montegue said. "I'll check it out. You need a photo if I can find one?"

"Yeah, we got one faxed from DMV. It's good enough to start with, but it's black and white and fuzzy."

"Sounds like a panda."

"Har, har," Fey said. "Listen, things are breaking. You get anything call my beeper." She gave Montegue the number. "And thanks."

Monk Lawson sauntered over. "I'm still bugged about the blue van," he said. "I know we think we've got it pinned down to Kenny Kingston. And I know that it has come up from three different sources. But none of the sources appear connected to me, and I still feel there is something else there—something else that we're missing."

"I don't know," Fey said. "I felt that same way too, but I don't know if it matters anymore."

Monk was still thoughtful. "The street kid and your brother who works the raves—I can see them moving in the same circles and getting the same information. But how does Darcy Wyatt come up with it?"

Fey dry-washed her face with her hands and yawned. "Beats me." She stood up and arched her back. "I know this is stupid, but I'm starved. I didn't get to chow down on any of that stuff Harry Cross put out for us at the Gunnery. Anybody want to order in a pizza?"

Fey stopped and looked at Monk. She felt chills.

Monk's eyes got big.

"Pizza," he said.

"Pizza," Fey said. "Damn it, that's it! Darcy Wyatt used a blue van to deliver pizzas."

"He borrowed it from another worker at the restaurant," Monk said. "What was the name of it?"

"Fratelli Pizza," Fey said. "And there's another connection."

"What?"

"On the directory of automatic numbers on the phone in JoJo's local town house. When we searched the place, I ran all the numbers. They were all fast-food joints, and one of them was Fratelli Pizza. If Darcy Wyatt has something to do with a blue van—"

"And if that blue van belongs to Kenny Kingston—" Monk continued.

"It's a lot of ifs, but if Darcy delivered pizzas to JoJo it could give an explanation for how the evidence got planted in the town house and why Darcy thinks he has something to trade." Fey ran the line of reasoning to completion.

Ash interrupted both of them. "Fratelli Pizza?" he asked.

"Yeah," Fey and Monk said in unison.

"Do either of you know what Fratelli means?"

"No," said Fey.

"I figured it was the owner's name," Monk said.

"Kenny Kingston must have been laughing his ass off," Ash said.

"Why?" Fey insisted.

"Fratelli," Ash said. "It's Italian for brothers."

✦ CHAPTER FIFTY-EIGHT

KENNY HAD A STACK OF NEWSPAPERS SPREAD OUT IN front of him and he was pissed. How in the hell could they let JoJo out of jail? JoJo was a murderer, a perverter of boys. How could they let him out?

The battery-powered portable radio to which he'd been listening had just spilled the news. JoJo had been released on bail. Kenny knew, however, that was only the tip of the iceberg. If JoJo's fancy lawyer could get him released on bail, then he could get JoJo off.

Kenny shuffled the papers around until he came to the transcript of the tape that Devon Wyatt had released to the media. He had been keeping up with the news about JoJo every day. It both excited and fascinated him. He'd scanned the article about the transcript earlier, but now the radio said that the tape was what had led to JoJo being given bail.

Kenny didn't understand how JoJo's lawyer got the tape, or even why anyone was paying attention to it. So, some bleeding-heart female police detective believed JoJo was innocent and told her shrink about it. So what? So, it made a bunch of people rally round and shout slogans. Again, so what? What the hell was this world coming to when fancy lawyers could make the police department roll over and play dead?

Kenny just didn't understand.

The radio said that the detectives were also pursuing other leads. Did that mean they knew about him?

With one arm, he swept the papers off of the cracked

counter and onto the floor. He reached over and picked up his basketball and began bouncing it. He was pissed. This wasn't in the plan. The cops were supposed to be stupid. Everyone was supposed to play by the rules, and the rules said cops were stupid.

The windows of the abandoned restaurant had long been boarded up, but Kenny had removed enough of the plywood to give him the illumination he needed. The Sea Otter had once been a successful oceanfront restaurant. Thick wooden pylons, buried into the sea floor, supported the half of the restaurant that jutted out over the gray waters of the Pacific.

Located on a wide turn of Pacific Coast Highway in Malibu, the Sea Otter had been one of California's preeminent feeding troughs, with top starring in every epicurean guide. It had been a mecca not only for lovers who wanted the romance of the ocean, but also for the gourmet who wanted the romance of exquisite food.

Huge picture windows had provided Sea Otter diners with a magnificent view of the Pacific Ocean and the rolling sets of waves that provided sustenance for surfers and boogie boarders. The food had been superb, the service excellent, the prices high, the atmosphere wonderful, and the reservations book filled a month in advance.

The parking lot in front of the restaurant was surprisingly generous, due to the fact that half of the restaurant jutted out into thin air. Now it was deserted and crumbling, the asphalt neglected and scarred.

Over the years the Sea Otter had survived many natural disasters. There had been raging storms that sent sets of twenty-foot waves crashing against the huge view windows. Twice, Malibu area brush fires had burnt down to the edge of the Sea Otter parking lot, licking hungrily for the structure but never feasting. Landslides and mudslides from the cliffs on the opposite side of Pacific Coast Highway had failed to do more than disturb business for a few hours at most. Through it all, the Sea Otter had stood as an impervious, almost cocky testament to the endurance of manmade structures.

Mother Nature, however, is a relentless mistress and when the 8.4 Northridge earthquake struck in January of 1994, the Sea Otter took a hit from which it couldn't recover. The pylons that were sunk into the sea bed crumpled, leaving the restaurant above them to twist and buckle. The restaurant had not been open at the time, and the owners gave blessings for small mercies, but the heart of the Sea Otter had been torn out and crushed.

The owners had wanted to rebuild. They were willing to do whatever it took to give new life to what had become a historical Malibu landmark. The bureaucrats, though, were not as enthusiastic. Try as they might, the owners could not get approval for rebuilding a restaurant that hung into space on a coastline where any second the next big one could hit.

The battle waged on. Meanwhile, the Sea Otter hung twisted, buckled, abandoned, and condemned—kept off limits by a chain-link fence surrounding the property on three sides and the sea on the other. The once warm and thriving restaurant was now nothing more than an empty, rotting carcass in an above-ground grave.

At least the owners believed the Sea Otter was empty, condemned, and abandoned. For a short time, Kenny Kingston had been a cook at the Sea Otter. He hadn't lasted long, as his culinary talents tended more toward flipping hamburgers than preparing trout amandine. There was also the problem of Kenny getting to work on time, if he came in at all. If he'd had a good day hustling the basketball courts, he saw no reason to hustle his buns all night over a hot stove under the direction of an ill-tempered chef.

However, before Kenny was given his walking papers, he'd made sure he had pilfered the keys to both the restaurant and the alarm system. If times got tough, Kenny knew he could always find an after-hours meal and shelter at the Sea Otter.

When the Sea Otter had been condemned, Kenny claimed it as his own personal castle. It had been a long time since he'd had a permanent place to call home—something more permanent than his van anyway—and the

Sea Otter was perfect for somebody with Kenny's dubious habits.

Dribbling the basketball, Kenny moved from the kitchen into what had once been the main dining area. Everything inside of the restaurant, booths, tables, fixtures, lighting, and anything else that was salable, had been removed and auctioned. Even the carpeting had been rolled up and sold, leaving the hard concrete floor naked. This suited Kenny just fine. Dribbling faster and faster, he turned one way and then another as if moving through imaginary opponents. With a final, fluid movement he jumped, twisted in the air, brought his arms up over his head, and flicked the ball toward a backboard and hoop he'd jerry-rigged to one wall. The ball swished through the hoop and the nylon net below.

"Two!" Kenny yelled. That was another thing Kenny liked about the Sea Otter—there were no other businesses or houses close enough to overhear any noises he, or one of his guests, might make.

Kenny let the ball trickle away until it came to rest against a wall. At six-five, his elongated frame was heavily muscled. He wore a sweatshirt with cut-off sleeves over baggy shorts, thick white socks, and high-top Nikes. He dropped down and cranked out a hundred pushups, and then flipped over to grind out five hundred crunches of various types. Not needing fancy exercise machines, Kenny used what was left behind in the restaurant to facilitate his workout.

He had removed the plywood from one of the picture windows through which hundreds of diners had once gazed out over the gray Pacific. The floor here was buckled and unstable—at several points there were actually holes that dropped through to the ocean below—but Kenny had learned where to step and where not to step. In front of the window, he moved through a series of stretching exercises. He could feel a need growing within him, but fought to deny it.

He was worried. The woman detective who had been taped said she thought that JoJo was innocent. Kenny had once believed that he was smarter than the cops. He thought he'd covered all the bases. He thought that he'd put JoJo in the frame beyond any question. Kenny hadn't thought that evidence could be looked at as—what was the term the woman detective had used?—too convenient.

Kenny went back to the kitchen and picked up the papers again. He read through the transcript of Fey's session with Dr. Winters. *Maybe she's as crazy as me,* Kenny thought, *having to go to a psychiatrist,* Kenny knew all about psychiatrists. He'd been to see enough of them. Apparently, hanging cats and dogs from neighborhood trees was not an acceptable childhood pastime.

But what the shrinks didn't realize was that the hanging of cats and dogs was a case of monkey see, monkey do. They didn't believe Kenny when he tried to tell them, said he was making it all up.

Nobody would believe that Kenny's dad would do the things Kenny said he was doing. Kenny's dad had been something special. Real special. He was a local hero. The basketball coach. Kenny and his brother Jim had been special also. They were the coach's kids and there was nobody better on the basketball court. How could a man who loved children so much be capable of doing the things Kenny said he was doing? It wasn't possible.

Anyway, Jim wasn't saying his dad did these things. Only Kenny—and it was clear there was a lot of sibling rivalry going on between those two. Kenny was a little shorter, a littler slower than Jim. He was also a year older than Jim, so it wasn't a matter of catching up. Everyone could understand how that might make Kenny a little disgruntled. But to say the things he did—well, that was going too far. The kid needed help.

People knew that Kenny's dad loved him. Loved his brother Jim as well. Loved JoJo, the little nigger he brought home to live with them. Also, Kenny's dad sure was admired for taking in JoJo and teaching him how to play b-ball. Kenny's dad sure loved kids. Knew what was good for them too—hard work and discipline.

Kenny's dad had loved him all right. Loved him nearly

to death when he found out that Kenny had told the shrinks about their special training sessions—the ones that would make Kenny a better basketball player.

The special training had begun when Kenny's dad had been coaching their YMCA team. Kenny and Jim had been the stars even then at eight years old. But in the championship game, Kenny had missed two critical free throws that had given the game away.

In the vernacular, Kenny had *choked*. His heart had filled his throat in response to the pressure and he'd been unable to do what needed to be done to win.

Jim had never choked.

Kenny's dad worried about Kenny choking. He couldn't have his kid blowing games because he choked under pressure. Something had to be done to teach the little shit—excuse me—kid not to choke.

The special training had started later that night when Kenny was getting out of the shower. Jim was out in the front yard, still practicing—had to do those hundred free throws for dad.

Dad had grabbed Kenny and demanded to know why he wasn't out practicing with his brother. Kenny had started to cry. He could smell the beer on his father's breath, knew something bad was going to happen. Kenny's mom had been at church that night. It seemed as if she was always at church.

Kenny was naked and his dad laughed at him. The big man spun him around, held him tight. He told Kenny he was going to teach him how not to choke, how he better never choke again.

Dad mounted Kenny like a dog, hurt him, made him scream. And to cut out the screams, Dad had put his hands around Kenny's throat. Dad said that if Kenny was going to choke, then he was going to give him something to choke about.

The special training had been practiced again many times. Kenny's dad had to make damn sure Kenny never choked in a game again. That was what it was all about—

conquering fear and pain so you didn't choke. You always had to make the other guy choke.

Kenny hated the training, but it was the one way he knew he was more special than his brother. If he could conquer the fear and the pain, if he didn't choke, then he made his dad proud—and that was all that Kenny had ever wanted.

So Kenny had suffered the special training almost without complaint. That was until daddy had brought home JoJo. Then everything had changed. Kenny's mom had left them because dad's obsession with basketball had become too much for her to deal with, but nobody seemed to miss her—least of all Kenny's dad. And wasn't it wonderful how Kenny's dad soldiered on as a single parent? How could that woman leave such a fine man?

Even the special training had changed. It got worse and worse once mom wasn't around and Kenny's dad didn't have to worry so much about being caught. Kenny was forced to dig holes in the backyard and lie there while his dad covered him up with earth. He had to lie, buried, trying not to suffocate and choke, holding still while his dad played with himself. He couldn't choke—had to lie there until dad was finished and told him he could claw his way out.

Even today, he could still taste the grave in his mouth.

Kenny could have put up with it though, could have lived through it if it hadn't been for JoJo. JoJo didn't have to do the things that Kenny had to do in order to be a better basketball player. Kenny's dad had promised Kenny that if he did the things that he was told to do, he'd be a better player—the best player—but it wasn't true. He could never beat JoJo. And JoJo got all the praise, while Kenny got all the fear and pain.

JoJo had stolen his father, had stolen his childhood, and had stolen the fame and glory that would have been Kenny's if his father had only had the time to spend with him instead of JoJo. His father had time to coach JoJo. All he had time to do with Kenny was the special training, the scary things, the painful things.

Kenny felt the anger rising inside of him. Like JoJo, Jim had never had to do the special training. Jim had just played basketball. He'd also been better than Kenny. Dad had said that was why Jim didn't have to do the special training. Jim didn't choke when the pressure was on.

Dad had been wrong.

Jim may have been a better basketball player than Kenny, but he wasn't stronger and he wasn't smarter. Kenny learned a lot about choking from the special training sessions.

He'd also learned a lot from roping and choking the animals in the neighborhood. That was until he'd got caught. He'd been sent to see a psychiatrist. Eventually, he told the shrink about the special training sessions, but nobody believed him.

And when dad found out he'd told—whoo whee! Dad told him he'd choked again, big time. You didn't tell people about the special training. That was secret. Now he'd have to teach Kenny about choking all over again.

So Kenny learned some more about choking. He also learned about being sly. Jim and JoJo didn't know these things. As he got older and became sexually aware on his own terms, Kenny began to see that it was up to him to teach them. He figured he'd start out with Jim. Practice, after all, made perfect.

He and Jim had been playing hoops in the dark one night down at the high school. They were alone in the gym. They could get in using dad's keys. Moonlight filtered in through the high windows, giving them just enough light to play by. They could have turned on the lights, but that wouldn't have been as much fun.

It was Jim's senior year—the year after Jim and Kenny and JoJo had led Mission Bay High to the state championship. It was almost time for graduation, and Jim was getting ready to go to university on a basketball scholarship. A full ride. Kenny had to admit, he was jealous.

Kenny had graduated a year earlier, but there had been no full scholarship offer. He wasn't as good at the game as his brother or JoJo. He was good, better than many others, but only good enough to rate a place leading the local junior college.

The special training session had also stopped. Kenny was both relieved and upset. With JoJo around, the special training sessions were the only real connection with his father he had left.

Kenny wasn't sure why the sessions had stopped. He figured it was something he'd done. And then one night he looked in his father's bedroom window and saw JoJo naked on the bed with his dad. And what they were doing were things that his dad had never done with him.

Kenny was angry then, more angry than he'd ever been. He began to watch his father, spy on him, and he discovered other dirty little secrets. Dad choked also, only he did it to himself with a big, black leather mask over his head while tied to a door handle.

Kenny guessed his father didn't need him anymore. Kenny guessed he'd been cured of choking.

That night at the gym, Kenny and Jim were playing one-on-one, using the darkness to hone their instincts. You had to know where your opponent was and where the basket was at all times.

Jim never comprehended what was happening when Kenny threw a rope around his neck and strung him up over the backboard. Kenny hadn't done anything like this since he'd strung up cats and dogs as a kid, and it excited him in incredible ways.

Kenny had danced around in joy watching Jim kick and scrabble, fighting against the rope that choked him. Kenny figured he now knew all about choking. He even kind of liked it. It burned him in its power to arouse—especially when it was somebody else doing the choking. Watching his brother Jim undergoing special training for the first time, Kenny got so excited he spent himself all over the floor.

After Jim had done the ultimate choke, as Kenny liked to think of it, Kenny had carried the body out to his blue van. Calmly, he drove away from the school and out to the local cemetery.

He'd been there earlier in the day. He'd been planning ahead. And things were as he needed them. Two new graves had been dug, six-foot-deep holes waiting for caskets to be lowered into them the following day.

That night it didn't take Kenny long to dig the grave a little deeper, lay Jim down, and cover him up with earth. Jim's arm had popped out, and for a second Kenny thought his brother was trying to claw his way out. Once he'd recovered his wits, he quickly reburied the arm.

Kenny knew that the following day a coffin would be dropped on top of his brother along with another six feet of earth. *Let's see him claw his way out of that*, Kenny thought.

Moving quickly and surely, he dug down in the next grave and buried a suitcase full of Jim's clothing and personal items. A new coffin on top would keep that lot well hidden also.

Kenny didn't give much thought to what he had done. It had been fun. It had been revenge.

The cops looked for Jim, of course. Kenny, dad, and JoJo were really worried. But Jim had just turned eighteen. He was an adult. He could do whatever he wanted. If he wanted to take off without telling anybody, that was his right. If he had choked and wanted to run away from the pressure of big-time college basketball, it was up to him.

The cops were stupid, Kenny thought. Didn't they know he was the one that choked under pressure? Not Jim. Jim only choked when there was a rope around his neck.

One death invariably leads to another. This was a law of nature that Kenny quickly discovered. Kenny thought that things would be different with Jim gone, but dad just got more and more into pushing JoJo.

Kenny became nothing more than another training aid to help JoJo excel. Kenny resented it. He resented that the next year JoJo was offered scholarships everywhere. All of Kenny's special training had been for nothing.

Kenny hated JoJo, but he hid it well. Couldn't do anything about it, because dad would never forgive him. Kenny still just wanted his dad to love him and approve of him, but he had never been good enough. He always choked.

Then Kenny's mind got another twisted idea. If dad wasn't around any more, Kenny could play whatever game he wanted with JoJo. Make it bad. Put JoJo under pressure. Make JoJo choke.

It was another three years before Kenny matched up both nerve and opportunity. Kenny was no longer living at home. He visited occasionally, but he'd already become a drifter, working odd jobs and hustling basketball.

Kenny had come home to be with his dad while watching JoJo and UCLA play in the Final Four tournament. For whatever reason, that night was almost too much for Kenny to take.

His dad's fanaticism in urging JoJo and his team to win was crushing. And when UCLA lost, watching his dad's tears tore Kenny up. His dad had never felt that way about him—but he felt that way about a little nigger kid he'd taken in off the street.

Biding his time, Kenny waited and watched until he was sure dad was going to have one of his private sex sessions. Kenny had watched him secretly before—put the mask on, tie the rope to the door, put it around his neck, lean forward and choke himself while he choked his monkey. This time, though, Kenny was there to add that bit of extra pressure. And what do you know? Dad choked, big time.

When the body was discovered, Kenny knew the police were really stupid because they said the death was an accident. Yeah, his dad had an accident all right. But if that's what the cops wanted to believe, it was okay with Kenny.

Kenny realized then that murder was pretty easy. If he took his time and planned, savored every minute of it, he could also get to JoJo. He wanted to get to JoJo, wanted to make him suffer for being better than he was, for taking his father away, for all the special training sessions that never made a difference.

Apparently, however, not all cops were stupid. Kenny thought he'd planned the murders to frame JoJo real well. He'd had fun taunting his adopted brother, sending him photos of the victims. Victims that Kenny had allowed JoJo to choose himself through his own perversions.

Kenny enjoyed looking through the photos he had taken of the victims. He liked listening over and over to the tapes of them dying. None of them could stand up to the special training sessions as he had. He was better than they were. He didn't choke.

He listened to the tapes and looked at the pictures while he masturbated. He thought about sending JoJo to prison. Maybe JoJo would hang himself. Now, wouldn't that be the coolest. The images of all of it gave him such intensity in his sexual completion he felt he could die.

Now Kenny could see that it was all unraveling.

Who was this cop who was hunting him, he wondered. Turning the pages of the newspaper, Kenny found the article with the transcript of the cop's shrink session. He read it through several times.

This cop, this Detective Fey Croaker, she was trying to make him choke. What she was really doing was making him mad. Maybe she could figure out who he was, but Kenny wasn't going to choke. He didn't choke under pressure anymore. Dad had taught him not to choke under pressure. He was better at not choking than anybody.

He felt the pressure rising up in his throat. He could smell the dirt of the shallow graves from which his father had made him crawl out. He felt like his head would implode from the pressure. No time left on the clock. The other team is one point ahead. Kenny could see himself at the free throw line. One for two. Make the first free throw. Tie the game. Make the second free throw. Win the game. Choke and miss the first shot and it's all over.

Kenny set the newspaper aside and went back to playing basketball. It helped him think. He threw up one free throw after another into his makeshift basket. Each one swished through the net. Somewhere in the mesmerizing activity, Kenny realized he knew what to do next.

Detective Fey Croaker wasn't going to make him choke. He was going to make her choke.

CHAPTER FIFTY-NINE

THERE WAS NO BLARING OF SIRENS OR FLASHING LIGHTS from the detective cars as they pulled into the front and back parking lots of the Fratelli Pizza franchise on La Cienega Boulevard.

La Cienega Boulevard cut like a knife across the city, forming a natural border between West Los Angeles area and Wilshire area. On the West Los Angeles side of the boulevard, decrepit apartment houses bent in toward each other like rotting teeth. On the Wilshire side, no-tell motels, dilapidated gas stations, liquor stores, and lower-end businesses lived off the welfare checks of the local residents.

The drug dealers, thieves, robbers, and gang members crossed the unmarked police department border without even knowing it existed.

Fratelli Pizza was located in a medium-sized strip mall on the West Los Angeles side. Montgomery Ward department store, Circuit City, Thrifty Drug, Payless Shoes, Wherehouse Records and Tapes, Woolworth, and several other smaller businesses all battled for customers along the L-shaped design. Most of them had been looted empty during the '92 riots, but somehow found a way to come back, and the most-robbed bank in West Los Angeles stood alone on the diagonal corner of the mall.

Fey, Ash, and Monk pulled into a parking spot well away from the front windows of Fratelli Pizza. All three were wearing bulletproof vests under dark blue raid jackets

371

with POLICE emblazoned across the back and a silk-screened LAPD badge on the front.

In two cars, Hammer and Nails and Alphabet and Brindle had pulled in to the rear of the eatery.

"8W613 to 8W619," Hammer reported over his hand-held rover radio. "No blue van back here."

The rovers were set on simplex to allow the detectives to communicate with each other without interfering with the normal flow of radio traffic.

"8W619, roger," Fey acknowledged. "No blue van out front either. We're going to go in and talk to the owner. You stay on the perimeter as discussed."

"8W613, roger," Hammer acknowledged.

Making sure her gun and handcuffs were easily accessible, Fey entered the pizza joint followed by Ash. Monk took up a position of advantage outside the front door.

"Just sit anywhere," a young female waitress said.

"Is the manager or the owner here?" Fey asked.

"Is there a problem?"

Fey hated when secretaries or other minions tried to run interference for their self-important bosses.

"Not if the owner or manager is here," she replied, proud of herself for not snapping the waitress's head off.

"I'll see," the young girl said. She moved toward a set of swinging doors that led back to the kitchen.

Standing in the entrance, Fey could see that the restaurant was fairly clean with long tables and bench seating for customers. Several big-screen televisions were broadcasting different sporting events with the sound turned down. There were advertisements for numerous types of beer scattered everywhere.

A short, fat man with a large black mustache came out through the swinging doors followed by the waitress. He stepped up to Fey.

"I'm Donald Norman," he said. "I'm the owner."

The waitress stood looking at the gathering, giving no indication of moving about her business.

"Detective Croaker, LAPD," Fey introduced herself

briefly. "And this is Special Agent Ash, FBI. Is there somewhere we can talk?"

Norman led the way back to a small office. The waitress stayed behind.

"Is this about Darcy Wyatt again?" Norman asked.

"In a roundabout way," Fey told him. "Do you have another employee by the name of Kenny Kingston?"

"Yeah. He used to be a cook here."

"Used to be?"

"Yeah. Few weeks back—right after your people arrested Darcy—he just didn't show up. Screwed me over, I can tell you. I had to cook two whole Saturday night shifts myself."

"Have you heard from him since?"

"Nope. He picked up his paycheck on Friday and on Saturday he didn't show."

"Is he owed any money?"

Norman shook his head. "Nah. Paid up to date on the Friday, like I said."

"Do you know where he cashes his checks?"

"Right here. I give him cash for it after closing."

"You have an employment application for him?"

Norman turned to a filing cabinet and rustled around inside. After a moment, he pulled out a manila file folder with Kenny Kingston's name on it. "I have to tell you that I don't think this will do you much good." He handed the folder over to Fey. "He turned up on a day when I needed help. He worked out pretty good while he was here, so I never needed to check out any of the stuff that's in there."

Fey opened the folder and looked at the job application. It was sparse. For his address Kenny had put down the same San Diego PO box number that had been on his van registration. Fey knew that was a dead end she didn't want to be chasing right now. There was no phone number, and Fey could tell by looking at it that the social security number wasn't correct. There were no references or emergency numbers listed.

When she placed the job application back in the folder,

she was delighted to see a Polaroid photo of Kenny clipped to the back cover. She pulled it free.

"Did you take this?" she asked Norman.

He snorted. "Yeah. It's a con job. Sometimes if you take a picture, they think twice before they rip you off."

"Kenny ever rip you off?"

"Nah. He got free food on his shift and he never worked the register. Couple of times I had to jump on him for not showing up for a shift, but he always had some kind of an excuse. I figured that's what happened when he didn't show up that Saturday, but he never came back." Norman stroked his mustache in a habitual manner. "Overall, he was better than a lot of guys that have worked here. I don't run a delivery van like the other Fratelli Pizza franchises—the insurance is too high around here—so the delivery guys have to provide their own ride. When I had to use Darcy Wyatt as a fill-in driver, Kenny was pretty good about letting Darcy Wyatt use his van since he didn't have wheels of his own. They seemed to become pretty good friends—drank together when they got off and stuff. Sometimes they would come to work together."

"How long did Kenny work for you?"

Norman shrugged. "A couple of months."

"Can I keep this?" Fey asked, holding up the photo. "Sure."

Fey handed Norman her business card. "If Kenny turns up here would you call 911 right away. It's important."

Norman took the card. "What did the guy do? Murder somebody?"

Fey smiled at Norman. "Poisoned some customers at a restaurant where he worked before starting to work for you."

Norman blanched.

"The civil suits are going to be horrendous. I'd make sure you call us right away if he shows up."

"Absolutely," Norman said, his voice rising an octave.

"Thanks for your help," Fey said. "And keep watching your newspapers and television for further developments."

◆ CHAPTER SIXTY

"POISONED CUSTOMERS AT ANOTHER RESTAURANT?" ASH questioned Fey incredulously when they exited the pizza place. He laughed. "You're too much."

"I wanted to make sure he'd call us if Kenny showed up."

"I think he'll call all right," Ash said as they climbed back into Fey's detective sedan. "Probably won't stop sweating about potential lawsuits for the next week."

Fey keyed her rover. "8W619 to 8W613. There's a code 4 here. Suspect hasn't been around for a couple of weeks. Let's head back to the station and do some more digging."

"8W619, roger," came the reply from Hammersmith's rear guard position.

Ash reached down to touch the pager that was vibrating on his belt. He pulled it off and checked the number.

"Recognize it?" Fey asked, referring to the pager's LED readout.

Ash shook his head. "May be a misdial."

"Use my cellular," Fey said, digging it out from her purse.

Ash flipped the phone open and dialed. When the phone was picked up, he immediately recognized the voice that answered.

"What do you want?" Ash said nastily.

"Don't hang up!" Zelman Tucker's voice was filled with urgency.

"You don't have anything to say that I want to hear."

"Wait! Give me a chance to redeem myself here. I've

got some solid info. It's going to blow your socks off.''

"Tucker, if you're blowing more smoke up my ass, I'm gonna have the Vermont Vampire released into my custody. We're gonna find you and I'm gonna let Vampy-baby suck you dry.''

"Hey, man!" Tucker sounded offended. "They're right when they say no good deed goes unpunished. I was only trying to do the right thing down in San Diego. So, it didn't pan out. What's the big deal? Are you such a crack-erjack detective that you've never followed a dead-end clue before?''

Ash rubbed his eyes and pinched the bridge of his nose between his fingers.

"You still there?" Tucker asked when Ash didn't respond.

"Yeah, I'm here.''

"You want this information or not?''

"Yeah. What have you got?''

"I spent some time doing some more digging in the department of social services records down here. Etta Carson still has a number of friends down there who gave me access.''

"The power of the almighty dollar," Ash said.

"Don't knock it. I'm making you look good.''

"Don't press your luck, Tucker. You're still under my skin.''

Tucker sang a few bars in his worst Sinatra imitation.

"Quit screwing around," Ash said gutturally, his voice straining between clenched teeth. "I'm not paying cell phone rates to listen to your bad Sinatra impersonation. Do you have anything for me, or not?''

"I do, monster man. Seems that there might be some squalid skeletons in the closet of the Kingston family who adopted JoJo.''

"We're ahead of you there, pal. We already know about daddy Kingston's kinky death—which is probably more than you do—and we know about brother Jim who did a Houdini without a curtain call.''

"How about momma Kingston telling tales out of

school about brother Kenny and daddy playing little
games?''

"We know about Kenny. In fact, as we speak we're hot
on his trail.''

"Man, I knew you were good.''

"You tracked momma down?''

"If truth be told, she came to me.''

"Isn't that special.''

Tucker ignored the jibe. "Apparently, her originally accepted story for leaving home was that she couldn't take
the family's basketball obsession.''

"But you found out different?''

"It cost a bundle, but we're ready to spill the story on
American Inquirer Tonight—that's the syndicated, tabloid
news show sponsored by *AI*—''

"I've seen it. A piece of dreck.''

"But everyone watches,'' Tucker said. "The demo-
graphics are through the roof.''

"Who cares?'' Ash said. "What's momma going to
break down and say?''

"She's admitted to running out on the family because
Richard Kingston threatened to track her down and kill
her.''

"Why?'' Ash asked.

"Young Kenny was caught hanging cats and dogs in
the neighborhood. He told a shrink that he did it because
daddy played kinky little games with him that involved
sex and suffocating.''

"Autoerotica,'' Ash confirmed.

"There's a fancy term for everything, isn't there?''

"What did momma do about it?'' Ash asked.

"Not much. Nobody believed the kid's story. Richard
Kingston was too much of a local celebrity for something
like that to be believed. Momma knew differently. She was
well aware that her sex life with daddy was a big zero. At
first she figured he had something on the side, but when
the kid talked to the shrink, she realized there was
something else going on.''

"And she didn't try to do anything about it?''

"She snooped around and caught them at it one day. However, daddy saw her watching and gave her hell. Beat the shit out of her and then wouldn't let her leave the house until the bruises healed." Tucker's voice had taken on a weary tinge.

"An old story," Ash said. "I take it she was so terrorized that she just split and left daddy and the kids to their fate?"

"Some mother, huh?"

"I'm beyond passing judgment in those situations," Ash said. "Nobody knows what that decision has cost her since."

"It's like the old joke," Tucker said. "What do fifty thousand battered women in LA have in common? They just won't listen."

Ash didn't laugh. "Anybody ever tell you you're an asshole Tucker?"

"I'm gonna have it carved on my gravestone."

"It's not something to be proud about."

Tucker's voice suddenly brightened. "This is going to make great television," he said. "Crying jags, screamed admissions, pain and suffering—there won't be a dry eye in a single Nielsen family house. A story like this could get me moved from the pages of *AI* to a regular anchor spot on the show."

"Bully for you."

"Give me a break. I'm giving you this first. If Kenny doesn't already know you're after him he will by the time the show runs."

"You're a regular solid citizen. If you really cared about what happens, *AI* wouldn't run the show until after we catch him."

"Are you crazy?" Tucker asked, appalled. "How could we claim *AI* cracked the case if we did that?"

Ash suddenly found himself holding a dead phone.

CHAPTER SIXTY-ONE

KENNY HAD HIS VAN UP AND ROLLING. IT WAS GIGGLES time. Behind the driver and passenger seat, Kenny had rigged a blanket on a wire to hide the back compartment of the van.

Behind the blanket, the van was almost empty except for a six-foot plank with one four-foot-long two-by-four lashed across the top and another across the bottom. Strong I-bolts had been screwed into the ends of the two-by-fours. Velcro straps were secured to each of the four I-bolts by leather thongs. Beside this contraption was a soft-sided half-moon sports bag containing a coil of rope and a roll of silver duct tape. A basketball rolled around freely over everything.

Kenny had freaked out when he saw his photo—the one taken by Butt Wipe Norman over at Fratelli Pizza—in the evening edition of the *Los Angeles Tribune*. Given time, he would have to go back and do something about old Butt Wipe.

Things, though, had gotten even worse when Kenny went to grab a beer and a burger at a snack shack along the coast.

The guy running the snack shack had been watching the news on a portable TV with a piece of tin foil wrapped around the antenna. The same photo of Kenny that had been in the evening paper was all over the screen. A couple of jerky talking heads were spouting stuff about Detective Fey Croaker searching for Kenny as a new suspect in the JoJo Cullen case. There was an explanation about Kenny and JoJo's relationship, and about the disappearance of Kenny's younger brother and the death of his father. The whole mess was coming out.

There wasn't anyone else in the snack shack except for Kenny and the guy doing the cooking. Kenny had pulled his baseball cap down low, and stuffed his burger in his mouth whenever the cook turned to look at him.

"What do ya think about that?" the cook had asked. "I knew that JoJo couldn't do that shit they said he did."

That really pissed Kenny off.

He kept watching the TV. Watched as Fey was filmed on the front steps of West Los Angeles area station making a statement about a warrant being issued for Kenny's arrest and asking for help from anyone who knew him.

What was this? Kenny felt like screaming. "*America's Most Wanted*"?

The sudden feeling of being hunted dropped on him like a boulder. He'd thrown a couple of bucks on the counter with the remains of his burger, and got the hell away from the damning insistence of the television's eye. He felt as if he were going to puke his cookies up any second.

In his van, he'd sat on the rotting carpet covering the floor and spun his basketball on the tip of his left middle finger time and time again until he had centered himself. He couldn't choke. He just couldn't choke.

He knew that every game had its high points and low points. This was just a low point. The other team was ahead, but Kenny knew he could come back if he just didn't choke.

After a while he was better. Maybe he wasn't that far behind after all. He'd really enjoyed making those kids choke—the ones he'd taken after JoJo had finished with them. But he couldn't do everything he'd wanted because he knew the cops had to find them with JoJo's goo inside them, not his.

And after JoJo was arrested, Kenny knew there had to be an end to the giggles for a while. More bodies couldn't turn up once JoJo was in custody.

But it had been a long time since then, and Kenny was

beginning to feel the pressure of his sexual desires—pressure that had to be released before he choked.

He had hoped that there would be several more bodies before JoJo was caught. He hadn't figured on the two cops who checked the beach where Kenny's phone call had lured JoJo. That was only supposed to be another way of screwing with JoJo's mind. You had to beat your opponent by making him be the first one to choke. Kenny's dad had always told him that during their special training sessions.

But while fate may have deprived Kenny of more sexual and mental games, it could not have served his purpose better when it came to making JoJo foul out of the game.

As he had sat in the back of his van, watching the basketball spin on his finger, feeling the sexual urges stirring within him, Kenny began to see that he had no reason to hold back anymore.

The cops knew who he was. They were running a full court press, and Kenny realized he couldn't avoid them forever. He'd learned other things playing b-ball besides choking, and one of them was that the best defense was a good offense.

Kenny was thinking about the transcript in the paper of the recording of Detective Croaker and her shrink. There was some interesting stuff in there. Not just the stuff about why Croaker thought JoJo was innocent, but other stuff. Stuff about Croaker's relationship with her brother.

What had struck Kenny the first time he'd read the article was that he knew Tommy Croaker. Moving in the circles he did, Kenny knew all about the rave scene. He'd even picked up the kid Rush from one of the raves that Kenny knew was staged by Tommy Croaker.

The more Kenny thought about it the more he liked it. He had savored making JoJo sweat. It had made the giggles with those kids even better.

Now, Kenny figured he had a way to make Detective Croaker sweat.

All he had to do was find where Tommy Croaker was staging his latest rave. Tommy was a puny little guy. Kenny wouldn't have any problem manhandling him. He'd probably even be easier than the kids he'd done before.

Kenny had put down his basketball and climbed into the van's driving seat. He'd need to put a giggles kit together, but that wouldn't take him long. And then he'd go hunting for his new target.

It was time for tip-off.

Let the giggles begin.

✦

CHAPTER SIXTY-TWO

FEY SAT AT HER DESK IN THE WEST LOS ANGELES AREA squad room as the clock ticked near midnight. Ash sat nearby at Monk Lawson's desk. His eyes were closed with his chin resting on his chest. In repose, Fey could see that he looked exhausted.

Her twenty-four hours was dwindling down. She thought that they had their break with the Fratelli Pizza angle, but it had failed to pan out. Zelman Tucker had forced their hand when it came to the search for Kenny Kingston, and since there was no stopping the *American Inquirer* from putting on their show, then it was best for Fey to do a press conference and try to achieve some measure of damage control.

Given a choice, Fey would not have held the impromptu press conference. She had the gut feeling Kingston was somewhere close—all of the murders had occurred in the immediate area—and would have preferred to sneak up on their quarry.

As soon as Kingston got wind the police were on to him, he could disappear anywhere. For that reason, Fey had not made public the information about the blue van.

She'd shared the information with selected patrol, uniformed CRASH, and special problems units, hoping that Kenny would still feel comfortable using the van and somebody would spot him.

At least one good point came from the press conference. It made Lieutenant Cahill and the other brass happy because it looked as if progress was being made—an arrest imminent. That statement was as much bullshit as a Devon Wyatt defense.

In reality, the press conference had turned out to be anticlimactic. There had been a number of crank calls pertaining to Kenny, but nothing that had panned out as a solid lead.

And then there had been nothing.

No clues. No leads.

Nothing.

The rest of Fey's crew had gone home an hour ago for a short break. Fey knew time was ticking away for her, but instead of continuing to pick up speed, the case seemed to have ground to a halt.

Fey was fresh out of ideas, but something had to give and give soon.

Midnight-thirty. The homicide unit line rang.

Fey picked it up.

"Homicide."

"Hey, boss. It's Hammer. Nails and I are just touching base to see if there is anything popping."

"All quiet," Fey told him.

The cell phone in Fey's purse chirped.

"Hang on," she told Hammer.

She set the receiver for the inside line down and answered the cell phone.

"Croaker."

"This is Kenny," a voice said. "I understand you're looking for me."

"Who is this?" Fey asked. "How did you get this number?" She clicked her fingers and Ash snapped to instant awareness.

"Don't jack around," Kenny said. "I just thought I'd

call you and let you know how much I enjoyed the recording of the tape you made with your shrink. You must be a right little basket case.''

"Look, Kenny. If this call is for real why don't you come down to the station and let's talk.''

"Man, you really are crazy,'' Kenny said. "Or do you think I am?''

"If you don't want to come down to the station then meet me somewhere,'' Fey said. "Anywhere. You name it.''

"How about hell, Detective Croaker? How about hell?''

"Come on, Kenny,'' Fey said. "Let's be serious.''

"Oh, I'm serious,'' Kenny said. "Serious as a heart attack.'' There were some muffled noises. "Hold on, I want you to listen to something.''

There were some more unintelligible sounds, as if Kenny had the mouthpiece of the phone receiver covered, and then another voice could be heard shouting from a distance.

"Fey! This guy is nuts! He's got me tied to a bunch of boards in the back of a van—''

"Do you know who that is?'' Kenny's voice came back on the line full blast.

Fey felt as if she'd been stabbed by an icicle.

"That's your little brother, Detective Croaker,'' Kenny said. "He can't talk to you anymore 'cause he's a bit tied up. Pretty soon he's going to be real tied up. And unless you can figure out where to look, he'll be pushing up daisies before morning. I'm talking worm food here. Of course, there's a lot of giggles I'm going to share with him before then.''

Fey's breathing had turned ragged. She was beyond speech.

"Let's see how good you are under pressure, Detective. Let's see which one of us chokes first.''

The line went dead.

CHAPTER SIXTY-THREE

KENNY HUNG UP THE PAY PHONE. INSIDE HIS CHEST, HE could feel his heart banging around between his ribs like a gorilla trying to escape from a cage. He realized he had an erection. Not just any erection, but an iron-dick erection. Damn, he felt good.

Kenny had chosen this particular phone because it was isolated along Pacific Coast Highway and he could back the rear doors of his van right up to it. That was important because he had wanted the detective to hear her brother yelling. It was all part of the game.

Picking up Tommy had been easier than Kenny had imagined. Word on the street was that Tommy Croaker's party crew had another rave planned. Tommy's functions were apparently still the flavor of the month with the kids and he was taking advantage of that by putting on as many as he could.

Talking to some of the head-bangers trying to score along the Venice boardwalk, Kenny had easily learned that the rave was set to take place in an auto wrecking yard.

Late in the evening, Kenny had parked near the auto yard. It was located in a heavily industrial area, virtually deserted at this time of night. From his van, he watched as Tommy and his crew set up the makeshift stage and bar. Cases of liquor were carried into the yard from a rusted pickup truck that looked as if it should be left behind when the happening was over.

Kenny knew who Tommy was. He'd been to raves before, getting drunk and high. It was there that he had first heard the kid named Rush bragging about being punked by JoJo. Those statements had been the stimulus for Kenny's thinking when it came to getting back at JoJo.

It was funny, Kenny thought as he sat and watched, *how things in life are circular.* He'd started at a rave and now he was back again for what was possibly the end.

Kenny knew he wanted to get to Tommy before things started really popping. When he saw Tommy walking out to the rusted pickup truck alone, Kenny made his move without hesitation.

Pulling the blue van next to the pickup, Kenny moved back though the interior of the van and opened the rear doors from the inside. Tommy, who was now standing by the pickup, had turned—startled by the van's sudden appearance.

"Hey, man," Kenny said with a smile. "What's happening?"

Tommy took the intruder to be somebody turning up too early for the party. He turned back to pick up another case of beer from the bed of the pickup.

"You're too early, man," Tommy said. "Party won't start for another couple of hours. The band isn't even here." Kenny didn't look like the normal raver, but it took all kinds. Tommy knew that for a fact. In his mind he dismissed Kenny and turned his thoughts back to the logistics of setting up in the open air.

When Tommy turned his back, Kenny reacted immediately and punched the much smaller man in the back of the head. Kenny hit him hard, just behind the left ear. Tommy groaned and slumped over the side of the pickup.

With a quick check to make sure nobody could see what was happening, Kenny bodily lifted Tommy up and threw him into the van. Seconds later Kenny was driving sedately away from the scene.

Nobody from the rest of Tommy's party crew noticed anything.

When he was a few blocks away, Kenny pulled over to the curb. Adrenaline was pumping through him in massive spurts. He loved this stuff.

Tommy was groaning in the back of the van. He tried to sit up. Kenny moved back and grabbed Tommy's right hand. Yanking it hard, he slammed it down on the top two-by-four and secured one of the Velcro straps around it.

"Ouch!" Tommy said. He was still groggy. "What are you doing?"

Kenny didn't answer. Instead, he moved quickly to secure Tommy's other wrist and both ankles with the Velcro straps attached to the I-bolts screwed into the two-by-fours. When Kenny was finished, Tommy was on his back, spread-eagled to the two-by-fours. The wider plank, to which the two-by-fours were lashed, ran underneath Tommy.

Starting to come out of his stupor, Tommy was beginning to panic.

"Hey! Hey!"

Kenny took a strip of duct tape and slapped it across Tommy's mouth. Then he brought out a fish-gutting knife and slit Tommy's clothes from his body like an ER nurse preparing a trauma patient.

Tommy's eyes were enormous. One second he'd been fat, dumb and happy, and the next moment he was tied up naked in the back of a van with a knife-wielding maniac.

Kenny riffled through the pockets of Tommy's shredded clothing. He opened Tommy's wallet and thumbed through the cards in there. One in particular caught his eye. It was one of Fey's police business cards with her cell phone number added in pen. She had given it to Tommy the night she and Ash had spoken to him during the rave at the warehouse. Kenny tossed the rest of the items on the van floor, but held onto the card.

"We're going to have a lot of giggles together," Kenny told Tommy conversationally. "But first, there's somebody we have to call."

After hanging up on Fey, Kenny reentered the van through the back doors, closing them behind him. He slapped the side of Tommy's naked ass. There were small amounts of blood running down Tommy's sides from where Kenny hadn't been too gentle cutting clothes off.

"Please don't kill me, man," Tommy said.

Kenny took a Polaroid camera out of the sports bag along with a small cassette recorder.

"How unoriginal," Kenny said. "Do you know how many times that has been said to me?"

Tommy was feeling faint. He twisted around on the I-shaped frame his tormentor had constructed. "Please, man," he begged.

"Pathetic," said Kenny. "You'll never hold up to the special training sessions." He turned the recorder on and then took a photograph of Tommy's helpless position.

Kenny had plans for Tommy. And when he was done with Tommy, he had plans for Fey Croaker. He wanted her to squirm first, though, and the tape and photos of Tommy should take care of that problem.

And after he was done with Fey Croaker, Kenny had thought of a whole list of other people who he needed to teach about choking.

But first things first. Kenny was getting very excited. He reached down and groped himself.

"How long can you hold your breath without choking?" he asked Tommy. Without waiting for an answer, he slapped another piece of duct tape over Tommy's mouth.

Kenny smiled at the terrified man attached to the two-by-fours. "Let's start out with a minute." Kenny checked his watch and then jammed duct tape over Tommy's nostrils.

◆◇◆
CHAPTER SIXTY-FOUR

FEY WAS STUNNED. HOW DID THIS GUY GET TO TOMMY? Worse yet, what was he going to do with Tommy? Fey thought of Ricky Long's body being uncovered in Will Rogers State Park. He'd been hog-tied and buried alive after being sexually violated. Her stomach flip-flopped and nausea swept through her body. Sweat broke out on her forehead.

"Fey?" Ash was suddenly wide awake. "What is it?"

"Kenny Kingston has got Tommy."

"What are you talking about?"

Fey jumped out of her chair. "The rat bastard has kidnapped my brother! He's got him somewhere, doing who knows what—"

"How can you be sure? Maybe Kingston is just screwing with you."

Fay turned blazing eyes on Ash. "I know the fear in my brother's voice. I hear it in all my nightmares. It's the voice he used when our father would hold a knife to Tommy's penis in order to make me do the disgusting things he wanted. It's the voice I've spent my whole damn life protecting!"

Fey snatched the metal file separator on her desk and slammed it down with a vengeance.

"Easy, Fey! Easy!" Ash said, reaching for her.

Fey pulled away. "Don't tell me to take it easy. I'm so sick to death of people like Kenny Kingston who think the terrible things that have happened to them are an excuse to do terrible things to others." She backhanded her coffee cup, sending it spinning across the deserted squad room. "I'm sick of sheep in wolves' clothing—sick of predators who claim they aren't responsible for their actions because they're victims too." She faced Ash full on. "You're dying. It's over with for you! You don't have to go on anymore. You can even pull the plug on yourself and do it early so you don't have to face the suffering. Some of us have to stick around and deal with it. Nobody—and I mean nobody—had a more horrifying childhood than I did, but I'm not out there killing and maiming in revenge for what was done to me. People don't have to do those things. There are choices, damn it!" Fey yelled this last pronouncement.

"My secrets have been blabbed all over the news thanks to Devon Wyatt, but that's still not all of it," she continued. "My father was a cop. One of the good guys while he was at work, but when he came home he was no better than Kenny Kingston or any other perverted animal out there." Fey pointed an arm dramatically in the general direction of the outside world. "My father screwed me nine ways to Sunday, beat me to a pulp when he felt like it, and then let his friends have at me. But I was stronger than him. I wouldn't let him defeat me. He couldn't touch the me inside. I could have turned out to be an animal— the seeds are all there—but I didn't. Instead, I've spent my life protecting others, saving them from beasts like my father—trying to make amends for him, for what he did to me! But somebody always comes along to drag everything back to the surface again. This time it's Kenny Kingston. Next time it will be somebody else. But I'm telling you right here and now, Kingston is going down."

Fey stepped back to her desk, a sudden frightening calm seeming to slip over her. She picked up the phone receiver for the inside line that Hammer had called her on.

"You still there?" she asked.

"I'm here," Hammer said.

Fey realized she hadn't put the phone on hold and Hammer must have heard all of her outburst.

"You and Nails call the others," she said. "Meet me

at county jail. We're going to ruin Darcy Wyatt's beauty sleep."

Ash and Fey were mostly silent in the car on the ride to county jail. Traffic was sparse and Fey kept the speedometer hovering around the eight-five mark and above. It was Ash's turn to ride shotgun.

At one point, Ash spoke quietly. "You obviously think that I'm taking the easy way out if I don't ride this disease out to its inevitable end."

"I'm sorry," Fey said. She took a deep breath. "I had no right to say what I did. I'm not walking in your shoes. You have the right to make your own decisions."

"But you don't think I'm right?" Ash persisted.

"I've lived with pain all my life," Fey said. "And the only thing I've learned from it is that you've got to spit in its eye and fight it with everything you have inside. You can't let it win. You're only a victim if you allow yourself to be a victim."

Ash went back to being silent.

At county jail, Fey jangled a sleepy deputy to arrange for Darcy Wyatt to be brought up from the cells. Fey and Ash were waiting when Darcy stumbled sleepily into the interrogation room.

"Sit down," Fey said.

There was no nonsense in her voice. Darcy recognized that right away. Quickly, he sat in the wooden chair that was the only piece of furniture Fey had not removed from the room.

Darcy realized that this was a whole different person with whom he was dealing. This might look like the same woman who'd originally interrogated him, but there was a universe of difference between the two. The first one had been calm and collected. This one was half a step away from going out of control.

Fey stood in front of Darcy. She reached out and grabbed him painfully by one shoulder, bringing her face in close to his.

"I'm not fucking around, Darcy," she said, her voice

coming from the depths inside her. "You tell me where I can find Kenny Kingston, and you tell me right now."

Darcy's eyes filled his face. His pupils darted to Ash leaning against the wall.

Fey saw the movement. "Leave us alone," she said to Ash.

"Fey—"

"Now," Fey commanded.

Ash didn't argue. He simply turned and walked out of the room.

Fey brought her face back to Darcy's. "Kenny Kingston," she said.

Darcy swallowed hard.

"Darcy, I know you know about Kenny Kingston, or you wouldn't be trying to make a deal with Hammersmith."

"Deal," Darcy said, hopefully. "I'll deal."

"Maybe you're willing to deal," Fey said. "But I'm not. You're an animal Darcy. You're no better than Kingston or any other perverted predator on the street. I'm not going to trade one of you to get another. You're going down for the rapes. Period. No room for argument."

"But he was with me," Darcy pleaded. "He started me doing it again. He knew I was weak. I couldn't help it."

"I don't give a shit, Darcy. You either tell me where Kenny Kingston is, or I will arrange for you to be sodomized every day that you're behind bars. You won't be safe for one breathing moment."

"You can't do that!"

"Oh, yes I can," Fey said. "And I will. Do you feel like taking a chance that I won't keep my word?"

Darcy felt cold fear choking in his throat.

"Kenny will kill me."

"Skip it," Fey told him. "My time is ticking. I can protect you from him. Nobody can protect you from me."

Darcy swallowed again. Fear swept out of him in waves of body odor. His eyes were bigger than ever, big enough to swim in.

"He crashes in an abandoned restaurant in Malibu," he

said. His voice was squeaky. "The Sea Something. I went there with him once to get stoned. The place is a death trap."

Fey reached over and slapped Darcy gently on the cheek. Darcy jumped a mile.

"Good boy," she told him. "Good boy."

✥ CHAPTER SIXTY-FIVE

"FEY, WE SHOULD WAIT FOR SWAT AND A HOSTAGE NE-gotiation team," Monk Lawson said.

"You want to wait for them, go ahead and wait," Fey told him. "I'm going in."

"This is crazy," Alphabet said. "There's no blue van around."

"I'm not concerned about the blue van," Fey said. "He's too smart to leave it in plain sight. When we have more time later, we'll probably find it nearby."

"Look," Alphabet gave it another try. "We have no idea of the layout inside. We don't even know for sure if this guy is in there."

"That's what I'm going to find out," Fey said. "Anyone who wants to handle it another way can stand back now. Tommy isn't much, but he is my brother, not yours. I'll understand."

None of the detectives clustered around Fey's detective sedan said anything. Nobody stepped back.

"Screw it," Alphabet said, capitulating. "What are we waiting for?" He jacked a round in the Ithica shotgun he was holding. "Let's do it."

When Darcy had coughed up the information on the

"Sea Something," Fey had immediately known what restaurant he was talking about. There was only one along the Malibu coast that had taken a hard enough hit to be left abandoned after the earthquake.

Leaving Darcy in the loving care of the county jail deputies, Fey had powered back to the parking lot dragging Ash in her wake.

Outside, she found that Hammer and Nails had arrived along with Alphabet and Monk Lawson. Brindle Jones pulled in while they were talking.

Everyone had their bulletproof vests and raid jackets in the back of their detective cars. There were shotguns also—one to a car—and everyone was carrying 9-millimeter automatics except for Fey who had her .38 strapped on.

Even in the light traffic, the ride out to the coast took close to forty minutes. They took three cars. Hammer and Nails were in the black war van. Alphabet and Brindle had paired up in the rear vehicle with Fey, Ash, and Monk leading the way. Moving in formation, the electricity of the situation seemed to crackle through the convoy.

Half a mile away from the target, Fey pulled into a McDonald's restaurant parking lot. Under the bright lights, the detectives geared up and then gathered around Fey's car.

After Alphabet and Monk had voiced their concerns, and Fey had offered to let anyone back out who didn't feel right about the situation, the focus came back to the task in hand.

"Darcy said this place is a death trap," Fey told her crew. "We all know it's been condemned since the earthquake—seen the pictures of the eating area twisting into space over the water. That makes things doubly dangerous. We don't just have to worry about Kenny Kingston. We also have to worry about getting hurt by the structure itself."

Everyone nodded. Each of them was thinking, *it won't happen to me.*

"We wouldn't be going in like this if there wasn't a life at stake," Fey said.

Nobody questioned her.

"All right," she said. "Once we get around the chain-link fence, I want Alphabet and Brindle on the outside in the front."

Both detectives nodded.

"Hammer and Nails, you two take the rear of the location. I don't want you to go down in the water, but make sure Kingston doesn't slip away."

"You got it," Hammer said.

"Ash and Monk will enter the structure with me."

The two men hefted pry-bars removed from the back of the detective cars.

"Any ideas about this guy, monster man?" Fey asked Ash.

"He knows you're coming," he said.

"How can you be sure?"

"Instinct. Experience." Ash shrugged. "Kenny might not realize it, but it's ultimately what he wants at this point. That's what the taunting game is all about. Consciously, he thinks it's about proving he's smarter than the cops. Unconsciously, I would say he's responding to you as he did to his father. He wants to submit, but he needs your approval of how brilliant he is before he can."

"Hell," Fey said. "I'm not planning on giving him the chance to submit. If he shows himself in any manner but full surrender, he's going down in flames."

She looked around her crew. "Everybody have good batteries on their rovers?"

All heads nodded.

"Everyone have flashlights?"

More head nodding.

"This is the sheriff's area," Fey said. "If at some point they find out about the party and decide to invite themselves, just play it cool. Make sure you identify yourselves. Don't get shot by the good guys."

There were some knowing, nervous chuckles. Worse scenarios had happened.

Fey checked her watch. "Looks as if were going to beat that twenty-four-hour deadline," she said.

The inside of the Sea Otter was almost pitch black. Fey used her six-cell Kelite to illuminate her way, but even its powerful beam seemed to get sucked away into the darkness. All around creaking beams and unsteady foundations made it hard to listen for surreptitious movement.

Behind Fey, Ash watched both sides with Monk acting as rear guard. All three had their guns out. Only Fey had her flashlight on. One lighted target was enough.

As they approached the edge of the restaurant floor that extended over the ocean, they could hear the crash of waves against the rocks below. Nobody spoke, their senses too concentrated on the surroundings.

They had entered the grounds by climbing around the end of the chain-link fence where it stopped at the edge of a low cliff that dropped down to the sea. The pry-bars had been used to tear plywood away from the front doors and then jimmy them open. The pry-bars were then abandoned in favor of freer hands.

The consensus of the detectives' opinions was that it didn't make sense to try and sneak in. It could take forever in the dark to find how Kenny came and went. He would probably hear them anyway, and he had the big advantage of knowing the lay of the land. Moving slowly from the front of the restaurant, the three detectives hoped to secure each section as they passed through.

The lobby and bathrooms had provided no clues. In the kitchen, in the glow of Fey's flashlight, they found signs of Kenny's recent eating habits.

Moving on, Fey flashed her light over the walls, stopping to focus on the jerry-rigged backboard and rim. She felt her heart thumping. Kenny had to be here somewhere. She had goose bumps all over, a sure sign to her that danger was imminent.

The abandoned restaurant continued to creak around them. Fey found herself straining to listen for screams or cries that would indicate that Kenny was working his perversions on Tommy. But Fey knew that if Kenny was choking Tommy somehow, he might not be able to scream. The thought of Ricky Long's bound, naked body again danced through her mind.

Concentrate, she screamed at herself mentally.

What if Kenny wasn't here? What if this was someplace he'd crashed once, but had moved on—moved on to someplace that Darcy hadn't known about?

What if? What if? What if? The refrain ran through her brain over and over.

There was a sudden crashing sound.

Fey whirled to see the top half of Monk's torso sticking out of the floor.

"Help!" he said.

In the light of her Kelite, Fey saw Ash move toward Monk. Something dropped around her neck. She brushed at it and moved forward, but was suddenly jerked backward and up—off her feet.

Her flashlight fell and rolled away, leaving everything in darkness. Fey also lost her gun, grabbing at her throat with both hands. The rope around it was crushing her windpipe and cutting into the sides of her neck.

"Urrrg!" she sputtered.

She was swinging in space, with no idea how far above the floor she was. Ten feet or two inches, it didn't matter, the result was going to be the same.

"Hee hee!"

Fey heard the laughter even over the pounding of the blood in her head.

Kenny had come charging out of the darkness and crashed into Ash with the power of a bull. Ash had gone flying into the darkness.

Kenny turned on a flashlight and shined it in Fey's eyes. "How does it feel, Detective? How does it feel to get all choked up?" His voice was high, tinny.

He suddenly pointed the flashlight down at the floor. "Look down, Detective. Look down."

Fey was struggling. Her left hand was digging at the rope on the side of her neck. Her right hand was grappling with the rope that vanished into the darkness above her, trying to pull her weight up—release the pressure.

"Look down! Damn it!" Kenny screamed at her.

Where was Ash? Where was Monk? Where was anybody?

Fey looked down to where Kenny was shining the light. There was a hole in the floor beneath her feet. Kenny shined the light through the hole. "What do you see?" he demanded.

Fey saw the sea below. It crashed in and then receded away. When it receded away, Fey looked down and saw Tommy still strapped to the infernal contraption Kenny had created. The plank and two-by-four structure had been wedged between the rocks below the restaurant floor. The waves crashed over it relentlessly, drowning Tommy again and again.

Fey could see the silver duct tape across Tommy's mouth. He stared at her with dead eyes.

"Nuuug!" Fey's screams caught in her throat.

Kenny was dancing with delight when Ash hit him across the back with a board.

Kenny went down, losing his flashlight. He was a strong man and the board hadn't done too much damage. He rolled away and came athletically to his feet.

"Come on," he taunted in the dark.

I'm dying! Fey screamed inside her mind. *I'm going to die! He's going to win!* Images of Kenny mixed with those of the original monster in her life. *My father's going to win!*

She bounced around on the rope Kenny had secured over a ceiling beam. Panic welled up around her.

Grunts and animal noises attested to the struggle of Ash and Kenny.

She couldn't swallow. Couldn't get breath.

Dropping her left hand to her side, Fey jammed it into the pocket of her jeans. Pulling her legs up toward her, she felt her fingers wrap around the small pocket knife she always carried when working.

With her other hand, she was opening the blade when

a body crashed into her and sent her swinging. The pocket knife spun away as if it had never existed.

Lights danced before her eyes in the darkness. She was slipping out of consciousness. She knew she was on her way to join Tommy.

A body slammed into her again. With the desperation of a drowner, she grabbed at the head and pulled it back into her. Instantly, she knew it was Kenny. The hair was thick and long. Ash had a lawnmower cut.

Kenny tried to pry her hands loose, but Ash was in front of him throwing punches into his midsection.

Fey raked her nails across Kenny's eyes, gouging and poking. Using his head for leverage, Fey brought her legs up and wrapped them around Kenny's neck in a scissor hold that she locked with her feet and ankles.

Raised up that way, the tension of the rope around her own neck lessened. With almost her last conscious thought, Fey flashed her hands to the rope and tore it away from her throat and over her head.

She gripped the rope tightly in her hands, holding herself up as she gasped for air. Through all of it, she never released her scissor hold.

Knowing there had been a hole in the floor directly below her when she'd been hanging, Fey pulled on the rope that had been choking her. By the force of her legs around his neck, she dragged Kenny backward. She felt him stumble below her, and then the rope was torn from her hands as Kenny stepped into the hole and collapsed.

Fey crashed to the floor, but with the force of every angry wound she had ever suffered, she twisted her legs with a vengeance. There was a snapping noise that was deafening even over the yells and shouts of the rest of her crew dashing into the restaurant.

"Freeze everybody!" Fey tried to shout. She wanted to warn them about the treacherous floor. The words didn't come out. Her throat was a raw wound.

Suddenly Ash was at her side. The flashlights of the other detectives were everywhere.

"You okay?" Ash asked.

He looks worse for the wear, Fey thought, seeing his face in the glow of a flashlight. She reached out and touched his face.

"Monk?" she asked. It came out, "Mnnnk?"

"I'm okay," came a response from off to her right.

"Tommy," she said.

"I don't know," Ash said. "We haven't looked yet."

"No," Fey said. "Below." She pointed down. "Under the restaurant in the water."

"Oh, shit," Ash said.

"I saw him. Kenny made me look."

She realized Kenny's broken neck was still twisted between her legs. She unlocked her ankles and kicked out with her feet, hitting the torso that was wedged in the hole in the floor that she'd seen Tommy through.

She kicked at Kenny's head again and again until Ash put his hands under her armpits and dragged her away.

"Fey! Fey!" he yelled at her. "He's dead! He's dead!"

She pulled away and kicked the body again.

"He's not dead until I say he's dead." She kicked out again and again—her father, her brother, her whole life exploding through her anger.

⌖

CHAPTER SIXTY-SIX

A MONTH LATER, FEY WAS WAITING IN THE HALLWAY outside Division 93 of the West Los Angeles courthouse. The preliminary hearing of the rape charges against Darcy Wyatt had been put over to the afternoon.

There had been a ton of fallout from the night at the Sea Otter. Fortunately, the department chose to put the best face they could on the whole situation surrounding the arrest of JoJo Cullen and the subsequent apprehension and death of Kenny Kingston.

The internal affairs investigation had cleared Fey without even an admonishment for her actions. Somewhere, somehow, Fey figured Hammer and Nails had a hand in that decision. The fact was there had been a number of kudos to go around for everyone.

There was always a fine line between victory and disaster.

Devon Wyatt suddenly materialized beside Fey. "Detective Croaker," he said, acknowledging her. "I was sorry to hear about your brother."

Fey nodded. "Thank you." She still didn't trust herself to say more. A week of compassionate leave from the department had been almost too much to bear. After the private funeral she had needed to get back to work as soon as possible.

The week, however, had been spent in what seemed like continuous sessions with Dr. Winters. The doctor had a new receptionist. Fey no longer let her sessions be recorded.

Sometimes the therapy helped. Sometimes it didn't. She hadn't been in time to save Tommy. Dr. Winters tried to convince Fey it wasn't her fault. Fey didn't believe it yet. It hurt her deeply.

"I have to tell you," Wyatt told her, "I admired the way you handle yourself. You're very, very tough—a worthy adversary. Even when you were telling me I'd won, you were still playing the game. You got what you wanted from me."

"I did my job. Nothing more," Fey said. "Just like I'm going to do my job today, in there, against your kid." She nodded toward the courtroom.

"I wouldn't expect anything less," Wyatt said.

Fey gave him a hard stare. "Don't even think of asking for your favor back today."

Wyatt smiled. "I wouldn't dream of it. I wouldn't waste something like that on a lost cause."

Fey shook her head. "You're a cold fish."

"I've heard the same thing said about you."

A bailiff came out and called Wyatt into the courtroom.

"JoJo asked me to give you this," Wyatt said. He handed Fey an envelope and walked away. "We'll cross swords again," he said over his shoulder.

When Fey looked up from the envelope, she saw Ash walking down the hall toward her. He had a cane and used it with noticeable effort.

"Hi," Fey said, smiling at him. They didn't ever mention the ALS. They simply took things one day at a time.

"Where are Hammer and Nails and the others?" Ash asked.

"They're going to meet us at the restaurant," Fey told him. "I think you'll like this place."

"I like any place with you," he said.

"Stop it," Fey told him. "You're embarrassing me."

"Then I guess you don't want these," Ash said taking a small bouquet of flowers out from behind his back in the hand not holding the cane.

"Good grief, Ash." Fey took the flowers. "What do you think we are? High school kids or something?" Secretly she was very pleased.

"What's in the envelope?" he asked. "A payoff?"

Fey slit it open with a fingernail and shook out the contents. "Would you look at these?" she said. "Center court tickets for the Lakers and Sails tonight. I understand JoJo Cullen has been ripping up the boards lately."

There had been times during the past weeks when she had felt a type of kinship with JoJo. His world had been torn apart, much as hers had, but he was continuing on despite his personal tragedies.

"Who are you going to take?" Ash asked, innocently.

She put her arm through his. "I'll take you," she said. "But you have to tell me something first." They turned and began walking toward the exit and lunch.

"Okay."

Fey smiled at him.

"Just what is your first name?"

A nineteen-year veteran of the Los Angeles Police Department, PAUL BISHOP is currently assigned as a detective supervisor with the West Los Angeles area sex crimes unit. He has worked many varied assignments, including homicide, vice, undercover narcotics, and a three-year stint with the department's anti-terrorist division.

In 1993 he was named Officer of the Year for LAPD's West Los Angeles area, and in 1994 he received the Quality and Productivity Commission Award for the city of Los Angeles.

The author of six previous novels, including the first Fey Croaker mystery, *Kill Me Again* (Avon Books, 1994), Bishop was born in England in 1954. He immigrated to America in 1962.

Between police work and writing he makes time for playing soccer, reading, teaching, and many other interests.